THE
RESURRECTION
GAME

THE
RESURRECTION
GAME

A NOVEL OF THE SHADOWSIDE

MICHELLE BELANGER

TITAN BOOKS

THE RESURRECTION GAME
Print edition ISBN: 9781783299560
Electronic edition ISBN: 9781783299577

Published by Titan Books
A division of Titan Publishing Group Ltd
144 Southwark Street, London SE1 0UP

First edition: November 2017

2 4 6 8 10 9 7 5 3 1

A CIP catalogue record for this title is available
from the British Library.

Printed and bound in the USA.

Did you enjoy this book? We love to hear from our readers.
Please email us at readerfeedback@titanemail.com
or write to us at Reader Feedback at the above address.

To receive advance information, news, competitions, and exclusive
offers online, please sign up for the Titan newsletter on our Web site:
www.titanbooks.com

For Vera Rubin

1

Miles of empty night sped away from the Kawasaki. Hugging the lines of the cruiser, I leaned forward and dared to spread my wings. The disguising cowl of energy that hid my more-than-human nature shredded as they unfurled across the road. The vast limbs of pale blue light didn't strictly exist in the physical world, but I felt the wind blowing through them all the same. Grinning beneath my helmet, I coaxed the Vulcan faster.

It was the closest thing to flying in the mortal world.

A sign for Chagrin River Park zipped past and I traded open highway for winding, narrow curves. A thin ribbon of asphalt—more a nature trail than a proper road—cut through a forest as deep as it was dark. I swerved around the chained stanchions with the "Park closes at eleven" sign, spitting mud and turf behind my wheels, and let the Vulcan go all-out. Mist spilled from the shadows between broad, lichen-covered trunks, and skirls of early autumn leaves scattered in the headlamp at every dip in the path. The hilly trail felt like riding a rollercoaster, and, giddy with the pulse of the wind and the motor, I took every turn a little too fast.

I could almost leave the nightmares behind me. Almost.

Again and again, I urged myself close to a skid, reveling in my body's hard twist and pull as I kept the Vulcan on the treacherous excuse for a road. Here, at least, was something I could conquer—as opposed to dream after dream where power sang a siren song and I lost all control. The world ran red in those dreams, and a part of me was hungry for it.

Pouring on the speed, I pretended I could outrun myself.

All too swiftly, the needle tipped toward E. I hadn't bothered to check the tank before heading out and that was hours ago. Stupid, but this current bout of insomnia hadn't been great for my skills at decision-making. Seeking a main road, I worked my way out of the damp hollows of the park. Riverwood Loop dumped me onto Rural, a street so aptly named, it wasn't much different from the nature trail I'd been joyriding. Rural led in the opposite direction of the highway, but the houses started getting closer together, and with all the lights in the distance, there had to be a gas station somewhere up ahead.

There were four. I passed each of them as I traveled from Rural to Reeves and finally onto Lakeshore, crossing the river that lent the park its unlikely name— Chagrin. Every single one of the stations, even the one in the middle of town, was dark and abandoned, their glassed-in storefronts locked against the night. Even on E, the bike still had miles in her, so I pressed onward, sticking to Lakeshore because it led straight to the city. Once I got closer to Cleveland, there was sure to be a gas station that shared my insomniac hours.

As the ride wore on, I regretted the decision. Like Rural before it, Lakeshore was a road named for the countryside through which it led. The mostly two-lane boulevard hugged the shore of Erie and, while I couldn't always see that stretch of dark water, there was no mistaking the brooding presence of the lake. Bleak and uncanny, it dragged at my senses, threatening to unravel all the calm I'd stitched together earlier on my ride.

The mortals couldn't see it—lucky bastards—but Erie wasn't any normal body of water. It was a vast abyss yawning far deeper than fathom charts could graph. In the heart of the lake's darkness, a doorway hung open, and crimson-eyed horrors slithered into our world from whatever hell they called home. I fought the cacodaimons on a regular basis, but rarely this close to the water. The lake held too many bad memories—and more that I could never recover.

Belatedly, I pulled my wings tight against my body. Cacodaimons had a keen scent for energy, and they knew mine all too well. The subtle magic didn't come easily, and I focused so hard that my palms cramped on the motorcycle's grips. Painfully, the scar on my left hand twitched. One thing lay at the bottom of the lake that I'd tried to lose intentionally, but the artifact had its hooks in me deep, and this was its reminder. If my nightmares were any indication, I had no hope of tearing free.

Shoving the bleak thoughts into a corner, I shifted my shoulders and settled into a more comfortable position across the bike. The low fuel light blinked on, letting me know I'd be stranded if a station didn't manifest soon.

The engine was sucking fumes when I finally spied the lighted sign of a twenty-four-hour gas station with the dubious name of "Qwik-Fill." Deep in East Collinwood, the off-brand establishment sat on a sad spit of asphalt warped by time and neglect. An empty lot stretched across from it, wild with sumac and chest-high weeds. A sign for the Ohio Lotto declared the weekly numbers, but it was missing half its bulbs and those still working stuttered weakly, taunting with their promised millions.

Coasting to the nearest pump, I slid off the bike, stretching as soon as it leaned on the kickstand. Both shoulders cracked like rifle shots and I unfastened my helmet so I could properly roll some of the tightness from my neck. Vertebrae crackled all the way up. I'd been riding for hours without a single cramp, but the dark ruminations inspired by the lake had made the last twenty minutes especially tense.

Hooking the helmet over one of the grips, I uncapped the gas tank and dug for my wallet, only to see a bright strip of yellow tape over the card reader at the pump. Flapping beneath it, like a flag of surrender, was a slip of receipt paper scrawled with big block letters.

SORRY. NOT WORKING.

It was the same story on the other side. All the card readers were down.

"Fuck me running," I muttered.

Unenthusiastically, I opened the billfold, pretty certain

I had no cash. One tattered dollar peeked out from behind a folded receipt from work. That wouldn't get me much, and my Platinum card was worthless if the station couldn't take plastic. Already scouring various pockets, I gestured to catch the attention of the solitary attendant mopping the tiles in front of the counter. He waved me closer cheerily, wiping lean brown fingers against a stained apron after propping the mop handle alongside a chip display. I tested the door, not really expecting it to open, but he had it unlocked even at this hour.

"A weary traveler, and so late," he called. He had a voice made for radio—expressive, rich, and resonant. "I'm sorry our card readers are down."

"Yeah, I noticed. In here, too?"

He nodded. If he caught my gruff irritation, his face betrayed no insult. He cracked an apologetic smile, wide and pleasant and short a few teeth.

"It was the storm earlier," he said. Nimbly, he scooted behind the counter, barely having to lift the little gate. His navy-blue polo shirt hung baggily on a frame more stick than flesh. Maybe fifty, his once-black hair was mostly gray. A curious patch of pallid scars puckered behind one ear and the hair that grew around them was white and wispy as cobwebs.

"Storm? Didn't rain where I was." I plunked down my ratty dollar and a handful of lint-sticky coins. It was all I could scavenge from my pockets. "If you can't take plastic, this is what I got."

Thick brows knitting over dark, intelligent eyes, he bent and started counting. Softly, he murmured all the numbers as if reminding himself of both their taste and sound. *One seventy-five. One eighty. Two dollars.* It nagged at me that I couldn't place the accent of his words. Languages were kind of one of my super-powers. I was tired enough that my mouth followed thought without filter and I blurted the question, whether it was polite or not. "Where you from?"

With a tolerant smile, he looked up from his counting. "Aleppo. But I taught history as a young man in Britain, so I get asked that a lot." Wasted circles stamped a silent testament under his eyes and I made the mistake of looking too deep. Before I could stop it, a harsh wave of images pummeled my over-tired brain—a street lined with dead children, their skin gray from the rubble's endless dust. Shattered ruins of buildings, businesses, homes...

"You were there for the bombings. Your family—" It escaped as less than a whisper, but I might as well have shouted for the way he recoiled.

"How do you know that?" he demanded. More images surged with his reaction—fire and running and blood. Digging for the corpse of his daughter. I didn't want any of it. I slammed up all of my shields, silently cursing my gifts.

"Sorry," I muttered.

"No," he objected, reaching to seize my fingers. With a stifled snarl, I jerked them out of reach. He stared, uncomprehending. "Sir, please. Tell me. How can you know these things?"

"Sorry," I choked again, back-pedaling hurriedly from the counter. "The money—just put it on pump one, OK?" Before he could ask anything further, I bolted for the door, scrubbing my eyes clear of visions. I didn't even see the woman when I slammed into her, but I couldn't miss her stink. A mix of sweat and stress and chemicals, all of it sharp and stinging in my sinuses. Meth-head, probably. I didn't want anything that was in her brain, so I redoubled my efforts, closing my perceptions until I felt almost blind. Staggering through the swinging door, I just kept my head down and my shields up as I rushed out to the bike.

Grabbing the hose, I fed gas into the tank, willing the scroll of decimals to hurry while I shoved all my psychic shit back under its lid. Fucking nightmares had me worn ragged.

The last penny of my pre-pay rolled forward on the display and the pump shut off. I replaced the nozzle, grabbing my helmet from the handlebars. But before I put it on, something stopped me—a creeping sense of scrutiny that teased the hairs on my neck. I turned toward the stretch of grimy windows, expecting to see the haunted eyes of the refugee clerk.

The woman's face was pressed against the glass. Empty-eyed, she gaped at me. Behind her, the history professor turned gas station attendant moved with his mop and bucket through the central aisle of the store. He bent without complaint to the lowly work, paying no attention to the woman at the windows. And why should he? She was just another peculiar customer on a long and lonely night.

Then came a chittering cry, one that I'd heard too many times before.

Cacodaimon.

The woman dragged her nails against the glass, eyes

gleaming crimson as her rider revealed itself at last. Once it had my attention, her face split in a hideous grin. Ghosted over by the maw of her rider, her mouth was all teeth, and I was struck with the certainty that at any moment her entire head would swing open on a hinge to reveal some jack-in-the-box skeleton screaming from the moist chasm of her throat.

Laughing—I could tell she was laughing—she rushed from the window and tackled the clerk. It happened so fast. Teeth and nails. That was all she had, but spurred by the frenzied strength of the cacodaimon, it was enough.

Arterial blood arced across the aisles before I fully processed her attack.

Dropping everything, I ran to the door, blurring Nephilim-quick. It was a trick learned from my brother Remy, and, while it was costly, it was handy in a crunch. I crossed the store in less time than it took to unsheathe the twin daggers concealed at my wrists.

Blue-white fire crackled around my fingers as I thrust the woman from her victim. She whirled and snapped wildly, blood coating the entire lower half of her face. Through her vacant eyes, the glare of the cacodaimon burned hateful and red. The thing was fully wedded to her—had to have been from the moment she walked through the door. And I'd been so mired in my own shit that I'd missed it completely.

Too late now.

Fingers hooking for my eyes, she threw herself at me. The cacodaimon hissed as I sought to pry it from her body, inky flesh cold and stinking in the light. The woman shrieked and ferociously clawed for my eyes, my throat, my face. With the pommel of one dagger, I struck a ringing blow against her temple. A concussion of light exploded at the impact and both woman and rider tumbled ragdoll-limp across a football-themed display of Budweiser cans.

At my feet, the dying clerk spasmed. He was bleeding out, and nothing could stop it. Three refugee camps, the wreckage of a life in Aleppo—he'd survived everything just to end with a possessed woman's teeth in his throat.

I blamed myself.

His out-flung arm twitched, and I caught skittering motion behind him on the tiles. A second cacodaimon slunk along his back like a fat, black leech, spindly legs worming into his nerves. He wasn't even dead and already it sought to claim his body for its own. Intoning the syllables of my Name, I called power to my blades and slashed at its central mass, severing every connection. The thing shrilled as I cut it to pieces.

An answering cry erupted from the possessed woman's throat. Conscious, but wobbly, she dragged herself from the spill of dented beer cans, lurching into a rack of chips as she scrambled for the door. Glossy packets of Doritos and Ruffles scattered every which way across the sticky tiles. I turned to sprint after her, but the clerk seized my ankle and clung with the strength of the doomed.

"I'm sorry," I said, as if that could change a damned thing. "I won't let it hurt anyone else." It was the best I could offer. His thin body spasmed once, a final spray of blood-flecked spittle erupting over the leather of my boots. His eyes fixed on the ceiling, staring past me to an incomprehensible vastness.

Yanking free from the vise of his dead fingers, I rushed to make good on my promise.

2

Outside, the cacodaimon-ridden woman ran pell-mell past the furthest row of pumps, already half way to the road. Flexing my will, I pulled the speed trick again, hurriedly sheathing my blades so I didn't impale myself if I tumbled. Closing the distance in an eyeblink, I streaked past my parked motorcycle and tackled her before she could get beyond the sallow lights of the gas station canopy.

I slammed into her hard and we hit the ground in a flailing jumble. The creature riding her shrieked with hateful fury, rearing back from its host to bare rows of razorblade teeth. Striking like a cobra, it darted for my face.

That was a mistake.

Spirit-fire blazing around my hands, I seized the incorporeal horror just under its flaring black hood. Its cold flesh sizzled on contact. Both host and rider fought with manic ferocity, the cacodaimon pushing the woman's body so hard her tendons crackled. She went for the throat, clawing and biting at the vulnerable flesh between jaw and neck. Roughly, I smashed her face with my shoulder so I could focus on the cacodaimon. Once I tore it from her nervous system, she would drop like a cast-off suit of clothes.

Contact with the soot-black flesh sent gnawing waves of numbness up to my wrists, but I didn't let up, throttling the invertebrate nightmare until its hold on its host finally began to slip. Long coils of sectioned tail unspooled from its vessel like some hellish tapeworm, the little scythes of its claws scrabbling against the thick leather of my biker jacket. The barbed tip finally ripped from the base of her spine and the woman shrieked once, back bowing until her head nearly met her heels. Ripping bloody gouges in her face, she did an awkward pirouette, then pitched heavily onto her side.

As she writhed on the pavement, pinkish-gray sludge seeped from her nose and her ears—her brains, leaking out of her head like pink slurry. The smell was somewhere between spoiled meat and rank sushi, and everything in my stomach threatened to come up at once. No matter how many times I killed these monsters, the wreck they left of their human hosts never failed to gut me.

Noticing my distraction, the cacodaimon twisted fiercely, whipping the spiny tip of its tail straight for my head. I brought my forearm up to deflect, but half a second too late. The impact sent me reeling and the parasitic nightmare jerked free of my grip. Shrieking with triumph and mockery, it zipped like a rocket for the dark growth of weeds in the vacant lot across the street.

Bellowing with pain and frustration, I raised my own

shout—three potent syllables that echoed through the night.

"*Za—qui—el.*"

My station. My power. My Name.

Light crackled with renewed fury around my fingertips, and I charged across the empty ribbon of street. Even so, I almost lost the creature in the deep shadows. Undeterred, I let my vision spill to the Shadowside, the realm of spirits one step off from mortal reality. There, the black-on-black nightmare sketched an unmistakable silhouette against a landscape of stark, amorphous gray. It moved stealthily now, gliding with the eerie grace of a beast born of deep water.

Stumbling over roots and weed-choked junk, I pursued with single-minded purpose. The treacherous footing gave the cacodaimon a growing lead.

Abruptly, I slammed into the mesh of a chain-link fence, and uttered a startled curse. With all my focus on the spirit-realm, I'd missed the thing completely.

Shaking the gathered power from my hands, I twined my fingers through the wire lattice and bodily dragged myself up. Near the top, my jacket snagged on a rusty bit of wire, and for a moment, I teetered, stuck. All at once, the jacket pulled free and I tumbled in a heap to the slick grass on the other side. Catching most of the impact on one shoulder, I rolled to my feet and charged onward.

The cacodaimon was yards ahead, making a swift beeline across a wide, flat park, heading for the erector-set sprawl of a public playground. Moray-swift it flew across the lawn. Glancing back, it loosed a taunting cry, the slitted crimson of its eyes gleaming in the dark.

Calling on a burst of speed again, I felt the strain

blossom under my ribs with a breath-hitching burn. My sprint covered less distance than before, fizzling as my feet traded grass for damp wood chips. The cacodaimon dove into the shadowy hulk of a jungle gym, disappearing into the tubes of a tunnel maze only to charge hissing from the other end like some obscene jack-in-the-box. I lost it at the base of an enclosed spiral side, staggering in circles as I strove to pick up the trail while fighting to catch my breath.

Another shrill screech told me I was off the mark entirely—the cacodaimon had doubled back and was halfway to the road again. A lone car crawled west along Lakeshore, its driver slaloming drunkenly from lane to lane. Its lights dimmed as a shadow flew past, and, for a terrible moment I feared the cacodaimon was intent on claiming another vessel—minds weakened through drugs or alcohol were easier to subvert.

But the creature twisted sharply, angling its body toward a distant arch of brick and concrete on the far side of the road. Broad marquee letters stretched between the twin towers of the gateway.

EUCLID BEACH PARK

It was heading for the lake.

I pelted after it, but couldn't move fast enough, and the burning stitch in my side that came with each breath was a warning. Nevertheless, I ignored it, and with the dregs of my physical reserves, I *pushed*.

This time, the speed didn't come. The thundering ache in my chest cut so sharp, for a minute I couldn't breathe.

My legs went all watery and I nearly pitched forward.

While I floundered, the cacodaimon arrowed toward escape. Once it reached the silt-choked waters of Erie, I might as well quit. Cacodaimons belonged to the deep places, and those were places I couldn't—and wouldn't—venture.

What I needed was a Crossing so I could face the creature on the Shadowside. That was my turf, the unique purview of the Anakim tribe. The transit had a price, of course—every power did—but it didn't grind me down as fast as the Nephilim speed. I needed the use of my wings. On that side, I didn't have to run—I could fly.

Concentrating to make my head stop spinning, I threw my senses wide, seeking the telltale stain of human trauma. Crossings required a special alchemy— the perfect blend of drawn-out violence, fear, and desolation. The gas station attendant's death had been brutal, but too swift. He'd been bleeding out before he even processed the attack.

Just as I was about to give up, there was a prickling presence. Turning toward the glimmer of distant apartments, I homed in on the source. If I could find the nexus and cross quickly, I could take to the air and get the drop on this monster so it couldn't return and claim another life.

Through the thunder of my pulse, I found the edge of the psychic imprint about thirty feet to the left of the archway. There, an incandescent moment of human suffering played against the landscape like a movie loop on endless repeat, invisible to mortal senses. My focus narrowed until the shadowy echo was all I could perceive—an elderly woman's brutal assault.

Details flooded over me in a rush, images and emotions twining indistinguishably. I seized them like a rope, and for a moment I was completely immersed. I saw the snowy cap of her hair, buzzed close to her scalp so she didn't have to fuss. Arthritis put a wobble in her gait that had embarrassed her twenty years back. Now, not so much. She was simply happy she had legs that carried her along. Too poor to own a car, she'd given up on cabs long ago. Cabbies didn't stop for folks so dark, not even with that much white in their hair.

The loops of heavy plastic grocery bags cut into her hands, and she fussed about the apples that fool of a clerk had dumped down at the bottom beneath the bread. She just knew she was going to lose one through a tear, and those apples were destined for a pie. A reward for a very special grandson. Straight A's another semester.

Boy was going places.

She was so proud.

As she paused to rearrange the bags, two men—teens by the look of them—sauntered up behind her. She daydreamed about her grandson standing tall in cap and gown, and was so fixated on the sight of that future diploma that she didn't notice the shadowy figures looming close by.

They didn't like the look of her. Their brutish emotions blurred in jagged bursts across the vision, momentarily blotting out the image of the elderly woman. The Shadowside gobbled the sounds of their voices, but it was easy to guess the slurs.

The scene stuttered forward and the woman was

locked in a desperate struggle. She didn't take their treatment quietly, never tolerated that sort of ugliness— not when she was young, and not now—but her days of fighting were long behind her. She swung the grocery bags at her attackers, it wrecked her balance, and she went down. Enraged by her defiance, they kicked and punched and beat her, mouths twisted in silent shouts.

She shielded her head from the worst of it, but her body rocked with every blow. I imagined I could hear the crackling of broken ribs, the high and tremulous keening of her pain.

They didn't kill her. When she didn't beg, they grew bored. In the end, the tallest stole an apple, cheerfully eating as they left her in a heap among her smashed and scattered groceries. His smug triumph filled my mouth with bitter bile—

And then I was through. Blinking, I swayed in the grayscale landscape, briefly uncertain where the imprinted emotions ended and my own began. The chittering cry of the cacodaimon lasered my attention back to the present. The sound dopplered in the distance. If I didn't hurry, the bastard would escape.

With a few solid strokes of my wings, I took to the sky.

3

Below me stretched the phantom of a bustling amusement park—Euclid Beach, gone for decades but so firmly imprinted in local memory that echoes of both park-goers and rides remained in the patchwork landscape of the Shadowside. Faded as photos on antique film, the coasters and crowds stuttered in and out of existence, shuffled over by other, less distinct imprints—the blocky hulks of construction equipment, barren fields, and the brittle ghosts of long-dead trees.

I spied it near the lusterless form of an endlessly spinning carousel—a shadow so black that light sank into its depths. The cacodaimon glided sinuously from one old-time ride to the next, swimming through the air as easily as water. In an instant, it became aware of my attention, doubling its speed to disappear beneath the cover of a broad, flat building perched on Lake Erie's edge.

Beyond the specter of that building, the great maw of the lake gobbled the horizon. As I pounded the air, that growing sharpness tightened within my chest. It was more than a holdover from the failed attempt at Nephilim-speed. Every minute in this twilit realm sucked precious vitality. Though I was technically immortal, if I overstayed my welcome I still could die—at least the physical part of me. The rest would drift, unmoored, while I struggled to attach myself to a new incarnation.

It was a process I hoped to avoid. I didn't trust it. Steeling myself, I scanned the ground and readied my weapons. Spirit-fire licked along the gleaming curves of my daggers, a perfect echo of the light streaming from my wings.

The cacodaimon finally darted from its cover and toward the sucking void of the lake. I dropped like a thunderbolt and caught up with it on a thin strip of sand perhaps ten feet from the edge of the blackness. With the yawning chasm of Erie at my back, I defiantly spread my wings. The cacodaimon reared and hissed in their glow, baring a maw bristling with teeth.

"Eeeeeat yyoouu, Sssskyborn. Ssssnuuufff yoouurrr liiightttt." The voice of the creature flensed the air, shrilling like metal collapsed beneath its own weight.

It lunged, and I lashed out in swift response. The cacodaimon dodged—but not fast enough. Half a dozen insectile limbs fell twitching at my feet. It recovered quickly. Feinting left, then right, it strove to snake beneath the living barrier at my back. Talons raked my side as I pivoted to block its escape. The thick leather of my biker jacket deflected most of the blow, but one stinging line of cold blossomed along the exposed flesh of my throat. Cloying numbness trailed in the cacodaimon's wake.

Shaking off the damage, I buffeted the creature with the joint of one great wing. Wherever it made contact, the light sizzled the nightmare's rubbery flesh. My breath hitched at the stink.

Though I was running on fumes, the lust of battle kept me moving. My curving daggers flashed once, then twice, tearing through the cacodaimon's central mass. Still dazed by the blow from my wing, the creature thrashed feebly, scything its tail toward my knees. The strike never connected. After a third pass from my daggers, the chittering horror disintegrated into chunks of black jelly—sticky as Napalm but with an arctic burn. They spread freezing numbness wherever they touched skin, then, like snow on hot pavement, melted clean away.

In the wake of the fight, I sucked air in heaving gulps. The stench of burned cacodaimon seared the back of my throat. I spat its foulness onto the ground, but it was the kind of taste that lingered. Tomorrow I'd wake up with it pasted to my tongue.

Wiping the gunk from my blades, I crossed back into the flesh-and-blood world. Dropping to my knees in the dirty sand, I struggled to get both daggers back into the Kydex sheaths that ran the lengths of my forearms. My hands shook with post-adrenaline tremors as I tugged the cuffs of my jacket down to conceal the rounded pommels. A fishy gust from the lake chilled streamers of sweat trickling down my face.

My whole neck felt wet. Tacky.

That wasn't sweat.

Blindly, I sought the edges of the wound, trying to get a sense of its length and depth. Scalpel-clean, it didn't hurt or sting, at least not yet. That probably wasn't good, but, so far, nothing spurted. A nick to jugular or carotid would have meant near-instant death.

While I shoved my fingers into the slice at my throat, someone uttered a harsh whisper.

Behind you.

It came so fast I couldn't tell if the voice belonged to a woman or a man. I wasn't even certain it was human. Awkwardly, I whirled to catch sight of the speaker. There was nothing—and no one—behind me. It wasn't uncommon for me to hear spirits, but Lailah was the only one I might expect to issue phantom warnings. Yet I'd know her voice, even in whispers.

This wasn't the Lady of Shades.

Overhead, the blind eye of the moon peeked through a scudding veil of clouds, making its first appearance in hours. As I scanned the silvered landscape, a rush of motion rustled the hair at my nape. It carried with it the strangest scent, like the wind scouring distant tundra. Frigid and desolate, it stirred emotions deep in the hinterlands of my brain—something familiar that I couldn't place. I lurched to my feet in an instant, yanking out both gleaming blades. Brandishing the weapons, I pivoted to meet an attacker.

Again, there was no one.

Either I'd lost more blood than I'd realized and was hallucinating, or someone was fucking with me. The soaring moon winked in and out, its light strobing the empty beach, making monsters of piles of driftwood. On high alert, I turned in every direction. From east to west, no living being stirred, only deep shadows. Even the sand showed only the footprints I'd made, beginning where I'd exited the Shadowside.

Nevertheless, I couldn't shake the sense I was being watched. So I wove a cowl to cloak the more-than-human parts of me, adding extra layers to distract and obscure my presence. Tentatively re-sheathing only one of the weapons, I lingered uncertainly on the gray stretch of beach, struggling to place that cold, desolate scent. Nothing came. Heart still surging, I shifted my vision to peer into the Shadowside.

No spirits. Nothing. Just the sucking chasm masquerading as a lake.

Baffled, I started limping back toward the road. The more distance I could put between me and those haunted waters, the better.

4

As I scrabbled up the steep embankment, a call came through on my cell.

At first, I just jumped at the manic buzz against my backside. The traitor moon had fled and, in the gloom, lights from the distant apartments were barely visible through a stand of second-growth trees. The phone buzzed again and I dug for it in my pocket, if only to shut the thing up.

A fine tracery of wards prickled my fingers when I brushed the slim case. I was proud of that work—the wards were probably the only reason the device had any charge. Ordinarily, Shadowside travel sucked the life from electronics, especially the delicate inner workings of smartphones. Over the summer, I'd done enough theorycrafting to sort out a fix. So far, the protective mesh of magic had held.

My first instinct was to send the call straight to voicemail. I'd done that so often, I could thumb the red CANCEL button without even looking. Then curiosity overrode my antisocial tendencies and I flipped over the screen. The upwash of light blew my already iffy night vision as I squinted at the name.

Bobby Park.

At this hour, if my detective friend was calling, he had to have good reason. I just hoped it wasn't related to the two corpses I'd recently left at the gas station. I didn't need any more WANTED bulletins in my life. Still, I hesitated a moment, but all my instincts screamed this call was important.

"Bobby," I said. My voice came out ragged and I roughly cleared my throat. Swallowing caused the cut to twinge beneath my jaw. "Hey."

"You answered your phone." He sounded stunned.

"People keep telling me to do that," I said, wavering near the crest of the embankment, reluctant to move forward with the afterimage still floating against my retinas. "What's happening? My name come over dispatch?"

"No," he answered cautiously. "You in trouble?" I pictured him rubbing restlessly at the back of his scalp— his stock gesture. He always looked shocked to find his hair so short.

"Hopefully not." With the back of my arm, I swiped a trickle of sweat before it made it into my eyes. The rough leather of my jacket found every scrape landed by the cacodaimon. "So what's up?" I asked. The muffled murmur of the wind rattled through the nearly naked branches of the trees.

"If this isn't a good time…" he offered.

I scanned the shadowed landscape for any sign of further threats. It was empty. Cacodaimons weren't subtle creatures—if there was another one, it would have already jumped me. "Good as any."

"OK," he answered skeptically. There was a pause and a brief rustle of fabric. "You remember those two women you had me looking for? The ones from your letter?"

"Marjory and Tabitha," I said. "Of course I remember." As my eyes adjusted, I headed deeper into the tangle of second-growth. The broad, flat field that had once been the midway for Euclid Beach Park stretched maybe twenty yards beyond the thicket. It hadn't seemed that far from the air. "They're supposed to have keys to some safe deposit box of mine. I have no idea what's in there."

"Well, there wasn't much to go on," he said. "Mother-daughter pair, maybe based in Parma. No last name. Every search kept coming up empty." Distantly, the sound of heels scuffing tile came through the phone. He was pacing. Echoes told me he was in an empty room— probably a back hall of the precinct.

"Something changed." It wasn't a question.

"Zack, before I say anything else, I've got to ask. Are you sure your parents live in Kenosha?"

That came out of left field. Startled, I paused, and something crashed noisily through the carpet of dead leaves.

"No, I'm not," I responded, glancing around. "Amnesia, remember? You're the one who told me about them." Nerves and exhaustion stropped an edge to my words, harsher than I'd intended. Squinting in the direction of the crackling twigs, I tried to make out the shape of an animal, but it was impossible to see in the gloom. Whatever it was, it sounded big. Even so, nothing appeared.

Probably just a deer. Sure—because, in my life, everything was harmless.

"How's any of this connected anyway?" I demanded.

Bobby ignored the question. "Then you haven't had *any* contact with your parents since your accident?"

"No," I snapped. "What the hell would I say? 'Hi, Mom. Hi, Dad. I don't fucking remember either of you, but here's a card for the occasion.'" The crunching sounds stopped.

"Zack, I'm not trying to be an asshole here."

"If you say so," I answered. "Spill it, Bobby." Three beats of silence. I counted as I started walking again, trying to duck low-hanging branches. Bobby sighed, and the sound rattled the mic like a windstorm. Finally, he spoke.

"I'm pretty sure I found Marjory," he said. "But you won't like it."

My stomach dropped.

"She's dead," I said flatly.

"Murdered," he answered. "And it's not pretty."

Quietly, I digested this. "Are you sure? With no last name, how do we know it's the right Marjory?"

"Residence in Parma. Daughter named Tabitha," he said. I could practically see him ticking off points on his fingers as he moved restlessly with the phone trapped between cheek and shoulder. "And—here's the kicker—she's got you in her contacts."

"Hunh," I murmured. The deer—or whatever—was long gone. "I suppose that's not a surprise. After all, I trusted her enough to leave her with the keys to… whatever," I said. "Why are you so knotted up about this?"

"I don't like laying this kind of news on somebody," he said. "Especially not a friend. This Marjory—she's more than just a business contact, Zack. After her daughter, she has you listed as her next of kin."

5

"I'm *what*?" I squawked. A startled night bird took to the air in a whirr of wings. I dropped my voice, making a token effort at becoming stealthy. "Are you *sure*? Does it mention how we're related?"

"No, and no," Bobby replied. "It just gives your name, and some address in Tremont."

A welter of questions roiled through my brain. After my beach-front fight with the cacodaimon, I felt ill-equipped to deal with any of them. It took all I had to put one foot in front of the other to get out of the damned trees. "Tremont" struck a chord, though.

"I've got a stash out there, but it's in an abandoned video store," I said. "No apartment, not that I know of."

"Nothing you remember, anyway," Bobby suggested. The near-pity in his voice would have rankled, had it come from anyone else, but with Bobby, empathy was a reflex, as irresistible as breathing. Not always an asset in his line of work.

Mounded leaves crunched underfoot, obscuring

knotted roots. My boots found every damned one, though. Switching to speaker, I angled the phone at the ground like a flashlight, but the bluish light was little help.

"What's her last name?" I asked.

"Kazinsky."

"Hunh," I muttered. Nothing rattled loose at the name.

"Look, Zack, I don't know what to make of the next-of-kin thing, but in this case, it works to our advantage," Bobby said, his voice tinny and distant. "I really need your eyes on this, and they still need someone to identify her remains."

"My Kawasaki's sitting at a gas station about a mile away." *Assuming it's not already been impounded.* "Wait a minute," I blurted, finally processing the last half of his statement. "Identify the body? Hasn't the daughter already done that?"

Silence. I still had four bars, so it wasn't the call.

"Bobby?" I urged.

"No one can reach her."

"You think she's dead, too."

"Can't rule it out," he allowed.

"Shit," I said.

"Yeah," Bobby concurred. "Look, I'm on shift until six-thirty," he said. "It's not my case, but I called in a favor, so I can meet you at the county morgue." Briskly, he rattled off the address for the medical examiner's offices. I was familiar with the building, though I had no conscious recollection of visiting the place. A moment later, Bobby's voice went all echoey, as if he'd cupped his hand over the phone. "If we do it tonight, I can get you direct access to the body." Another long pause. "You need to see this, Zack. This attack was personal."

"Personal?" I echoed. "Are you talking about Marjory, or me?"

On the other end of the phone a door opened, unoiled hinges creaking. Booted footsteps—not Bobby's—grew loud. Abruptly his whole tone changed, getting louder, flippantly casual.

"So, yeah," he said. Cloth rustled. "We can do breakfast. No later than seven, 'K?"

"Bobby?" I started, and then thought better of it.

"Gotta go, hun," he said. The call ended.

"Dammit!" I hissed, scowling at the phone.

I was about to thumb the CALLBACK button when another crash rattled the underbrush. This time, it was practically on top of me. That prickling sense of observation returned, sweeping along my spine to end in a vise-like tightness at my throat. I swallowed hard, and regretted it immediately.

Deep in the shadows between the trees, two red eyes slid open. Baleful and gleaming, they fixed instantly on me. A chittering cry brought all my neck hairs to stiff attention.

"You sneaky bastard," I breathed. "You've been stalking me this whole time." Quickly, I traded phone for blades, cursing my muddy-headed distraction. I should have known to stay vigilant, especially after the weirdness with that phantom voice on the shore. Just because I couldn't see the monsters didn't mean they weren't out to get me.

Marshaling my focus, I crossed my blades.

"Bring it," I hissed.

With gnashing teeth, the third cacodaimon erupted

from the trees. This one was bigger than the others, and just as ugly. Weak and sputtering, spirit-fire ignited my blades.

A torrent of leaves skirled in its wake. That wasn't right. Cacodaimons were spirits—they couldn't properly touch things in the physical world. There was no way its passage should crackle branches and stir up leaves.

They can't change the rules, can they?

The thought was fleeting. The slithery horror barreled straight for me, and all my focus narrowed to the work of staying alive. I didn't have a lot of juice left, but I wouldn't go down without a fight.

The guttering flames of my daggers did little to deter the chittering nightmare. Maw open, it dove at me. I struck for the center of its body, but the creature reared up and back, nimbly evading my weapons. It slithered through the air with the grace of a serpent, utterly unfettered by gravity. With rapid undulations, it swept high above my head, unfolding countless jointed limbs to lash at my face, scalp, and neck. Points of bitter cold blossomed across every inch of exposed flesh.

Waves of dizzying numbness swiftly followed.

Instinctively, I spread my wings to leap and meet my attacker—but this wasn't the Shadowside. I was grounded. Snarling in frustration, I pummeled the cacodaimon in a sweep of gleaming pinions—the wings might have no substance in the flesh-and-blood world, but to the cacodaimon, they still carried a wallop.

Staggered, the creature lurched close enough for me to tag its belly. I plunged a dagger into the sectioned torso, opening a gash as long as my forearm. Viscous fluid came flooding out, covering my hand in stinking goo. Straining upward, I slashed to sever its lower half completely, but the cacodaimon whipped its twitching coils beyond my reach. The bony spike at the end of its tail narrowly missed my face.

For a moment, the creature hung suspended in the air above me, madly shrilling its pain. Then it tucked its head and dove straight for the middle of my back. Swiping with my wings, I pivoted sharply, only partly deflecting the impact. Instead of my spine, it crashed thunderingly against one shoulder, spinning me around with the force of a battering ram.

I kept my feet—just barely. Bringing my blades up to counter, I cut a swath of legs to steaming stumps as they scrabbled to pierce the armor of my leather. It had plenty more to work with. Little points of stinging chill erupted as a few of them burrowed past my defenses. The numbing contact drained some of the fight from me—those legs weren't just cutting into my flesh. They were seeking purchase in my nervous system. That was how the cacodaimons rode their victims—and ultimately how they killed them. Immortal or not, I'd seen more powerful beings than me devoured by these horrors. It was a shitty way to die.

Slashing wildly, I severed its connections—any I could reach—but it was a losing battle.

The cacodaimon draped itself across my shoulders. How had it gotten to my back again? Hadn't I dodged? It settled the center of its weight into that unreachable span between shoulderblades and wings. In tightening coils, it wound itself past my knees and I braced my legs, fighting to keep my footing.

I couldn't remember when the beast had trapped my hands, but then they hung against my sides, the light around my weapons snuffed completely. All of it was happening too fast and my brain limped uselessly. The coils tightened and the hilts of my daggers slid from nerveless fingers. Dimly, as if from a vast and echoing distance, I felt the impact of the weapons as they thudded to the leaves.

Thoughts came in disjointed flashes.

Frustration. Fury. Panic.

I needed to get away—didn't I?

Too much effort. Even standing was a strain.

Fight, you idiot!

The voice came from everywhere and nowhere. Maybe just inside my head. It didn't matter. I sank on trembling knees.

In a slow-motion slink, the cacodaimon maneuvered its black nubbin of a head around from behind my right shoulder. Eyes cut into the black void of its flesh studied me, so close I was drowning. It had no pupils, just slits of unrelieved crimson. A membrane flickered, and—for a moment—a green as pale as poison bubbled up to drown the red. The color shift lasted only an instant, but something about that brief transition stopped my breath more completely than the coils constricting my body.

"Knoww yyooouuu, Aannnakiimm. Huunntt yyoouuu."

Row upon row of wickedly edged teeth rippled the length of its gullet. Its mouth gaped wide enough to swallow my face and, for a terrible instant, it seemed to consider exactly that course of action. Then, quizzical as a hound, it cocked its head.

"*Whhyyyyyy?*"

Drawn far beyond the span of its single syllable, the question scrabbled at the air with creeping urgency. My slack lips hung empty of answers. I barely remembered the taste of words.

It repeated its plaintive question, growing strangely docile. Without warning, the invertebrate horror released me, its coils unspooling so rapidly that I dropped heavily to the ground. With an eye-tricking swiftness, it vaulted heavenward, the contours of its alien form so dark they sketched a void against the night's gathering clouds. In mid-air, it screeched, then twisted, plummeting past the edge of the embankment to disappear into the lake.

Gasping, I sprawled in the damp nest of leaves.

6

For an interminable stretch of minutes, my brain clamored orders at a body that stubbornly refused to respond. Eventually, my arm twitched—that was something. Then I made a fist, and it felt like a triumph.

With the angry ants of nerve pain swarming beneath my skin, I dragged myself into a sitting position. My head throbbed and the world swung wildly, so I didn't try to stand right away. Feeling around in the shadows and tree clutter for my blades, I found first one and then the other, wiping them on my jeans with an unsteady grip.

Sheathing them was an adventure. I still couldn't fully feel my hands.

Head clearing, I levered myself up and leaned my back against the nearest trunk. A sighing wind stirred the branches and I tensed, half-expecting the hollow clack and rattle to herald the return of the cacodaimon. But the chittering horror had fled deep beneath Erie's waves.

At least, I hoped it had. Things had gone bad so fast. I still couldn't figure out how the thing had gotten the upper hand, or why it hadn't pressed its advantage. The creature's bizarre behavior was the only reason I wasn't a corpse oozing gray matter out of my ears. If it decided to return for another attack, I didn't like the odds for my survival.

All questions and no answers. My head ached.

Heaving to my feet, I took a few, halting steps to make sure I could walk without pitching over. Every muscle burned with exhaustion, but I needed to get across town. Marjory's body lay on some anonymous slab, and I needed to see what had Bobby so rattled. More than that, I needed to get the hell away from the lake.

One foot in front of the other...

My inner cheerleader sounded pretty weak.

Slogging out of the woods, I started across the broad, flat field that was all that remained of the old midway. Halfway to the gas station it started to rain—a gentle fall of drops that made the night smell strongly of damp stone and turning leaves. Then a wind gusted from across the lake, tearing the bellies from the clouds. In an instant, the soft patter became a deluge. Rain pasted my hair against my scalp, sluicing down my neck to soak the T-shirt under my jacket. The gash on my neck stung like hell—as did every other nick and scrape landed by the cacodaimons.

The half-mile to my bike was starting to feel like half a million. I wanted my Vulcan, but I wasn't even certain I could trust myself to ride it, especially not with all this rain. Peeling my phone from my pocket, I started texting Bobby, but remembered that he was on shift.

I hit backspace until all the letters disappeared.

Sluggishly ticking through my narrow options, I

dithered on the side of the road as the storm cut tiny rivers through the gravel at my feet. Father Frank didn't own a vehicle, and he sure as hell wasn't calling Sanjeet at this hour. Cabs didn't run this late—not on this side of town, and what cabbie in his right mind would pick me up anyway?

Remy? I'd been avoiding him of late, but my brother owed me one. No question he'd be awake, too—all the Nephilim were essentially vampires, right down to the pointy little fangs.

Hell, no. Dealing with Remy meant dealing with his boss Saliriel, and I'd be safer with the cacodaimons.

Doggedly I lurched onward, swiping rain from my eyes and struggling to ignore the way the muscles trembled across my back and legs. Coming within sight of the gas station, I kept to the shadows, taking shelter under an expansive sycamore that had yet to surrender its autumn wealth of leaves.

My bike stood off to one side, just outside of the pool of light. The helmet lay on the pavement where I'd dropped it. But getting to the Kawasaki wasn't going to be easy.

Emergency responders crowded the lot, most of them clustered around a seizing heap sprawled at the threshold of the convenience store. Amazingly, it was the woman, and she wasn't yet dead. Brains leaking out of her ears, somehow, she had managed to drag herself past the first row of pumps to get all the way to the swinging door. Two sets of EMTs struggled to get her on a stretcher, and she fought with bloodied teeth and nails.

Horrified pity swelled in a gutting surge as I huddled in the shadow of the tree. Those poor bastards had no way of knowing she was only a husk of meat and instinct, everything else devoured by the cacodaimon. Still, they struggled to save her.

Things like this are why I can't sleep.

One of the medical techs finally pinned her shoulders, holding her prone while she struggled to take chunks out of his forearm. Another got her legs, narrowly dodging a kick to the jaw. The two remaining worked hurriedly to strap her in place.

While they wrestled, a small, uniformed officer exited a squad car parked on the other side of the building. Something told me it was a woman. She wore a clear, shapeless poncho that draped her so thoroughly, she could've passed for a Jawa. Opening the back door of her vehicle, she motioned impatiently. The lanky figure that unfolded was dressed head-to-toe in black, so he was even harder to see than she was, but something about him riveted my attention. He hunched self-consciously in the rain, his back turned to me. He wore a leather jacket. From this angle, it looked a lot like my own.

Maybe that was what caught my eye.

They spoke in a rapid series of exchanges, the tall man mainly nodding as the woman replied with animated gestures. Rain lashed sideways as the storm intensified and then she turned abruptly, seeking the cover of the canopy. The tall man hesitated long enough to sweep his dripping hair from his eyes, then, with loping strides, he jogged after the tiny officer.

When he stepped into the glow of the overhead lights, I shivered down to my marrow. The stark brow, the long, angular features—the finer details were lost to the needling rain, but the guy could've passed for my twin brother. Even his clothes were the same, right down to the biker jacket. Hurriedly, I teased open my perceptions to examine the man's echo on the Shadowside.

What the hell?

The guy was just a hollow spot knocking against my vision. If he had a cowl or some other kind of cloaking magic, it was wrapped so tightly, I couldn't spot any metaphysical seams.

A gnawing sense of familiarity grew and blossomed the longer I watched the guy, like notes of music heard from a vast distance. I *almost* understood what lay in front of me—knew with absolute certainty that I *should*—but each attempt to pluck at that thread of recognition only caused the surrounding details to unravel. With mounting trepidation, I realized this was knowledge that had been taken from me, one more crumb of understanding denied post-mortem by Dorimiel.

That couldn't be good. All my hackles went up, and it took everything I had to stay under that tree.

With painful effort, I quashed the impulse to tackle him, my fingers digging so deep into the mottled bark of the sycamore, little splinters shivved under my nails.

The lady cop said something, and he gestured impatiently toward my motorcycle. She scowled, but he spoke again and, under the rain-speckled folds of her poncho, her shoulders slumped in something like resignation. With a brusque note of warning, she tossed him a set of keys. They sketched a perfect arc in the air, and even in the rain it was impossible to mistake the distinctive shape of the pewter Millennium Falcon I kept on my keychain.

Where the hell did they get those? I patted my pockets, including the ones inside of my jacket, and swallowed a curse. *Shit.* I'd dropped them in the chaos earlier.

Fury spiked again, hot and choking.

My doppelganger looked up as if he could hear the very intensity of my emotion. Eyes questing in my direction, he plucked the keys from the air with a negligent dexterity just this side of human. Keeping to the shadows behind the broad trunk of the tree, I clamped down so hard on my cowl it felt like I'd been shoved out an airlock.

His gaze faltered. I didn't let myself relax—I couldn't. The bastard with my face scooped up the helmet, popping it onto his head. A moment later the bike growled to life, and I froze in a paroxysm of indecision. I needed that motorcycle, but I couldn't blithely march over and tear it away from him—not with all those cops around. It wasn't just that they might arrest me—there were plenty of strings I could pull. No, it was that in situations like this one, the mortals around me had an ugly habit of dying.

Whoever this guy was, every instinct told me he was dangerous.

No more death tonight.

So I ground my teeth and watched him ride out of the lot on my bike. As he coasted past my hiding spot, a gust of pressure shoved against my cowl, like nothing I'd ever felt. The reflective visor of the helmet swiveled slowly in my direction. The sheen of lights on beading rain obscured his features, but I knew with bone-deep certainty he was staring right at me.

7

The roar of the four-stroke retreated in the distance. Westbound, toward Cleveland. I needed to get moving. That set of keys didn't just work the Vulcan—there was a full set for locks on my apartment. Given his appearance, I had to assume my evil twin knew where I lived—and, if he knew that, he probably knew what I had there.

Things were going to get ugly.

The keys wouldn't get him past the aggressive layers of wards I'd worked around my place, but that didn't make me feel any better. If my doppelganger suspected the existence of even *one* of the things stashed in that apartment, he'd find a way inside.

Moving slowly, I quitted the cover of the sycamore. Every instinct jangled for me to rush, but I forced myself to play it cool so I didn't attract attention. Head down, I shuffled along like some unfortunate caught in the fierce autumn storm. It was an easy enough ruse. From the tail of my eye, I kept watch over the activity at the Qwik-

Fill. No one looked up, and no one raised an alarm.

Free and clear.

Finding a bench near the playground, I dared to pull out my phone, huddling over the harshly glowing screen in a weak attempt to protect it from the sheeting rain. The battery was so far into the red, I could barely see the sliver of color. With luck, it would last for one call. Choking down a double helping of stiff-necked pride, I pulled up Remiel's number.

His phone went straight to voicemail. I left a long and rambling message. A beep cut me off about halfway through. The phone buzzed once as I pulled it from my ear and, excited, went to thumb the answer button. But it wasn't a call. The screen flashed a low battery warning. 1%.

Quickly hammering a text, I cursed as the device refused to register a full half of my keystrokes. My fingers were too cold—not that I could feel them. Eventually, I managed.

> Need a favor. Pick me up in Collinwood. Old
> Euclid Beach gate.

Remy would know the landmark—every long-term resident of the city did, and he'd been living in Cleveland since the 1800s. Racing to beat the last gasp of battery life, I appended the word URGENT in all caps and hit send. Hawkishly, I watched the screen to see if it went through.

It did. After a breathless hesitation, three little dots in a bubble told me Remy was typing. He'd gotten the message. Before his text appeared, the phone's screen winked out. Morosely, I stared at my reflection in its black mirror.

He'd come. I had to trust it.

Haggard and weary, I retraced my path. It was a long walk in the punishing rain, but I didn't dare stick close to the gas station. Reaching the arching brick landmark, I sat at the base of one of the tower-styled pillars, huddled against the downpour. Ugly whiffs of violence seeped through my shields from the nearby Crossing. Tired as I was, I couldn't hold my walls against it. Tightening the layered cowl with flagging mental focus, I did my best to ignore it. The woman's plight was long over, although the winking lights of the distant apartment building made me wonder if she were still alive—and if it would do any good for her to know that I'd borne witness to her suffering.

Probably not. Sympathy only salved my own conscience.

I settled in for a long wait. My thoughts drifted, and, despite the aches and the rain, I slipped from wakefulness by slow degrees. Weeks of insomnia didn't help. The ugly emotions imprinted scant yards away colored my dreams, and I was plagued by fitful images of a woman calling my name. She was in danger, and I couldn't save her. First she was Lailah, my lover lost on the lake. Then, the elderly black woman from the Crossing. Finally, she was a face seen only distantly, one I didn't know but felt I should have—a round face, apple cheeks, piercing eyes.

The frantic notes of her voice chased me back to the waking world where someone gripped me by the shoulder. He shook fiercely, calling my name—first Zack, and then the older one. Needling shards of nightmare scattered, and I surged at my attacker.

I was scrabbling for a hold on Remy's throat before my brain came awake enough to realize what I was doing.

"Goodness," he said, utterly unfazed by my frenzied reaction. "You look a fright."

With little effort, the Nephilim plucked me off to hold me at arm's length until I stopped thrashing. My toes barely touched the ground—his casual strength was almost insulting. Blearily, I processed my surroundings. The nearby Crossing, the looming arch, the high grasses of the field crushed to sodden heaps by the storm. The rain had stopped, but every inch of me was soaked, and it was a good thing I didn't really feel the cold, or else I'd have been hypothermic.

"Sorry," I breathed. One of his lapels jutted at an awkward angle where I'd rumpled his expensive jacket, and I fought an urge to fix it. Instead, I shoved my hands in my pockets. Remy followed my gaze, putting me down, then fastidiously smoothing the wrinkles in the red and gold damask.

"No need to apologize." His pale lips twisted in a fond, if rueful, grin. "I knew what manner of bear I was poking."

Awkward silence fell as I tried for something else to say. Months had passed since I'd last spoken with Remy. He was, of all my many siblings, one of the few I counted as both a brother and a friend—but his ties to Sal made things complicated.

"It's been a rough night," I hedged.

"I can see that," he replied. A subtle accent clung to his vowels, impossible to accurately place. Vaguely

British, it made everything he said sound sardonic. "Do you need medical attention? You've got a gash on your neck that's still bleeding."

With a grimace, I touched my fingers to the stinging line of heat below my jaw. They came away slick.

"Must've reopened it fighting you off," I grumbled. "It can't be too deep or I wouldn't have made it this far, right?"

"You were passed out when I found you."

"Not passed out," I said. "I was sleeping."

One brow arched eloquently. "On the pavement," he said. "In the rain."

"I haven't slept for shit in weeks," I responded. "That's why I was out here in the first place. I thought a ride would clear my head. Insomnia's got its teeth in me again."

"More than insomnia, judging from the state of your face."

"That was the cacodaimons," I explained, sagging against the pillar.

Remy's eyes, an uncanny shade of azure, glimmered with their own light as he studied the wounds more carefully. We stood in a pool of shadow cast by the looming gate of Euclid Beach, but the darkness was hardly a deterrent for the Nephilim's preternatural vision.

"A hospital won't do," he murmured. "They'll have questions. I'll take you to one of my people."

"I need to get to my apartment," I said flatly. "I'll clean it up there."

Remy waggled a lean, pale finger in my face. "Your text phrased this as a favor, dear brother," he reminded. "Favors come with a price."

"Taking lessons from Sal?" I rankled. "This is important."

At the comparison, the light glittered in his eyes. "Do you think I'm stupid?" he growled. "If you weren't completely out of options, you wouldn't have bothered to call me at all."

"No, I—"

Brusquely, he cut me off. "You have been avoiding me as if I have something contagious." He was annoyed enough to lisp around his fangs. "Now get in the car. I'd prefer not to have this conversation in public."

His midnight blue Lexus idled at the curb, the driver's side door slightly ajar. A soft, persistent "ding" emanated from the interior. I started for the vehicle, but lurched unexpectedly when a wave of vertigo spun my internal gyroscope. The whole world took on a sharp tilt. Instinctively, I threw my arms out for balance. Without a word, Remy seized me by the elbow, then steadied my steps till we made it to the sedan. Brusquely, he folded me into the passenger seat, and I did my best to help. Mostly I flopped like a flounder.

Inside, the vehicle was spotless, its gray leather seats smelling vaguely of mink oil. I almost felt bad for sitting on them.

"Seatbelt," he reminded me tersely, then he closed the door. I was still fumbling to fit the metal tongue in the clasp when he slid into the driver's seat. With a little frown, he took the apparatus from my hand and clicked the belt home for me. Offering no further comment, he put the car in gear and pulled back onto Lakeshore.

The tires of the Lexus whispered wetly against pavement as we sat in strained silence, each waiting for the other to begin what could only prove to be a difficult conversation. Neither of us was brave enough to take the first step. The quiet was so absolute, I wasn't certain he even bothered to breathe—didn't even know if he had to.

When I couldn't stand it any longer, I reached for the radio. Faster than I could track, Remy slapped my hand away from the knob.

"No." He uttered it firmly, but without heat.

The lights of the dash glittered on the gold trim along his cuffs, and for the first time, I fully processed what he was wearing. Frock coat of elaborate damask, ruffled shirt, velvet pants so tight they might have been painted onto his legs and—was that make-up? His long, black hair hung in carefully dressed waves, as rich as any kingly wig.

"Did you mug Louis Quatorze?" I choked. My brother had flamboyant tastes, but normally they ran toward fedoras and zoot suits. This was weird, even for Remy. Once I'd noticed, I couldn't stop staring.

"I beg your pardon?" Remy asked.

"This." I gestured at his get-up.

Flicking his eyes from the road, Remy offered me a disdainful moue. "Three months without contact, and the first thing you do is criticize my clothes?"

"But look at them!" I insisted.

"I did," he replied. "In the mirror, when I selected them quite specifically for the occasion." The fact that he wasn't yelling only accentuated his irritation. "Perhaps, dear Anakim brother, if you'd paid any attention at all to my personal affairs, you would know that we had a performance tonight at Club Heaven. It went beautifully, by the way, right up until my unexpected departure."

"Oh," I managed.

"*Oh*," he echoed in withering mockery. "What, no witty repartee? I would expect, at least, some *Interview with a Vampire* comment."

"The book or the movie?" I ventured. Snark was preferable to stinging guilt.

"You forced me to watch the movie," he sniffed. "The book was *not* to my taste."

I tried to picture us binge-watching Anne Rice together. The image was ludicrous, and despite everything, I cackled. That actually eased the tension. Even Remy chuckled softly. Idling at a light, he regarded me with a wistful expression.

"When you're not being a caustic ass, you are entirely ridiculous," he said. "And I miss that."

No words felt adequate, and even if I'd found them, they wouldn't have fit past the knot in my throat. So I just hung my head. Remy mistook it for more evasion.

"I can understand why you are reluctant," he began as the light changed. "What Dorimiel did to you onboard the *Scylla* was unforgivable. The depth of your loss—I cannot even begin to imagine." He wasn't just talking about Lailah, although her death rested firmly in Dorimiel's hands. The power-mad decimus of the Nephilim had used his tribe's stolen icon to attack my mind, sucking away memories until I was left a stranger in my own life. Remy seemed to divine these thoughts.

"I can see how my presence might serve as a bitter reminder, but you *must* know that he and his ilk do not represent all of my tribe." With a gleam of hope, he glanced in my direction, easing down on the brakes as we approached another red light. The light turned green before the car came to a complete stop, and he coasted through it.

Squirming beneath his unearthly blue gaze, I struggled with everything I wanted to say, and couldn't. This time, it wasn't an overwelling of regret that stilled my tongue, but a magical compulsion. Remy's boss, Saliriel, had bound me to an oath, and there were sweeping details about the Dorimiel incident that I simply couldn't share.

Again, Remy misread my silence.

"Zaquiel," he said. "You and I have very different worldviews, and it would be foolish to pretend that relations are functional between our two tribes, but despite all of that, we've been friends for a very long while. Why must that change now?"

Awaiting a response, he swung the Lexus into a parking spot along Euclid Heights. Somehow, we'd already made it to my Coventry apartment. The lights were still off in all the windows, and there was no sign of my Vulcan on the street. Hopefully that was a good thing. Beside me, Remy cut the ignition, slipping the keys into an interior pocket of his frock coat. Self-consciously, he smoothed its lines, but made no move to get out.

I put my palm on the handle, then hesitated.

"Look, it's not—" I started, but the oath closed my throat before I could finish. Superficially, I was bound to keep silent about the Eye of Nefer-Ka, but so many of Dorimiel's atrocities revolved around that ancient icon. The damned thing lay at the bottom of Lake Erie, but its power still wove creeping tendrils through my life.

Nothing I can do about that now.

In silence, Remy studied the chase of emotions that flickered across my features. After a moment, he spoke.

"You're not the only person in the world laboring under an oath, you know."

I stared at him, thunderstruck.

"*What?*" he asked. "I told you that I knew."

"No," I said flatly. "You didn't."

"Yes, of course I did," he insisted.

A light scrim of steam began to cloud my window as I kept one eye on the apartment. Internally, I flailed.

"When?" I demanded.

"Back at the hospital," he said.

"The hospital," I echoed, rubbing my brow. "Which time?"

"After Saliriel resuscitated you on the lake."

"*What?*" That revelation didn't just derail my thoughts—it switched the tracks, sent me barreling over a chasm, and dynamited the trestle behind me. My stomach lurched. "You never said it was Sal," I choked. Remy dipped his head so his long hair partially obscured his features.

"I hadn't intended to let that bit slip."

"Well, too damned late," I said, striving not to picture it—but my brain was regrettably visual. Cheerfully, it disgorged images of Saliriel's plump, pink mouth descending upon mine, then opening to reveal her unnaturally pointy grin. It was the fangs that did it. Shuddering, I scrubbed my lips with the back of my hand, wondering what kind of toll Sal would exact, and when.

Probably saving up for a special occasion.

"Saliriel was the only one who knew the proper... technique." Helpfully, he added, "I've made a point to learn it since then, just in case."

"I don't plan on drowning again," I grumbled.

He sniffed. "I didn't think you'd planned on it the first two times."

On that point, he was wrong, but I tried to get back to the original topic. Tried to say, *"Yes, I'm oathed,"* but my throat locked tight around the statement. Instead of words, only a whistle of air came out. Resisting the urge to pummel the armrest, I counted silently to ten and made a second attempt.

The results were identical.

"Look, we really should continue this inside my apartment," I managed.

In a blur of motion, Remy hit the locks. I didn't have to test my door to know my own button wouldn't work. Remy was one of the nicer ones, but he was still a Nephilim. I wasn't getting out until he was good and ready.

The heat ticked up on my temper.

"There are always loopholes," he urged. "Just talk around it."

Deep in my throat, I growled my irritation. Remy was unimpressed. I lost the fight to save the armrest, pounding it viciously with the heel of my hand.

"I can't even talk about what I can't talk about!" I bellowed.

With a disapproving frown, Remy seized my wrist before I could savage his Lexus any further. The odd chill of his fingers clung wherever they touched my flesh. "Is this really why you've been avoiding me all summer?" he asked. "Honestly, Zaquiel, it's like you're fifteen again."

"Give me a break," I snarled, twisting to break his grip, but he kept my arm locked with no apparent effort.

"No," he said. "I shall only let you go if you promise not to hit things."

"More oaths," I spat.

He reeled as if the words were a fist.

"I would never do that to you, Zaquiel."

His quiet fervor sobered me. I was being a jerk. Remy wasn't the enemy—far from it. The soft-spoken Nephilim was a dedicated friend and mentor. When I awoke in this lifetime there were gaps in my memory, as with all members of my tribe, and Remy had dutifully shepherded me through the early years of confusion. My blood-sucking Obi-Wan Kenobi. That couldn't have been an easy job, but he'd done it for several lifetimes, primarily because of an oath he'd sworn to me.

I stopped struggling.

Remy relinquished my wrist. Across the street, a light went on in the unit beneath mine, a pale testament to how late the night had grown. For some, it was already morning.

"I know we're not done talking," I said, "but I really have to check my apartment."

Skeptically, he quirked a brow, but released the locks. I was out the door and starting across the street before his hand was off the button. The car chirped as he armed the security system. Quickly, he caught up, trailing only a pace or two behind.

"Dare I ask what's the crisis of the week?"

"It's complicated," I muttered.

"When isn't it, with you?"

Instead of heading for the main entrance, I altered course for the back, stepping between the side of the building and a line of decorative firs. Mud and damp mulch squelched under my boot, making the footing slick. It had rained here, too.

"You're skulking," Remy observed. Mincingly he followed my path, somehow managing to avoid all the mud. "You said nothing about stealth. Should I expect a fight once we're inside?"

"Maybe," I replied quietly. "I don't know." Pausing at the back corner, I gestured for him to keep his voice down. From this vantage point, I had a clear view of the small lot set aside for residents, as well as the alley that threaded between units to the next street over. Aside from one old Ford Taurus trailing exhaust as its motor heated up, the place was empty. The Taurus belonged to one of my downstairs neighbors—the guy with the brutally early work schedule. "Some asshole made off with my bike," I explained. "And my keys."

"That would have been useful to know before now," Remy chided. "But unless you keep your home address stamped upon your keychain, a simple thief shouldn't end up at your door."

"This guy was anything but simple," I said. "For one thing, he looked like me."

"How do you mean?" Remy hovered so close to my shoulder, I should have felt him breathe.

"Like full-on evil twin," I said. "Biker jacket and everything." My voice was barely above a whisper, pitched for his ears only—the Nephilim had unnervingly keen hearing. "The cops had him, and he fooled even them. Skated right out of there like it was nothing."

Remy's silence was so deep, I had to look over my shoulder to make sure he was still behind me. His features—normally porcelain-perfect and schooled into a pleasant mask—registered deep unease.

"Yeah, I know," I said. "It can't be good, especially not paired with cacodaimons. I don't know how he's doing it, and I don't know why, but it has to be personal. I mean, how can it *not* be?"

"You really should have mentioned this earlier," Remy said tightly. His lips barely moved.

"You wanted to talk about oaths," I replied, creeping forward so I could catch sight of the furthest corner of the lot—the dumpster. That part was in deepest shadow, the week's trash spilling out of the battered metal bin. A weathered fence rose behind it, and behind that, a tall, leaning pole that should have held a security light, but didn't. The damned thing hadn't worked since I'd started living here again.

"Doesn't look like he ended up here, so that's something."

"Unless he was smart enough to leave that motorcycle of yours on another street," Remy suggested. "It's a distinctive vehicle."

He had a point. I scanned the lot again, this time

tipping my vision to take in more than the physical landscape. The shadows stretched and deepened as my vision spilled to the Shadowside, simultaneously becoming starker and more visible. The cars and other structures in the lot grew insubstantial as smoke. Only the wall beside me didn't change.

My apartment building was one of the few structures along this stretch of street that held solid weight in the realm of spirits. The faint gleam of wards shimmered along the façade—my work, worn into the bricks over years of residence. Convenient, because it meant the walls stood as barriers against threats from both sides of reality.

Nothing lurked in the gray spaces that I didn't already expect to see—a few restless spirits, the faded shuffle of imprinted foot traffic near the street. Nodding to myself, I rose from my crouch and stepped around the corner, gesturing toward the back door.

"I think we're clear."

Remy hesitated a moment, finally trotting after me. Softly, the leather of his boots creaked.

"Without your keys, how do you plan on getting in?"

"Like this." I yanked on the back door. The rusted hinges squealed, but swung open uneasily. We stepped into the apartment's shared laundry room, one dryer gently whirring. "Someone broke the lock, right after they installed that annoying buzzer system up front," I said. "No one's bothered fixing it."

"Charming," Remy breathed. He stood backlit in the entrance. Framed in silhouette, the long hair draping his shoulders could have passed for a lush cape. I padded toward the door to the stairwell, and didn't bother reaching for the light. I knew the route by heart. "What about your apartment door?" he asked. "I know the kinds of locks you typically keep."

Pausing at the stairwell, I shrugged. "I'll figure it out once I'm there—assuming it's not already wide open."

8

My doppelganger hadn't beaten us to my apartment—but someone else had. Halfway up the second flight of stairs, I spotted a familiar figure pacing outside my door.

Lil.

Fuming like a caged tigress, the Lady of Beasts traced a restless figure eight near the threshold, the legs of her pantsuit flaring with every step. She held her jacket folded over a little white clutch-purse, both tucked in the crook of one arm. Her clinging V-neck had a smear of mud across the rondure of one breast and her wild, red curls seemed unusually disheveled. The instant she caught sight of me, all her pent-up fury swung heavily in my direction.

"Where the *hell* have you been?" she demanded.

"Me?" I responded as I jogged the rest of the way up. "You've been MIA since Lake View. What are you even doing here?"

"What's it look like, Einstein?" she snapped. "I'm

waiting for you." With a disapproving scowl, she reached for the cut at my throat. "Mother's Tears, what's this? You lose a fight with a weed-whacker?"

"Cacodaimons," I said, slapping her hand away. "And don't touch."

"Well, that's just perfect," she grumbled. "Now, open your fucking door."

Her voice echoed all the way to where Remy stood frozen a few steps down. His face was just visible from where I lingered near the landing, pale features caught uncomfortably between uncertainty and trepidation.

"Lilliana?" he called up.

"Damn it, Remiel," she said, raising her voice. "How many times do I have to tell you? It's *Lil* now."

I winced at her volume. "For fuck's sake, keep your voices down." If we didn't attract the attention of my neighbors, it would be a miracle. "Normal people are sleeping."

Lil snorted dismissively, bulling past me to the top of the stairs. She planted her hands on her hips to glower down at my foppishly dressed brother. Her glinting gaze took in every detail of his elaborate costume—from the delicate swirls around his eyes down to the poured-on velvet pants. "Shouldn't you be running an event?" she sneered.

"I was," he replied stiffly. His hand hesitated on the railing, long nails gleaming in contrast to the dark wood. At the top, Lil spread her stance, making it clear that he wasn't getting to my floor without going through her first. With a pleading look, Remy flicked his attention to me, but there wasn't much I could offer in the way of help. Their train wreck of a relationship was an on-again, off-again exercise in mutual masochism that left me feeling baffled that they hadn't yet killed each other.

At least with Lil here, I knew no one had gotten through that door.

"Funny, *Remington*," she spat. "I was supposed to be at that event."

Remy swallowed hard enough that muscles clicked audibly in his throat. He shot me that pleading look again. Guiltily, I turned away. I wasn't getting tangled in their fight, not if I could help it. Instead, I studied the lines of wards around my door.

Everything was solid.

"Lillia—" he started, but swiftly corrected, "*Lil*. If you're still mad about the burlesque troupe, I told you it was nothing personal."

A scent like spice and vanilla wafted through the hall, underscored by the sharp bite of ozone—Lil's fatal mix of pheromones. In the backwash of her power, all the sigils scribed on my threshold lit up like Christmas.

"Oh, it's *never* personal with you, is it?"

"I had to make room for local talent," Remy insisted. "It wasn't a good fit for the Windy City Vixens anyway. You would have found the formality... stifling." Slowly, my brother mounted the stairs, stopping two down from where she loomed. With his height, this put them roughly eye-to-eye. Lil leaned in until their foreheads nearly touched.

"I've danced for *kings*, Remiel," she hissed. "You think my girls and I can't do classy?"

With effort, Remy kept his head high, but mostly he ended up looking like a condemned man staring down his sentencing judge.

"I said nothing of the sort."

She leaned closer. "Which one of them are you sleeping with?"

"Hey," I said, interrupting. "We need to figure out how to open this door." I reached toward Lil and almost grabbed her by the shoulder. Then I stopped myself short. I liked my fingers too much. Lil side-eyed my hand like it was something that slithered.

"It's your door," she said. "Open it already."

"No keys," I responded.

That got her attention. "Why the fuck don't you have your keys, flyboy?" Her mouth crimped like she'd just bitten down on something sour.

"I dropped them chasing bad guys."

She looked to Remy for confirmation. He had backed down a couple of steps, the better to watch from a safe distance. He offered her an empty-handed gesture.

"Fine," she grumbled. "As usual, I have to do everything myself." Seizing her little clutch-purse, she fished around inside and pulled out a slim roll of velveteen material. The item was longer than the purse was deep. Something inside rattled lightly as she unrolled the package on her open palm. Lock picks. She selected two slender tools and gestured impatiently toward my sealed door. "Take down your wards."

"You carry lock picks?" I marveled.

"Of course I've got lock picks," she said. "What do you think this is, amateur hour?"

"But…" I fumbled. "Why didn't you just let yourself in?"

She lashed out with her knuckles so fast her hand

blurred. The leather of my jacket caught the brunt of the blow, but it still knocked the breath out of me. With the kind of night I was having, I was tempted to reply in kind. But with Lil, it was a casual gesture. If she'd intended real harm, she'd have opened up my throat.

"Wards, numbskull," she said. "I'm not touching that door until you disarm them. I kind of like this body." She did a little lift and wiggle. I stared away from her mesmerizing cleavage.

At least, I tried.

"Is that mud?" Remy asked. He lost the game.

Lil rolled her eyes. "That's why we need to talk. There's a problem." Her chin lifted suddenly. Remy and I exchanged puzzled glances. Canting her head like an attentive hound, Lil closed her eyes as she focused on whatever it was she'd heard. Her features grew both intense and distant.

The lines of her body blurred as little tendrils of gleaming power stretched through the air. The spectral faces of animals manifested at the furthest edges of the bleed—fox and ferret, lion and owl. Lil's spirit companions. From the azure fire that kindled in my brother's eyes, he sensed them, too. With a sudden shake of her head, she snapped out of it, marching over to the banister to peer down the stairwell. Deep in her throat, she made a thoughtful sound, almost a growl.

"Not out here," she said, gesturing toward the door again, her hand trailing wisps. Whatever she'd done, she was finished—for the moment. "Get a move on, Anakim. I've wasted too much of my night already."

The thrum of Lil's magic still buzzing in my head, I

stepped around her to lay my hand flat against the door. Tiny rows of painstakingly etched sigils flared briefly at the contact, and I whispered the pass-phrase, framing the words more with my mind than with my mouth. Even Remy would've had trouble making them out.

Power rode on my breath, flowing down my arm to connect with the complex mesh of magic barring the entrance. My head throbbed, but at least I had enough juice for this. As the spells responded to me, blue-white fire ignited every symbol in a brilliant burst visible only to those who could see past physical reality. Lines spun and twisted in my vision, rearranging themselves until the door was just a door again, all its otherworldly protections momentarily inert.

The instant the wards were down, Lil bent to the locks, moving swiftly to open first one and then the other. She even got the deadbolt—which my highly paid locksmith had assured me could never be picked. With a flourish, Lil turned the knob, and the door swung wide.

"Glad you're on our side," I muttered, reaching for the light switch to the right of the frame.

"For now," she replied. Primly, she tucked her lock picks back into her purse.

9

The apartment was cleaner than usual. Lil still clicked her tongue against her teeth, eyes skipping from the abandoned coffee mugs on the table, mantelpiece, and floor, to the spill of books and papers that nearly buried my laptop on the desk.

"No time to play housekeeper," I said.

"That's obvious," she replied with a snort.

Remy turned in a slow three-sixty near the back of my couch, his brows knitting as he gaped at the empty walls.

"Where are they?" he murmured in a hollow voice.

"Where are what?" I asked.

He gestured stiffly. "The manuscript pages. The illuminations. The art." With a glimmer of hope, he peered down the hallway that led to my room, shaking his head dolefully when he realized those walls also were bare. "What have you done with them?"

"A night like this, and you're worried that Zack redecorated," Lil sighed. "Husband, your priorities have always baffled me." She pivoted in my direction. "Get that door closed, and be sure to seal the wards again. I think he's still out there somewhere."

"Who?" Remy inquired.

"The imposter," she spat. Her lips perched around more, but she refused to give it voice as she glared at the open threshold. Hurriedly, I shut and locked everything, then whispered the phrase that re-armed the wards. Gleaming lines of power flashed against my retinas as all the spells snapped into place.

"You've seen him, too, then," I said, shrugging out of my leather. I tossed it across the spine of the couch, angling the throw to avoid hitting Remy, so lost in his contemplation of my home. He didn't even flinch, instead fixating on every surface of the numerous bookshelves, searching for some vestige of the missing art. He was going to be disappointed—I'd taken down all of my framed pieces to scour them for hidden ciphers. Pre-amnesia me had used them to leave notes to myself. More than a few were curled in the mess on my desk, partly decoded.

"You knew about this joker," Lil spat, "and you didn't tell me?"

"Tell you how, exactly?" I retorted. Moving to the kitchenette, I grabbed a dishtowel and waited for the water from the sink to run hot. Only a breakfast bar separated me from the living room, and Lil planted her hands on this, shooting me the stink-eye.

"You have my number, Anakim," she said.

I gave the towel a good soaking and started dabbing at my throat. The cut stung like a sonofabitch. As I leaned over the sink, flakes of blood drifted down, running crimson to the drain.

"You so sure about that?" I asked. "The number I have doesn't work—hasn't for a while."

"You actually tried to call someone without a gun to your head?" Remy sniped.

With a grunt of irritation, I yanked the shirt over my head, wadding it up to toss it at my brother. He snapped it from the air with a frown.

"What do you mean it doesn't work?" Lil demanded.

"Exactly what I said," I replied. A sharp, raw sensation twinged my neck as the damned cut reopened. "Perfect," I muttered. Disgusted, I chucked the stained dishcloth into the sink. "Hang on. This requires more than a band-aid." Swinging out of the kitchenette, I started down the hall. All my first-aid stuff was in the bathroom, and I needed to get eyes on the wound. The fucking cacodaimon had tagged me good.

"Where do you think you're going?" she growled.

"In case you hadn't noticed, I got my ass handed to me," I called as I ducked into the bathroom. "I'd like to stop bleeding all over the hardwood."

Huffing, she stormed after me. "Well, you can't just walk away like that." Remy hesitated, then remained in the living room. The Lady of Beasts scowled from the bathroom threshold—I'd known better than to try to close the door. Lil was like a cat that way. If you closed a door on her, she *had* to find a way to the other side. Easier just to leave it open.

"Let me see your phone," she demanded.

"It's dead," I said, angling toward the mirror in an attempt to get a good look at the laceration. It was further back than I'd suspected, running from behind my ear in a clean slash that stopped just short of all the major blood vessels. Good thing, too. Half an inch further and just a hair deeper, and I wouldn't have been around to argue with Lil. "Go check my pockets."

"If it's dead, what good will that do me?"

"Not a thing," I said as I fished a bottle of rubbing alcohol out from under the sink, unscrewing the cap. "I just want to get you out of my hair for a minute." Leaning over the tub, I dumped half the bottle across my throat, sucking air through my teeth as white fire spread along every millimeter of the cut.

"Gimme that," Lil growled, sweeping into the cramped room and yanking the alcohol from my grip. She grabbed a clean washcloth from the rack and soaked it with the rest of the bottle, dropping the empty into the tub. The plastic sounded hollow as it hit the porcelain.

"Is there anything I can do to help?" Remy called.

"No!" Lil and I cried in unison. From her look, she trusted him as little as I did—not that close to my blood. He'd never crossed the line like that, but the Nephilim as a tribe had an unnerving relationship to the red stuff. I didn't want to take any chances.

Lil seized my jaw, twisting me to get a better look at the cut. Our height difference made it hard for her to get the right angle. With a muttered curse, she went up on one foot and I thought she was going to kick me out of sheer spite, but all she did was slam the toilet seat shut with the toe of one boot. Roughly, she shoved me in that direction.

"Sit."

Mutely, I did. When Lil took that tone, arguments were futile.

"Close your eyes," she ordered. I narrowed them instead, skeptical as fuck. She lofted the alcohol-soaked washcloth and started for my face. "This'll sting a hell of a lot worse with them open," she said. "But suit yourself."

Just as the cloth descended, I squeezed them shut. Roughly, she scrubbed the material across my face, grinding the nap into every scrape and abrasion from my earlier battle. Much more delicately, she daubed the bigger wound, teasing the edges apart with the fingers of her other hand to gauge its depth.

"Ow," I objected.

She only probed deeper. A little slip of her long nail at the outermost corner felt intentional. I peeled open my eyes to glower. Lil stood so close, I could see striations of gold and green in the center of her steely irises.

"Good news?" she said. "It went through both layers of the dermis, but it doesn't seem to have hit anything beneath that."

"Peachy," I snapped. "I figured that much because I can still move my head." The fumes of the alcohol made me tear up and I blinked rapidly to clear away the sting. "And the bad news?"

"If you were anyone else, I'd send you somewhere for stitches," she answered. "You're healing for shit and the cut's long enough, it'll just keep opening whenever you stretch the skin."

"So, like, every time I move," I grumbled.

"Pretty much." Straightening, she pushed loose curls back from her face. "What do you have in your kit here? Butterflies? Steri-strips?" Before I could answer, she started rooting around in the medicine cabinet. "Some superglue would be nice."

"Not there," I said. "Under the sink."

Crouching down, she continued her search, discovering the hefty first-aid kit I kept in a long tackle box in the back of the cabinet. With an appreciative sound, she pulled it out and balanced it on the side of the tub. Throwing the latches, she scanned the many compartments.

"At least you're prepared."

"I like my body, too," I said, leaving off the flirty lift and wiggle—with me, the gesture wouldn't have been nearly as impressive. A soft step resounded from the hall and Remy peeked in through the open door.

"Are you certain there's nothing I can do to help?" His eyes flicked from me to Lil to the bloody washcloth she'd abandoned to the floor. A stitch of worry creased his brow. Seizing a pack of steri-strips, Lil shoved them at him.

"Open these."

Obediently, he took the package, tracing one manicured nail along a seam. Peeling away the plastic-coated paper, he withdrew a single sheet of the long wound closures. Wordlessly, he held them out. Lil made an impatient gesture.

"Give them to me one at a time," she said. "But be careful. Only touch them along one edge. I need them to stick tight." Remy nodded. Before long, he wore half a dozen of the thin, white bandage strips, tacking them to the tips of his fingers like streamers. Lil plucked them off one at a time.

"Hold still," she told me, turning my chin in the direction of the bathtub. "And angle your face like that."

Huffing, she slapped my leg with the back of her hand. "Relax your neck, already. You're cording your tendons, and that's not gonna help."

"Little tense here," I said through gritted teeth.

"Well untense, unless you want this thing to be a bunched-up mess." She slapped the side of my thigh again, just enough for me to feel it. Doggedly I focused on the pattern in the tiles on the far side of the tub. It didn't help.

"I really don't like being touched," I grumbled. Lil's fingers pressed against my neck and I was struck with the warmth of her hands. We were rarely in such close contact.

"Cry me a river," she shot back, pressing another of the steri-strips into place. Remy loomed in my peripheral vision, a silent statue blocking the door. I didn't think of myself as claustrophobic, but this many people in so small a room wasn't helping to keep my blood pressure low.

"You almost done?" I demanded. My voice cracked.

"This is precision work, Anakim," she answered. "Don't rush me."

The sound of adhesive unsticking from skin—that was Lil taking another closure from Remy. The press of fingers, fever-hot. Through my nose, I exhaled a long stream of breath, struggling not to move—or punch anyone. Some people had a fight or flight response. Mine was all fight.

"So tell me about this imposter," Lil said as she fixed another strip across the wound. Maybe it was her idea of soothing me. It sort of worked. "When did you first notice him?"

"Earlier tonight," I answered. My hands fisted in my

lap, fingernails digging shallow half-moons into my palms. "Couldn't sleep. Went out for a ride. Stopped at this gas station when the tank ran low and shit went sideways."

"You always have the most colorful expressions," Remy mused.

"Pear-shaped. FUBAR, fuck-o bazoo," I supplied. "I could go on."

"Please don't," the vampire said.

Lil chuckled as she worked.

Again, I loosed a long breath, this time trying to ease the tension crawling up my neck. Holding this position was awkward. Muscles were starting to cramp all across my shoulders and back. "There were a couple of cacodaimons," I said, squeezing my eyes shut again. "One was a sleeper. I think it woke up because I was there."

"They do that," Remy observed.

"Well," I sighed, "it killed the guy working night shift and its buddy made a move to ride his skin. I put an end to that, but the first one made a break for it." Vividly, the whole scene replayed on the insides of my eyelids. I blinked. "Anyway, I chased the fucker down before it slunk back in the lake." I almost told them about the third cacodaimon—the weird one that trailed me after that—but something held me back. Nothing so clear as an inner voice, just… a feeling. Chewing on too many layered implications to unpack, I fell into silence. Lil nudged my arm.

"Not to diminish your crusade to rid the world of the Unmakers," she said, "but how's this tie to your imposter?"

"Asshole stole my bike," I spat. At the memory, I clenched my fists so hard the nails bit into the crease of each palm. One of them tagged the scar and I stopped as it ticced in protest. "When I got back from fighting the bastards, the police were all over the station. My Vulcan was still at the pump, along with my helmet and keys."

"You left the keys with your motorcycle?" Remy choked. "In *that* neighborhood?"

"Cacodaimons," I reminded. Without thinking, I started to turn so I could face him. Lil sharply caught my chin.

"Not done here," she snapped.

I scowled and focused on the tiles again. "I'd wanted to save the clerk." I sighed. "Dropped everything once I saw the first one go after him, but it was already too late." My body held its rigid posture, but my wings slumped. No one could yell at me for that.

"So, your motorcycle thief," Lil urged. "Notice anything odd about him?"

"Aside from the fact he was wearing my face?" I asked. "He even had a twin of my jacket."

"Yeah," she replied. "He was wearing that when he rolled up here."

"He was here?" Fuck holding still—I whirled on her so fast, she didn't have time to react. Lil glared with her hand still raised, strip dangling from the tip of her middle finger.

"You're lucky this is the last one," she snapped. "That would have ripped the whole thing open again."

"What were you even doing here?" Remy asked her.

Lil tossed her wealth of red curls in an extravagant gesture of derision. "I have a life outside of your club, husband dearest," she sneered. "You're hardly the only thing that interests me in this town."

"So you're stalking me again," I said.

Her full lips curled provocatively. "Again?" she mused. "That implies I stopped at some point, doesn't it?"

Annoyed, I lurched off the toilet seat, pushing past her to the mirror. Lil had an uncanny way of keeping track of me—one I hadn't been able to spot. Yet. Making a show of checking her work, I stretched over the bowl of the sink. This put me directly between Remy and Lil.

"All that crap about my wards," I grumbled. "Was that just some kind of misdirection?"

She shook her head, rising fluidly from where she crouched on the floor. Darting in close, she applied the final steri-strip with a triumphant flourish. This took her perilously near all my bare skin, and she pressed the advantage—literally. The crush of her soft curves along my naked side made it hard to concentrate.

"Your wards are solid." Warm breath tickled the lobe of my ear. "I was just checking your defenses. I do that every once in a while." A rush of spice and vanilla filled the tiled room. She'd held her angler-fish tactics in check while patching my cut. Now the floodgates were wide open. Tingling gooseflesh rushed down my neck, chasing itself across my chest and arms. Without a shirt, there was no way to hide the reaction. Lil loosed a throaty chuckle.

"Mmm," she purred. "Good boy."

I flinched away before she could pat me on the ass. I knew she was thinking about it. Remy observed our interaction with mild curiosity, one brow delicately Spocked. If he had any objections, he wisely didn't voice them.

"Do we know why someone is trying to impersonate

you?" he asked after Lil gave up on groping me.

"I'm more interested in how," I said. The room was still too cramped, and Lil wouldn't budge to give me space. A teasing grin split her face. I shouldered past her, then Remy with a muttered "sorry," making for the living room. I dug through the pantry along the way, snagging one of my protein bars. My body needed fuel. The flat rectangle of soy and peanut butter wasn't steak and potatoes, but it would have to do. "If I understand how, maybe I can counter it. When I checked for a cowl or some other kind of obscuring magic, the guy came up blank—like he wasn't even there."

Lil trailed after me, stopping at the mouth of the back hall. Remy lurked a few steps behind, his impossibly blue eyes reflecting the light from the living room. Weary and frustrated, I dropped onto my couch, ripping open the wrapper of the bar. The line of steri-strips along my neck itched as I chewed. I stretched against the tension bunched across my shoulders, rolling my neck as far as the bandages would allow. The motion through the cushions sent my jacket sliding heavily to the floor. The SIG inside thunked against the hardwood. Lil grew tired of her game, going from sultry to serious in the blink of an eye.

"The first time I saw him, I thought he was you," she pronounced. "I don't make mistakes like that." She strode into my kitchenette like she owned the place and started rinsing out my coffee pot. Her voice, flat with annoyance, rose to carry over the sound of running water. "Whatever spell he's got, it's tight—but it isn't foolproof." Regarding me from across the breakfast bar, she laid one finger along the length of her nose.

Rhinestones glittered from her nail. "He didn't have a scent. That's what tipped his hand. Nothing natural is like that."

"You mean it isn't Lil-proof," I corrected. "Not all of us have the nose of a bloodhound."

"Or a fox," she mused. Dumping a double handful of fresh beans into the grinder, she muttered a polite warning. Then she hit the button. Ear-shredding sound ratcheted through the apartment. Remy clapped a hand to his ear, but in spite of this, he still winced.

The energy bar was already gone. Somewhat baffled by its rapid disappearance, I crumpled the wrapper, aiming for the nearest trash can. I missed it by a mile. Didn't care. Reaching over the side of the couch, I snagged my jacket, fishing through the pockets for my phone. The charger lay on the coffee table and I plugged it into the power strip I kept on the floor. The phone was so dead, only the charging screen came on. Bobby had to be going crazy, wondering where I was.

Hopefully he could wait another few minutes.

"I'm going to guess by the state of your clothes that you fought him," I said.

"Of course I fought him," she replied, plucking a filter from the stack and filling it directly from the grinder. "He knew how to handle himself, too. Definitely not mortal." Pushing her heavy curls back from one ear, she revealed an uncharacteristic bruise. Remy made a startled sound. Lil was virtually impervious to harm, so if this guy had managed to tag her, he wasn't fucking around. My own expression wasn't lost on her. "He wasn't interested in me, Zack," she said. "The minute I got the upper hand, he disappeared." Snapping the basket into place, she stabbed the button with a painted nail and set the whole thing to brew.

"I've seen how you operate, Lil," I responded. "How does anyone get away from you once you've got them in your crosshairs?"

"No," she insisted, "I meant it literally. He disappeared into thin air." She swept from the kitchenette and settled onto the cushions, dangerously close. Poignantly, I became aware that I still wasn't wearing a shirt.

"Disappeared?" Remy echoed.

"Poof," she said, gesturing for emphasis. "Not just invisible, but *gone*." She jabbed a pointy nail into my ribs, causing me to twitch. "Only one tribe can do that."

I slapped her hand away. "You think he's Anakim?" The thought was staggering. Outside of the four trapped in binding jars, I had yet to encounter any member of my own tribe. From all the research I'd done, only a rare few still roamed free in the world. Someone had been hunting us for a couple hundred years.

Rising from the couch, I stepped well out of Lil's reach, in case she felt a further need to poke. I needed to think without distraction. Drifting to the kitchen, I helped myself to some of the coffee. It wasn't finished brewing and I was too tired to care. Steady spatters sizzled on the hot plate while I stole the pot to pour.

"If he was one of my tribe, shouldn't I be able to tell?"

"I don't know," she mused. "How good's your memory?"

"Low blow," I growled.

"But not untrue," she retorted.

Scowling, I took a sip of bitter coffee. It was hot enough to scald. "How the fuck is he even doing it?" I demanded. "I should be able to see these things. So should you."

"Forget about how," Lil said. "You've seen Tuscanetti magic. They could do it, so could a dozen others. But for an illusion like that to be this convincing, you either need a boatload of personal items—hair, blood, nails—or you've got to know the subject really, *really* well." She pivoted on the cushions, the better to fix me with her steely glare. "So what you've got to ask yourself, flyboy, isn't how, but who. Who's got that kind of access? And what do they want from you?"

Behind her, Remy fell unnervingly still, like he'd forgotten how a body was supposed to work.

"Where did this fight even go down?" I asked. I swept from the kitchenette to pace a loping circuit before the hearth. "There isn't a Crossing near here he could have used. The closest one is at the entrance to Lake View Cemetery, and that's a mile away."

"He could have used a relic," Lil reminded. "Either way, I don't think he was casing your apartment with the intent of dropping off a gift." She cut her gaze pointedly in the direction of my desk. We both knew what lay in the locked and warded bottom drawer—the four jars containing my tribe's Primus and his lieutenants. Those jars were the tip of the proverbial iceberg.

With a sharp heave of breath, Remy came suddenly to life. He moved so unexpectedly, I sloshed coffee over the lip of the mug.

"Are we certain it's one of the Anakim using a disguise?" he asked.

"I know Shadowside transit when I feel it," Lil said, insulted by the question.

He shook his head like she hadn't fully understood, then, with a shrug of dismissal, joined me at the hearth. The look he fixed on me was strange, almost pitying. "If another has come," he said, "then it is time we discuss why you live in a city run by Nephilim."

"You say that like I'm here as a punishment," I ventured.

Tellingly, he refused to meet my eyes.

Suddenly, a memory came flooding back—something our sibling Malphael once said. He'd wagered the life of a very special girl—Halley Davis—to get me to join a crusade. Malphael was Gibburim, and throughout their bloody history they had hunted Nephilim and Rephaim alike—with the full support of the Anakim. As we'd dueled for Halley's survival, he'd made it clear he saw me as a traitor—not just to him, but to both our tribes.

"Remy," I growled. "You'd better start talking. *Now*."

10

Glints of gold shimmered from the rich fabric of the Nephilim's jacket as Remy shifted uneasily on the balls of his feet. The supple leather of his tall boots creaked, but otherwise, that—and our collective breathing—were the only sounds in my apartment. Remy's gaze flicked from Lil to me and back again, hesitation pursing his painted lips.

"Oh, for fuck's sake," she snapped. "You think any of this is going to be news to me?" At her look, he frowned, but still said nothing. With a huff of irritation, Lil shoved off from the couch, crossing to Remy in a few, swift steps. Absurdly, she reached up and pinched his cheek, cooing like a spinster aunt. Remy stiffened, too stunned to respond. Releasing the skin, she gave the slightly pinkened spot a loving pat. Her irony dripped.

"If that weren't so endearingly naïve of you, Remy, I'd be offended."

"Lilianna—" he choked.

In an instant, her smile went feral and she leaned

into him, baring all her teeth. "If you can switch up all the pronouns for your transsexual decimus, you'd best get my name right, lover boy." As Remy sputtered a response, I joined their little party, risking my arm by sticking it between them.

"You two can work out your marital problems on your own time," I said. "I've been up all night, I'm beat to shit, and I still got places I need to be." I turned my glare on my brother. "Spill it, Remy."

Muttering her annoyance, Lil pivoted sharply away. She stomped toward the burbling coffee maker, the rifle-crack of her heels making me sorry for my downstairs neighbors. Digging a clean mug from the dishwasher, she started fixing herself a cup, adding an uncharacteristic amount of sugar and cream.

The Nephilim met my gaze, anxiety plainly writ upon his features. I understood his concerns about Lil, even commiserated with them. She was the single most unpredictable person I knew, and I still hadn't sussed out whether she was an ally or an enemy. Probably both.

"I don't have time to dick around with this, Remy," I said. "Just tell me what I need to know."

His lips twisted to make words, but nothing came out. In the kitchen, Lil stirred her coffee with such vigor that the spoon struck the mug like the clapper of a bell. The harsh and rhythmic clinking set my teeth on edge. I redoubled my focus.

"Some time this week, Remiel."

The Nephilim struggled to speak again. Once more, his throat seized up before he could bring forth any answer. He shot me a despairing look. Knitting her fingers around the mug, Lil watched keenly through the rising tendrils of steam. Remy extended his hands, palms-up, his mouth tugged unhappily down. Finally, I got the message.

Someone had him oathed.

"You can't even talk about this, can you?" I asked.

His eyes flicked to Lil. "I can speak under the proper circumstances," he said tightly.

"Then damn it, Remy, why even bring it up?"

"As you've said," he responded, "it's something you need to know."

I vented my frustration with a wordless yell. To hell with the neighbors.

"Perhaps if you gave direct permission?" Remy ventured. "But, Zaquiel, be *very* specific in your phrasing."

Frustration gave way to misgiving and I swallowed hard against a rush of unease. Maybe it was a shred of memory, maybe just the way he looked at me, but in that instant, I knew.

"It was me, wasn't it?" I murmured, breath stolen by sick shock. "This was something I made you swear."

His jaw tensed. The fact that he couldn't answer was answer enough.

"Well, fuck," I hissed.

"Zaquiel—" he choked, but couldn't finish.

Lil chortled from the kitchenette. "If you boys are going to fuck, how about I give you a little privacy?" At our appalled expressions, laughter cascaded from her throat. "Always so serious." She took a long sip of coffee, licking her upper lip for traces of cream. "I'll do you a favor. No charge—this time." With an exaggerated sashay, she sauntered from the kitchen and headed down the hall. Disappearing through the door to my room, she closed it behind her.

The lock latched audibly.

Remy and I exchanged uneasy glances.

"Did she just give you an out?" I asked.

"She'll still be able to hear," he whispered. "Even through the door. I know I would."

Music began blaring from the back room—Gabriella Cilmi's "Sweet About Me." I had no idea where she'd gotten the track—it wasn't anything in my collection.

"Hunh," I muttered. "Does that fix it?"

Remy hesitated, then shrugged uncertainly. Grabbing his elbow, I guided us toward the front bay window, as far away from Lil as the apartment's narrow floor plan would allow.

"How about this?" I asked. The music blared loud enough that the bassline rattled the leaded panes.

Remy considered, then shook his head. "It was *very* specific," he managed.

Curling my fists again, I resisted the urge to hit something—especially my brother. Outside, the gray and watery light of early morning filtered through a break in the churning clouds. Pre-dawn. In another hour, Bobby's shift would be ending—and with it, my opportunity to view Marjory's body.

"How the fuck am I supposed to give you orders on an oath I don't even remember making you swear?"

"The oath remembers," he urged.

"I don't have time for riddles, Remy," I grumbled. "There are always loopholes. Isn't that what you told me in the car? Find a way around it."

He scowled, remaining mute as the seconds ticked by. I counted their limping progress, striving to quell my rising temper. Finally, he heaved a tremulous breath, sweeping the heavy tresses of hair from his face. Putting self-conscious distance between us, he twitched a curtain back from the far side of the window, gazing out at the flow of early morning commuters.

"Do you recall our first dinner together last November?" His nonchalance felt brittle and contrived. "The one at that charming family place in Lakewood?"

I ground my teeth, slow to realize this change in subject wasn't an evasion, exactly.

"Yeah, I remember," I answered. "You taught me to use some of my powers again." I moved to step closer so we could talk face to face, but, instantly, he stiffened. Getting the hint, I hung back to let it play out at his speed. "I think you were also testing me to see if my amnesia was legit."

"For that, I do apologize," he murmured, still watching the cars rather than looking directly at me. "I understand how difficult those moments must have been. The confusion, the guilt—"

"Guilt?" I snapped, instantly suspicious.

"Of not knowing if even you, yourself, could be trusted."

That struck a nerve.

"Is that what this is about?" I demanded. "You think *I* can't be trusted? You're the one who's practically in bed with the snakiest manipulator I know."

"Saliriel is a survivor," he responded tightly. "If ever

you remember, you will understand."

That did it. I seized his shoulder to spin him from the window. It was like tugging on a marble statue. He didn't even budge. So I stalked over to my computer desk. A couple of old T-shirts lay draped across the back of the chair—my idea of a laundry way station. Snatching up the top one, I sniffed it—*clean enough*—and pulled it over my head.

Feeling less exposed, though only slightly, I paced a restless course from bookcases to hearth and back again. Lil's music gave way from Gabrielle Cilmi to Meghan Trainor. I recognized the voice, but not the song. The bassline thudded. If the couple downstairs could sleep through that racket, they deserved medals.

"Saliriel practically sold me up-river to that asshat Dorimiel," I growled. "Does Sal have some connection to this?" I prodded. "That'd be just like her."

"No," Remy said. The feeble light from the window traced a geography of shadow across his porcelain features. The only life was in his lips.

"Then how does any of this tie to a rogue Anakim running around with my face?" I grumbled. When he replied, however, something changed in his voice, lilting as if he recited some long-memorized prayer.

"There is a mathematical elegance to the hierarchies of the tribes," he said. "Primus, decimus, centesimus." Crisply, he ticked off the titles, only two of which I had heard previously. "The primus is the font of the tribe. Ten chiefs of ten rule the hundred beneath." At the mantel, I caught myself swaying in time with his rhythm. The words and the way he said them stirred things deep in the shattered halls of memory. "Within each decade are three sets of three *shalish*, plus one who stands apart from the nine. The *shalish*, as groups, work in synergy. The tenth serves as the hand of the decimus."

Shalish.

The term was a leviathan that just breached the surface, its hulk a massive shadow spreading beneath the waves. My arms broke instantly to gooseflesh and such a surge of emotion crashed over me, I was reminded of drowning—so deep in the water that up and down became distant abstractions. Lil's pounding music merged with Remy's rhythmic patter until I no longer heard any of the words. The room fell away in a wash of memory. No visual details, just a deep and bitter longing. A sense of being severed from something so integral, its loss had no name. A weighty feeling of purpose. Regret sharper than any blade, and…

Isolation. Such a tallied burden of it, I knew it stretched across decades.

Centuries. The thought was mine, its clarity strangely jarring. *But I had to walk away. Someone had to choose to end it.*

That was ominous, and without context. Nothing further crossed the Lethean precipice. Blinking, I found myself with moisture on my lashes, my hand locked on the mantle in a grip of such ferocity, all feeling had fled my fingers. At the window, Remy's stance changed, less statue and more a living man again. With a mournful huff, he turned from his view of the street, letting the curtain drop behind him.

"I still can't break it," he said.

"What?" Hurriedly, I dashed a hand across my eyes.

"The oath," he said. If he'd caught that I was crying, he pretended not to notice. "I can only talk around it."

I peeled my hand from the mantel and dropped heavily onto the couch. I left my half-finished cup of coffee behind, and I didn't care enough to get back up for it.

"I think you said enough."

"Have I?"

"I walked away from my own tribe." I clenched my fists until the knuckles cracked. Scars stood whitely against pale skin—badges from battles I no longer remembered. "That's it, isn't it? Malphael said something about it. I didn't understand at the time."

Remiel made an aggravated noise. "While all of that is true, you've completely missed my point."

"What?" I demanded. "That some of my people might be pissed at me? They're gonna have to get in line."

"No, Zaquiel. Stop being so angry and actually listen." That only made me angrier and he knew it—but anger was preferable to the gutting sense of loss inspired by that strange, haunting word. *Shalish.* "Are you the hand of a decimus?" he asked.

The answer came on reflex. "No."

"Good," he encouraged. "Now ask yourself, where are the two who stood with you closer than brothers?"

"I don't fucking know," I snapped.

Remy bent his rouged lips in a moue of annoyance. "To understand my point with all I am obliged to leave unsaid right now, you must answer that question as well as one other."

"What is the airspeed velocity of an unladen swallow?" I griped.

He ignored the petty jest, features going stony. "How far do you think you might go to protect those who've earned your loyalty?"

I didn't like the implications of his question, nor the weird slew of feelings it dredged up. "I'm not that guy anymore," I muttered. Coffee welled bitter at the back of my throat and I fought an unreasoning desire to storm from the room before he asked anything else. On the coffee table, my phone buzzed so hard, it danced spastically across the slick surface. Happy for the distraction, I snatched it up and thumbed the answer button in one brisk motion.

"It's Bobby," I said. Remy swept close to lay fingers on my shoulder. Irritably, I shrugged him away. "I've got to take this."

"Jesus, Zack," the detective said in a rush. "Are you OK? What happened out there?"

Remy continued to hover. I turned and mouthed, "*Later.*" Lips perched on an objection, he reluctantly withdrew.

"Phone died," I said. Despite Remy's distance, I held no pretense that my call was private. With the vampire's hearing, it probably sounded like Bobby was in the same room—even with Lil's music rumbling in the background.

"Time's almost up on my offer," Bobby said. "Night shift's just about done, and as soon as the morning people start showing, I won't be able to sneak you in to see her."

I glanced to the clock in the kitchen. During that weird exchange with Remy, time had flown.

"How long?" I asked.

"Can you get here in the next ten minutes?"

I'd been up for almost twenty-four hours. What was another few?

"Sure," I said. "I'll find a way."

"I'll meet you around back by the loading dock," he answered. "And I'll wait for twenty, but then I have to go home. It's been a hell of a night."

"You're telling me," I said. I almost hung up, then paused with my finger over the red button. "Thanks, Bobby. I owe you."

"Just help us find the daughter."

He ended the call.

11

"So, we're going to see Bobby," Lil purred.

Her voice came from directly over my shoulder. I turned to find her leaning over the back of the couch, so close, I nearly faceplanted into her cleavage. She grinned like that had been her intention. Quickly, I scrambled to my feet. Music still blared from the back room, and it had covered her approach.

"Dammit, Lil." I bent to unplug the cellphone's charger, winding it up to stuff it in a pocket. "Why do you always have to do things like that?"

"Why do you always notice?" she countered. Provocatively, she rolled her shoulders, making a dance of everything between and beneath.

Heat swept to my ears. Scooping up my jacket, I pulled out the SIG, checking its magazine and chamber. The Legion was full. I knew that already, but my hands needed the distraction.

Remy cleared his throat with a "hrmph," that managed to sound both annoyed and relieved. He picked imaginary lint from the arm of his frockcoat.

"You should meet me at Club Heaven later so we can discuss this in private."

"Oh, we're not done." I slipped the handgun back into its holster, then shrugged into the jacket. The arms snagged on my wrist sheaths, and I tugged everything into place with the ease of habit. "Not by a long shot, but this has to come first. Bobby's on a schedule."

"How *is* your little Korean-American friend?" Lil taunted.

"Is that supposed to be funny?" I snapped. "You shot his partner. Garrett still can't use that arm."

She made a noise of disgust. "For this kind of grief, next time I'll shoot to kill." Hoisting herself from the couch, she moved to retrieve her white leather purse from a side table. With prim, curt gestures, she tucked it under one arm. "The guy was possessed, Zack. I solved your problem. You should thank me, not complain."

A host of objections wrangled just behind my lips. I managed to choke them all back. Pointedly, I looked to the clock in the kitchen.

"I don't have time for this." Stepping over to the door, I took down the wards, then started work on the more conventional locks. "You two have to leave."

"You know that guy's going to try again," Lil warned. Instead of following, she stepped into my kitchen. When I gave her a look, she shot me one right back. "What? I'm turning off your coffee maker. You want to burn the place down?"

"No," I responded.

She marched across the hardwood. "You're putting a

lot of trust in your wards, Zack."

"What do you want me to do?"

"Leave one of us to babysit."

"I don't trust either of you in here, not unattended—no offense, Remy." If the Nephilim felt any rancor, he didn't let it show. He was doing that statue thing again. I was close enough to be certain that he really wasn't breathing. A little creeped out, I faced off with Lil. "Even you didn't want to tangle with my wards," I said. "That speaks volumes."

"The defenses are good," she allowed, "but nothing's perfect, flyboy. Wouldn't want your precious collection of action figures to take a walk." Lil glanced at my desk, her gaze fixed tellingly on a slim wooden case angled between my memorial figurines of Han and General Leia. She'd guessed what it had inside.

The Anakim equal to the Eye of Nefer-Ka, the Stylus of Anak contained all the most devastating powers of my tribe in one easy-to-use package. If a rogue member of the Anakim was after anything in this apartment, it was that. No way I was going to leave it.

"Your concern has been noted," I said. Maneuvering around Remy, I threw open the door. "Now get out so I can reset the first layer of my defenses." I all but shoved them both into the hall.

"You can't just—"

I cut her off by slamming the door in her face. She snarled her outrage from the other side, furiously working the knob. I barely beat her to the lock.

"You'll want to move that hand," I warned.

The manic twisting of the doorknob abruptly ceased.

Whispering the sigil phrase, I breathed power into the waiting lines of magic. Row upon row of minutely etched symbols glimmered to life, pulsing blue and silver, and then fading from sight. Lil's hissing intake of breath, muffled through the door, brought a smile. If I could get that kind of reaction from the Lady of Beasts, I was doing something right.

Before locking the final layers into place, I scooped up the container with the Stylus of Anak from where it rested in its invisible circle of protection. Spidery threads of power snapped as I lifted it away, their aggressive defenses fizzling in response to my signature. Had anyone else touched it, those defenses would have blasted them into their next incarnation.

The wooden case, crafted to hold something the size of a single cigar, hummed softly against my palm. Every inch of it was covered with runes, the rows of sinuous script carved so finely that they faded into the dark grain of the wood. To open the container, you had to slide the top, but it had been crafted so cunningly, you also had to know exactly where to put your thumb and forefinger. I'd found the richly stained puzzle box at an antique shop a few months back, adding a soft scrap of runed garment leather to its interior. It had become the perfect home for the bone stylus that nestled within.

Fighting a wicked twinge of déjà vu, I tucked the wooden case into the innermost pocket of my jacket. Opposite the heavy imprint of my SIG, the warded box traced a hard line against my ribs. It wouldn't be much safer than leaving it in my apartment, but it was the best I was going to manage given the circumstances.

With luck, it wouldn't bite me in the ass.

From a bowl on my desk, I scooped up my spare set of keys, locking the rest of my wards into place as I pulled the door shut behind me. Remy was already gone, but Lil was still there, fury etched into her features. As I worked the key, the magical barriers snapped around the latches and deadbolt, reinforcing the physical locks. The power behind the wards crackled for an instant, fading as the obscuring magics kicked in.

Despite herself, Lil made an appreciative sound.

"You've added some real finesse to your set-up," she said.

"A compliment?" I responded dryly. "Lil, I'm touched." Pushing past her and heading for the stairs, I started down them two at a time, plotting the quickest route to the Cuyahoga County Medical Examiner's offices. It was only about a mile and a half from the apartment, but if I got mired in morning traffic, that wouldn't matter. Lil followed close behind, and at the bottom she nearly crashed into me. I paused long enough to glower at her.

"You're still not invited."

"Someone's got to watch your back," she said.

"No," I growled.

She lofted her smartphone. A stopwatch app ticked down prominently on the screen. "Less than seven minutes to go, flyboy," she prodded. "Still want to argue?"

"You're a brat," I grumbled.

"The word you're looking for is bitch," she corrected. "And I wear it with pride."

12

A space opened up on Cedar less than a block from the Medical Examiner's compound, and I backed my Dodge Hellcat in before anyone else could snag it. Early morning traffic inched past us, clogging both lanes, but the drive out had been lucky—most of Euclid Heights and Cedar Glen had been clear.

"You're not coming inside," I said flatly.

"Who said I wanted to?" she asked.

"I thought that's why you tagged along," I grumbled. "To loom over my shoulder and make inappropriate comments."

Lil grinned, Cheshire-wide. "I wouldn't want to embarrass you in front of your friend."

With a groan, I unstrapped my seatbelt and opened the door. "You're impossible." Stepping onto the curb, I slammed the door harder than was necessary. Lil shot out of the passenger side in the next instant.

"You're not leaving me cooped up in there."

"Well, you're not getting my keys," I said, clicking the fob so all the doors locked. Then I armed the security system. "I don't trust you."

"Come on, Zack," she replied. "If I really wanted your big, slick muscle car, believe me, I could take it before you even realized it was gone."

Frowning, I waited for the punch line, certain she was leading up to some sort of innuendo. For once, though, it seemed she actually meant my car. Still, my imagination took me places I really didn't want to go. It didn't help that her spice and vanilla come-hither overpowered even the asphalt stink of the street.

That was my brain, on Lil.

"My eyes are up here," she purred. "Something on your mind, flyboy?"

Dragging my gaze from where it had settled, I muttered something indecipherable, then rushed across Cedar before I further embarrassed myself. That guilty flush was back at my ears, and it wasn't lost on the Lady of Beasts. Her rich, throaty laughter followed tauntingly all the way to the door.

To my shock, Lil stayed put.

The big concrete block of the main building squatted on a thin strip of lawn behind a token iron fence. Freshly painted, the waist-high metal barrier looked like its sole purpose was to accent the landscaping. Beyond it, the entire façade of the boxy gray structure was gridded with windows. At this hour, only a few of them flickered with life.

A boldly lettered sign prohibiting the carrying of weapons was posted prominently beside the main entrance. Self-consciously, I tugged the cuffs of my jacket over the rounded bulge of pommels at my wrists, hoping they wouldn't have metal detectors. Bobby knew what kind of arsenal I carried, and that may have been why he'd asked me to meet him at the loading bay.

Problem was, I couldn't recall where it was.

A cursory study of the lot led to a promising spit of pavement emblazoned with yellow one-way arrows. Those led around the side of the building. The truck-sized lane twined between the main office and a nearby parking structure. One entire side was lined with signs.

NO PARKING: TOW AWAY ZONE

These were tacked to a sagging chain-link fence that separated the truck lane from the parking garage beyond. Vagabond weeds sprouted among clusters of trash at its base, the plastic tatters of abandoned grocery bags flicking in the wind.

Turning a corner, I finally spotted Bobby. The young detective hunched with his back to the wind just beyond the pool of light cast by a halogen mounted over a metal receiving door. A few feet to the left of the loading bay stood a dented fire door with a security box mounted next to it—the kind with speakers. Bobby was in his shirtsleeves, and the wind pasted his pants to his slim legs as he fervently tapped on the glowing screen of his smartphone. My own phone buzzed with an incoming text. Grabbing the device, I lofted it in his direction.

"Hey," I called. "Got your text. Hope I'm not too late."

Bobby jumped at the sound of my voice. His nerves had to be frazzled—I wasn't even sneaking.

"Zack," he said. "I was afraid you wouldn't make it."

The little lines at the corners of his eyes deepened once he got a good look at me. Quizzically, he tapped the side of his throat, echoing the placement of the bandages. "What happened here?"

"Lost a fight," I replied, resisting the urge to fuss with the row of steri-strips.

"Ouch," he said. "I'd hate to see what you lost to." His eyes cut to a surveillance camera mounted on a pole between the service lane and the parking structure. Its blank, black eye stared directly at the pool of light around the receiving door. "Let's get inside. We don't have time to waste if we want to keep this under the radar." So saying, Bobby pressed his thumb to a buzzer in the metal housing. A tinny speaker built into the box crackled with a voice that could have been human, although it was so distorted, it left room for debate.

"I've got my guy," Bobby announced. "Buzz us in."

The voice said nothing in acknowledgement, but the lock mechanism vibrated hard enough to make the whole fixture shake. Straining, Bobby yanked on the handle. Something loose at the bottom dragged with a tortured-metal shriek, adding to a rusty half-arc scored into the cement.

"Didn't need that ear anyway," I muttered.

"Take a deep breath," Bobby cautioned, then he ushered me inside. Beyond the door lay a narrow hallway with bare walls the color of old fingernail clippings. Dull gray tile covered the floor, so freshly scrubbed, it squeaked beneath my boots. A thick miasma of antiseptic cleaner rose from the tiles. Instantly, my eyes stung.

"Holy fuck," I choked. Bobby simply nodded. He stepped swiftly across the still-glistening tiles while I lagged behind, gulping air that tasted like bleach. "At least we know the place is hygienic."

"The gal on nights takes her cleaning seriously."

I scrubbed at my eyes. "Ya think?"

"Come on," he urged. "Only a little further and it'll clear up." The hall bent left and then broke into a T.

Bobby took us left again, moving at a brisk pace. As promised, the choking pall of bleach-water began to fade. We came to a security checkpoint, unmanned, and Bobby swiped his ID card through a reader. The lock on the door buzzed and he held it open, all but pushing me through. Highly strung on a good day, he moved like a clockwork doll wound tight enough to burst. He wasn't just in a hurry—he was spooked.

"What are we walking into?" I asked, as we pivoted around another bend. Bobby practically scurried past a line of stainless steel doors, each of them locked tight, with gleaming security pads mounted next to them. He shot me a strained look over his shoulder.

"I'm just glad it's you and not the daughter that has to see the body," he said.

"That bad?"

He quickened his pace, gripping his ID card hard enough to crimp the lamination. "You know I've seen a lot of awful shit, especially after Garrett," he began. Impulsively, his hand went to his short hairs, scrubbing like there was something he sought to wipe from his skin. "But this lady—Zack, she was tortured. And whoever did it knew how to make it last. Probably for days."

"When did they find her?" I asked.

"The Parma police have had the case a couple of weeks."

"Parma's a little out of your jurisdiction," I said. "How'd you even hear about it?"

"One look at the symbols and they kicked it to me."

"Symbols?" I asked. My gut twisted.

"You know how it is," Bobby said. "I'm the go-to guy for all the weird shit, especially after the busts last March with Garrett and that... *thing*." Even knowing Malphael was my brother, Bobby couldn't bring himself to acknowledge the connection. To him, the Gibburim would always be a demon. I didn't correct him. "The detective in charge—Lopez—she didn't relinquish the case, but she has me consulting."

"What kind of symbols are we talking about this time?" I pressed.

Footsteps echoed at the end of the hall, and we froze in guilty silence. A petite woman in scrubs and carrying a clipboard briskly turned the corner. A bindi marked her faintly lined brow. As she passed, she looked up briefly from her paperwork, glancing past me to Bobby. She flashed the detective a broad, white grin.

"Good morning, Detective Park."

"Hey, Priya," he replied. Tension ratcheted across his narrow shoulders, but the smile he gave her was warm and genuine.

"A little late for you, isn't it?" she mused. "I almost never see you here at the changing of the guard."

"Yeah." He ducked his head in a nod. "Last-minute appointment. Only time we could fit it in."

Her gaze shifted briefly back to me, but she didn't ask any questions, just tipped her head in greeting and continued on her way. The metronomic click of her low heels echoed loud and hollow in the long and barren hall. She stopped at a doorway just before the next bend, rattling through a pocket full of keys. Producing her own ID card, she swiped and tapped a passcode into the mounted pad. Before disappearing into her work space, Priya smiled again at Bobby.

"You have a good day now, Detective Park."

Hurriedly, he nodded, turning back to me. "Priya's day shift," he whispered. "She's always early, but this place will fill up fast." He swiped his own card through the key pad nearest us, punching in a series of six numbers. "We've got to make this quick... and, Zack," he added, with an ominous note. "However bad you think this is. Trust me. It's actually worse."

13

Stainless steel, tile, and antiseptic so strong it nearly covered the stench of death, marked the dimly lit room. Bobby swept ahead, flicking on a bank of overhead lights. Under their dull, insect drone, the walls echoed hollowly with the sound of our footfalls. I tried to walk softly, but body and thoughts felt oddly out of step. Struggling to marshal my focus, I swayed near the threshold.

With nervous efficiency, Bobby moved straight for the refrigerated units along the back wall. Each of the square stainless steel doors bore a placard with a number-letter combination. Without hesitation, he reached for number 4-9A, top row, far right, one from the end. He waited with his fingers poised on the handle. I moved gingerly past equipment I'd thus far only seen on crime shows—at least since my rebirth on the lake. Little blips and flashes of memory told me this wasn't my first time in a place like this.

Finally stepping to Bobby's side, I held tight to my shields, having little interest in picking up stray psychic impressions. A morgue wasn't as bad as a hospital, where every day the living imprinted brittle hopes and grinding misery, but corpses held their own memories, even once the soul had flown.

In Marjory's case, I was counting on it. Her death was the only one here I was willing to let inside my head.

"Ready?" Bobby asked.

Cautiously, I nodded. Despite his warnings, however, I wasn't certain I could properly prepare. I'd seen dead bodies before—even made a few myself—but the heat of battle was altogether different than this hushed vault of stainless steel.

"Go ahead," I murmured.

A grim set to his features, Bobby pulled the drawer.

The gray-haired woman lay on her back, a Y-incision spread between her collarbones. Soft folds of skin bunched roundly between the stitches, alternately pale and mottled. Cozily plump, she was covered with a crisp vinyl sheet from about her armpits down—and that was a blessing.

Deep bruising on her face and shoulders showed that she had been severely beaten. Purple, green, yellow—the colors told the story of a lengthy assault where some of the wounds had been given time to start healing.

I'd hoped to recognize Marjory—at least some glimmer—but the damage was so extensive, her face looked more like a horror movie mask than anything that had once been human. Whoever had processed her had washed away the clotted blood, but cuts still stood out on her cheek and mouth and forehead, where the sheer force of impact had split her skin. One eye socket sagged inward, all the bones around it shattered. From the lumpy shape of her jaw, that, too, had been broken.

"Wow," I breathed. It was all I could manage.

Bobby tugged at the sheet, revealing further damage—bruises so deep their purpled centers looked black, burns bubbling in soft folds of skin.

"We had to get her dental records because of what they did to her hands."

I followed his gesture and, at first, my brain refused to process the tattered stumps of meat and skin as fingers. Gray and yellow tendons hung like grisly ribbons around the exposed knobs of rounded bones. What flesh remained was ragged, the bruising raw in a way that suggested this damage had been inflicted while Marjory yet lived.

"They didn't break her fingers," I said numbly.

"No. They tore them off," Bobby replied. "One by one, probably with vise-grips." His voice came as if from across a chasm. "They did the same to her toes."

"Torture," I said flatly. He'd said it already, but it was the only word that came. Grimly, Bobby nodded. Forcing myself to examine each burn and point of impact, I leaned closer. Someone had wanted something very badly from this woman, and she had fought like hell not to give it up.

My secrets.

I wanted to deny the thought, but couldn't.

"Where did they find her?" I asked.

"Her home," Bobby answered, "but that's not where they killed her. The place is pristine."

"Staged, then?" I ventured.

"Without a doubt."

I walked a slow circuit around the corpse. My stomach lurched every time my eyes strayed to her mutilated hands.

"Why?"

"Best guess? They wanted someone to find her there."

"Not just anyone," I answered in a hush. "A family member."

Reluctantly, he nodded.

I bent back to the body, not yet willing to touch it. I wanted a clear inventory of all the physical details before I dove into the psychic aspect of things. The stringent scent of disinfectant rose pungently from her skin, but under that, no stink of decomposition.

"I expected a smell," I muttered, "even with the refrigeration. How long has she been dead?"

"That's one of the weird things," Bobby answered. He fidgeted with his tie, tugging the knot from his throat. Tiny Rebel Alliance insignias masqueraded as polka dots against a background of black. "She's been here a couple weeks. Before that, no one's sure. Time of death was hard to quantify. Decomp hasn't progressed like it should."

A deep shiver clutched at my innards, only partly connected with the abused corpse. A fleeting tease of memory, almost cogent…

Then gone.

"Any idea why?" I asked.

"I was hoping you would know."

Thickly, I swallowed. Some part of me did know. The rest of me didn't want to.

114

"You said there were symbols," I prompted.

"A circle in the center of her chest." He put on blue gloves, then bent forward, spreading her heavy breasts. "The Y-incision cuts right through it, but you can still make out most of it." Not quite touching, he traced a raised, red pattern with the tip of a finger. "The work is intricate. We think he used a wood-burning tool, or maybe a heated needle."

"I hope someone got a picture before they cut into her," I said. "That incision makes it hard to read."

"Lopez sent me copies on my phone, but I wanted you to see it in context." He shifted position so he didn't block any light. "Besides, I know how you work. You don't get the same kind of read from a photo."

"No, I don't," I assented.

Leaning closer, I struggled to read what was there. Within the mottled bruising, almost invisible against the severe discoloration, rows of carefully incised symbols flowed in a tight series of concentric circles. Sinuous and angular by turns, the letters were burned directly into Marjory's skin. The Y-incision distorted several of the lines, but one set of glyphs I recognized with thundering immediacy.

It was a Name.

"Zuriel." The syllables shivered through me as I whispered. No clear recollections emerged, but in the depths of my soul I knew him. On the heels of that awareness welled a sense of loss so sharp, it left me reeling. Remy's word, *shalish*, returned.

"You OK, Zack?" Bobby asked. "You're really pale all of a sudden."

"He—he's woven dense layers of magic here," I

muttered, not exactly answering. I could unpack that reaction once I sorted the rest of the words. The lettering was delicate, none of the symbols larger than the nail on my pinky. "With all this damage, I'm fumbling."

"I can bring the pics up on my phone," he offered.

Shaking my head, I held one hand poised above the pattern of sigils, keenly aware of what physical contact would bring.

"I'll get more this way."

"There's a box of gloves on that counter," Bobby suggested.

"Can't do gloves," I said. "It dulls the perceptions." Bobby frowned. "I think, at some point, I trained myself to see gloves and even clothes as psychic barriers— convenient for shielding from a barrage of random perceptions every time I bump into someone, but I haven't figured out how to turn it off for something like this."

"She's already been processed, but it's not a good idea to touch her directly—"

My hand was already descending. I needed to see what they'd done to her, not just the physical assault, but everything that had led up to it.

The first thing I heard was her scream.

14

She knew no one could hear her. That didn't stop her from wailing as loud as she could every time he left her in the dark.

Her voice was long past ragged. No idea what anyone would do if they found her. She was beyond saving. On some level, she knew that, wasn't really sure how she'd lasted this long. Funny, the will for survival. She hadn't understood it with Sammy, a husk full of tubes, whittled to nothing by the cancer, still fighting for each painful breath.

Now, she got it. Grokked it on a deep and unequivocal level. The body didn't like quitting, even when the mind knew there was no other escape...

I'd dropped straight into the vision. Everything came from Marjory's perspective—not exactly through her eyes, but certainly filtered through her head. She hunched in darkness, bound to something. Probably a chair, though she didn't remember any more. It could have been an elephant for all that she could feel it. Pain had cycled her to some distant place where sensation was just a river that occasionally broke its banks.

Every time it flooded, more of her eroded. Longer and longer bouts of empty dark.

Really, it was a blessing.

She longed to descend and never surface, but her stubborn body wouldn't let her. *He* wouldn't let her, either. So much anger in that one. Always, he shoved her over the edge only to drag her back and do it again. He asked his questions. She wouldn't answer.

Rinse, repeat.

Rinse, repeat.

What did you do with Tashiel? I know he came out here, you stupid cow. Why can't I hear him? What do you know about it?

Tashiel, Tashiel. The endless refrain. Tashiel was a name in a dead man's journal.

Why was your name in his ledger? You have something that belongs to him, don't you? You cunt! Give it up.

Travelogues. Her guilty pleasure. She'd spent thousands on first-hand accounts of other peoples' adventures, the more doomed the better. She loved the survive-against-all-odds narrative.

Not so thrilling as the survivor.

You think I can't see my brother's mark on you? You can't fool me. Look at me when I'm talking to you! Where is he?

She sent herself on one of those journeys every time his questions started. Among headhunters in Borneo. Through the pioneer wilds of America. The Congo.

Everest. Antarctica. The Tashiel book wasn't even that interesting. Tired stuff, really, but it had meant something to Zaquiel—and for that, she kept its secrets. Zaquiel's, too. So many secrets.

That was her life. One big closet.

Poor Sam. Patient unto death.

The endless stream of consciousness was a riptide, dragging me under. Flailing, I fought for traction. Marjory's thoughts were so terribly present, it felt as if she was still living every second of her torture. The information was useful, though. I recalled nothing of a travelogue, but Tashiel I knew.

At least, I knew *of* him. He was another of the Anakim.

There was a memory, gleaned from the stolen stores of Dorimiel in our life-or-death struggle above the lake—the sole time I'd willingly used the powers of the Eye. The Nephilim decimus had shoved the knowledge as a distraction in my path while I'd ripped through his mind for my real prize—the sigil-phrase that unlocked the seal of Lailah's binding jar.

Tash had been traveling with Anakesiel and other members of my tribe through what might have been the Swiss Alps. It was the early eighteen hundreds, moments before Dorimiel had ambushed the Anakim Primus in a bid to acquire the Stylus. Tashiel had been scouting ahead. He'd just returned to warn of the impending attack.

The intel came too late.

I had nothing on the actual fight, but I knew its result. Anak and three of his lieutenants captured, their souls trapped in jars—the same vessels now hidden in my desk. Notably, Tash wasn't among them. Had he been

Marjory's sole survivor, recording the events in a personal journal? It wouldn't have been the first time some scrap of our history had weathered a centuries-long trip. Yet how could that journal be worth so much torture?

The things Zuriel did to her…

Zaquiel, is that you? Have you come to save me?

Her voice clutched at my thoughts with desperate ferocity.

Let me out, she pleaded. *I want to see my Sammy again.*

My head whirled as I struggled to process what was happening. All those half-lucid ramblings—I wasn't reading some fragment of past events caught in the amber of her skin. Her ghost was trapped in there.

It was a corpse. It shouldn't be.

Please, Zack. He won't let me leave!

"Jesus, Zack, what's wrong?" From a vast distance, Bobby's voice battered my awareness. I felt a harsh tug on my arm. "Come on Zack, let go. Snap out of it!"

At the mere possibility that she might see release, Marjory flailed in a welter of need. Lucidity drowned in a stupefying rush of sensation—the misery of her torture, determination to keep her promises, rising horror when she realized how she'd survived for so long.

She hadn't.

That was his worst cheat, locking her to the wreck of dead flesh. Maddened, we clawed against the insensible shell, desperate for any response.

All the bindings held.

Her screams chased me all the way to the surface. Finally, I tore my hand free.

I was on the floor, with no recollection of my transit from her body to the tiles. Half of the vinyl sheet had been dragged down with me, and Marjory's arm draped lifeless over the edge of her cold metal resting place.

In the room of buzzing lights and sterile steel, Bobby shook me until my teeth rattled. I bit my tongue. The pain—*my* pain—gave me some traction. Gasping, I recoiled, overwhelmed with revulsion.

"She's in there," I blurted. "She's in there. Holy fuck. She's still inside her dead skin."

15

Flesh and gray tendons hung like grisly streamers from the absence of fingers. Hot bile rose bitter at the back of my throat.

Bobby was at my side, his voice low and urgent. I didn't process anything that he was saying. With firm persistence, he strove to drag me to my feet. With our difference in height, it was comical. The rhythmic patter of his words brought me back in stages. Eventually, I scrambled from the floor, putting some distance between myself and those tortured fingers.

The screaming dulled, but didn't stop.

"What just happened?" Bobby demanded. Now that I stood, his words rang sharp—my collapse had left him rattled. That made two of us. With trembling hands, I gripped my head.

"He left her in that body," I choked.

All my horror echoed back from Bobby's face. Eyes creeping to the spectacle of the cadaver, he groped for composure.

"Why?"

Not *"how."* Bobby had been down that rabbit hole before. The smartly dressed detective might not understand my world, but he knew about its truths. This was just one incomprehensible horror among many, and he didn't need to know the how of it in order to offer me his help.

"She didn't give him what he wanted."

"Good for her," he said.

Marjory's voice, hushed but still panicked, reverberated just beyond hearing. Endlessly, she pleaded. With reluctant steps, I approached her corpse once more.

"I've got to release her," I said. "This isn't fair—she suffered to protect me."

"So this *is* personal?"

I nodded. Steeling myself, I went to place my palm over the sigil burned into her flesh. Those three rings of text were the key. Bobby seized my wrist before I could make contact.

"Whoa, whoa," he said angrily. "What are you doing?"

"I've got to get a better feel for the spell," I explained, tugging away. Bobby relinquished my wrist, but inserted himself between me and the body.

"A minute ago, you touched her and it put you on the floor," he said. "How is this a good idea?"

"I can't leave her like this, Bobby."

A muscle ticked in his jaw as he glared up at me. "No," he insisted. "First you tell me how to fix things if this goes sideways."

"What?"

He pushed me away from the drawer, back braced

against its metal lip. Stunned by this uncharacteristic resistance, I gave ground—a single step. Marjory's lifeless arm dangled behind him. I still couldn't look at it.

"I can't believe you can stand there with her looking like that, and not worry that this is a trap," he said. "Someone knew enough to find this woman and to carve that thing into her skin. That person obviously knows you, so they know what you'd do to access that magic—am I right?"

Grudgingly, I nodded. With a soft grunt of vindication, Bobby folded his arms over his narrow chest. The gesture crimped his tie.

"Bobby—" I started.

Gruffly, he cut me off. "Maybe it's normal for you, people using human beings as stationery, but it's not normal in my world, Zack," he said. "I have no idea what to expect here, and I'm not going to stand around feeling useless. I *can't*." His voice faltered, a bitter reminder that I had shut Bobby out when his partner had needed him the most. Things might have turned out very differently for Garrett if I'd shown my friend a little trust.

"Look, I don't know what to expect any more than you do," I countered. Bobby's dark brows stitched as he scanned my face for dissemblance. I wasn't lying—wouldn't do him that injustice, not again. "If I've ever encountered something like this, I don't remember. You know how it is."

His grip on his elbows tightened until he all but hugged himself.

"You can't do it some other way?"

Abruptly, footsteps resounded through the hall,

and we both froze. Closer and closer, they halted near our door. Keys jingled. Bobby poised with his hand on Marjory's drawer, ready to roll her back into darkness the instant we heard someone try to get in.

After a nerve-wracking silence, the steps moved away. We let ourselves breathe. I slipped around Bobby to face the corpse.

"I can't do it any other way, not if you want us out of here before someone kicks us out," I said. He hovered near my elbow, doing a nervous shuffle.

"You start screaming again and they'll kick us out regardless."

"I was screaming?"

He nodded. "And not in English."

"Hit me." At his startled look, I repeated the instruction. "I'm serious. If I do it again, smack me in the face or something. I bit my tongue when you shook me earlier, and that pulled me out of it."

"That is a shitty plan, Zack," he grumbled.

"I've had almost zero sleep over the past five days," I said. "It's all I got."

My friend didn't look happy, but when I reached again for Marjory's body, he didn't stop me. He retreated a few paces away, so tense he vibrated. I closed my eyes for a moment, cutting him from my awareness. With a deep breath that hardly left me feeling any steadier, I concentrated on the three concentric rings of symbols scored into Marjory's chest.

The layered magic of the sigil stung the tips of my fingers before I even made contact. As I watched, the rings ignited with a pale, arctic glow against the deep bruising, lifting like a hologram to hover in the air before me. Each on its own axis, the rings twirled and spun, dials on a combination lock crafted from pure energy.

Zuriel's Name burned brightly, repeating in a pattern through the graduated circles. In shadows beneath it, I could just make out another triad of syllables. I expected this Name to be Tashiel's. Instead, it was my own.

The symbols twisted weirdly together with Zuriel's. It gave me the strangest feeling. All of Bobby's warnings clamored in my head.

Too late.

The whirl of characters burst in a soundless explosion. Arctic fire drowned my vision. Trailing light like a comet, the heart of the sigil crashed into the center of my chest. The impact rocked me backward and I staggered away from the open drawer. Marjory started shrieking. She seized my wrist with the stumps of her fingers, and I felt the slick press of each exposed knuckle.

"He knows," she cried, the words mushy around the edges. Shards of teeth tumbled from dead lips as she worked her broken jaw. "What you did to Tashiel. He knows." I strained in her grip, but the ragged nubs held fast.

"Let go." I clawed wildly. Where the fuck was Bobby?

She clambered from her cold slab, the vinyl sheet spilling to the floor. Still gripping my wrist, she pulled me into a tight embrace, sagging breasts crushed against my jacket. She pressed her cheek to mine, flaccid lips against my ear.

"Everything you took, he'll take from you," she whispered. "You broke your promise. You're a traitor to your brothers. Traitors pay." She hissed the words fiercely, her voice distorting until his voice emerged, the sound as familiar as my own.

I'm coming for you, Zaquiel, it said. *You're going to suffer for what you stole from me.* In a lightning-stroke, a face leapt the chasm of memory. A near twin of my own, only older. Drawn and haggard.

Tashiel. I knew it without thinking.

On the heels of this vision, there was a crushing weight of guilt devoid of context. A cascade of confusing images. White sheets. Sharp hospital smell. The rhythmic huff of some machine. The shreds of knowledge blew through me so fast, I caught no sense of their meaning. They spun like blasted cinders, and I reeled in the void they left behind.

Shouting wordless negation, I flailed against the message-bringer, finally tearing my wrist from her noxious grip. With ferocious effort, I shoved the dead woman away. She stumbled back, clouded eyes blinking dumbly. This wasn't the person I'd first encountered, the one locked in darkness, pleading for release.

Marjory.

I called her name in a silent scream.

Marjory Kazinsky.

Abruptly, the milky corneas cleared. All the brutal damage dropped away. A face emerged, alive and vibrant. One I'd seen in nightmares—as recently as my nap by Euclid Beach. For weeks, she'd haunted me, calling, pleading. She hadn't been some guilt-born dream. She'd reached through our connection. In that instant, I knew we had one. A psychic bond.

More than that.

The knowledge almost surfaced, then sank out of

reach. The next words she spoke were her own again, free of Zuriel's influence. They bypassed her lips to ring directly inside my brain.

Help me, Zaquiel. I can't endure this one more day.

Her desperate, lucid contact brought me back to myself. With mounting clarity, I caught the flaws in the room that surrounded us. Too many shining doors lined either side. The sterile walls stretched like a gleaming funhouse tunnel. All of it spun, flat and distorted.

Bobby was nowhere to be seen.

"It's a projection," I breathed. "I'm in my head. This isn't real."

The whirling sigils cycled through all of it, three rings of gleaming magic fueling the façade. His power had a taste—close to my own, but colder and sharper, like the bite of air on a brisk winter's day. Something about it was hauntingly familiar. Hate and anger seethed in its chill.

Marjory—as she must have appeared in life—stood rigidly against the drawer that was her current resting place. Her battered corpse stretched behind her.

I'm real, she pleaded. *Get me out of here, Zack. Please.*

Recognition teased just beyond reach. "How do I know you?" I asked. She gave me the saddest smile.

Find Tabby before he does. She's always trusted you.

"Is she still alive?" I demanded. "Do you know where to find her? Why did you die for me?" I surged forward to shake her for the answers, but something yanked me back. A hand on my arm—it had to be Bobby, pulling me out—but I didn't want to go. I needed her answers. I tried to jerk free of his grip, twisting around until I could see him.

"Let me finish!" I bellowed.

The pull was hard enough to knock me off balance. Something wasn't right. Bobby's face—it started melting, like a cheap candle left in the sun. Waxen rivulets of skin dripped to obliterate his features. From beneath, another face bulged.

My face, but a mockery. The mouth split.

"You mad, bro?" my tormentor cackled.

I shoved him away violently. "Get out of my head!"

The Bobby-Thing rocked back on its heels, springing right back up like one of those clown-faced punching dolls. "It's not that easy," he taunted. The grin never wavered. "I got her, which means I got you." Gleaming tendrils of energy trailed from the back of his head, skulljacking him to Marjory's dead body. A second set of psychic cables sprouted from the whirling circles between her breasts. Those ran between her and me, hooking just under my ribs—exactly where the explosion of magic had crashed against my chest.

I needed to unpack the layers of that spell, and fast.

Lazily, the rings of the sigil spun, a tiny echo of the larger version reflected from every gleaming surface in the room. The burning letters shimmered and streaked, making them hard to read, but I managed. The outer ring—that was Marjory's binding. It locked her soul to her body. The inner ring, blazing with his Name and my Name, let Zuriel leapfrog to me. The middle one, I wasn't certain. The symbols rearranged themselves as I struggled for focus. Only one word stood out with any clarity.

Rage.

"You mad, bro?" he asked again. The question was ridiculous.

"Why are you doing this?"

"You know," he spat. Taffy-stretched ribbons dangled from the lips of his melted simulacrum. "How about I give you time to reflect?" Locking the fingers of both hands, he shoved. Abruptly the floor tilted, and I hurtled backward, scrabbling for purchase.

As I thrashed, cracks spiderwebbed through walls and lights and autopsy equipment. Massive pieces sheered away in my hands. With a shattering explosion, the whole scene burst into a rain of jagged shards. They pelted my face and my jacket, stinging against my wings. Empty blackness hung behind them. The whirling sigil was an ultraviolet ghost against the void.

I stopped my fall with a downstroke, one arm shielding my eyes. The raining shards expanded, folding outward until they penned me in with mirrors. Front, back, top, down, Zuriel cackled in every one, wearing endless iterations of my face. Only the sneer of the lips was different. Petty.

"You been two-faced so long, you wouldn't know the real one if it bit you," he growled. Jacked in through Marjory, he skimmed my thoughts. I didn't know how deep he could go, but I could feel those cords at my chest. They were like vipers, poisonous and burrowing.

I needed to cut myself free and put an end to this, but that meant slashing my ties to Marjory. At the thought, I felt a welling reluctance. She was dead. I knew it, but I didn't want to lose her.

Let me go. Find Tabitha.

That made sense—so why did the prospect hurt so much?

Around me, banks of mirrors folded and refolded themselves in a whirl of kaleidoscope physics. Weightless, I drifted among shifting angles, seeking a way through the ever-warping maze. At every turn, I was confronted by a mockery of my stolen face.

"You know what I'm after," he spat.

"No," I said. "I really don't."

"Liar!" he shouted. The mirrors rattled with the force of it, a brittle cascade of tinkling notes. "He came here to meet with you. I know he did. I plucked it from her head."

"Now who's lying?" I demanded. "You never broke her, not even when you bound her to her corpse."

Fifteen versions of my face folded into masks of ugly rage. "I'm psychic, you dumb shit. I didn't have to break her."

"But she beat you any way," I needled. "Bet that pisses you off."

He launched into a long and gratifying rant of barely cogent fury. While he distracted himself, I groped for the root of my tie to Marjory. Hooked deep, it was nearly hidden by Zuriel's own cobbled connections. Her mind chimed like distant music. Even in the midst of this psychic assault, she was still fighting.

She'd walled herself away in one of her travel stories, doggedly imagining the majesty of the Himalayas. Bypassing the mirrors, I arrowed for the tiny sanctuary. The snow-bright image held a soothing nostalgia. I'd never been to this place, but I'd heard it read to me.

That's it, she urged. *Follow the path to the summit.*

Through tenuous threads of recognition, I dove until I found her. Behind me, Zuriel lashed the air, but I held tight to my purpose. My brother might have crafted this space, but he'd built its foundation on Marjory. If I found her, I could free both of us.

She hung in a gray expanse, suspended at the center of the burning sigil. The three rings spun in mad gyrations, whirling so fast they painted a sphere of light around her. His power gleamed in its inscribed symbols, arctic-white and cold as her dreams of Everest.

Here, the devious cruelty of Zuriel's gambit became apparent. The threads connecting us went far deeper than those he'd cobbled together. Marjory was an anchor—a mortal into whom I'd placed a portion of my power. Anchors were more than friends or allies. They were family—often literally. When life left my mortal body, it was through an anchor that I'd instinctively seek rebirth.

I should have seen it. The deep connection. The haunting recognition. She'd listed me as next of kin. Marjory was about the right age—

Don't think about it, I told myself.

I couldn't afford to waver, so I drew my daggers. The curving blades sang as I pulled them free, their glinting steel catching slivers of my face. One eye spilled light, pale as the moon on a midnight lake, and glimmers of answering fire licked along the steel. Weapons primed, I studied the whirling sigil. This work came down to timing. The knots of power were so enmeshed, any cut that freed us both would sever her ties to me.

But I had to get to her first.

"Do it," Zuriel coaxed. "Cut her. I want to see you hurt like me."

I didn't ask or try to reason. There was no way to contend with that kind of hate. Tucking my wings, I plummeted at top speed through the rotating rings, catching an open space before they all scythed together. But I couldn't move fast enough. The middle ring cut a swath of fire across my brow. Ducking, I curled my body into a tight ball to avoid decapitation. Icicle shards of magic burst against my vision as an edge caught me a second time.

Then I made it. Marjory hung deep in her dreams of distant places, backpacking with the love of her life. In those dreams, she sometimes had a son, and Tabitha was safe.

Zuriel's power bore down with suffocating intensity. Sere tongues of white flame leapt from the physical inscriptions writ large upon the spinning sigil to the ethereal strands woven within and throughout Marjory. I aimed my daggers.

"I am so sorry," I breathed.

Power surged. Her lids fluttered, and our eyes met. I knew her smile. Loss welled at the impending amputation, but I refused to hesitate.

In a clash of light that drowned my vision, I cut Marjory free.

16

The stink of scorched skin chased the winter-sharp bite of Zuriel's power as I emerged. My ears thudded with the rush of my heart. The room felt strange and hollow around me, and I stared at each reflective surface, making sure I was truly out of his crafted nightmare.

The severed-limb ache of Marjory's absence should have been answer enough. Her corpse was just a corpse again, brutalized, mutilated, but with no soul attached.

Bobby stared like he expected me to collapse at any moment, stepping close in case he had to catch me. Irritably, I waved him off.

"I'm fine," I insisted. We both knew it was a lie.

"What next?" he asked.

"I need... I need to see her things, Bobby." I struggled to get the words past the dry and ragged feeling in my throat. I hunched around a deep burn beneath my ribs that might have been my heart, but was probably something worse.

Both of my blades were drawn. Out of habit, I wiped

the daggers on the leg of my jeans before hiding them away in their sheaths. As I sagged against one of the nearby drawers, Bobby put Marjory back roughly the way we had found her, fussily settling her sheet a little higher on the Y-incision. Neither of us mentioned the blackened streak of damage I'd left burned across her chest.

We exited the room, and Bobby hustled me toward the far end of the section. We moved through the halls swiftly, but no longer had the complex to ourselves. Activity had picked up as the night shift gave way to the day crew. Still hunching around that dull ache where my connection to Marjory had been severed, I kept my head down and avoided eye contact. I had zero interest in talking with anyone, but at least half of the new arrivals knew Bobby on sight, so they slowed our progress with a seemingly endless stream of "good mornings" and "hellos."

Everything rankled. All the pleasantries were empty recitations, the reflex of a polite society. It was different for Bobby. He met the eyes of each person who greeted him, making a point to acknowledge them by name. He didn't talk long—we were both in too much of a hurry to waste that kind of time—but he made every salutation count.

"Mr. Popularity," I muttered once we had a little stretch of hall to ourselves. Bobby just shrugged, as if his level of earnest amiability was nothing special at all.

"It's not hard to be nice to people," he responded, a little perplexed.

"Says you."

"Seriously, Zack. Who's to say they're not having the same kind of day we are?" he said. "This kind of job, people see awful shit nearly every hour, and that's just the work front. We don't know their lives—we only see a sliver, and they're putting their best face on, just like we are." A little too pointedly, he added, "Everyone's carrying some hidden pain. A little kindness goes a long way."

"Don't start with the lecture," I grumbled. "Not now."

"Sorry," he said—and he meant it. He started to say something else, but I quelled it with a look. My breath felt shallow in a way I really didn't like, and I couldn't nail down the extent of the damage I'd done to myself. Waves of wounded anger thudded against my skull, some of it directed at Zuriel, but the rest bleeding through all of my thoughts. I wanted to snarl at the fake smiles around me, just draw my blades and cut the hypocrisy from their skin.

You mad, bro?

I'd cut Zuriel's access, but the taunt lingered persistently.

"Pissed as hell," I muttered.

"I didn't catch that," Bobby said.

I stuffed my hands in my pockets to hide the clenched fists. Muscles across my shoulders bunched beneath the jacket. "Shut up and get a move on."

Bobby's mouth tugged downward. He was smart enough not to say anything, but he quickened his steps, angling away from me. A growing distance opened between us in the hallway. If he thought that made him safe, fine by me.

We marched in silence until we came to the door of the properties room. Bobby scooted ahead, approaching the gal behind the counter. I let him do the talking. He kept glancing back over his shoulder. I looked away. The properties clerk was new to her job, so he had to introduce himself. Somewhat subdued, he still managed to be charming. She only frowned once in my direction. Bobby diverted her attention and, after a few exchanged pleasantries, she happily signed Marjory's effects out to me.

Avoiding my eyes, she pushed the clipboard through the window dividing us. I scribbled a rough approximation of my name—it still felt foreign, even after a year—then shoved pen and clipboard back at her.

"Thanks," she muttered, peeling back a layer of the ditto paper. She tore off the bottommost sheet and placed it on the counter. "That's your copy. Let me get the box of her things."

"We appreciate it," Bobby said.

She gave him a weak smile and then, softly humming, disappeared down the rows of metal shelving piled high with box after box. Folding the receipt for Marjory's things into something manageable, I tucked it into a pocket. Without warning, an aftershock of pain lanced through my chest. The world grayed and I seized the counter.

"Are you sure you're ok?" Bobby asked.

"No," I snapped.

"What happened back there?" His eyes flicked in the direction of the clerk and he dropped his voice to a whisper. "I know what I saw wasn't half of it."

"I don't want to talk about it," I said. Swift as it arrived, the pain started fading. I held my breath in anticipation of another wave. Nothing came. Tentatively, I straightened.

The girl returned with a small-lidded carton sealed with orange tape. "Marjory Kazinsky," she pronounced. "This is all she came in with." She placed the box into a metal drawer set under the counter. It opened on both sides. I reached for the handle, but Bobby interposed himself with a cautious glance toward me.

"What'd you do that for?" I demanded.

Bobby took the package and tucked it under one arm, then turned back to the girl.

"Is there a room free, where we can look over these before he takes them home?" he asked. "The case is ongoing."

"Sure," she said, pointing. "Right over there."

Box in hand, he muttered his thanks and headed toward the door she'd indicated. Choking on annoyance, I stalked after him. Twice, I almost ripped the package from his grip. All I wanted was to grab her things and get the hell home. All the chattering mortals made my skin crawl.

Oblivious to the violent scenes of carnage scrolling behind my eyeballs, Bobby ushered me through the door. He locked it behind us the minute I was through. Slamming the box onto the desk in the center, he whirled to confront me.

"Tell me what happened." He kept his voice low, conscious of the clerk, but the way the tendons corded on his neck, it was obvious he wanted to shout.

"I said, I don't want to talk about it," I snarled. Shouldering him aside, I grabbed the box and ripped through its seal. Tossing the lid to the floor, I upended the container, dumping all of its contents into a messy heap on the desk. They were depressingly sparse—a green purse of worn leather, house keys, and two rings—both with a Southwestern theme.

No cellphone.

Anticipating my question, Bobby said, "If she had a cellphone, it's in evidence for sure."

"That doesn't help me," I groused.

He made an empty-handed gesture. "I might be able to get access from Lopez, if I fake the right reason, but don't hold your breath."

"Useless," I muttered. "Fucking useless."

"Come on, Zack," Bobby urged, pulling out the chair. It rolled on heavy casters over a thick square of plastic sheeting meant to protect the tile. Age had left the plastic warped and yellowed, the edges curling up. "Take a few minutes and calm down. Whatever you went through back there, it couldn't have been easy." He reached for my elbow. I jerked away so violently I nearly clocked him in the forehead. Hesitantly, he backed off. "To be honest," he said, "you're kind of scaring me."

"Good," I snapped. "You should be scared. You know the kinds of things I'm capable of."

"Zack—" he persisted, but I ignored him. Rooting around in the whale of a handbag, I searched for Marjory's wallet. I wanted to see her pictures—nearly everyone her age still kept printed ones. The main pocket was a bust. Breath mints, a tube of lipstick, half a dozen crinkled candy wrappers. Werther's Originals. They were everywhere. A sense-memory of their taste rose swiftly at the back of my throat, blindsiding me with wrenching nostalgia. Cozy home feelings.

They did nothing to allay my rising fear and anger. Spitting an incoherent string of curses, I shook the handbag as if it might disgorge its secrets under threat of violence.

"Where the *hell* is her wallet?"

"Try the middle pocket," Bobby offered. "That's where my mom usually keeps hers."

I didn't thank him, just went straight to the central section. Something caught in the teeth of the zipper, and it snagged halfway open. I tried to force it, but my strength was more than the metal could bear. The zipper's tag ripped off in my hand and, snarling, I hurled it against the wall. It hit with enough force, it scored the plaster.

"Fuck it all," I grumbled.

Bobby took a halting step backward. One hand twitched in the direction of his firearm. Then he caught himself, straightening the lines of his shirt instead.

"I've… never seen you like this, Zack," he said.

"What's the matter?" I snapped. "I remind you of Garrett?" The words leapt all of my filters. I knew better, but I couldn't stop. "We're more alike than you realize, you know."

Bobby rocked as if slapped. "That's not fair—not to any of us."

"Don't talk to me about fair," I said. "Not with what I had to do back in that meat locker." With a *snkkt* of metal against Kydex, I pulled one of my daggers. Bobby's eyes flew wide. I adjusted my grip and the curve of the weapon caught the light of the stuttering fluorescents. He backed up until he could go no further, narrow shoulders smacking the door, one hand perched upon the knob.

"Zack, what are you doing?" he asked uncertainly.

Without comment, I plunged the blade into the lining, gutting Marjory's purse. Bobby's face seesawed in a bewilderment of shock and relief.

"You can't do that," he objected.

"She's dead," I reminded. "I can do what I want." Angling my hand out of the way, I re-sheathed the dagger with a snap.

"Yeah, but..." He trailed off.

"I need to see her wallet," I said insistently.

A long, fat monster of turquoise, I dragged it through the slice in her purse. Cards from local businesses came tumbling out the minute I opened it—tons of them. Most had notes scribbled on the back, names of employees and managers along with details like "has a precious kitty," and "birthday in March."

Marjory kept track of everyone she enjoyed doing business with. Probably sent each of them holiday cards.

That wasn't what I was after. I scattered the cards anyway, just in case something important was sandwiched between her mementos for Rito's Bakery, Three Brothers Plumbing, and all the rest.

It wasn't.

One side of the wallet had a pocket with a clear plastic window. It held her driver's license. The thing had been in there so long, it had adhered to the plastic. I teased it out with a little effort, holding it vaguely in Bobby's direction.

"This her current address?" I asked.

"That's where they found her," he responded tightly.

I memorized it and shoved it into my jacket. The

license was useful, but it still wasn't what I wanted. There was a fan of clear vinyl sleeves tacked in place with a little closure. It was fat with credit cards and—I hoped—something that would prove or disprove all my awful suspicions about why she'd marked me as next of kin. Wedging my nail under the snap, I popped it open. Insurance cards, emergency contacts—including my name and the mysterious Tremont address—an old-school card for the Clevenet Public Library system.

Not a single photo.

"Fucking hell!" I shouted. Her two rings jumped as I slammed my fist onto the desk's metal surface.

"Could you at least tell me what you're looking for?" Bobby demanded.

"I'll have to find it in her house," I snarled. Grabbing Marjory's keys, I stuffed them in my pocket. Everything else, I left in a heap on the desk. I shoved at Bobby. "Out of my way."

Mutely, he complied.

17

Imagining all the creative ways I wanted to torture Zuriel for what he'd done to Marjory, I stalked past the properties clerk and toward the nearest exit. The halls were thick with people now. Most took one look at my expression and got the fuck out of my way. Bobby trailed for a few steps behind me, asking useless questions. He had the box with the rest of Marjory's possessions tucked under one arm. He kept trying to give them to me, but I had what I wanted—her address and her keys. Eventually, he gave up and retreated.

No one tried to stop me, which was good for them.

Outside, I dug for my own keys as I neared the Hellcat, clicking the fob to disarm the security system. At its chirp, Lil popped her head up from the other side of the roof. I'd forgotten all about my wild-eyed escort.

"What took you so long?" she called.

Fists clenched, I wavered on the curb. "Go away," I snapped.

"Fat chance," she scoffed. "Someone has to play

babysitter." She held out one hand, the little gems set in her manicure catching the light as she beckoned. "Give me the keys."

"Like hell," I snapped. Blinking against the grit of sleep in my eyes, I debated the wisdom of walking the mile and a half back to my apartment. On any other day, it would have been easy, but I felt like hammered horse shit. Lil marched past the Hellcat to where I lingered on the curb, hands on her hips as she glared up at me. Quick as a snake, she made a move to snatch my keys, and I fended her off—barely. Sealing my fist around the bristling metal, I decided to take my chances and turned toward Cedar Glen.

Lil darted quickly after.

"What do you think you're doing?" she demanded.

"Walking home."

She tugged at the arm attached to my keys, trying to drag my hand out from where I'd stuffed it in my pocket. "Stop being such a stubborn ass and hand them over," she said. "The way you look, you're not making it to the end of the block, let alone your apartment."

"Let. *Go.*" I yanked my arm from her grip, bringing my elbow up and angling for a strike. I almost went through with it, too, aiming for the vulnerable spot at her temple. Immortal badass or not, that would ring her bell. "I'm not fucking around," I warned, arm still lofted.

For once, she backed off. "No, you're not," she said, hovering an arm's length away, and I started off again. She easily matched my stumping pace. The light went red at the crosswalk and I charged forward anyway, walking right up to the edge of an old Buick Regal as it flew through the intersection. It missed me by inches, the driver honking wildly. I graced him with a single finger salute. On the opposite corner, an old man dragging a wheeled suitcase gave me a wide berth. Lil jogged after me, cursing.

"You're not going to make it, you know," she observed. "If you could see yourself, you'd know that I'm right." I kept walking. "You look worse now than when you went into that place, and you didn't look so good to start out with."

"Like you fucking care," I snarled.

"Who pulled your ass out of the fire the last three times you had your back against the wall?" she demanded. Not even pausing for my response, she answered her own question, legs pumping. "Oh, that'd be me."

"I don't need your help, Lil," I said through gritted teeth.

"Of course not," she chirped. "You'll just stomp up the hill to Coventry, maybe stop and eat someone along the way."

A hot wash of guilt swept over me, followed swiftly by waves of seething fury. I rounded on her, fire kindling in my eyes. She met my inhuman gaze without blinking.

"Why do you think I came along, flyboy?" she prodded. "The last time you looked this rough, you killed a woman with your bare hands just to get the power you needed to heal yourself. Or did you conveniently forget that ugly little incident?"

I clenched my fists so hard, the knuckles ground with an ugly crackle, blue-white fire licking from between my fingers. "Do you think I enjoyed that?" I snarled. "I'm not some kind of monster. I know better than anyone exactly how awful it is to have someone reach in and tear your fucking soul apart just to get what they want!"

The draft of mounting power stirred the hair at my brow, and I was about to launch a fistful at her face—but when I drew back my hand, the flames sputtered. Irritably, I shook off the clinging remnants. My pulse thundered from the effort, and an echo of its rhythm ticked with urgent heat through the scar in my palm.

"I will never forget," I growled.

"Well, that's good," she said. "Because you've tied yourself to a corrupting artifact of tremendous power, and I don't think you fully appreciate what that thing is doing to you."

"Shut up about this, Lil," I warned and started walking again. "I've got it under control."

"Yeah?" she demanded. "How would anyone around you know? You can't even talk about the thing because Sal oathed you into silence." Working herself into a real lather, she matched me step for step, stabbing a finger accusingly into my side. With unnerving accuracy, she found the box with the Stylus. It banged against my ribs. "So tell me again how you're just going home to sleep it off. I'm *sure* to believe you."

I seized her wrist before she could poke me again. "You don't know what you're talking about." I twisted angrily until I could feel the grind of bone against bone. With a wracking, full-body memory, I flashed back to Zuriel's psychic dreamspace of mirrors and illusions.

You mad, bro?

Mad didn't begin to cover it.

Lil went motionless in my grip. With a calm more threatening than any show of fury, she tilted her head to meet my seething gaze. Her lips were inches from my own.

"Find someone to bang." She nipped the ends of her words. "Sex generates a hell of a lot of energy, and you need it right now."

Disgusted, I shoved her away. "You've got to be kidding," I snarled. "I'm not having this conversation." Muttering a blistering string of curses, I stomped down the sidewalk, making it as far as the loop of Cedar, Carnegie, and MLK. The five-way intersection was a tangle of cars and pedestrians and I had no choice but to stand at the corner waiting for the light to change. Lil took full advantage of the situation, smacking my shoulder to make sure she had my attention.

There wasn't even a handprint on her wrist.

"I'm dead serious, Zack," she said. "You're squeamish about taking what you need from crowds or strangers, but if you keep depriving yourself like this, the Eye is going to take over." A woman heading to the crosswalk caught the barest snippet of our argument and abruptly turned in the opposite direction. The rapid retreat of her heels beat a stark counterpoint to the thud of blood in my ears. Lil stepped in front of me, bodily blocking my access to the street. "You're being such an ass about this because you know I'm right. You're just too scared to admit it."

The WALK sign switched on. I shoved past her.

"If you won't take my advice, I'm going to keep following you so I can stop you before the inevitable happens and you hate yourself even more than you do now," she promised, sticking close to my heels. "You don't remember what those Icons can do. I've witnessed the things at the height of their power."

"Glad to know you'll be here to kill me the instant I'm no longer convenient to you," I grumbled. Head down, I lengthened my stride, forcing her to trot to keep up.

"That's not what I said, you idiot," she snapped. "Look at yourself. Look at how you're acting. This is crazy even for you. Take a fucking breath and assess for a minute."

We reached the crumbling overpass of train tracks on Cedar Glen Parkway. Pitted concrete stanchions divided the lanes of the causeway, one of them so weathered the lattice-work of rebar showed through. Graffitied walls rose to either side of us, trapping sound and shadow in the hollow space between. It was the perfect place to kill someone.

"You should stop following me now," I said. My hands rested on the pommels of my daggers. Angling my back toward the nearest wall, I found the surest bit of footing on the neglected sidewalk and dropped into a fighting stance. We were well away from prying eyes. "I've got my blades, and I'm pretty sure I can murder you, if I really put my mind to it."

"Bleeding Mother, you're really going to do this?"

"You're the one threatening me," I barked. "If you don't want to do this, back the fuck away."

Rolling her eyes, she took a step sideways, going for something in her little white clutch purse. I had the daggers out in the next instant, their flame-kissed metal alive with the thready dregs of my strength. To my utter bewilderment, Lil produced nothing more deadly than a tube of lipstick, twisting it to freshen her smile. Mutely, I stared, the guttering spirit-fire casting weird shadows around us. Lil shot me the reddest of grins.

"Poor Zack," she said. "Don't say I didn't warn you."

With a coughing roar, a huge and tawny specter erupted in my peripheral vision. Before I could process what I was seeing, Lil's ferocious lioness descended. Conjured purely in spirit, the animal's massive paw nevertheless struck with stunning velocity. The ringing blow spun me, and I retained just enough clarity to realize that Lulu kept her claws carefully retracted even as she forced me to the pavement.

Then Lil hit me with a neat little sap, and stars chased me down to darkness.

18

Stiff and aching, I woke in the trunk of my car. My jacket was gone, as were the blades and wrist-sheaths. My face was shoved against the canvas of a duffle bag of gym clothes I kept in the Hellcat but never managed to use anymore, and I was drooling on myself. With a click, the lid popped open, needling my eyes with a flood of light. Against the brilliance, Lil stood over me, smiling cheerfully.

The expression was utterly unnerving.

"Have a nice nap, Anakim?" she purred.

I answered her with a swift right hook—or, at least, I tried. My hands were so numb I'd completely missed the zip ties. Lil snorted amused annoyance, shoving me back with next to no effort, and slammed the trunk shut again.

"We can do this hard or easy, Anakim," she said from the street outside. "We both know you don't have the strength to fight me—and whose fault is that, anyway?"

"What the fuck did you do with my things?" I demanded. "I want my blades back, and my jacket!" Furiously, I kicked at the trunk around me. The space was too cramped to get any kind of leverage and, humiliatingly, Lil was right. There was no strength left in any of my blows. I'd spent the last of my dwindling power posturing under the Cedar Glen overpass.

"I know what you really want, Anarch," she said. "I've had the Stylus once before, and, if you remember, I gave it back nicely." In punctuation, she thumped the top of the trunk soundly from outside. The thunder of it made my ears ring. "I told you then—I don't want the damned thing, but I wasn't going to let you anywhere near it, not with the crap you had lodged in your chest."

"What?" My voice cracked.

"I cleared it for you," she responded. "You can thank me any time."

Stilling in the dark enclosure, I gave my body a chance to check in. My head still throbbed where both Lil and the lioness had clobbered me, and the circulation was shit in my hands. But that tugging fishhook beneath my ribs was gone, along with the blinding haze of fury that had clamored in my mind.

Rage.

The only word I'd deciphered from the middle ring of Zuriel's sigil. Combined with my brother's repeated taunt, it started to make sense. He'd bound Marjory and used her as a conduit, not merely to get into my head, but to leave behind a present. Something that festered. Anger in excess of any reason.

"You mad, bro?"

He knew I was, and he'd used his ridiculous refrain as a trigger. Over and over again, he'd primed me to respond with the fury always simmering in the dark spaces of my psyche. And it had worked like gangbusters.

I'd been such an ass to Bobby. Lil, too.

"What'd you find exactly?" I asked.

"Are you ready to cooperate?" she replied.

Impatient, I banged on the carpeted roof of my prison. "Just let me out, and stop fucking around, Lil."

"Before I let you out, I need you to promise not to fight me or try to run away unless I'm actively harming you," she said. "Swear it for the space of one hour, starting once I cut the zip ties."

"An oath?" I barked, kicking uselessly again. "Are you fucking kidding me?"

"Take it or leave it, flyboy," she answered. I twisted against the plastic bonds. They bit tight into my skin. Her heels clicked on pavement—she was walking away. "You've got enough air in there for a little while, yet," she called from a growing distance.

"Wait," I cried. The retreating footsteps halted. "One hour?"

"One hour," she confirmed, her voice somewhat less muffled as she took a step nearer. "And I promise—I'm not trying to hurt you, Zaquiel. This is for your own good."

I tested the restraints again. They showed no sign of breaking.

"Fuck me running," I sighed. "Fine. I swear it."

As the binding power of the oath shivered through me, the lid opened to reveal a cloudless stretch of autumn sky.

19

The Hellcat was parked in front of a three-story white farmhouse complete with slate gray shutters, old-school lightning rods, and a weather vane in the shape of a tin rooster. Set near the back of a rolling green lot slightly larger than all those around it, the house looked like a relic from the forties that had probably once commanded acres of land, but had gotten parceled out as times grew lean.

In the intervening years, suburbia had crept around it like a pastel contagion. Neatly trimmed lawns and perfectly spaced houses—each a variation on one of three styles—spread as far as the eye could see. It was picture-perfect, and a little stifling.

From the sun's position, at least an hour had passed since I'd parted ways with Bobby at the Medical Examiner's complex.

"Where the fuck are we?" I asked. Circulation returned reluctantly to my legs as I stumbled against the back of the car. Lil steadied me, cutting through the zip ties with a wickedly sharp switchblade she then returned to her bottomless purse.

"A charming little neighborhood in Mentor," she replied crisply.

Turning around so I could face my redheaded abductor, I tried to massage feeling back into my hands. Blood surged to the tips of my fingers in a rush of pins and needles, and I muttered some choice words in conjecture of Lil's parentage. Unruffled by my insults, she smiled primly a few feet away near the curb, tucking the severed zip ties after the switchblade. The little purse wasn't particularly deep or even wide, but the items went in as if she'd dropped them down a well. I wondered if that was where my jacket and other things had gone. They weren't visible anywhere inside the car.

"One of these days, you're going to tell me how that thing works," I said.

"Dream on, Anakim," she laughed. She pointed a bedazzled nail in the direction of the farmhouse. "Now march."

I balked. "Not until you tell me why we're here."

"Mother's Tears," she sighed. "You're still going to argue?"

"Look who's talking," I snapped.

Feeling a little naked without my jacket or the blades, I dug in, daring her to try to move me by force. We faced off in stiff silence. From its perch on the nearby power lines, a mourning dove took up its plaintive call. A dog yipped a few yards away. The only thing lacking was the whirr of a lawnmower.

Neither Lil nor I blinked. I was fully prepared to

park my ass on the back bumper of the car and just wait until the hour had passed. That would satisfy the barest requirements of the oath and frustrate whatever Lil had cooked up with this latest stunt of hers. She might have saved me from Zuriel's spell, but I still didn't entirely trust her.

The Lady of Beasts huffed her displeasure. "It's not a trap, Zack," she said. "I've got some friends inside who can help you." The wind whipped long curls of red hair across her face and, impatiently, she shoved them behind one ear. The bright morning light caught the fire from a diamond stud in that lobe. I didn't remember seeing the piercing before. "If you keep running around in crisis mode without taking a breath, you're going to fall flat on your face. Look me in the eye and tell me you don't need to rest and feed, at least a little."

The breathless fishhook under my ribs was gone, but in its absence, the hollow burn of hunger was unmistakable. I'd been running on fumes since before the fight with the cacodaimons, and she knew it. Squirming, I looked away.

"Thought so," she responded. "I'm really doing you a favor, Zack. A big one."

She was probably right—and I couldn't help but argue. "By abducting me, stripping me, and forcing me into an oath," I spat.

"Stripping you? I could have taken way more than just your jacket," she purred. She took a step closer. The backs of my legs hit the bumper. Lil smiled up at me, all teeth. "Of course, you don't know what I did or didn't do while you were unconscious." With slow seduction,

159

she trailed a decorated nail lightly down the center of my chest. With nothing but a thin T-shirt between us, gooseflesh shivered immediately down my arms. I held my breath and she laughed. "Your ass hurt at all?"

"You're not helping with the trust issues," I gritted.

"You know I'm just having a little fun," Lil said. She backed up a step, just enough to give me some breathing room. The cloying scent of her come-hither lessened somewhat. Above us, the mourning dove continued to cry. "The way you blush, I can't resist it."

"Also, not helping."

"I'm plenty helpful," she objected. She twirled a red strand around one finger, curling and uncurling the long lock of hair. "Your head feels better, doesn't it?"

Bitterly, I snorted. "Mostly it feels like somebody whacked me across the back of it with a sock full of quarters."

"They were ball bearings," she corrected. "But that's not what I meant, and you know it." She moved close again and I tensed against the car, prepared for some new trap, but she just tilted her head to study my features. The storm-gray depths of her eyes glittered. "Whose spell was it, anyway?"

I almost didn't answer, but she wasn't going to let me get away with that. "His Name is Zuriel." I shivered as I spoke the syllables. If they held any spark of recognition for her, Lil did a bang-up job at hiding it. This close, I could see her pores.

"He's your look-alike asshole?"

I nodded.

"Well," she said, shifting to stand next to me, still uncomfortably close. "He's good." She settled one hip against the edge of the trunk, most of her weight on the car. The wind plucked strands of her hair into a wild halo. The ends lashed my bare arm. "He disguised it as a tracking spell, but then I realized it was hooked deeper. He had it piggybacking a freshly severed link."

"Marjory." The name escaped as a whisper.

"Was that the body you went to see?" she pursued. A wave of emotion tightened my throat and I couldn't answer. The morning air felt suddenly chilly, and I resisted the urge to hug myself. Lil read enough in my look. Her voice softened. "That spell was meant to isolate you, Zack, trick you into driving all your allies away—or killing them," she added darkly. "This guy means business."

"I didn't see it," I responded. "I know that's a lame excuse, but, in the moment, every outburst felt completely justified." Restlessly, I ran my hand through the tousled mess of my hair. "I could tell I was a little cranky, but I had all these reasons for everything I did—"

She cut me off with a flat look. "Pulling your blades on me in the middle of the street, no matter how secluded, is more than a little cranky, Zack." In an unexpected gesture, Lil laid a hand on my shoulder and gave a gentle squeeze. All her cat-and-mouse flirtation was tellingly absent. "Now can you see why I'm trying to help you?" she asked. "You're being hunted by a member of your own tribe, and that guy has at his disposal every trick you've got—and then some. You need all the strength and clarity you can get."

"And what do you get out of it?" I asked petulantly.

Pushing off the bumper, she laughed as the wind

played in her hair. "I get to tease you, for starters," she responded. "And my sister would never forgive me if you were dead by the time she came back." She started walking. "Let's go."

Leaning back against the trunk of the Hellcat, I stared into a sky so blue it hurt my eyes. Nothing up there was going to help me, and I knew it. Against my better judgment, I followed.

A long, graveled walk led up to the farmhouse, little white pebbles crunching under our boots. The wraparound porch came complete with rocking chairs and an antique milk jug painted with Holsteins in tutus. That almost convinced me I was hallucinating the entire trip, and then I spied a discreet little sign by the door.

In elegant, black letters, it read, "Cat House." Suddenly, the reason for the folksy camouflage became all too clear.

"Is this a brothel?" I squawked.

"It's a cat house," she said. "Stop being so dramatic."

"You can't just force-feed me on women, Lil," I objected. "That's not how I operate."

"You're being ridiculous," she huffed. She pushed me front and center, then rang the bell.

I fell into awkward silence when a lean woman with nut-brown skin answered the door. She didn't *look* like my idea of a madam—her bright, sweeping skirts cried "hippie" more than anything else—but it wasn't like I was up to date on the fashion protocols. Long gray cornrows tipped with multicolored beads swung heavily forward as she nodded in greeting. To me, she was cautiously pleasant, but her whole face lit up when she caught sight of Lil.

"Lucy!" she cried. "Oh, it's so good to see you. Shareen said you might be dropping in."

Baffled, I turned and mouthed the name at Lil. I got an elbow in the ribs for my trouble. Stepping smoothly forward from the gesture, she took the madam's hand warmly in both of her own.

"Ivy! You look great." Then, to my utter astonishment, they hugged—and Lil looked like she *meant* it. Maybe the ballerinas on the milk jug really were a sign, and I'd slipped through the cracks to an alternate reality.

"Um, hi," I managed, utterly at a loss for any cogent response.

"Oh, I'm sorry," Ivy said, disentangling herself from Lil. "We're being rude." To me, she extended a hand. "I'm Ivy. Hello, and welcome."

A little stiffly, I demurred. "I got a thing about handshakes."

Ivy just smiled, not in the least offended. Lil stepped in, seizing me by the elbow. She gripped harder than was strictly necessary, as if she could somehow telegraph instructions through the nerves at my funny bone. I keenly missed the armor of my leather.

"He's got a thing about a lot of things," she explained. "Which is why I brought Captain Tight-Ass here to loosen up a bit."

"Captain Tight-Ass?" I sputtered.

Ivy laughed, deep and rich, and all the beads in her hair clicked musically as she shook her head with her amusement. Moving out of the doorway, she gestured with warm enthusiasm for us to enter. "Well, your friend Lucy brought you to the right place if you need to relax," she smiled. "It's a little early, but I know a couple of girls who'll be *thrilled* to curl up with you."

Still digging into my arm, Lil steered me into the little foyer. What might have once been a parlor had been converted into a kind of receiving room decorated with framed bits of needlepoint, wind chimes, and rainbow-colored mobiles. A fat guestbook sat on a burled counter with a computer on a short desk beyond. A couple of over-stuffed couches in gaudy floral prints were arranged along both walls to provide seating for customers.

"Who's available?" Lil asked.

Ivy scooted behind the counter, perching a pair of reading glasses on the end of her nose as she consulted the guestbook.

"Sunny and Kabuki just got their breakfast," she said. "They're in the Tea Room, and they'll be ready to go in a few minutes. Does that work for you both?"

"Sure," Lil said. "They'll be just his speed."

I tugged my arm from her grip. "I'm *really* not sure about this."

Ivy shot me a wide, sympathetic smile. "This is your first time, isn't it?" she asked. Rubbing Lil's fingerprints from my arm, I refused to answer. Undaunted, Ivy continued, as effusive as I was reluctant. "It's OK to feel awkward, but touch and companionship—they're healthy, needful things," she insisted. "You've got to give yourself permission to seek joy once in a while."

"I'm not sure my friend and I have the same definition of joy," I muttered.

"He'll be fine," Lil said, reclaiming my arm. "He just doesn't know it yet." This time, there was no escape unless

I wanted to straight-up clobber her. I flexed my hand as my fingers tingled. "Could you send Shareen around once she's done feeding everyone?" Lil inquired, and she tilted her head toward a wallpapered hall beyond one of the ugly couches. "The Tea Room's that way, right?"

Ivy nodded. Lil started moving us in that direction.

"I'll be sure to tell Shareen you're here," Ivy said. "She'll be so happy to see you." She made a note in the massive log, putting her reading glasses away. Calling after us, she said, "Shareen will take good care of you, Captain. Try to have a little fun."

"My name's Zack," I choked.

Purposefully, Lil marched us down the narrow hall. I started dragging my feet as we passed door after door, each of them bearing nameplates with unlikely titles like "Lola's Lily Pad" and "The Jungle Room." All were closed tight this early in the morning.

A peculiar wailing sound, like the cries of an infant, drifted from somewhere further down the hallway. I *so* didn't want to know who was doing that, or why. Digging my heels into the carpet, I forced Lil to halt her relentless advance. She tipped her head up, glaring.

"Just so we're clear," I hissed, "I agreed to come along. That's it. I made no promise of participation."

"You *seriously* need to lighten up, Zack," she chided. "This isn't going to kill you."

"You made your point outside," I said. "Agreed, I need to take better care of myself, but this isn't going to work for me. For fuck's sake—Sunny and Kabuki? How am I even supposed to take them seriously?"

"They're both really sweet," Lil responded. We

reached a bend in the hall and she grabbed for the door, never relinquishing my arm. "See for yourself. At least give it a try."

"Stop leading me around like an ill-tempered toddler, and maybe I'll consider it."

At that she eased up, pulling open the door. Sunlight flooded from the room beyond. Lil urged me ahead with a shooing motion.

"Well?" she said. "Go on."

Squirmingly uncertain about what I might find, I reluctantly stepped into the room.

20

Long, and somewhat narrow, the Tea Room was done up in an antique rose motif, from the print on the little loveseat to a border of decorative wallpaper that traced a circuit just below the ceiling. A huge bay window, draped with sheer gold curtains, opened onto the expansive yard.

In one corner sat a small, circular table set with a fancy silver tea service that looked like it had fallen through some time-space anomaly from the set of Jeeves & Wooster. Near it, a fluffy orange tabby cat blinked sleepily from where she had draped herself across the back of one chair. On seeing us, she loosed a querying tribble, then rose with an extravagant stretch that shivered from nose to tail-tip. The gesture jingled a heart-shaped tag that dangled from her collar. In looping, cursive letters, the tag read, "Sunny."

Her companion, a petite calico with bright golden eyes and a distinctive mask-like pattern on her face, stared fixedly from her perch on the windowsill at the far end of the room. From this distance, I couldn't make out the name on her collar, but from the face alone, she had to be Kabuki.

"They're cats," I said.

"This *is* the Cat House," Lil replied. "Of course they're cats." Then, with belated comprehension, her eyes flew wide. "Mother's Tears. You were *serious* about the brothel." At my chagrined expression, she started laughing so hard she nearly choked. Tears stood out on her lashes. "Oh, Zack, you glorious idiot," she gasped. "I thought you were just being a pain in my ass."

"But… cats?"

"They're therapy animals," Lil explained, dabbing at her eyes. "Shareen and Ivy train them here, then place most of them in nursing homes or long-term care facilities for disabled children." She sucked a rasping breath, still not quite recovered from her laughing fit. "A few—like Sunny and Kabuki—stay at the house for visitors who need help with stress-management. That would be you, by the way," she added pointedly. Pulling out a chair, she stabbed a finger toward the seat. "So, sit down, get comfy, and pet a cat."

"You're joking."

I lingered uncertainly near the door, still trying to convince myself I wasn't hallucinating. While I dithered, Sunny sauntered over, sniffed delicately at Lil's boots, then unceremoniously dropped onto them. Rolling over luxuriously, she put her broad white belly in the air, purring like an outboard motor. Smiling, Lil bent down, rubbing her knuckles along the underside of the cat's chin. Sunny closed her eyes, gratuitously pleased with this arrangement.

"Companion animals are proven to combat depression, lower blood pressure, and even boost a person's immune system," Lil said with such ardency I felt I was caught in some surreal infomercial. "People with companion animals demonstrably live longer—and so do the animals. It's a mutually beneficial arrangement."

At her feet, Sunny rolled over to be sure Lil distributed her scritches evenly. With a possessive air, the cat curled a paw around Lil's wrist, drawing her hand even closer. Lil cheerfully complied, her grin widening. Until this moment, I'd never seen the Lady of Beasts smile in a way that didn't look predatory. Her unfeigned delight only heightened my detached feeling of unreality.

"And then there's the dopamine response," she added. "A cat's purr isn't merely soothing. Humans get an instant chemical reward for their actions." She looked up from the full-body massage she was lavishing on the animal. "Shall I go on?"

"You're a walking Wikipedia article. It's kind of creepy."

"Lady of Beasts," she quipped. "It's not just a fancy name." Smoothly, she scooped Sunny up to her shoulders. The cat burrowed into the wild tangle of her hair, finally draping herself around Lil's neck like a purring fur stole. Taking careful steps so the cat maintained her balance, Lil minced over to the other side of the tea table and eased into one of the high-backed chairs. Withdrawing her smartphone, she lofted its screen up so I could see its timer on countdown.

"Also, you're oathed to stick around for another forty-two minutes, so you might as well enjoy yourself.

Miss Kabuki looks lonely over there."

Scrubbing grit from my eyes, I wavered by the door a moment longer before finally succumbing to the inevitable and plunking down heavily down into the chair across from Lil. Its ornate upholstery was way too pink for my tastes, but there was no denying it was comfortable. For the moment, however, all the comfort did was highlight my many aches.

I groaned. "I'm not sure I'm really awake at this point."

Lil clucked her tongue speculatively. "Not surprising, since your version of awake is two steps away from sleepwalking these days." Reaching toward a silver bowl in the middle of the tea setting, she lifted the lid. I expected the thing to hold sugar, and hoped that would foreshadow a breakfast of some sort—I should at least get something useful out of this—but instead it brimmed with cat treats. My expression fell, but Sunny perked up immediately, and even the aloof Kabuki jumped down from her warm patch to investigate. "When was the last time you slept, flyboy?" Lil asked. "Passed out doesn't count."

"I dozed a little waiting for Remy in Collinwood," I said defensively.

"And before that?" She handed me a treat, and I took it automatically. Near my feet, Kabuki rose onto her haunches like a meerkat, peering quizzically toward the stained and rumpled landscape of my jeans. With a little trill, she announced her intent to claim my lap, then made the leap. Tribbling again, she butted her head into the heel of the hand holding the treat, reminding me whose mouth it was destined to enter.

Melting in spite of myself, I handed it over. The cat took it delicately, whiskers tickling my fingers. Reaching with a paw to hold my arm in place much as her roommate had done with Lil, Kabuki licked what remained of the crumbs. When she was done, she headbutted my hand again, glancing pointedly toward the treat-bowl.

"Bossy little thing," I chuckled.

"The tiny ones have to be," Lil said. "If they're on their own, they fight for every scrap."

Relenting to the demands of my five-pound, furry dictator, I scooped up a few more morsels and began doling them out. They almost smelled like food. That protein bar hadn't done much for my empty stomach. The calico took the treats from my fingers, fangs diligently crunching.

"Feel better?" Lil asked. I was tempted to say no, but the idiot smile on my face made denial impossible.

"Thought so," she mused. Kabuki finished the last of the treats, then did a little half-turn in my lap, settling herself into a tight little ball. I could feel her purr vibrating all the way up to my molars. Lil replaced the lid on the bowl and Sunny took that as a sign that she, too, should settle in. Hunching on the Lady of Beasts' shoulder, she curled her tail around Lil's neck like a lavish feather boa. "Now we can talk about what you need to do if you're going to survive the next few days."

"I've been doing pretty well so far," I objected. "Barring that spell."

"Is that a fact?" Lil replied. "Because from where I'm sitting, all I see is someone who's been avoiding his problems by taking long rides on his motorcycle and picking fights with cacodaimons."

"I didn't go looking for that fight," I reminded her. "It found me."

She continued as if I hadn't even spoken. "And then you jump straight into an obvious trap, because you're so sleep-deprived your brain checked out some time last week. Do you have a deathwish?"

"I didn't blunder into that as blindly as you make it sound," I protested. "Bobby thought it might be a trap. I didn't disagree, but with what that guy did to Marjory, I had to do something."

"So you went ahead and stuck your hand in it," she snapped.

"I thought I could handle it," I said.

Lil emitted a sound of strangled fury. Sunny peeled back one lid and glared disapprovingly, resettling herself into a more comfortable position. "This—*exactly* this— is why you need a few hours to rest and regroup," Lil said. "Even with your memory in shambles, the Zack I know wouldn't have let things escalate like that. You'd have checked yourself."

"If the point is to relax," I grumbled, "the lecture's not really helping."

"Then shut up and pet Kabuki," she said. The little pinpricks of claws kneading my thigh signaled the cat's approval of this plan. Sullenly, I laid a hand across the back of the petite calico. She was so tiny, my palm alone nearly covered her from shoulders to haunch. "Have you even considered what kind of damage control you'll need in order to handle the guy running around with your face?" Lil prodded. "And I'm not just talking his magic. I'm talking mortal-world issues."

"I'm working on it," I responded. The soft rumble of the tiny beast, combined with the warmth of her soft fur against my palm, did seem to help clear some of the fog from my thoughts. Not that I was going to admit it to Lil. "I've got keys to Marjory's place. I was going to head home, get some rest, and then track him from there."

"And then what?" Lil pursued.

"I don't know," I said. "Her daughter's still missing. I've got to find her. I'll figure the rest out as I go."

"Because that works so well for you."

"You've got a better idea?"

"Of course I do," she said.

Beleaguered, I let my head drop against the high back of the chair. I missed the cushy part and whacked rattlingly against a flourish of carved wood. I was too exhausted to give a shit.

"Go ahead," I sighed. "Enlighten me, oh Great and Powerful Oz."

"That's Ozma, to you," she quipped. I was surprised she even got the reference. Lil scooched forward on her own chair, gray eyes glittering intensely as she ticked off points on her fingers. "First, you need to change the locks to your apartment. The wards you've got are potent, but why make it easy?" I couldn't really disagree with that, although I still felt the niggling impulse to do so. Burying my fingers into Kabuki's thick fur, I briefly slid shut my eyes, doing my honest best to just shut up and hear Lil out. I came perilously close to dozing.

"After that, you need to report the theft of your Vulcan. Thanks to whatever spell he's using, this Zuriel has your looks, but that kind of magic has its limits. Scent, fingerprints, DNA—those are all harder to reproduce, and that's a good thing—especially if his point is to ruin you."

"Ruin me?" I asked thickly.

"Think about that spell for a minute, flyboy," she said insistently. "You have a life among the mortals—it's the strength and weakness of your tribe. A life on record, with all the pros and cons that go with it. Friends, apartment, even a day job at the art museum, when you bother."

"Since when do you care whether I go to work or not?"

She let out an exasperated sigh. "I don't. You do," she said. "And that's my point. A façade like that is ridiculously delicate. Think of all the hoops you have to jump through just to keep your name out of police reports. That's why you've got your pet detective."

"Hey, Bobby's a friend," I objected. "I don't just *use* him."

"That's not the issue here, flyboy. What if he goes on a crime spree, wearing your face? Riding your bike? Until you report that it's missing, any crime he commits will lead them right to your door."

Kabuki stretched under my hand, the soothing thrum of her purr making my skin tingle. Suddenly I realized that I'd closed my eyes again. Jerking upright, I blinked rapidly, trying to focus.

"Are you ready to jettison the persona you've built?" she asked.

"All right," I conceded thickly. "You've got a point." Stifling a yawn, I stretched against the high, stiff back of the chair, wings ghosting through the floral upholstery. My eyes threatened to slide shut again. I squinted until they watered. "I'll have to make up some shit, though. As far as the Collinwood cops are concerned, I'm the one who rode off with the Vulcan at the gas station last night."

Dragging a hand across my eyes, I grimaced at the trail of cat hair this left behind. Kabuki lightly dug her claws into my thigh.

"I should really count my blessings," I added. "The cops let my doppelganger leave an active homicide investigation. If they'd been dealing with the real me, my smart mouth probably would've landed me in the back of a squad car."

"Which brings me to my next point," Lil said. "You need that police report."

"Why?" I asked. "I know what happened, and whatever Zuriel told them, it couldn't have been the truth. They wouldn't have let him go if he'd blamed it all on demons."

"Again, you're making my point, Anakim," she said. At my blank look, she reached across the table and flicked me on the forehead. "Think it through, Einstein. There were dead people, and cops, and a witness. At some point, they'll have a trial. That's what mortals do when they find people with blood running out of them."

"Yeah," I replied. "I suppose." Absently, I rubbed the spot where her finger had connected, my thoughts lurching to keep up. Mostly I ended up fixating on the cat hairs still stuck to my face.

"What if you get called to testify?" Lil pressed. "Unless you know what was in that report, you'll look like an idiot." When I still didn't look as distressed as she clearly thought I should be, Lil raised her hand again. I flinched away, but instead of hitting me, she smacked her open palm hard on the table. The tea service leapt, and the impact rocked up her arm to the cat snoozing on her shoulder. Sunny sneezed in protest, flicking her tail against Lil's cheek. When Lil ignored her, the cat hopped down, ears stiff with annoyance.

"Worse than an idiot, you'll look like a liar," Lil continued, "and cops tend to think liars are guilty. In this case, 'guilty' means fifteen to life. You may take it for granted, but for you, life is a good, long time."

Finally, I followed—and couldn't find any holes in her argument. I just wished she didn't look so damned smug about it. So I decided to change the subject.

"Isn't a tea room supposed to come with tea?" I asked. "I could really use some caffeine or something."

"I could pinch you," Lil offered wickedly.

"Thanks, but no thanks," I grumbled. The little cat under my hand abruptly pitched over, wriggling to position my fingers on her belly. Sleepily, I complied, then found myself pierced by half a dozen needle-sharp claws as she gripped fiercely with all four paws. With a hissing intake of breath, I yanked my hand back, but she clung like a fuzzy burr, purring even as she gnawed on the tip of my thumb.

"Gah!" I cried.

Lil snorted. "Awake now, flyboy?"

The calico loosened her grip just as I was tempted to hurl her to the floor, switching from biting to grooming my thumb as if that was what she'd intended from the very beginning. Grumpily, I glared first at the cat and then at Lil. Both regarded me with Sphinx-like expressions.

"You did that on purpose," I accused.

"Oh?" Lil perched her chin upon her hand, red hair swinging forward. With exaggerated care, I pried my shredded fingers free of the cat.

"Admit it," I said. "You made her do that."

Lil's smile only widened. "There's nothing I can do to improve on the nature of cats," she said. "They do fine without outside encouragement."

I was searching for a fitting comeback when the soft sound of steps distracted my attention. They minced down the carpet along the hall, pausing just outside our door. A woman's muffled voice called from the other side.

"Knock, knock."

"Shareen!" Lil cried with undisguised pleasure. Fluidly, she rose from her chair, practically leaping the few feet between the tea table and the door. Throwing it wide, she greeted the woman beyond with a beaming smile. "Thank you so much for doing this on such short notice," she gushed, filling the doorway. All I could see of the woman beyond was the curve of one shoulder and her small, bare feet. A bright silver ring adorned one of her toes. "The cats have been great, but we could really use your special skills."

The woman in the hall laughed warmly. From the sound of clinking plates, she bore a tray of breakfast foods. The rich scent of coffee, not tea, wafted past Lil into the room. Heartily, I approved.

"I take it he has a high-stress job?" Shareen asked in hushed tones.

"Law enforcement," Lil said glibly. It wasn't exactly a lie. "He hasn't had a break in ages. Last night was especially rough, not that the bandages won't give that away. He could use the works."

Suddenly, I wondered if my original impression had been closer to the mark than Lil had led me to believe. That notion gained greater currency once the Lady of Beasts stepped aside to usher her friend through the door. The woman wore nothing but a tight halter top of a sheer beige material, and a pair of what looked like flowing harem pants. Glossy black hair fell in heavy waves to her shoulders and her smooth brown skin was dusted with something that shimmered warmly of gold. With her heart-shaped face and huge, dark eyes, she looked startlingly like Lailah.

Accusingly, I glowered at Lil.

"You don't play fair," I growled.

The Lady of Beasts twisted her lips into a *Mona Lisa* grin. "You should never expect otherwise."

21

Shareen set down her tray, leaning past me to arrange a plate of pastries on the table. The silken fabric of her halter top rustled as she moved, and I stared stalwartly at a spot on the far wall to avoid ogling the enticing curves her movements brought so close to my face. Oblivious to my awkward tension, she nudged the silver teapot to one side, setting the carafe of coffee in its place.

She hummed softly to herself as she worked, brass bangles on her wrist gently clinking. A scent like roses and cardamom wafted from her richly colored skin and I crushed further and further back into the padding of the chair to avoid accidental contact.

The cats were neither awkward nor polite. Sunny sauntered across the table to investigate the rearrangement of her domain, quizzically sniffing the edge of the pastry tray. Determining that the pastries were not, in fact, intended for cats, she strode boldly to Shareen with her tail in the air, loudly chattering her complaint. The woman ignored her, intent on her task, so the tabby settled onto her haunches, reaching out with one paw to pat repeatedly at Shareen's bare arm.

This, too, Shareen ignored with the determined air of a mother inured to the begging of a child. Drawn by the activity, Kabuki stirred on my lap. Ducking out from under my hand, she slunk closer to the table, placing two paws on the edge so she could draw herself up and peer at her garrulous roommate.

Her antics would have amused me if not for a persistent thread of creeping horror wending its way through my sluggish brain. Shareen's heady perfume, her uncanny resemblance to Lailah, combined to give the impression that she and Lil might be related.

I found the prospect unnerving.

It should have been easy enough to check by peering across to the Shadowside, but I was worn so thin I could barely muster even that tiny show of power. Nevertheless, I gave it my best—and was rewarded with an instant stab of blinding pain that started over my left eye socket and drilled its way through the back of my skull. It was all I could do not to utter a sound.

In the wake of that brilliant agony, I was left to stew in mute conjecture. Asking Lil would have been laughable—she never gave straight answers, especially not where her family was concerned. I only knew there were more sisters than Lailah—how many more, I'd never been able to determine. At best, I had a vague notion that each of Lil's spirit animals held some essential tie to one of her siblings. An owl for Lailah, soot-gray, with silent wings. The lioness was Lulu, and somewhere in the world there stalked a fierce and tawny woman who was her living counterpart. That left the two ferrets whose names I'd never caught, a fox that I had only ever seen in Lil's aura, and half a dozen more similarly cryptic creatures.

Shareen could be any one of them. From her willow-thin frame and lithe, hypnotic movements, I'd have put money on her animal being a serpent. As she finished emptying her tray of breakfast, she turned those huge, dark eyes on me. All I saw was my own reflection in their depths.

"Cute cats," I managed.

She chuckled, and her smile could melt glaciers. "That's why we keep them around." Lofting the carafe of coffee, she indicated a nearby teacup. "I had a feeling you were more a coffee guy. You want some?"

"Yeah," I said stiffly. "That'd be great."

As her friend poured, "Lucy" sat back in her frilly chair, amusement stamped across her bronze features. Every ounce of pleasure she felt was being extracted at my expense, and that only heightened her enjoyment. She nudged her own little cup into Shareen's orbit, murmuring her gratitude proactively.

"Ivy said this was your first time at a place like this," the woman continued, deftly pouring the steaming black brew first into my cup and then into Lil's. Although there were four teacups on the little table, each perched on its own matching saucer, she didn't pour any coffee for herself.

"Yeah," I replied uncertainly. At a loss for anything further, I filled my hands with the tiny cup—it was hardly up to the task—peering pensively into the rising steam. Kabuki, half-forgotten, levered herself onto the table and stared reproachfully, squatting on her haunches to my left, the tip of her tail tapping with impatience.

"*Someone's* upset you stopped petting her," Shareen observed. She set the carafe down, stepping lightly behind me. "Be careful not to spill—I want to see what I'll be dealing with." Without any further warning, she grabbed the flesh between my neck and shoulders and started kneading with surprisingly strong fingers. She was careful to avoid the cuts. "Oh my, Lucy's right. You are tense."

I nearly dropped the teacup.

From the other side of the table, Lil smirked at my dismay.

"I must have forgotten to tell you," she said. "Shareen's certified in massotherapy. You're getting a rub-down."

"I'll get you back for this," I promised. The words came out strangled as I struggled not to melt. The corded muscles along my shoulders and neck telegraphed both their unhappy state of tension and their stupefying pleasure at having someone—anyone—finally offer some relief.

"Oh, I'm sure you'll try." Lil's grin grew rictus-wide— less a smile and more the baring of predator's teeth.

Shareen thoroughly misinterpreted our exchange. "It's nice to see you looking out for each other," she said blithely. The grinding pressure of her hands was a stark contrast to the soft lilt of her words. "More people need to practice kindness, you know? Spread some joy now and then."

"Nnggh," I responded as her fingers found a particularly nasty knot. My hand twitched as tingles of sensation jolted all the way down to my fingertips.

"Oh, poor Zack," Lil cooed. "You can ask her to stop at any time, you know."

"Yes, of course. I'm so sorry," Shareen said in a rush. "You looked so tense sitting there, I totally forgot to tell you the ground rules." She paused in her ministrations long enough to step around and make eye contact. I tried to respond in kind, but it was a struggle just to focus. Bonelessly, I slumped against the chair. Kabuki took advantage and crawled back into my lap, further distracting me with the soporific thrum of her purr.

"This morning's all about you, Zack. Only what you want, nothing that you don't. There's a massage table in the spa room, and once you've relaxed a little longer with Sunny and Kabuki, I can take you there for a full-body treatment."

"Full... body?" I asked thickly, groping for why I even wanted clarification.

"Mm-hmm." Shareen nodded. "Feet and facial, neck, back, legs, and hands—not necessarily in that order." She ticked off the body parts on her fingers. I tried to offer some meaningful response, but a yawn overtook me. Belatedly, I covered my mouth with the back of one hand. She smiled tolerantly.

"He's been up for a while," Lil supplied. "Add insomnia to the list of his issues."

"Insomnia, too? You poor dear," Shareen said.

"It's a long list," Lil sniped.

"Well, Zack, I'm certified in crystal therapy and

aromatherapy, too, so if you'll let me, I'll whip up a little take-home sachet you can put under your pillow to help with your sleep. Do you have nightmares?" Vaguely, I nodded, but she might as well have been speaking Cantonese at that point—I could barely follow. Then an oddly hesitant look creased her otherwise smooth brow.

Chewing her lip, she cast a furtive glance toward Lil.

"What?" I asked, instantly suspicious and much more awake. Lil offered no help to either of us. Shareen didn't exactly squirm, but some internal debate played out clearly across her features.

"Well," she began. "I'm a Reiki Three also, and, with your permission, I'd like to do some work on your energy." She hesitated again, eyes flicking once more to the redheaded schemer seated across from us. Lil's only response was her usual Sphinx-like smirk.

That just left me annoyed—and more awake.

"Spit it out," I said.

Shareen looked briefly miserable, then gave a sigh of surrender. When again she spoke, her whole attitude had changed, moving from easy-going to guarded. Her honeyed voice was half apologetic, half patronizing.

"I know a lot of people in law enforcement, and I understand that your world can be pretty black and white," she said. "I get it. It kind of needs to be." Cautiously, I nodded, urging her on. After a pause, she continued haltingly. "And... some of the things I do might seem pretty hippy-dippy to you—seriously, it's impressive that you even agreed to come here, to try and find some peace and mindfulness among all these blessed little creatures."

"You really need to get to your point." At the harshness in my tone, her brows ticked up and, for a minute, I thought she was going to yell back at me. With a visible effort, she reclaimed at least a superficial calm.

"You've got really strange energy," she said tightly. "I can tell you've been through a lot recently, but there's more to it than that. There's... well, there's a weight resting on your back—it's why all the muscles there are so tight. I can—"

Before she could say another word, I threw my head back and started cackling. I couldn't help it—and I couldn't stop. Sunny dashed from the table, and Kabuki was so startled, she launched herself in a hail of claws from her resting spot on my lap. I barely felt the stinging impact. It was all too much. Laughter stole my breath and tears streamed from my eyes.

Lil stared blankly, completely at a loss.

Shareen, however, bristled with undisguised offense.

"If you don't believe in energy work, that's fine," she said sharply. "But you don't have to be so rude."

"No, that's not it," I gasped, sniffling and wiping at my eyes. "That's not it at all." Even so, Shareen planted her fists on her hips and glared from me to Lil.

"He's your friend," she said. "*You* explain it to him. I thought you would have, bringing him here."

"Shareen, normally I wouldn't forgive him for anything," Lil said, "but just this once, give the guy a pass. He's really not trying to be an asshole. It's just his factory default."

"I'm not laughing at the energy work," I insisted—choking hard on the irony. "Reiki. I get it. It's just...

what I've got on my back." Another peal of laughter wracked me like a seizure. Once it had passed, I hunched, struggling to catch my breath. Through a film of tears, I faced the annoyance in Shareen's dark eyes. "You're not going to fix it, lady, but you can give it your best shot."

22

One hour and an extensive deep tissue massage later—well beyond the deadline for the oath—Shareen led me back to the lobby where her counterpart Ivy stood chatting with the Lady of Beasts. On the counter between them sat a grizzled old tom with a lopped ear, black as a panther and built along similar proportions. He perched like a monarch enshrined on his throne, and Ivy rested one hand lightly against his glossy flank.

As she talked, the gray-haired woman swayed from hip to hip, keeping time to some internal music that was hers alone. No part of her remained still save the hand on the cat, as if that connection was her only anchor to the world the rest of us inhabited.

I could have used that kind of anchor in the wake of Shareen's massage. Her work left me feeling so profoundly relaxed, I was in danger of floating away. Stumbling after her like a sleepwalker, I moved on legs all gone to jelly. Lil would never get me to admit it, but this hour-long respite had been everything I'd needed.

At least, it was a start.

Shareen swept past me as we moved toward the counter, making a beeline for the massive beast seated beside the guest book. As if conscious of her attention, he drew himself up stiffly, puffing his chest and giving his chin a lift.

"Kingsley," she said, her tone caught somewhere between affection and admonishment. "How did you get in here?" She held out the fingers of one hand, which the cat sniffed lightly, as if bestowing his approval.

Ivy chuckled. "You know Kingsley. He goes where he wants, when he wants, and to hell with doors," she said. "I've given up fighting with him."

"I can see that much," Shareen said, and she laughed.

"Kingsley is a special guy," Lil chimed in. "You're both lucky he chose this place for his home." As Shareen had done before her, she extended a hand to the cat, not to pet him, but to invite him to respond on his own terms. After intense consideration, he bumped his head into her open palm, then rose and sauntered to the edge of the counter. Settling down again, he turned golden eyes on me and stared with a focused intensity that would have been unnerving in a human.

"Do I smell funny, cat?" I asked. I tugged at the collar of my T-shirt where it hadn't settled right when I pulled it back on. My fingers came away slick from a smear of massage oil. "Pretty sure it's just sandalwood."

The cat blinked once, a slow lowering and raising of fringed velvet lids. Other than that, he held statue-still. Not even a whisker twitched. Lil strode over to join him in his soul-piercing scrutiny.

"What do you think, Kingsley?" she asked, tilting her head in my direction. "He ready yet?"

I couldn't help but laugh. They made quite the pair.

"I need approval from a cat now?"

"Not from a cat," Lil replied. Her face remained placid, but I could hear the smirk in her tone. There was a joke I wasn't getting, but if she wanted me to play guessing games, she should have tried at least an hour earlier. After Shareen's thorough pounding, all I wanted was my bed.

I yawned to drive the point home.

"Kingsley doesn't bother to come out for just anyone," Ivy observed. Untethered from the solid presence of the feline, she floated behind the counter like dandelion fluff, skirts rustling as she tidied stacks of papers and rearranged random items on the shelves.

"Oh, he's not just anyone," Shareen murmured. Lil shot her friend an appraising glance, then speared me with a similarly inquiring expression. I kept my mouth shut. That was a conversation best left for the car.

Shareen was no psychic, but she had pretty good instincts for energy. She'd framed all her perceptions in flighty light-worker talk—star-seed this and indigo child that—so I didn't feel in the least bit threatened. But while she was doing her Reiki, she'd picked up some genuine impressions. The fact that she'd picked up anything at all was... interesting. All that energy work had helped passively replenish some of my spent power, too—which no doubt Lil had intended from the start.

"I'm sure Mr. Kingsley is a very nice cat," I said, "but

I only agreed to be here for an hour, and it's well past that." Pointedly, I glared at the Lady of Beasts. "I've got an investigation that needs my attention. The bad guys never wait, especially not for spa days."

Upon hearing this, Kingsley huffed as if he fully understood the nature of the dismissal. Rolling his eyes in an almost human fashion, the cat stood, stretched, then jumped down from the counter to disappear among the shelves at Ivy's feet.

"Guess you didn't pass his test, flyboy," Lil sighed. She sounded genuinely aggrieved.

"I'm crushed," I said, walking to the door. "Let's go."

Lil shook her head, then thanked her friends, hugging them both before joining me. Despite the humming calm that lingered post-massage, I found all her effusive affection unnerving. Like her work with the Windy City Vixens burlesque troupe, this was a side of Lil I had trouble integrating with the stone-cold killer I had come to know and occasionally appreciate.

She unlocked the car so I could finally get at all my things, which she'd neatly hidden under the front seat. Heedless of any observers in this sleepy suburban neighborhood, I strapped the blades to my wrists, eager for their rigid comfort. The jacket came next, zippered and buckled into place, with the weight of my firearm heavy against my ribs. Opposite the SIG, I checked for the slender box of the Stylus. Its presence was less of a comfort and more of a weighty necessity. When I didn't feel it, I started to panic. Wordlessly, Lil produced it from her handbag, handing its runed puzzle box over to me.

"You didn't think I'd just leave that thing lying around out here, did you?"

Fighting back a scowl, I took it, tucking it back into the deepest inner pocket of my jacket where it settled in a hard line. For the first time in more than an hour, I didn't feel utterly naked.

Lil minced over to the driver's side. Tauntingly, she dangled the keys.

"No argument?"

"Nope," I said. "I'd fall asleep and put us in a ditch."

"I should kidnap you more often," she smirked. "You're being reasonable for once."

"Don't push your luck."

Laughing, she ducked inside the Hellcat. I followed shortly after, settling languidly in the seat. She stabbed a painted fingernail toward the radio and I lightly batted her away.

"Not right now," I said. "Just let me enjoy the quiet while it lasts. Everything is shot to hell, but for the moment I feel all right."

For once, she complied with neither snark nor argument, keying the ignition and peeling away from the curb. Lil's breakneck driving was typically hair-raising, but I felt too mellow to really care. I just strapped on the seatbelt and tipped my head back on the neck rest, closing my eyes.

Sleep overtook me immediately, deep and dreamless.

Lil firmly shook my shoulder. We sat in the lot outside of my apartment.

"This is your stop, Anakim," she said.

My response was confused and nonverbal. Clumsily, I swiped at her hand. She shook a little harder.

"Come on," she insisted. "I'm not carrying you up two flights of stairs."

She must have anyway—I had the barest recollection of making the transit from car to front door. Half in a dream, I took down my wards. Lil kept her arm around my waist, making sure I didn't stumble.

"Oh, the things I could do to you," she murmured. Her head tilted against my chest. I could smell her hair—not spice and vanilla, for once. Plain old shampoo. Something vaguely fruity.

"But you won't," I said. It was a struggle to enunciate. Sleep had thickened my tongue. "Mean Lil's a front. I know you. You're a really good friend."

With a snort, she pushed me into my apartment, then lingered in the door frame. Hands perched on her hips, she watched as I staggered toward the couch. Going around took too much effort, so I rolled right over the back. In an unceremonious heap, I tumbled onto the cushions, still in boots and jacket.

"You're so sleepy, it's like you're drunk," she observed. The smile in her voice made a color in my head, red as the lipstick she wore. Not a bad red, like Nephilim or anger or blood.

Lil red. Foxy.

"Booze doesn't help," I babbled. Clumsily, I gestured to dismiss her suggestion. The arm ended draped over my eyes. "Tried that. Pills, too. Nothin'."

"Sucks to be immortal, doesn't it?" she said gently.

"I'm not immortal till I die and come back," I objected. "But then I won't be me. Can't let that happen. Not-me's kind of a monster."

Deep in her throat, Lil made a speculative sound. "We're all monsters, Zack. It's just a matter of degrees." There was no judgment in her words, just a kind of sympathetic reassurance. I grunted a non-comment, too sleepy to debate the point. Turning, she started for the hall. I called her back, waving madly from the will-sucking cushions of the couch.

"Lil, hey!" I cried, as if she stood ten yards and not ten feet away. I didn't try to get up. Most of my body was pretty sure it was asleep already. The brain just hadn't caught up. Not quite.

"What now?" she sighed.

"You were right," I said.

She snorted. "Of course I'm right. What am I right about now?"

"I'm serious," I responded. My tongue felt loose in my mouth, as if its hinge had come undone. If I wasn't careful, it would slip right out and wiggle away.

The image had me cackling for a solid minute.

"Sleep it off, flyboy," Lil urged gently. "I'm going to lock up behind me. Hope you can set the wards from over there."

"Of course I can," I protested. "I'm a wizard." As proof, I wiggled my fingers in imitation of a grandiose spell.

"You're ridiculous, is what you are," she chuckled. The door closed and locks started throwing themselves, even though she stood on the other side. Blearily, I squinted from under the shield of my arm. I didn't know she could do that.

"Why do you keep lock picks? You're a wizard, too," I observed. I yelled so she could hear me.

"Not a deaf one, as it turns out," she said from the hall. "Go back to sleep, Zaquiel. I'll keep an eye on things as long as I can."

She did that a lot, and I knew it. I didn't always know why.

"Thank you," I called earnestly with my last shred of coherence. My whole body felt heavy as sleep dragged me back down. There was no answer, though, just the soft step of her boots as she descended the stairs. The sound followed me into dreams—of cats and foxes, spectral lions, and one old woman made young again, hiking to meet a lover in a mountain range draped with pristine snow.

In a moment of brief lucidity, as I flew above live, wooden horses endlessly riding around a haunted carousel, I remembered to mutter the words that re-sealed the wards.

23

Sleep claimed me so completely, I didn't even shift position until a loud, persistent rhythm dragged me unwillingly from the depths. Blearily, I fumbled for my phone, too muzzy-headed to realize that the sound wasn't an alarm. Uselessly, I stabbed at the screen anyway.

The rhythmic sound continued. Someone was at my door.

"Go away," I shouted finally. My tongue felt like a crusty piece of driftwood had found its way into my mouth. Tasted like it, too. Maybe it had escaped after all to slither across the floor.

"Zack," a stentorian voice called from beyond the door. "It's Father Frank. Saturday. Three o'clock. Did you forget?"

Sleep-thick and struggling through thoughts like cold molasses, my weary brain groped for any significance behind the particular date and time. I just wanted to go back to sleep. My neck itched and every conceivable muscle from my shoulders downward ached from last night's exertions—not to mention Shareen's relentless massage. Finally, limping awareness blundered through the haze of discomfort and exhaustion.

Halley's lesson.

"Shit," I hissed, scrambling from the couch. My legs didn't work as fast as the rest of me, so mostly I just tumbled to the hardwood, whacking a shoulder against the edge of the coffee table. The impact knocked a stack of books to the floor. The small avalanche of sound carried into the hall.

"Hey, you OK in there?"

"Gimme a minute," I called back, heaving myself to my feet. The world wobbled, and my head felt three sizes too big. "Fucking timing," I grumbled, then staggered to the door. Grabbing the knob, I flipped the lock and then the dead bolt, vaguely recalling that I hadn't been the one to lock them. Lil's telekinetic display—or whatever it had been—niggled uncomfortably in the back of my brain. She'd even gotten the chain lock. That thing was a bitch to work with flesh-and-blood hands.

That woman was dangerous, no doubt. I had no idea why she hadn't killed me yet.

The chain swung like a pendulum as I whispered down the wards and pulled open the door. In the hallway, a tall, lean man with a high, craggy brow stood in a position strikingly similar to mine. His black shirt with the white tab at the collar proclaimed his clerical vocation, although he still held himself with the rigid readiness of the Marine he once had been. I knew from long association that a Desert Eagle settled somewhere under his jacket, as much a part of his identity as the collar. As the wards unspooled, the gust of power rustled the iron-gray hair at his temples. Blinking bright-penny eyes, he took in the whole of my appearance—wild hair, bandaged neck, rumpled shirt, and jeans stained with mud, blood, cat hair, and nastier substances.

"Rough night?" he asked sardonically.

"Yeah," I said.

His mouth quirked in a paternal expression that seamlessly blended sympathy with disapproval and concern. Maybe because the severing of Marjory was so fresh and sharp, I could feel the steadying thrum of his connection. The lean, rangy priest was another anchor—one upon whom I drew with great regularity. The deep pulse of banked power that he carried struck a persistent bassline in my chest, telegraphing his emotions.

"What time did you go to bed?"

"Ten-thirty this morning." I scraped a palm across stubble that was verging on a beard, and found another clinging cat hair. "I think. Might've been later. I wasn't awake enough to check."

"No wonder you didn't hear me knocking," he chuckled. With well-earned familiarity, he moved to come inside. I shifted to block his entry. "What?" he demanded, more bemused than piqued. "You're not going to let us in?"

"Look, Padre," I hedged. "Today's not so good for a—"

Everything else I had planned to say fled my lips the instant a waifish girl with enormous brown eyes peeked out from behind him. Her tangle of dark hair had been swept back from her face and tamed into twin braids that hung heavily past her shoulders. She'd been so quiet and held her cowl so tight as she huddled in the rangy man's shadow, I'd completely missed her presence.

"Wingy!" she cried, delighted.

The nickname was ridiculous, but at its sound I melted. Smiling despite everything, I shuffled back from the door. Almost instantly, Halley collided with me. In an uncharacteristic show of affection, she clasped my side, then ducked away to arrow for my couch. With single-minded focus, she clambered onto the rumpled cushions, taking up her usual position pressed against one of the arms. Kicking off her shoes, she drew her knees up to her thin chest, hugging them as she stared fixedly at her toes. She wore no socks, the nails painted brightly.

"Hello, Halley," I said with undisguised affection.

"Lesson time, Wingy," the girl announced, mumbling the words into her jeans. Her gaze never wavered from her feet, but that was to be expected. Halley rarely made eye contact with anyone, even her closest friends. It was just part of her wiring. Among the girl's many challenges, Halley was autistic.

"I'm glad you were actually home," Father Frank said, kicking off his boots. As soon as he was through the door, I re-sealed the wards. "She's been looking forward to this all week, especially after we had to cancel when they switched up her appointment for the MRI. I swear, they've run so many tests on that poor kid, she should glow in the dark."

On the couch, Halley gently rocked as she poked at her toenail polish. Her gaze remained fixated, but I could feel the real focus of her attention. Little tendrils of psychic force inquisitively played across my shields. A

few almost slipped under, and I allowed the intrusion…
to a point, giving her confirmation that what she tried
was working. But my head was an ugly place even on
the best of days, so I shut her out before she could grab
anything more than surface emotions. With a gentle
push, I shifted the layers of protection. She chuffed
unhappily through her nose, the only indication that she
was aware of the interaction.

"You get further every time," I affirmed. Crushing
her face into her knees, Halley hid a wide, pleased grin.
"Pretty soon, I won't catch you before you're through.
Just be careful, OK?" I urged. "I say a lot of bad words
inside of my head."

"Bad words outside, too," she murmured, her diction
somewhat twisted as her bottom lip dragged on denim.

"She's got you there, Zack." The old priest chuckled,
accustomed to our psychic games.

"Like you should talk," I teased dryly. "We didn't
call you Foul-Mouthed Frankie back in the rice paddies
because you forgot to brush."

Halley collapsed into peals of laughter. She'd heard
the nickname before, but it never failed to get a reaction.
As she writhed delightedly on the cushions, I moved to
the far edge of the living room. Silently, I gestured for
Father Frank. He quirked a bristling brow.

"You sit tight for a minute, will you, Halley?" I called.
"I've got to talk with the padre. In private," I added. "So
no tricks to listen in."

"Aww, Wingy," Halley objected.

"No arguments," I said. "You know the rules."

She slumped like a toddler told to eat all her peas.

"What's wrong?" Father Frank mouthed. I gestured for him to join me at the mouth of the hall. Deceptively preoccupied, Halley plucked at a thread in the seam of the cushion by her foot, striving to make that part look the same as all the rest.

"I'll be OK, Wingy," she said without looking up from her self-appointed task. A reassuring note to her words suggested that she'd already been paying close attention to the underlying emotions of our discreet exchange.

Grabbing the old priest by the elbow, I marched us both into my room, shutting the door behind us. As Lil had done a scant nine hours earlier, I turned on the music, cranking the volume. Billy Joel's "Goodnight, Saigon" blared jarringly mid-chorus, telling me how we'd all go down together. Not consoling in the least. Disgusted, I flipped the dial back off again.

"Not funny, Lailah," I called to the empty air. Even if I couldn't see her, when the music got that pointed, it was safe to assume her will guided the tunes.

Twisting his big-knuckled hands, Father Frank dropped onto the side of my mattress. Springs creaked under his settling weight. From the play of shadows that haunted his eyes, he didn't appreciate the musical reminder any more than I had. Through that bitter jungle war, he'd survived only because I'd made him my anchor.

I'd come home in a body bag.

Sometimes, I couldn't tell which of us had gotten the shittier end of the deal.

"Talk to me, Zack," he said with quiet urgency. "I haven't seen you look this spooked in a while."

In the narrow strip of floor between footboard and

dresser, I restlessly paced. "Do you know a guy named Zuriel?" I asked, striving to keep my voice down.

His shoulders raised, then slumped. "Should I?"

"Maybe. I don't know," I said. "He's one of my tribe—and possibly a little more."

"I thought they were all missing," he responded. The priest tracked my stumping transit, crowsfeet nesting his eyes. "Locked up in jars."

"Yeah, that's what I thought, too." I dashed my fingers through the wild tangle of my hair. Sand tumbled out, left over from the fight at the beach, a few grains cascading down the neck of my T-shirt. Disgusted, I squirmed, flicking the remains from my hands. "This guy blew into town maybe a couple weeks ago. He killed that woman, Marjory. The one from the letter." Sand teased the fine hairs at the small of my back, seeking points further south. Untucking, I tried to shake them out before they made it into my jeans.

"I remember you talking about her." He arched a brow at my writhing antics. "You OK, Zack?"

"I'm filthy, and it's driving me nuts," I explained, finally ripping the whole shirt over my head. I chucked it into the dirty pile beside the door. I hadn't even been wearing that shirt at the beach. Fucking sand.

"I can see that," Father Frank said mildly. He politely averted his gaze as I stripped. Clean clothes were mounded in a laundry basket near the closet, and I rifled through them, grabbing fresh jeans and another T-shirt at random. I added a clean pair of boxer briefs from a drawer. "Didn't that letter also mention a daughter?" he queried, staring fixedly at my curtains. "Don't tell me she's dead, too."

Stepping into the jeans, I fumbled for the tongue of the zipper. It was wedged in the folds of the denim.

"Not yet—at least, I don't think so," I said, trying to tease it out so I didn't rip the thing apart like I had with Marjory's purse. "That's one of the things I need to find out, but I've got a shit-ton of stuff to do first." Finally zipped, I yanked my belt from the cast-off pants. The buckle chattered noisily as the leather slid through the loops. "Zuriel's running around with my Vulcan and a set of keys to this place. I've got to report the theft and get the locks changed before I do anything else."

"All this happened last night?" he asked.

Bitterly, I laughed. "I'm only giving you the high points, Padre," I said. "We'd be here for hours if I went over everything. I don't have that kind of time." Leaning over, I tried to shake the lingering sand from my hair before pulling the fresh shirt over my head. What I needed was a shower, but that wasn't happening. "Worse than the keys, the guy has some kind of spell that lets him wear my face. We look identical." The old priest's back went ramrod straight as he digested this revelation. Tucking my shirt, I tapped him on the shoulder so he knew it was safe to turn around. "It could be the spell, but he also matched my clothes, right down to the jacket. I get the feeling he's been watching me for a while."

The iron gray of his brows thatched. "You have any idea what this guy wants?" I must have telegraphed some measure of my wounded horror, because he leaned forward urgently, just short of rising from the bed. "What haven't you told me?"

"He made me burn my connection to Marjory," I answered thickly. "She was an anchor, just like you. And he wanted to watch." The severed hole panged where she had been. "This is intensely personal, Padre. Something connected with another of my brethren—Tashiel."

A muscle in his jaw ticked. "I've heard that name before."

"What?" I demanded. "When?" Narrowly, I resisted the urge to shake him. Instead, I crossed to the far side of the room, the muscles on my forearms cording beneath the black webwork of the sheaths. I held my hands in fists, clenching and unclenching. Father Frank rose, shaking loose his own tension.

"Couple years ago," he said. "You'd learned about something he'd done. It had to be awful, given your reaction, but you wanted to hear it from his lips before you passed judgment. Those were your exact words, by the way." He threaded fingers through his hair as he remembered.

"Do you know what it was about?"

Unhelpfully, he shrugged. "No clue," he said. "Whatever it was, it really pissed you off. I asked a couple times. You clammed up about it. I knew when to stop asking. You don't always tell me your business."

"Figures," I said. "The old Zack compartmentalized his whole life. Secrets inside of secrets."

Keenly studying my face, Father Frank leaned a shoulder against the bend of wall separating my closet from the entrance. "You know, I worry a little when you talk about yourself in the third person."

"You should try it in my head sometime," I scoffed.

"With so many memories gone, that guy really doesn't feel like me." Looking away, he pensively rubbed the hard angle of his jaw. The gesture was uncannily close to one of my own—like facing a mirror fast-forwarded forty years.

"You got a lot on your plate, Zack," he said finally. Heaving himself from the wall, he took a step toward the door. "I'll let Halley know lessons are canceled for the time being. After I walk her home, I'll head back here and handle the locksmith."

"You fucking walked?"

"It's less than a mile on a beautiful day," he answered. "Of course we walked. Poor kid's got to get out some time. Think it's any kind of life cooped up in a single room?"

"Did you hear *anything* I just said?" I demanded. "There's another Anakim on the loose who's hell-bent on destroying any person connected to me. That means you and that means Halley. This guy's not fucking around, Padre. He didn't just torture Marjory. He inflicted maximum pain and then he bound her spirit to her dead corpse so he could keep going. Wrap your head around that for a minute."

The man I'd once intended to become my father speared me with a look of steel first forged in the jungles of Vietnam.

"If you're trying to scare me off, Zaquiel, you can stop," he said. "As for Halley, take her home. With all those wards and spells, you got her place locked up tighter than Fort Knox."

"This guy can walk through walls and I don't know what else," I insisted.

He squared his broad shoulders, facing off with me in

the narrow space between closet, dresser, and door. Even with the years stamped upon his brow, I could see the fierce, young soldier he had been.

"Could you get in the Davis place if they weren't your wards?" he asked.

"That's not my point," I said.

"I know your point," he responded. "You're worried for us, and I appreciate that." Sputtering heated objections, I tried to interrupt, but he only raised his voice to drown me out. "Halley, I understand. She's an innocent, and her life's hard enough without your people breathing down her back. But me? I knew what I signed on for, Zack. So give it a rest. You may carry wings on your back, but you're still just one person. Accept my help with the locksmith, and get on with the rest of your day. When I'm done, I'll go keep an eye on Halley." Pointedly, he touched the hard lines of the gun at his back. "You know I can handle myself."

I glanced to the clock on the dresser. The afternoon was already winding down.

"I'm not going to win this one, am I?"

He snorted. "You won this argument yet?"

24

Still, I took precautions. Three times, I had Father Frank take down and re-arm the wards, just to show me that he could. Never mind that I'd taught him how to do it months ago. That knowledge had never been put to the test, not like this.

"Come on, Zack, this is getting old," Father Frank said.

"Just one more time," I insisted. "I don't want this guy in my apartment, especially not with you inside."

Through the door, I heard him grumble, but the old priest did as he was told. I wouldn't have been so pushy if it had been anyone else. My chest still ached with the gnawing emptiness where my link to Marjory had been. I couldn't even remember forging my tie to her, yet severing it had hurt as much as cutting off my own hand. I didn't want to imagine what it would feel like to lose Father Frank.

"Satisfied?" He raised his voice to carry from inside, making no effort to mask his growing impatience. From my position in the hallway, I pressed a hand against the webwork of energy, testing its tensile strength. The barrier held firm. Delicately, I prodded at the moorings, trying to unwind them without the use of the pass phrase. All the sigils around the doorframe flared briefly, and a warning surge prickled against my palm. A scent like hot metal teased my nose.

"Yeah," I said. "It'll hold."

With a harsh whisper of syllables, he took the whole thing down again. The bubble-pop of power blew cold fingers through my hair. Locks rattled and, a moment later, the door swung open. Father Frank leaned an elbow against the jamb.

"Of course it will hold," he said. "You made it. Now get going. Locksmith'll be here in less than an hour. I won't be stuck here for long."

"I still think you should head back with Halley," I said. "It'll be safer for both of you."

"We've been over this, Zack." He sighed. "Get out of here already. You've got a missing woman to track down. I'll have the new keys waiting for you at the Davis house."

At the sound of her last name, Halley quitted the couch and slipped past the big man, ducking under his outstretched arm. She maneuvered her passage in such a way that she avoided all physical contact with both the priest and the door, as if folding space halfway through the narrow aperture. Taking up a position at the top of the stairs, she curled her toes over the first step through the thin soles of her shoes, rocking precariously over the edge. She didn't say it was time to leave, but there was no missing her message.

"All right, fine," I relented. "Let's go."

Ushering Halley to my car, I held the passenger side door open as she clambered inside. She sat woodenly in the deep bucket seat of the Hellcat, although she fussed when I grabbed the seatbelt and started fastening it for her.

"I'm sorry, Halley, but you're going to have to put up with that," I said, adjusting the lap belt so it didn't bind. "It's against the law for you to ride without it, and I really wouldn't want you to get hurt if something happened with the car."

Mewling unhappily, she plucked at the chest-strap where it angled across her shoulder. It rode a little high, so the edge brushed her throat on one side. I tried to adjust it, but there wasn't much I could do, given her size.

"I hate those things, too," I admitted. "If you really don't like it, you could always ride in the back," I offered. "You'd only need a lap-belt there."

She shook her head with such conviction, her thick braids whipped wildly around her head. I drew back sharply to avoid catching one with my face. Her hand fell away from the troublesome strap, alighting briefly on the edge of the driver's seat.

"I get it," I said. The girl said nothing in response, but I'd spent enough time around Halley to catch the little shift in where her eyes were focused—from her knees to my hand, then quickly back again. The movement was subtle enough, most other people would have dismissed it. But, sometimes with Halley, all you got was a blink. That was the best she could manage when crossing the vast gulf between her brain and the outside world. "You're always welcome to sit with me, Halley, you know that," I assured. "Now, I'm going to close this door and come around to the driver's side. I want to see you still in that seatbelt when I sit down."

She made it clear that she didn't like it, but she complied. Once I settled in, I fastened my own belt and started the car. Pulling out onto Euclid Heights, I turned in the direction of Lancashire. Halley's head swiveled around and she stared morosely back toward Coventry Road—that was the route she was accustomed to taking. Her dark brows drew together and she started fussing with the seatbelt again.

"I know this isn't the way Father Frank normally takes you," I said. "Just bear with me—this is going to involve some creative threading through back streets."

She continued plucking at the seatbelt where it touched her neck, falling into a rhythm that grew less restless and more self-soothing. I didn't try to stop her. The girl's head drooped forward, one braid partly unraveled from where she'd pulled it free of the hair tie.

"Why?" she asked.

"I don't like driving past the cemetery," I explained, taking the turn at Overlook and following the curve of the road. "With everything that happened there, I thought you'd want to avoid it, too. That place is full of bad memories."

"It helps to see," she replied. She offered nothing further, lips pouting around her thoughts. Her gaze drifted to the window and she tracked the slow progression of blazing red maples that lined the lane. The heavily tinted glass caught a sliver of her face, reflecting the curving landscape of one broad cheekbone.

Her dark iris glimmered above it, a deep and placid lake. In silence, I wondered how many horror-tinged memories drifted like specters beneath that deceptively calm surface. The girl had endured so much at that cemetery—not just Terhuziel's brutal attentions, but threats from the Gibburim-ridden Garrett, the tumble from the edge of the Garfield Monument, and a near-disastrous trip through the Shadowside with me.

I'd saved her life and killed her, all in the space of five minutes. If not for Bobby's quick-thinking CPR—

The tightness that gripped my throat threatened to choke me. I swallowed hard against the surging mess of emotions that scattered my thoughts. Shifting tensely in my seat, I refocused my attention to the unfolding of the present—the car, the girl, the quiet lane threading through post-war bungalows and brick apartment buildings, all of it edged with trees. Those horrors were behind us. Halley was safe, at least for the time being.

I'd do anything to keep her that way.

"Who is the red man?" she asked suddenly.

It sounded like a left-field question, an utter non-sequitur spilling from the disorganized chaos of a scattered mind, but I knew better. With convulsive intensity, that tightness returned, and a sick little thread of guilt slithered through my gut.

"What did you say, Halley?"

"The red man," she repeated. "At the cemetery. He stands behind you."

She was talking about the Crossing near the mouth of the Mayfield Gate. I'd almost died there, and, in the imprint left from that event, it was possible to see the

Nephilim Primus like a great red shadow stretching behind my back. She could see it as clearly as I could—a little too clearly for comfort. The scar on my palm twisted like a snake inside my skin, and I gripped the wheel to hide the sudden tremor in my hands.

"That's something I can't actually talk about," I hedged, astounded I was able to get even that much past the gag-order of Sal's oath.

Halley made a thoughtful sound, edged with disappointment. Her hand on the seatbelt fell still for the first time since we'd started the conversation. A long silence followed, long enough for me to hope her thoughts had taken her to some arena of interest far removed from the grim events linked irrevocably to Lake View. I really didn't want to talk about this, not with Halley. She needed her hero unsullied, and with the Eye, I was anything but.

Stewing in a welter of my own unpleasant recollections, I numbly guided the Hellcat along the winding road, slowing as the light ahead switched from green to yellow.

"She said you wouldn't be able to answer." Halley blurted the statement so matter-of-factly, it was a good thing I was already stopping at an intersection. I didn't trust my hands on the wheel.

"You're talking about Lailah again, aren't you?" I didn't really need to ask. Knuckles whitening, I fought a rush of conflicting emotions—not the least among them, jealousy. For months, the only contact I'd had with Lailah's spirit came fitfully through music and dreams, but somehow, Halley saw her clearly. The girl's blood pulsed with the gifts of my tribe, but I had no explanation for the disparity.

"Lailah teaches me, when you can't," the girl replied. Her skinny hand drifted toward mine, hesitating a moment, then alighting with the delicate brush of a butterfly's gossamer wings. A staggering jolt of power at odds with the lightness of her touch leapt between us as she made contact. "It hurts. I know. Come and see."

A haze of lavender light clouded my vision and the road slipped abruptly away. For a moment, I tumbled in a free-fall, wings beating spastically in an effort to gain any purchase—up or down or sideways. I couldn't tell the direction of my plummet, and then I appeared in a courtyard paved with white and black marble in a chevron design. High towers ranged all around, the brilliant white of their limestone façades reflecting the rosy light of a setting sun.

Halley stood before me—a very different Halley than the skinny child huddled in the distant seat of the Hellcat. This was Halley as she saw herself, the young woman she was meant to be—willowy, tall, extremely self-possessed. In her glittering, floor-length dress, she looked every minute of her fifteen years, and then some. Long waves of dark hair fell about her shoulders like a cloak, cascading to the ground. Twin sections at her temples were tightly braided, swept back from her smooth brow and pinned in place beneath a delicate, jeweled tiara.

She was always a princess in her mind-palace, although more and more she looked like a queen. The sight momentarily stole my breath with that sweet, aching pride I imagined a parent must feel for a favored child.

"You look tired, Wingy," she said, the fond nickname somewhat at odds with her regal deportment—but here, I earned it. Blue-white structures comprised of gleaming light spread behind me as I alighted on the rich paving stones, the wings sprouting unimpeded through the leather of my jacket.

"I *am* tired, Halley," I answered, settling the extra limbs tightly against my back. The tips trailed the ground behind my boots. "It's been a long few weeks. But you shouldn't bring me in here when I'm driving. We could wreck."

"The car's stopped," she responded, picking up her skirts and sweeping ahead of me along a crooked path. "This won't take long, not out there. She needed to tell you herself."

"What?" I asked, jogging after her. "Who?" But I knew the answer, and it spurred my chase. In silence, Halley glided ahead of me, always a few steps out of reach. Slowly, I caught up with her, but only with effort. Her glass-slippered feet were deceptively swift.

By the time I reached her, we were no longer near the palace, but on the verge of an enormous garden spilling through a hole in the wall. Halley stepped lightly over tumbled masonry, lifting her skirts to rush deep into the riot of flowers. Through twists and turns of soft lavender leaves, we followed a hedge maze that spiraled ever inward. At each turn, the leaves of the towering bushes grew darker, until the purple foliage around us shimmered in hues almost black. The sun above us fled by stages and, before I fully processed it, we stood at a central well, surrounded by whispering night. Halley paused at the edge of the clearing, pointing to a twining arbor of greenery, its archway cloaked in billowing mist. The scent of jasmine hung heavy upon the cool, damp air.

"There," she announced.

The woman's name left my lips on a susurrus of breath even before I spied her sinuous figure through the roiling curtain of fog. Then the mist parted and Lailah stepped forth, clad in a gray feathered robe that rippled with her every movement. Her eyes were caught between woman and owl, huge pupils dark as the space between stars.

"Hello, *majnun*," she murmured in a voice rich as velvet. "You're in danger, and we don't have much time. Halley can't hold the between-space for long."

25

"Halley's doing this?" I asked. "How?"

The girl stood rigidly at the mouth of the clearing, her fingers locked around a glowing sigil of power that cast a purple faery light against the spangles on her dress. Concentration creased her uplit features, and her lips moved around a rhythmic incantation that carried softly on her breath. As Halley strained, Lailah slipped from the mists of the arbor, advancing a few more steps.

"She found the well here all on her own," Lailah responded with a note of pride.

"This isn't her mind-palace," I said. "I didn't teach her any of this."

Lailah laid one finger against her pursed lips, cautioning silence. Her black nails curled like talons, startling against the softly brown flesh of her face. Choking down all my questions, I remained rooted to the little path beside the well. I didn't fully understand what was happening, or how, but some gut instinct clamored that if I touched Lailah or even dared come too close, she would shiver to nothingness.

"You didn't teach her this," she said. "I did. Someone had to, and you don't remember enough."

"You're here, then," I responded in a rush. "For real. This isn't just some vision."

"It's along the edge of one," she replied. "But that's not why I asked her to bring you here, Zaquiel. Your brother is tracking you as we speak, and there is very little you can do about it." She spoke urgently. "He's stalked you for a while now, and he knows enough about the different layers of the Shadowside that he's made it difficult for me to stalk him back." She shook clinging tatters of fog from her heels as if they burned. "He's good at hiding, and he's made some unexpected allies."

"The cacodaimon?" I asked.

Hair twitched against her shoulders as she shook her head. "No. That's a very different problem, one that cannot be left for too long—much like the red man." She halted opposite me on the far side of the well. Between us, its still waters gazed like a solitary eye up at the starless heavens, glimmers of silver shimmering across its surface from the soft light cast by my tucked wings. "But your brother is an immediate concern. He seeks to hurt everyone around you, and he will not stop. You took something irreplaceable from him, and his own pain drives him like a madness. Once your world has been ground to bitter ash, he means to bind you—all in retaliation for Tashiel."

"How can he bind me?" I asked. "He doesn't have the Stylus."

The feathers of her gray robe rustled in a wind I didn't feel. It teased her hair, making the long strands dance like charmed cobras. "Consider how the Gibburim sealed Terhuziel in the shattered husk of his form," she responded. "From the moment your people swore to bury the Icons and end the Blood Wars, they have been seeking creative ways to visit their powers upon one another, regardless of their oaths."

"I don't think you understand," I insisted. "Oaths aren't just empty words to us, Lailah. We literally cannot speak if we've sworn ourselves silence."

"And yet you can speak with me, all because of a single word in that oath, *majnun*," she said. "Your people uphold the wording but not the spirit, so oaths become more lip-service than obstacle."

"You're saying that we cheat," I said. My anger rose in excess of the accusation, rumbling through the space with the threat of a rising storm. Lailah lifted a hand to soothe me.

"No," she said. "I am telling you the rules."

"Fuck the rules." Lightning the shade of my wings flashed from sky to treetops, reflected in the depths of the well. "If this guy wants to turn my life into bitter ash, I need to get back to Father Frank. I should never have let him talk me into leaving—"

"The old man is fine, at least for the moment," she interrupted. "Please believe me. He's handled worse." She cast a woeful glance over her shoulder at the arbor. "You need to listen. We waste precious time by arguing. The path collapses even now." At her words, the mists in its archway boiled ominously, lashing tendrils seeking to snag the edges of her robe. She winced as they swirled up to her ankles. "Shortly, I'll have to go. I'll have no choice."

"But—"

"As with the intricacies of oaths, you've forgotten the many layers to this space and how they intersect. Your enemy has not. He can move in directions you cannot predict. You need to watch your back, *majnun*, in every literal sense."

"Lailah, please—I'm terrible at riddles."

A poignant, mournful look weighed heavily upon her brow. "It only sounds like a riddle because you've lost the sense of the words," she said. "I would help you further, but too many gates stand between us, and strict rules govern my interactions. I am close, I promise—closer than I have been since my death, but you might not want me back if you fully understood the price." With a sudden shudder, she pulled the feathered cloak more tightly around herself. Not all of the shape beneath it seemed human. The light from my wings turned her tears to mercury as she fretted. "When the time comes, please remember. There is such a thing as a necessary evil, and, in loss, we sometimes find life."

"What evil?" I choked. "Lailah, what are you even talking about?"

"Watch the shadows, Zaquiel," she said. "They are not all what they appear." Behind her, the arbor belched a blinding cloud, thick and choking. Halley let loose a startled whimper, tumbling boneless to the ground. The roiling billows engulfed Lailah and she cried out as she vanished.

Shouting her name, I surged forward to seize her, but even as I did so, the projection shivered to pieces with the musical crackle of shattering glass.

26

Joltingly, I was propelled back to my seat in the Hellcat. Halley's fingers twitched hard against my hand, nails snagging skin. Behind us, a car horn honked. Given how long the driver let it blare, it wasn't the first time they'd tried to get us to move. Shaking clinging bits of the vision from my spinning gray matter, I stomped on the gas and rabbited forward, trading Overlook for Edgehill.

Halley pulled her hand away with a regret-filled sigh.

"I'm sorry, Wingy," she said. A greasy sweat beaded her brow.

"You don't need to apologize, Halley," I responded. The sound of my voice seemed to reach my ears from a great distance. Everything felt out of joint, like getting dragged prematurely from a dream. With effort, I focused on the steeply climbing road. "You did good."

"Sleepy," she murmured. Her head dropped heavily against the seat, dark lashes fluttering.

"You rest, kiddo," I said. "You earned it."

She stretched and sighed, relaxing.

The rest of the drive to the Davis home was uneventful, leaving me to wrestle with a head full of questions about bindings and vengeance and the kindled fury of forgotten brothers. On the heels of Lailah's cryptic message, Remy's needling question boomeranged through my thoughts.

How far might you go to protect those who've earned your loyalty?

Father Frank had said I wanted to talk with Tashiel before casting judgment. Zuriel held me responsible for that brother's disappearance, which made me think that judgment had been harsh. It was no coincidence that Tashiel was named in one of Marjory's beloved travelogues. I wondered if that journal described an ill-fated passage through the Alps. Tash had been with Anakesiel at the end. He'd seen the ambush—and reported it too late.

That couldn't have been enough for me to judge and find him guilty.

But what if the travelogue had revealed another version, one where Tashiel delayed his report on the ambush because he'd played some crucial role in its set-up?

The very notion chilled me and I knew from the convulsive way my hands seized upon the wheel that I'd hit upon some dark, significant truth. I already knew that the Nephilim were not solely to blame for the systematic disappearance of my tribe. But to consider that one of our own had sold us out... I didn't want to believe it, but I could imagine old Zack meting out one hell of a punishment if he'd gotten solid proof.

As I followed Murray Hill through the heart of

Little Italy, I tried to soothe my roiling thoughts. Until I saw that proof myself, all of this was mere conjecture. Diligently, I focused on the road. The tires of the Hellcat buzzed softly against the old-style paving bricks of the skinny, sloping lane. Parked vehicles, crowding nose to tailpipe, further narrowed the one-way and bustling foot traffic poured from the shops.

Halley stirred fretfully in her seat, ashen smudges beneath her eyes a testament to the effort she'd expended to facilitate my communication with the Lady of Shades.

"You're real loud, Wingy," she murmured. She slid a hand across her eyes, blinking as the sun switched directions when I turned onto her street.

"I'm sorry, Halley," I said. "You gave me a lot to think about." Pulling in front of her house, I hit the locks to release her door. "Ready to go?"

She nodded, fumbling out of her seatbelt. I went around to give her a hand out of the car, but she held herself stiffly, making it clear she wanted to do everything herself. Still, she tottered coltishly on her way to the front porch, so I followed a step or two behind, ready to catch her if she stumbled. She pushed the buzzer, leaving her finger on it as it shrilled in the room beyond. After a rush of feet, Sanjeet answered the door. The instant she saw me, the young Sikh woman's features went stony.

"Professor Westland," she said, rigidly polite.

"Just Zack," I reminded.

Behind her, Tyson, Halley's little brother, came pelting from the kitchen.

"Who's at the door? Who's at the door?" he cried. Crumbs tumbled from the side of his mouth as he threw himself bodily at the back of Sanjeet's legs. With a deceptively casual gesture, she caught him by the shoulder before he fully connected, neatly deflecting the impact and spinning him around so she could scoop him into her arms. It was an impressive, if unorthodox, application of the mixed martial arts training she'd received from Father Frank.

"Whoa. Cool!" Tyson chortled. "Do it again!"

"No," Sanjeet said firmly. With one arm bracing his back, she perched him atop her hip. Legs kicking, he squirmed a moment, then settled, poking at her glasses. She endured the attention impassively. "Where's Father Frank?" she asked.

I craned my neck to peer beyond her into the familiar living room. It was neat, as usual, with a homey scattering of Tyson's toys. "Are Tammy or Joe around?" I asked. As we spoke, Halley slipped past Sanjeet and shuffled toward the hallway that led to her room. Neither of us stopped her.

"Tammy's still at work," Sanjeet replied. "And NASA called Joe maybe an hour ago. It was supposed to be his day off."

"So you get baby-sitting duty," I said.

She shrugged. "I like it." She poked an exposed bit of Tyson's belly where his shirt rode up, inspiring an ear-splitting peal of giggles. Her smile vanished the instant she turned back to me. "What did you want?"

Sanjeet didn't like me, and it wasn't in her temperament to pretend otherwise. The best I'd ever gotten out of her was that I reminded her of an unpleasant someone from her past. That left a world of conjecture—stepfather, maybe, or an abusive ex-boyfriend. Whoever it was, he had to have been a grade-A asshole to leave such a sweeping instinct of distrust.

What I had to say next wasn't going to help it any.

"This is probably going to sound weird," I began, then faltered.

Her brow quirked. "From you? No."

"Right," I said, restlessly scrubbing my jaw. "Weirder than usual, then."

Sanjeet remained largely ignorant of my world, and I was inclined to keep it that way. I didn't trust a whole lot of people with the truth, and the fact that the young Sikh woman already viewed me as a menace gave me good reason to avoid shoveling fuel onto the fire. But with so many tricks at Zuriel's disposal, Sanjeet needed to know the shape—if not the specifics—of the danger.

"If I happen to come back here later," I said, "unless Father Frank is with me and he confirms that I'm actually me, don't open the door."

She blinked, struggling to digest this. "You're right," she said. "That's weirder than usual." With her middle finger, she adjusted her glasses where Tyson had knocked them askew. "Do you have an evil twin I should worry about?"

"Just make sure Tammy knows—and Joe, too, whenever he gets back," I hedged. "And, no matter what, keep that door locked."

"I always lock the door, Mr. Westland," she answered tersely. So saying, she pushed it shut while Tyson frenetically waved goodbye with the same hand he held fisted around a hunk of her hair.

I lingered on the porch until I heard all the bolts slam home. With a covert gesture, I tested the wards. All the layered protections stood firm, including what amounted to a cowl across the entire house, obscuring its very presence.

I hoped it was enough to keep Zuriel away.

Thumbing the button on my key fob, I crossed the yard and slipped behind the wheel of the Hellcat. The engine thrummed in a steady, soothing rhythm. Pulling back onto Mayfield, I turned toward the ripening brilliance of the afternoon sun and started the trek to Parma. Once I caught I-77, I dug my smartphone from where I'd stuffed it in a pocket. When Lil, Father Frank, and Halley all agreed on roughly the same point, even I wasn't stubborn enough to ignore it.

I needed to suck it up and ask for help.

27

My first call went to Lil's new number. After three rings, a computerized voice recited a canned message so anonymous it could have belonged to anyone, from a broker to a hitman. I hoped it was the right number.

"Hey, Lil," I said, guiding the car around a rusted-out sedan sitting in the breakdown lane. "You told me to start asking for help, so I'm asking." Thoughts and mouth still ran at odds, so it took a little effort to choke through the words. "Could you... drop by Halley's house tonight?" I faltered again and hoped she'd have the patience to listen through all my fumbling pauses. "I need someone to keep eyes on the kid and the padre." Just before the voicemail beep cut me off, I managed one more word. It was the hardest. "*Please.*"

Wiping an unaccustomed slickness from my palms, I waited a few miles before attempting my next call. The setting sun painted glare across my windshield, and I sat straighter in the driver's seat, trying to get the right angle with the visor so I could see the other cars around me. The world bled to hues of gold and orange and the highway shimmered like a molten river.

Using the voice function, I pulled up Bobby's number, then hovered with my thumb over the green call button. A mile streaked by, then two. The screen faded to black. Eyes sweeping cautiously between the phone and the road, I tapped my passcode into the lock screen, then brought the number back up.

And then I choked. Again.

Asking Lil for a favor had been a cakewalk by comparison. Bobby deserved an apology, but what could I possibly say? I'd been a royal ass to him. The real bitch of it was, I could recall every vicious comment I'd uttered, and they still felt justified. I knew it was Zuriel's spell talking—*you mad, bro?*—but that didn't change the emotions. They lingered in stark contrast to any reason.

Finally, I worked up the nerve and jammed my thumb onto the call button. One ring. Two. On the third, I almost hung up. By the fourth, I didn't have to. Bobby's phone went to voicemail, just like Lil's had. Unlike Lil's, his message was personal, his voice both business-like and cheery as it rose crisply from my phone.

"This is Park. Leave a message. I'll get back to you."

When I opened my mouth, nothing came out. The only sound his voicemail recorded was the whirr of the tires on pavement and the soft thrum of the Hellcat's engine. I fumbled for something—anything—I could say, but all I managed was his name. Then the beep cut me off.

"Shit," I grumbled, then tapped the brakes, guiltily dipping the phone out of sight. A State Trooper had his cruiser angled in the median. He stood in the open driver's-side door, back against the sun, the black cannon of a radar detector aimed at oncoming traffic—my lane. The Hellcat was on cruise, so my speed was fine, but I didn't want a ticket for using the cellphone.

Hitting my turn signal, I slipped behind an intervening semi like I'd been meaning to for miles. Once I'd skated passed the trooper, I hit the call button again, waiting for the now-familiar greeting.

"This is Park. Leave a message. I'll get back to you."

I drew a breath. "Hey, Bobby," I said. My voice still came out tight. Awkwardly, I cleared my throat. "So... this morning. Kind of a cluster fuck. All those things I said..." I trailed off, keenly aware how short his voicemail ran. Struggling for brevity, I tried again. "I was an ass. I'm sorry. I can explain more later, but if you don't want to hear it, I understand." My mouth felt dry at the prospect. "One more thing," I added quickly. "A favor, but only if you're willing. I need a report filed for the Vulcan, but I don't have time right now. Can you take care of it? Shoot me a message if you can."

The beep cut me off before I could fit in a "thanks." Changing lanes again, I resisted the urge to call back and clutter his voicemail with yet another message. If he wanted to talk, he'd text, sooner or later.

I hoped.

As I merged from I-77 to 480, the sun dipped lower, reaching that point on the horizon where no amount of adjustment could block it with the visor. I dug around as best I could for sunglasses, then after a few miles I resigned myself to squinting through the glare. It made my head pound, and my stomach roiled sourly in tandem. The food at the Cat House had been hours ago, and I hadn't grabbed anything at the apartment after waking up. There wasn't so much as a breath mint in the car. That was dumb.

Lil was right on one point—when it came to looking after my own needs, I failed. Miserably.

Traffic on 480 hit a snag about ten minutes from my exit. Brake lights flashed, and everyone slowed to a crawl. As I inched forward, a state trooper—probably the same one running the speed trap—zoomed past, wheels spitting plumes of dust as he drove half on the shoulder. Shortly after, he was followed by a fire truck, its horn whooping to get people out of the way. Despite the racket, almost no one moved—there was nowhere for any of us to go.

The left and middle lanes were shut down completely, and everyone was jockeying to get ahead. Between that and the rubbernecking, what could have been a fairly simple situation turned the highway into a parking lot.

The ten minutes to my exit dragged into twenty. I filled the time with my final and longest call of the afternoon—the one to my insurance company.

No human answered the phone. Instead, I got to navigate a seemingly endless series of computerized menus, each narrated by a canned female voice that reminded me of GLaDOS. By the fifth menu, I expected her to passive-aggressively begin goading me toward a murderous rampage.

It wouldn't have taken much at that point.

While I negotiated the voice-recognition program,

the battery on the phone drained rapidly. Digging the cord from my pocket, I switched the phone to speaker and balanced it in a cup-holder, plugging it in so it didn't die. I didn't think I could go through all those menus again—not without punching something.

The only upside to being stuck in phone-menu hell was that it kept my mind off of my real-world worries, especially those revolving around Marjory. In the back of my mind, though, I wondered what I was going do if I got to her house and found my baby pictures all over her walls.

28

I wrapped up the insurance call just in time to hit the exit and switch my phone to the map function. The speed limit dropped to twenty-five miles an hour, and I drove through street after street of anonymous, pastel colonials, tension crackling through my shoulders. The houses in this section of Parma were arranged with uniform precision, their postage-stamp lawns so picture-perfect, they belonged in the backdrop of some charming '50s sitcom, or maybe a *Twilight Zone* episode. As I followed the directions toward Marjory's address, no recognition stirred—although that didn't really mean much, not with the holes in my memory.

The instant I turned onto Marjory's street—Parmenter—my phone declared "You have arrived," and I began scanning for number 635. No lurid "X" of yellow police tape marked the door where death had so recently come knocking, and no mailboxes sprouted alongside the sloping concrete driveways as I crawled well below the posted speed. The houses were set just far enough back in their yards that even when they sported numbers, it was impossible to make them out—the fours looked like sevens, and the threes, fives, and eights were even worse.

Rolling through a stop sign at a cross street, I thought I finally had it, but then the numbers jumped abruptly from three to four digits. With a grumbled curse, I did a three-point turn and started over again, slowing my speed ever further. It wasn't like I had to worry about traffic—the street was empty. No one was even out in the yards.

The *Twilight Zone* vibe grew oppressively persistent. Scouring the tatters of my memories, I strove to find some detail that felt remotely familiar—a color, a particular twist in one of the trees, the shape of drawn curtains behind a window. But there was nothing. If ever I'd been here before, that knowledge was gone from my brain.

Abruptly, I swung the Hellcat to the side of the road and parked with the wheels halfway up on the curb. Flipping through all the little doodads on her keychain, I searched for *anything* that might offer a clue, then got out and marched toward the nearest yard. The idiot babble of a television drifted from somewhere on the other side of the street, so there had to be someone on Parmenter Road. It only felt like a post-Apocalyptic wasteland.

The first house I checked didn't have a number posted, not even on the little brass mail slot beside the front door. Baffled, I went around to the side door, looking there. Nothing. No car in the drive and nothing I could see through the spattered windows of the garage.

Feeling like a stalker, I craned my neck to peer into the side window of the house itself. Kitchen cabinetry, a spider plant, a tin clock shaped like a crowing rooster—nothing that looked familiar, and no sign of any living residents. I knocked anyway.

No answer—that figured. So I moved to the next home. This one had a grinning frog statue hidden partially behind a line of shaped hedges that spanned the front of the house. Ridiculously, the frog lofted a sign above its flat head—633. There was no fucking way I could have seen that from the road. With a rush of elation, I darted quickly across the neatly trimmed grass toward the little green two-story house that sat next door.

No number, but it had to be Marjory's.

As I approached the front door, my breath caught in my throat, the anxious spike of emotion at odds with the house's bland appearance. Curtains were drawn at all the windows, and in the gloom of dusk, the sheer fabric turned all the furniture ghostly. A festive autumn wreath hung sandwiched between the front and the storm doors, its bright plastic berries and glitter-sprayed twigs bristling against the glass.

When I tried it, the storm door was locked. Sorting through her mess of keys, I couldn't find one that fit. Unwilling to break anything yet, I stuffed the keys back into my pocket and tested the psychic feel of the entrance, looking for my usual cheat. Most doors were used so frequently that they held no existence on the Shadowside, making it possible for me to skate right through. All I had to do was find a Crossing.

Not in this case.

As I pressed my fingers against the glass above the wreath, there was only a dull emptiness. Not even a flickering impression remained. Unsettled for reasons I couldn't quite articulate, I headed around to the side of the house. Another door nestled beneath a green aluminum awning. Two fat pots of wisteria sat on either side of a shallow step, the naked runners of their vines twisting up the awning's thin metal supports. Beyond the makeshift trellis, the screen door hung slightly ajar, shifting rhythmically with the breeze so that the house appeared to be breathing.

Mindful of both Lailah's warnings and Zuriel's proven treachery, I braced the screen door open with my shoulder and laid my palm flat against the flaking paint.

Again, no impression.

Baffled, I quested for any sign of wards or other magic that might be obscuring the energy of the house. Yet again, I came up blank. Whatever Zuriel had done to scrub the place—and it had to have been Zuriel—it had been scarily effective.

Visually scanning the doorframe for inscriptions, I tested key after key until one of them fit. Relatively certain no wards were going to fry me, I closed my hand around the knob and pushed. No magic exploded—at least, not yet—and I took a halting step inside. The door opened onto a cramped landing made smaller by the crush of coats hanging from a set of pegs directly behind the entrance. Beyond the coats, stairs led down to a musty basement, a washer and dryer just visible in the patch of dim light filtering from behind me. A hamper of laundry rested atop the dryer, as if Marjory still planned to come back for it at any minute.

The hollow knock of the psychic space teased all my hackles to stiff attention. Drawing one of my blades, I moved to the basement, pulling a cord to turn on an overhead light. Nothing lurked down there but cobwebs and moldering boxes of old Christmas decorations.

Back at the top of the stairs, I followed a short flight of three steps into a cheery kitchen with white cabinets and yellow tile. Collector's plates featuring characters from the *Wizard of Oz* grinned from a display above the sink. Everything was neat and orderly, from the placement of the toaster, coffeemaker, and knife block, to the arrangement of tea tins across the back of the bread box. This made it easier to spot evidence that the police had been there.

The silverware drawer hung partly open, smudges of fingerprint dust still visible on the lip and the handle. A slot in the knife block was empty—one of the big ones, from the look of it. More fingerprint dust stood out on the wooden surface of the kitchen table. An arc of the black dust speckled one of the nearby curtains where someone had been sloppy.

The oppressive absence of psychic impressions continued from the landing, through the kitchen, and onward to the living room, dogging my every step. My ears rang with the weight of it, as if my physical senses were compelled to invent some sensation to make up for the utter void. Doing my best to ignore it, I moved methodically through each room. At every new door or archway I paused, hugging the edge to visually inspect the corners before stepping through.

The house was as empty physically as it was psychically. Even some of the furniture was missing, likely carried off to the forensics lab to aid in the investigation. In the living room, there still was some outside light filtering through the curtains, so I just turned on one table lamp. Framed photos decorated every wall, but here and there a brighter rectangle in the paint betrayed the recent absence of an image. A large square of carpet had been cut from the center of the floor.

One whole wall featured a pastiche of travel photos arranged above a glassed-in bookshelf crammed with leather bound volumes—her precious collection of travelogues. I scoured the titles, but none of them matched the time and place of Anakesiel's attack. If she'd kept the damning journal that named Tashiel, she'd stored it someplace else.

Like a safe deposit box.

That tracked—and it would be just my luck. But I wasn't here only for the journal. There were other things that nagged me about Marjory, conjectures about our connection that might have their proof in pictures.

With a thrill of trepidation, I closely studied all the photos above the shelf. The search derailed my thoughts about the journal. I was looking for something much more personal—younger iterations of my face. But no evidence of little Zack peered back at me. No Tabitha, either. A significantly younger Marjory grinned, often windswept, from all of the pictures. In many of the photos another woman's face—always the same— repeated alongside Marjory's. Stocky build, short hair, she might have been a sister. They both smiled giddily.

For a span of what looked like ten or fifteen years, she and Marjory had done everything together.

None of the photos with her were recent.

The missing photos on the other walls grew increasingly ominous—and more deliberate.

Goaded by suspicion, I moved quickly from frame to frame, intentionally avoiding the missing square of carpet. Most of the remaining photos appeared to be graduation portraits. A host of bright-eyed young people smiled stiffly, wearing suits and fancy dresses. I couldn't think of them as family images. Black, white, yellow, and various shades of brown, they couldn't all have been related. Maybe Marjory had been a teacher and the photos were mementos of every proud success.

Still no Zack, and no one I could identify with any certainty as Tabitha. Searchingly, I pressed my hand to a rectangle of paint two shades lighter than the rest of the wall. The psychic space was just as blank—as if all emotional significance had been scoured with the magical equivalent of a sandblaster.

Perhaps I'd met her as a student, or even a co-worker.

Co-workers don't get claimed as next-of-kin.

Turning toward the center, I stared uneasily at the four-foot square cutout. That had to have been where the body was found. Impressions in the carpet to either side suggested that a heavy piece of furniture had stood there—probably a sofa. So, either he'd laid her on the couch and enough fluid had dripped to make that carpet swatch useful to the police, or he'd dumped her in a heap at the foot of the sofa. Either way, the furniture itself was missing, and nothing lingered on the exposed floorboards except the hint of a brownish stain.

Accustomed to the layers of information that normally lingered on the Shadowside, I pressed my fingers to the wood. Zuriel's touch was here, too. He'd left me nothing.

Tired of all the strangers' faces staring at me from the walls, I quit the living room, passed some stairs that led upward, and moved into what appeared to be a home office. Marjory's computer was gone, but the desk appeared relatively untouched. The cops must have figured there was nothing else of use here. Removing a hemorrhoid cushion from her swivel chair, I sat down, turned on a desk lamp, and dug methodically through each drawer. Stationery, postcards, little modular baskets full of neatly sorted paperclips and thumbtacks—nothing at all unusual, but also no memory sticks or external hard drives that might take the place of the missing computer.

In one drawer, there were two stacks of old letters tied together with faded pink ribbon. Their postmarks dated to the fifties. I got excited for a minute, but they turned out to be love letters between Marjory's mother and father, neither of whom bore names that seemed to have any bearing for me. I scanned a few of them anyway. The contents were steamy, and I felt like a peeping Tom. As often as I ended up rifling through other people's business, voyeurism wasn't really my thing.

The filing cabinet seemed a safer bet. All the drawers were sealed, and I couldn't match them to a key on the ring, but the locks were cheap and easy to pick. I had the top drawer open in under a minute. Tugging the handle, the casters squealed as it swung heavily open.

The thing was packed. Marjory was an obsessive records-keeper, and the more I paged through her meticulous ranks of tax returns, utility bills, and credit card statements, the more her absence from searchable records seemed to have been orchestrated. Bobby and I had spent months trying to track this woman down, and neither of us were amateurs. We should have turned up something.

Here was an obvious paper trail—years of it. She did her taxes. She had a driver's license, social security card, even a passport. The woman hadn't been living off the grid. Someone had to have buried her records for a reason.

With my luck, it was me, I thought. It felt like the punch line to a bad joke, but all too probable. Dragging open the second drawer, I hit the mother lode—literally. Every file had a person's name, and the contents matched the graduation photos in the living room.

Marjory had been a foster parent.

Again, Marjory saved everything. The folders were alphabetical, each containing birth records, photographs, test scores for college entrance exams, and even newspaper clippings. The first file—Marlon Baylor—had Xerox copies of a high school diploma, then a Bachelor's in Science, and finally a Masters in engineering. Clippings from the student newspaper showing his name on the Dean's list. The back of the file held a graduation photo. I recognized him immediately— the young black man with wire-rimmed glasses and a shy, crooked smile.

According to her records, Marjory had fostered him

between the ages of seven and twelve, but she'd never lost contact, encouraging his pursuit of his education and, judging from some of the receipts in the file, also helping to finance it. That didn't come cheap—and I hadn't seen anything in her tax records to suggest she had that kind of money.

I didn't devote too much brain to the puzzle of where she got the funds, fixated instead on finding my own name on a file, rushing back toward the W's. This had to be our connection. In my current life, Remy had been teaching me since I was fifteen. He'd let the number slip several times in casual conversation, and I'd never asked for clarification.

Supposedly my parents lived in Kenosha, Wisconsin. How, then, had they let me come all the way to Cleveland, Ohio to learn weird things from an even weirder man?

What if they hadn't? There were no photos of them in my apartment. Nothing in my wallet. No numbers written down. Maybe they were both dead, or we were estranged.

Questions I'd been avoiding, and there were no answers to be found in Marjory's foster drawer—but I did find Tabitha, tucked all the way back in the V's. She'd started life as Tadhana Villanueva, and her picture was out there in the living room. I'd passed it up completely, expecting Marjory's daughter to be a white girl. Tabitha was mixed Asian, probably Filipina, especially with that Spanish last name.

Chastened, I studied the file to see what else I might have missed. Of all the fosters, Tabitha had stayed with Marjory the longest, beginning when she was only four years old. Curious, I flipped through the records of her life. There was the usual collection of academic paperwork—award in middle school for language and writing, first place in the regional Spelling Bee. More art than science, but lots of strong grades. Scanning forward, I expected to find report cards from high school, but a fat wad of paperwork got in the way.

In the summer between seventh and eighth grade, Tabitha had been adopted.

At first everything seemed routine—nothing in this stack could tell me Tabitha's current whereabouts—but then a name leapt out next to Marjory's, on the line marked "husband." I'd assumed she'd been married to a man named Samuel.

The name was "J. Remington Broussard."

29

I nearly choked. Broussard was my brother Remy's last name—at least, the current one. Lil still called him Remington, at least when he slipped up and called her Lillianna.

That couldn't be coincidence.

With too many bizarre scenarios vying for space in my head, I reached for my phone to call Remy. I deserved some answers about this.

"Fuck me running," I snarled. The phone wasn't in its usual place in my back pocket—I'd left the damned thing in the car, attached to the charger.

Tugging the sheet with his name out of the stack, I hastily pocketed it. He wasn't going to talk his way around this one. Slamming the drawer shut, I went back to the one that held all of Marjory's tax and personal records. If a marriage certificate existed, that was where she would keep it.

As I dug through page after page of bureaucratic effluvia, a muffled thump came from somewhere beyond the tidy office. Whatever it was, it sounded like it was inside the house.

I froze, listening, one hand drifting to the hilt of a dagger. With my other elbow, I slowly eased the drawer shut. Before it closed completely, the sound came again—a soft thump and then a clatter—from the direction of the kitchen.

If it's not inside the house, it's damned close.

Switching off the lamp, I crept to the door of the office, moving on the balls of my feet and pressing myself into the tiniest space possible against the inside of the jamb. Taking shallow sips of breath to minimize my noise, I peered around the corner to study the room beyond.

Full dark had fallen in the time I'd taken to sort through Marjory's files. I'd left the single lamp burning on a side table in the living room, and the rest was a chamber of shadows. Wan faces stared dolefully from their frames on the walls, all their grins transformed into snarls. At the mouth of the kitchen, a patch of darkness convulsed, deeper than all the rest.

Holding tight to my cowl, I teased open my psychic perceptions. It took every ounce of concentration I had to both sense that side of reality and obscure myself from it. I got nothing for my effort—whatever the fleeting shadow might have been, it left no trace upon the Shadowside. The whole of the house rang as empty as when I'd first entered.

Lailah's warning clamored in my head.

I almost drew the dagger, then reconsidered. From the sounds, whatever was out there seemed physical, but if it wasn't, the blade's arcing power would give me away as surely as a spotlight. Partly unzipping my jacket, I put my hand instead on the butt of the Legion, stopping just short of drawing the firearm.

Moving with as much stealth as I could muster given my lanky frame, I quitted the door to the office and stalked to the edge of the living room. I stayed out of line of sight from the other doorways, hugging close to the walls—using the shadows to my advantage, even though Lailah's warning made me wary.

The bulb on the lamp flickered unexpectedly and I halted, half expecting it to fizzle out with a sudden pop. Then the light steadied, just as the sound came again—a little different this time, more a rattle than a thump.

Drawing the gun, I pointed the muzzle toward the ceiling and moved cautiously forward. Despite the crowding dark in the living room, nothing spectral jumped me as I crossed closer to the kitchen. Shoulders angled to the wall, I halted just this side of the doorway, reluctant to trade soft carpet for the noisy expanse of tile. In silence I waited, struggling to listen over the thudding in my ears.

I measured a minute by the hammer strokes of my heart.

Two minutes, and nothing. I couldn't hold still any longer. With a flickering rush of motion, I swept around the corner, sighting every potential hiding spot down the barrel of my gun.

The kitchen was empty. And then—*clack, slam!*—so close, I jumped and nearly squeezed off a stray round. But I knew that sound. Aluminum and an ill-fitting screen, banging together in the wind.

To confirm, I descended the short flight of stairs to the coat-cramped landing. The basement door was still closed, just as I had left it—that was a comfort. Twitching back the checkered curtains from the window on the side door, I peered into the driveway. Aluminum banged again, practically in my face.

The screen door hadn't latched.

Feeling like an idiot, I stepped out into a night grown restless with wind. It was going to rain again. Hadn't I seen that damned screen door heaving when I'd first entered? Even so, I had to test it, just to be sure, so I pulled it back and let it bang. It was *almost* the same sound. Maybe inside the house, it had an echo.

So why were all of my neck hairs still crawling?

Staring up and down the lane, I was struck again by the stifling quiet of Marjory's street. Lights burned behind curtains in the house across the way, but otherwise, the whole neighborhood felt abandoned.

Shaking off a deep unease, I holstered my gun and turned to go back inside. The house had yet to reveal all its secrets—I still hadn't ferreted out any mention of the safe deposit box, or found a way to search for Tabitha.

Something—not a sound this time—caught my attention. I halted with the screen door part way open. Poised between the rustling vines of dead wisteria, I wavered as an odd pulse twisted the air. Faint and distant, it thrummed like the subsonic kick of bass from a car, and it spread a rancid taste on the wind.

If I hadn't come outside, I might have missed it.

The pulse faded, and I strained to catch a sense of it again. It returned a moment later, stronger this time. Gooseflesh prickled in a rush all down my neck and forearms. That pulse didn't feel like anything that belonged in the mortal world. It was something deeper, stranger, and altogether sinister.

Like a sleepwalker, I drifted away from the house and into the front yard, head cocked and psychic senses flung wide as I struggled to pinpoint the source. It wasn't Marjory's house or her immediate neighbors', but the epicenter wasn't far.

As I reached the end of the driveway, the not-sound surged again and a reflex of power crackled from the tips of my fingers all the way to the ends of my wings. From the murky depths of memory, fragments of recognition welled into consciousness—no details I could name, but a feeling as certain as the heart that heaved against my ribs.

Somewhere along this quiet suburban street, someone was working magic. And it tasted like sacrifice.

30

Guided by instinct, I turned to the left, half-jogging along the sidewalk. Porch lights glimmered up and down the lane, but all the houses were locked tight, their windows bulwarked by thick curtains drawn against the rest of the world. Throwing wide my psychic perceptions, I plucked at their brittle façades, seeking for the focal point of that awful magic. As I rushed toward the end of the street, the gut-twisting pulse grew more frequent, my boot heels thudding in counterpoint.

At the first cross street, I could tell I was close. Two homes from the end there sat a little bungalow with a FOR SALE sign staked in the yard. Faded by weeks in the sun, the grinning face of a realtor peered hopefully across the lawn. Tufts of dandelions gone to seed attested to its neglect. There was a lull in the pulse, and I almost moved on, but something drew my eye to the garage at the back of the lot.

Gotcha.

Tucked to one side of the house, a Vulcan 900 was

parked in the drive. No lights burned in the yard, so I couldn't make out the license plate, but there was no mistaking it. That was my bike.

Hugging the side of the house, I arrowed for the motorcycle. Definitely mine—right down to the decals for the Rebel Alliance over the gas tank. The engine ticked softly, still faintly warm. He must have parked it shortly after I'd started my search at Marjory's. Trailing my fingers along the grips and the handlebars, I sought hopefully for some impression left behind by Zuriel. Nothing. The bike had been psychically sanitized, just like every inch of Marjory's house.

Still can't hide whatever you're doing in there, I thought, moving toward the empty home.

The lock on the back door had been jimmied, and I took advantage of it. The door opened onto a kind of mud room, oppressively dark. Easing it shut, I waited for my eyes to adjust. No curtains covered the nearby windows, and while the dim gray filtering through them hardly qualified as light, it was better than nothing. Mindful of my heavy boots, I crept forward to the kitchen.

When I was halfway to the dining room, a staggering wave of twisted power came crashing up from the floor. Dazzling whorls of arctic light burst against my vision and I wavered, blinking away searing after-images. The basement—that had to be where he was working. I needed to find the stairs.

The house's layout was nothing like Marjory's. The stairs to the basement weren't off the mudroom or the kitchen, but they had to be close—the place wasn't that large. Every instinct clamored for me to rush, but

I forced myself to move with exaggerated care, doubling down on the layers of my cowl to hide my presence for as long as possible—assuming Zuriel didn't already know I was here.

This whole thing stank of convenience, and the trap he'd tied to Marjory had me checking every corner and doorway as I delved deeper. The pulses of power rose to a cycling rhythm, surges of sound and magic that painted weird shapes against my retinas. Trailing my free hand lightly along the nearest wall, I guided my progress by touch as much as any other sense, striving to shield my thoughts against the flickering assault.

Ahead, near a bend in the hallway, a reddish light guttered in a short line along the baseboards. At first, I mistook it for more visual bleed-over from the magic, but, when I scrubbed the back of my hand against my eyes, it stayed—candlelight spilling through a sliver of space beneath a door. The thin vein of light prickled my eyes after such oppressive darkness, and I groped blindly for the doorknob.

Finally, I pulled one of my daggers, clamping down on the spirit-fire that eagerly rose to lick along its blade. Plastering myself to one side of the frame, I eased the door open and listened. The mounting energy of the spell made my ears ring, but I thought I heard a hitch of breath and a sob—muffled, as if through a gag.

Sidling onto the first step, I peered down the steep flight of wooden stairs. They hugged a cinderblock wall to my left, blank and unadorned. Orange and gold flickers danced across its pitted surface, the candles themselves still out of sight. A plywood half-wall on the other side blocked my view of all but the bottom landing, and it had scraps of paper tacked all over it. Photos, I thought. A dark smear of crimson led from that landing deeper into the basement.

Blood. The air was thick with it—raw and dank and briny.

Blade in hand, I eased onto the first step. It creaked the instant I put any kind of weight on it. In the wake of the sound, the cycling of power abruptly ceased.

So much for trying to be stealthy. Tightening my grip on the dagger, I rushed down the steps, angling so my back was to the cinder block. I tried to sense what lay beyond that plywood wall, but the whole room was drowned in a haze of power. Here was the exact opposite of Marjory's home—a space so flooded with impressions that I couldn't separate one from the next. As I reached the bottom, the molten wax of scented candles vied with the briny tang of carnage. My stomach flipped, then clenched into a tiny, miserable knot when I saw the source of the stink.

Blood flooded the center of the concrete floor, stubs of candles puddling around it in a broad and flickering ring. In the spaces between the candles, sigils flared, so obscured by the jellied gore they were impossible to read. The grinning realtor from the sign outside sprawled in a messy heap just outside of the circle. His throat had been slit, dead eyes fixed on the ceiling in a startled accusation.

It was his blood filling the circle—it had to be, because the woman dangling at its center was still moving. Pale, limp, and silenced with a gag, she hung by her wrists from a sturdy metal pipe that ran through the exposed rafters. Loops of rope swallowed her hands in their coils, so thick the metal glint of handcuffs beneath seemed like overkill. Her shoulders strained to the point of dislocation, toes barely touching the floor. Tauntingly, a little stool tilted on its side just beyond where her feet could reach it.

"Tabitha!" I cried.

At the sound of the name, her head snapped up. Eyes racooned with a broken nose, she squinted blearily through a clotted veil of hair. Purpling bruises marred her cheeks, her jaw—she'd been severely beaten. When she finally got her eyes to focus on my black-clad form, she recoiled as if mistaking me for her attacker. Then she stilled with apparent recognition. Wild-eyed and urgent, she shook her head.

"I get it," I said. "He's close—but I've got to get you out of here."

31

Eyes peeled for any sign of Zuriel, I moved swiftly to the edge of the circle, but couldn't cross beyond the sigiled ring. The harsh prickle of magic halted me, thrumming in a palpable wall from ceiling to floor. Pressing my hand to the stinging mesh of energy, I tested the strength of the barrier. At my touch, the power leapt angrily, sending jolts of pain all the way up to my shoulder. Answering energy swept defiantly along my wings.

The circle was potent, but I'd made stronger wards. Zuriel would have to do better if he wanted to keep me out.

Hissing the syllables of my Name, I slashed my dagger across the wall of the circle. Sparks flew, a vein-like pattern flashed on the air, and a tear opened up. Tabitha yelped, eyes bulging as she stared at the lightshow. She shouldn't have seen it—not if she were an ordinary mortal. There wasn't the sort of pull I'd have felt if she was an anchor, but there was so much psychic interference, I couldn't be sure.

"Just close your eyes," I said. "I'll get through."

Aiming for the same spot I'd already weakened, I hammered the blade into the magic, my power and Zuriel's clashing in a burst of brilliance. The stench of singed blood wafted up as one of the sigils on the floor ignited, pale flames sizzling through the gore. I drove the blade forward and the sigil sputtered, burning out completely.

The runes to either side began to smoke. A third strike, and the mesh of woven will and magic shredded with an audible crackle. Ozone and scorched blood stung the back of my throat as I shouldered my way through the breach.

This close, Tabitha looked rough. Both eyes were black and swollen. Blood clotted both nostrils, and with that gag in her mouth it was a miracle she could even breathe. I reached for the dirty wad of cloth, but she flinched before I could touch her. With an insistent grunt, she jerked her bound arms until the pipe rattled. Dust rained down from the rafters.

"All right," I said, "but watch your fingers."

The rope was a Gordian nightmare, looped so many times I couldn't see how the handcuff played into the mess. That cuff was the real problem—I wasn't sure I could pick the lock—but I had to get to it first. Covering her fingers to protect them, I started hacking where the twisted strands attached to the pipe. Tabitha's skin was shockingly cold to the touch. She had to have been tied up like this for hours. As I sawed at the bindings, I kept expecting Zuriel to leap from the shadows, but there was still no sign of the bastard.

"I wish I could have gotten here sooner," I whispered.

"I'm so sorry—both for you and your mother."

I shouldn't have said anything. Tabitha's grunts rose angrily, rage and heartbreak crashing from her in dizzying waves.

"I'm sorry," I said again. "Hold still. I don't want to cut you."

She only thrashed harder. I paused my work with the dagger, and the instant I did, she twisted suddenly beneath me. She moved so fast, I had no time to react. Before I understood what was happening, she heaved herself up by the ropes at her wrists, wrapping her legs like a vise around my midsection.

"What the hell?" I choked.

Staggering beneath her unexpected weight, I nearly pitched backward. Still clinging fiercely, she pulled her hands free from the knotted bindings, slipping out of the tangle with a single, deft tug. The whole wad of rope unwound abruptly, dropping in a long tongue down to the floor. She seized a loop and trapped my upraised hand—the one with the dagger—pulling it closer to the pipe overhead. Handcuffs jangled, and even as I processed that this was an attack, she slammed the metal ring tightly shut around my wrist.

"Tabitha!" I yelled. A flare of arctic-white sigils burst in a ring around the steel restraint, sending a jolt of power all the way up my arm. My hand spasmed, and the fire of my dagger winked out as if snuffed. The heavy blade dropped from nerveless fingers, tumbling tip over pommel to clatter ringingly on the floor. I yanked against the numbing bite of the magic, fighting panic.

"What the fuck?"

Furiously, she grimaced around the gag, clinging tightly. I flailed with my free hand, still unwilling to hurt her, and she strove to catch that wrist in a second loop of dangling rope. This close, it was hard to get any leverage against her, especially with one arm already pinned above my head. With every movement, she shifted my balance, and I strove not to lose my footing in the jellied blood. It felt as if my ribs might break, and we twisted madly around the fulcrum of my trapped hand. The steel of the handcuff bit deep into straining tendons. A worrisome, bitter chill wound gnawingly down my arm.

Zuriel's magic felt... *hungry.*

Tabitha worked the gag off and sank teeth into my wrist, biting until the blood ran. Bellowing with shock and rage, I shook her off—but not before she'd looped the thick coils of rope twice around that arm. She wrapped me wrist to bicep until I had no range of motion at the elbow, and spat my own blood back in my face.

"You monster!" she snarled. With one hand, she relinquished her hold on the rope, but only so she could flail that fist repeatedly against my face and chest and shoulders. Fury made her incredibly strong. "That's for my mother," she cried. She struck blindly, knuckles thudding against bone. "And that's for me. How do you like it? How do you like it now?" She caught me on the jaw, in the eye, across the throat, still tender from the wound. I swung crazily as I dodged what blows I could.

"For fuck's sake, Tabitha, stop," I choked. "It's Zack. I'm *helping* you."

"He told me you'd say that," she hissed. The dim candles made her tears look like blood. She blinked them away as she pummeled me. "You even look like him now. I didn't want to believe it. I *didn't*!"

"You think I'm him?" I roared. "He's the one who stole *my* face." A shrilling note of urgency rose in the back of my brain, fixated on the enchanted handcuff and what it was doing. The nerveless cold spread all the way to my elbow, and a breath-stealing pressure built in my chest as its advance continued.

I needed to get free, and I needed to do it quickly.

My strength waning, I pivoted into a spin, throwing my shoulder hard as Marjory's adopted daughter came at me. I didn't want to hurt her—I only wanted to throw her off, but the blow caught her right in the center of her broken nose. Cartilage ground against bone and she made a startled huffing noise as her head rocked backward. Her ankle-lock faltered, and she hurtled to the ground.

Tabitha landed badly, sprawled on her back in the sticky morass of gelling blood. Her head whacked the concrete.

"Shit," I choked. The breath burned in my lungs. "*Tabitha?*"

She didn't move.

"Fuck," I breathed. "Fuck, fuck, fuck!" Frantically I shouted her name, caught between the urge for survival and a drive to protect her. I couldn't even tell if she was breathing. Shaking free of the rope, I clawed at the handcuffed wrist, struggling to unsheathe that dagger. It was useless. She'd snapped the handcuff around the pommel. It dug deep into my tendons, as trapped as my wrist.

A soft, slow clapping came from under the stairs. Emerging from a space he hadn't occupied before, Zuriel flickered from the shadows, wearing my likeness from heel to hair. My brain leapt several uncanny valleys. I even knew the *feel* of that lopsided grin. The laugh he brayed in the next instant ruined the illusion.

"You should see your face," he said.

"I'm looking at it."

The golf clap continued, as infuriating as his smile. "Easiest trap I ever made," he bragged. "Dangle something helpless, throw up a shitty barrier so you think it's hard, and—*boom*—in you charge like a blind fool." Dipping his head in Tabitha's direction, he gave an exaggerated pout. "I think you broke my puppet, though," he said. "Nice touch, having her try to warn you away, don't you think?"

"You sick fuck!" I snarled.

I couldn't get at my blades, but I still had my gun. The SIG was holstered for a left-hand draw. Only my right was free. I dragged it from my jacket while my doppelganger gloated. The Legion snagged briefly on the zipper, but I had it out and aimed before he could blink.

"*Boom*," I breathed and fired straight at that disgusting grin. The .45 crackled into the stairs behind him, coughing splinters to the floor. That couldn't be. I was dangling like a side of beef and shooting with my off-hand, but there was no way I'd missed that shot—not at this distance. Sighting him again, I squeezed off a second round. The gun roared and my hearing dropped to a muted hiss.

Zuriel didn't even flinch.

"You actually thought I'd be standing here," he taunted. Spreading his arms wide, he offered me a stationary target. "I'm not that stupid."

The handcuff bit deep into my wrist, throbbing every time I sought to concentrate. I shoved the pain into a box in the back of my head. Closing my eyes so I could focus on his energy rather than his appearance, I strove to sense where he actually stood in the gore-soaked room. But there was too much chaff on my psychic radar. I couldn't tell where *anything* was.

"I thought of that, too, bro." With the smarmiest fucking grin, he paced a slow circuit just beyond the puddled wax of the candles. He walked straight through the tacky edge of the pooling blood. His boots left no tread. "I thought of everything, so you're just wasting bullets, and a noisy thing like that attracts the wrong kind of attention."

"Fuck you," I spat, squeezing off another round just to spite him. It was dangerous, especially firing such big, slow slugs around all this concrete, but ricochet was as bad for him as it was for me—both of us wore mortal bodies, and his had to be somewhere.

The bullet crashed through some boxes over the dead realtor's corpse, whining off the cinder block behind them and finally hitting something that made it stop.

Sadly, it wasn't Zuriel.

"Bro, you get stupid when you're desperate," he laughed. "You want to try again? Maybe I'm in the ceiling. You got, what, eight rounds in that magazine, max? One in the chamber, if you shoot smart," he said. "Five more to go, then, maybe less. You got no reload, not with one hand."

"You have a point?"

"I've got plenty of—"

Whatever it was, I didn't get to hear.

Tabitha twitched upright with a groan, and he danced back, genuinely startled. The faintest scuff of boots came from the furnace side of the room. I heard it, just barely, over the ringing in my ears. I strained to catch any further tells, but Tabitha's hiccupping cries echoed through the room.

Flopping as if her limbs refused to work, she floundered into a sitting position. Clotted blood from the floor covered her in messy streaks.

"Hunh," he said, recovering. "Guess she has some life left."

Frantically trying to wipe away the gore, Tabitha scrabbled backward as if trying to crawl away from herself. She didn't seem to fully process where she was. A terrible keening erupted through her clenched teeth. When she reached the edge of the circle, magic crackled and she flinched away, yelping as if burned.

"Tabitha, run," I cried. "Don't trust either of us. Just pick yourself up and get out of here!"

She slumped on the floor. Inexplicably, she started tearing at the neck of her blouse. Buttons sailed and plinked into the blood. Half-exposing her breasts, she kept pulling, nails hooked to score her flesh. I yelled for her to stop, couldn't figure what she was doing.

And then I saw it, cut deeply over her sternum—a ring of sigils, just like the one he'd carved into Marjory.

The one that made a prison of her corpse.

"No!" I bellowed. Wretched loss hit in a smothering wave and white-hot fury came galloping after. My power rose sharply in response—but the handcuff bit deep, drinking everything down. Blue-white fire kindled at my hands, then sputtered. Gasping, I dragged against the thick metal pipe as my knees refused my weight.

"Shit, bro, you think I'd let her live?" He brayed nastily. "That bitch is mine now, named and sealed. How else do you think I got her to stay put long enough to trap you with that cuff?" He snapped his fingers, derisive and imperious. "Tabitha Marie Kazinsky." At the sound of her name, her head jerked up. Blind eyes stared without focus. "You lazy slut. Get off your ass and take that fucking gun. That guy murdered your mother, remember?"

Tabitha moved like a doll whose batteries were running low, limbs stiff and lurching. She dragged herself onto her hands and knees and started crawling in my direction.

"No," I breathed. Shock robbed me of any volume. The dead woman stretched stiff fingers toward my pants leg, seizing it to claw her way up my body. Slow as seduction, she pressed cold flesh against mine, reaching for the gun. "No!"

"That's it," he encouraged. "Isn't she sweet? Almost looks like she's gonna give you a kiss."

Straining from her noxious touch, I lofted the weapon above both our heads. Tabitha pawed mechanically, as if clear thought fled as her strength wound down. With nauseating clarity, all the pieces tumbled together— the taste of sacrificial magic, the spilled blood of the unfortunate realtor. He'd tied her to her corpse, but that wasn't insult enough. He'd needed to make her his ally—

willing or not. Everything in the circle was focused on animating Tabitha. The sparking wall of magic wasn't just there to keep me out. That had been a convenient misdirect. The barrier held all that spilled life force in one concentrated space, the better to channel it into her.

Dimly, I even recalled fragments of a similar spell, something that allowed murder victims to confront their attackers. Post-mortem justice. I shrank from the gruesome memory. It was my hand that scribed the forbidden formula.

Zuriel watched closely as the emotions chased one after the other. "Now you're catching up with the rest of the class," he crowed. Fighting to concentrate, I twisted on the pivot of the handcuff as Tabitha flailed weakly against me.

There was something else, just on the edge of recollection.

Something about Names.

At the core, ours never altered, but mortals were tricky. They changed their names all the time. Even when we bound them, it made them hard to control.

Tadhana.

Her name called her spirit, but Tabitha wasn't the first name she had known. I couldn't release her from his binding—not hobbled as I was—but maybe I didn't have to.

"Tadhana," I cried. "Tadhana Villanueva. Listen to me!"

"Shut up, bro," Zuriel said. "You lost her." I tuned him out, devoting all my focus to Tabitha. She groped like a malfunctioning robot, but a spark of awareness kindled in her bloodshot eyes. Before it could fade, I spoke again, breathing life and power into the syllables of her birth name.

"Tadhana Villanueva." As I worked my magic, icy agony flared beneath the cuff. I pushed past it. "He doesn't own you. No one has that power. You're bound in that body, but you still decide what you do with it."

"Idiot," he growled. "She's not going to listen to you. Far as that girl knows, I'm the one who came to her rescue. You're the one that tied her up and smashed that pretty face." He picked dirt from under his thumbnail, flicking it disdainfully toward the circle. "I've got her so twisted, she doesn't even know that she's dead."

Tabitha's brows twitched.

Dead. Bruise-colored lips tasted the word.

Yeah, that's right, I thought. *Figure it out.*

"Tadhana," I said again, but this time the handcuff's bite stole the rest of my words. Gasping, I nearly lost my grip on the gun.

"Aren't those cuffs great?" Zuriel asked. He postured on the outside of the circle, blithely avoiding direct confrontation. The gun bothered him more than he was willing to admit. "Tashiel designed them. Called them Thorns of Lugallu or some puffed-up shit like that." He strutted, confident to the point of arrogance. I strained to hear the least sign of his actual location. Nothing drifted from the direction of the furnace. "They're brilliant," he continued. "They feed on your power every time you try to tap it. Loop it right back into the spell. The cuffs get stronger, while you just fade away."

"Tadhana," I repeated doggedly. "There's a cord that

ties him to you. You'll find it, if you look."

"Shut up," he snapped. "Tell me what you did with Tashiel."

I had a few guesses, but Remy was probably the only one who knew for sure. Not that it mattered now. Another wave of agony got me in its teeth. Gasping, I locked my gaze to Tabitha's.

"Follow that cord," I wheezed. Suddenly still, she met my eyes. Hers seemed to clear. "That's how you know who's yanking your chain."

"Shut up," he yelled. She flinched at the sound, turning slowly in his direction.

"She's going to see through you," I said. "The dead know their murderers. That's how we used this ritual. Back in the day. Once they get a hold of themselves, they can feel their killer's guilt. It shines like a beacon."

"Shut up, shut up, *shut up*," he bellowed—and his voice cracked, as if he was a petulant teenager too used to getting his own way. "Tabitha, take his gun, you stupid cunt!"

She turned from him to me, blinking matted lashes.

"He lied about everything," she breathed.

With a roar of righteous fury, she wheeled and launched herself straight for the barrier of the circle. Completely airborne, she hit the crackling energy like a diver, head tucked and arms outstretched. Her fingers hooked like claws, ready to tear his face off—but as soon as she passed through the sputtering power, the life sloughed from her body as if yanked on a ripcord. In a heavy heap, she dropped to the floor, ragdoll limbs tumbling in every direction.

She came to rest against the foot of the furnace, her head twisted beneath one arm—but I had him. Following the line of her initial charge, I caught sight of the vaguest shimmer in the shadows at that end of the room. Man-shaped, it crouched in the cover of the hot water heater. Tabitha's body gave a final twitch, and that shadow recoiled.

Thumbing off the safety, I aimed for that shimmer and fired. The bullets sang off cinder block, missing the mark. My fingers trembled, further numbed by the weapon's recoil. My second shot went wild and I lost control of the weapon. The Legion clattered to the floor, going off as it struck. The final bullet whined past my kneecap, so close, my jeans singed in the wind of its passage.

Some shrapnel must have caught him. That broke the spell. Zuriel loosed a coughing yelp and abruptly flickered into view. Finally, I had eyes on my nemesis.

He was a boy.

32

"Are you even old enough to vote?" I squawked. "Shut up!"

Zuriel's face creased with petulant fury. A rangy kid, he was sixteen, seventeen tops, with a straw-colored mop darkening at the roots. He was clad in a conscious mockery of my get-up—leather jacket, black jeans, dark T-shirt—with the addition of a silver locket on a chain around his neck. I'd missed the necklace back at the gas station. The locket glimmered with strange magic, dancing motes of power that I'd only ever seen in the hands of the Tuscanetti witches.

That explained a lot. Their spells could twist perception like nobody's business. Unexpected allies for sure.

Even without the eye-tricking illusion, Zuriel's features eerily echoed my own. He had the same craggy brow and, while it hadn't fully filled out, I could see a match to my long jaw under his unshaven peach fuzz. It was like looking through an hourglass at a younger version of myself—and it confirmed everything I'd begun to suspect. Zuriel and I were twined together. Brothers who were closer than brothers. *Shalish*.

This little shit was so vile—I didn't want to accept the truth.

"You haven't even out-grown your pimples," I muttered.

"Oh, give it a rest," he snapped. "You know how this works."

"No wonder you stole my fucking motorcycle. Daddy wouldn't give you the keys to the car."

"I said shut up!"

"Come over here and make me."

"No," he spat. "You're beat, bro. I wanted to just sit back and watch you tear your life apart, but you caught that little bit of magic and yanked it back out. My bad, but I'll take this." Shoving Tabitha's fallen corpse disdainfully out of his way, he flipped over an old plastic milk crate and took a seat. He pulled a small ring of keys from his pocket, twirling them idly in one hand, then palmed them tauntingly. "All I got to do is wait. You dropped your gun. You dropped your blade. You can't get at the other one, and the spell on that handcuff is sucking your strength. You've got zero access to the Shadowside, and if you try, it'll drain you faster."

Noisily, he scooted forward on the crate, an avid look of sadism twisting his youthful features. "You've still got a hand free. Want to try breaking your thumb? It won't work, but I'll fap to the sound." He spread his knees and mimed the gesture at his crotch, keys jangling with the rhythm.

"You're a sick little fuck," I spat.

"That's not what Tabby said last night," he gloated. "I think she kind of liked it." Reaching to where she lay behind him, he seized the corpse by the hair, turning her head so her eyes stared blindly into the circle. All the life animating her was gone, but I had no doubt her soul was still in there, forced to watch and helpless to do anything about it.

"Oh, your face, Zack, your face!" He slapped his knee, braying nastily. "Why the hell do you care so much? They're fruit flies. Here and gone again." He snapped his fingers inches from the corpse's nose, then flicked her eyeball. "Like that."

"Leave her alone," I said.

"Or you'll what?"

Wordless rage erupted from my throat. It ended in a thready wheeze. He wasn't bluffing about the handcuff. A tunnel of narrowing lights chewed my vision. Gripping my trapped wrist, I put all my weight on the pipe above me. If I couldn't get out of the cuff itself, maybe I could yank it from its mooring. For incentive, I envisioned closing my hands around Zuriel's throat until his face turned purple. As I thrashed, vibrations ratcheted from one end of the basement to the other, shaking down a rain of plaster and cobwebs, some of which landed on my lashes.

The pipe barely budged.

"Fuck you," I yelled, flinging the invective at the handcuff, the pipe, my brother Zuriel, and the whole damned situation. I thumped the metal uselessly with the stinging heel of my free hand. "Fuck, fuck, *fuck!*"

"They don't build 'em like they used to. Good thing this house is old as shit," my captor said. "Ready to talk yet?"

In excruciating detail, I explained what he could do with his questions.

"And you act like I'm crude," he laughed. "No skin off my back. You'll pass out soon enough, and then the real fun can start." He tented his fingers, tapping them lightly against his lips. I could almost see the shadow of wings rising behind him in the weak, jumping light of the candles. Or maybe it was just shadows. My head was spinning. "You can save yourself a lot of pain and tell me what you did with Tashiel. I know you must've killed him, but how'd you keep him from coming back?" For an instant, his arrogant mask slipped, and all I saw was a scared little boy. His voice shrilled with hate and hurt and longing. "Why won't he come back like he promised?"

That was it, then. The reason for all of this. The kid felt abandoned and I was to blame.

If Tashiel was half as bad as Zuriel, the fucker deserved whatever I'd done.

Dryly, I cackled. "For a guy who seems to know me so well, there are some gaping holes in your recon," I said. "I don't remember Tashiel. Even if I wanted, I couldn't help."

"You don't forget your brothers," he hissed. "You can walk away because you're a spineless shit, but you *never* forget."

"Fine, whatever." I groaned. My tongue felt like it didn't fit in my mouth any more. "Torture me. Murder me. It won't get you what you want." My head dropped forward and I almost gave myself whiplash when I jerked it back up. My thoughts stumbled.

Zuriel was standing. I'd missed him getting off the

crate. Rapidly, I blinked my eyes, fighting to focus, but the room was smeared with patches of darkness. The rush of blood in my ears sounded like the flurry of soft wings.

"Oh, I'm not going to hurt you, bro," he promised. "I've fought beside you long enough to know that you don't care what happens to you." Casually, he kicked at Tabitha's corpse. "I'm going to hurt *them*. Rip them to pieces while you watch." Nastily he grinned, and the anticipation of torture gleamed with sick light in his eyes. "The priest. The cop. Even that little black chick who drools on herself."

The others were bad enough, but his mere mention of Halley threw me into a panicked frenzy. For her sake, I tried to suppress the reaction, but there was no containing the flood of rage at what this monster would likely do to the girl. Triumphant, Zuriel tapped both fists to his chest, following it up with a taunting gesture like some wannabe white gangster.

"How's my recon now, bitch?" He looked ridiculous, but the naked bloodlust in his eyes was deadly serious. Straining against the short chain of the cuff, I surged forward in the circle, screaming my fury in a language older than Western Civilization. Zuriel basked in the reaction, so pleased with himself, he didn't notice Tabitha's hand twitch near the heel of his boot.

Her fingers curled, then went limp again.

That wasn't right. Beyond the circle, nothing powered her broken flesh.

Just rigor mortis. Has to be.

Again she twitched. Zuriel caught the motion this time and glanced in her direction. His brows knit, but he shrugged to himself—dismissing it as I had—and turned his attention back to me. When he did, a shadow briefly darkened her features. My first thought was cacodaimon, then the fetid air of the cellar blossomed inexplicably with the scent of jasmine. My head filled with the muffled flight of downy wings.

That shadow came again, like a hawk in overhead passage.

Not a hawk, I thought. *An owl.*

The Lady of Shades fluttered on the edge of perception—it was her, or a hopeful delusion. I didn't know what she could do to help. My thoughts spun drunkenly, consciousness circling like water down a drain. Even so, I shouted obscenities until my lungs ached, keeping my brother fixated on me. He seemed oblivious to her presence.

Maybe she wasn't really there.

"Won't be long now," he chuckled. "You're losing it, bro." Dangling the keys from one finger, Zuriel softly applauded my failing swansong with his favorite mocking clap. Abruptly, his haughty assurance melted.

Tabitha jumped him from behind.

Lailah's owl hovered like a standard behind her—visible outside of my dreams for the first time in months. Soot-gray wings outstretched, the strigiform avatar rained a benediction of power upon the dead woman. Not godly rays of light, but a surging stream of shadows, strong and subtle as silk. Tabitha didn't need Zuriel's spell or his circle. From beyond the grave, Lailah flooded her with a memory of life.

But how long could she sustain it?

The effort stole the air from the low-ceilinged basement. The pooling candles died away, until only one remained. In a welter of near-darkness, Zuriel danced and thrashed as the dead woman wrapped an arm around his throat. Power, cold as light through a glacier, shimmered at his fingers, casting wild shapes across both their faces as he clawed to get away.

Wherever he touched, sparks trailed, raising red welts along her skin. With the plodding persistence of the dead, she ignored the pain, prying the keys from his hand. Her other arm never left his neck. Heaving air into her stagnant lungs, she whipped her hand backward and aimed for where I hung in the circle.

"Get yourself out of here!" Her voice rattled wetly.

The jangling ring of keys flew in a tall arc that brushed the rafters. Shouting incoherently, he tried to lurch after them, but she held him back, clinging with the same tenacity that had marked her struggle with me. He bucked like a mechanical bull cranked to its most dangerous setting, but she locked her ankles around him and hugged his throat. He tried to get his jaw under the crook of her elbow, but she shoved on the back of his head, keeping him firmly in a sleeper hold that robbed him of breath. The magic wreathing his fingers arced and hissed, scorching her skin, but nothing convinced her to slacken that grip.

Only dumb luck enabled me to catch the keys as they crashed into me. I missed them the first time and they smacked against my jacket, snagging on a zipper then sliding toward the floor. With a spastic movement borne of pure desperation, I slapped them against my stomach, stabbing the palm of my hand with one of the bristles of metal, but stalling their descent.

My fingers trembled as I reached for the encircling cuff, and half expected to drop the whole ring before I even got to the damned lock.

"Get the fuck off me, you crazy bitch!" Zuriel shrieked. Half the words were a garbled slur. His face was purpling, eyes bulging as he choked. A thread of spittle ran from lips to chin.

Tabitha never faltered, and I didn't feel so bad that she had handed me my ass. She was all joint locks and tricky holds—not big, but agile and tenacious. His more-than-human strength didn't count for much when she robbed him of leverage at every turn.

The sleeper hold was working. He had one of his blades out, a short, wicked punch-dagger alive with magnesium flame, but he hadn't brain enough to use it. Blindly, he stabbed upward instead of sawing at her legs or the arm still choking him. She dodged him easily, face buried safely between his shoulders.

In the light of the solitary candle, I could barely see the keyhole. Metal rattled against metal as I fumbled to hit it, but repeatedly missed the mark. Finally, I got it, but for a sick instant I feared the key wouldn't get the job done. The cuff would open, but the binding would remain, snaring me in a web of will and power until all of my consciousness drained to black.

A muffled click, and the cuff came loose.

Glinting sigils flared needle-sharp and white as winter. Power bit one last time into my arm, and the sigils faded—then the whole thing swung loose and my dead limb dropped nerveless against my side.

Nearly pitching forward, I bent to scoop my fallen dagger from the sticky floor. With one arm flopping, I had to work the blade's point into my concealed holster. Otherwise I might accidentally gut myself. It hung awkwardly inside of my jacket. The pistol I tucked at the small of my back. With all my ammo spent, it was useless.

Unsteadily, I turned toward the fight.

I had to do something.

"Don't tarry, *majnun*," Tabitha cried.

Before I could wonder at her use of that word, Zuriel fumbled something pale and small from one of his pockets. Even in the magic-saturated pall of the stinking basement, I could taste the item's thrumming power. It was a relic— one of a rare few objects that acted as a portable Crossing to the Shadowside. With the final reserves of his strength, Zuriel used it. There was a sound like ripping canvas and the air around them distorted. Then, in a hiss of shadows, both angel and corpse vanished.

Lailah's owl was nowhere to be found.

33

As the final candle sizzled to an ember, darkness choked all direction from the room. I lurched in the vicinity of the stairs only to crash noisily over a tumble of boxes. The meaty thump of my boot told me I'd found the dead realtor. At least *he* hadn't gone anywhere.

I toed him again, just to be sure. The thready giggle that erupted from my throat seemed worrisome, but I didn't have enough brain left to process the reason. Too many of my overtaxed synapses were flailing around the problem of Tabitha.

She shouldn't have gone with Zuriel. Not that it was strictly impossible for an Anakim to carry another person into the Shadowside—it was just damned difficult. But the confluence of abilities and the effort involved... I couldn't grok it. Not with those two. She should have sloughed off when he made the transition.

Maybe because she was dead already, that somehow changed the rules. Or maybe Lailah changed the rules for everyone. But the owl was gone. I couldn't ask her.

"Worry about it later and move," I muttered, less concerned about talking to myself than the breathless wheeze my voice had become. The searing numbness running from shoulder to fingers reminded me that nothing was fine right now, and I'd be royally fucked if Zuriel popped back to attack again.

Orienting off the murdered realtor, I staggered for the exit. Climbing the stairs was a little better—the choking miasma of death grew distant, along with the brain-numbing buzz of sacrificial magic. My head began to clear, though the rest of me still felt like shit. Once out into the night, I took heaving lungfuls of the cool September air, trading the stink of corpses and clotted blood for damp grass and the subtle burn of turning leaves.

I stared at my parked motorcycle, slow to process the problem it created. Its very presence was incriminating. Despite the gunfire, no sirens shrilled in the distance, but that wasn't going to last. Police would find this mess eventually, and the less evidence I left of myself, the better. Bullets and casings peppered the basement. That was bad enough. I needed to get the Vulcan out of sight and put another call to Bobby. Remy, too—especially if Bobby didn't have the traction necessary to make my presence disappear.

Remy. *Remington.*

Sensation was returning to my dead arm, but not fast enough. I couldn't ride the motorcycle one-handed. Maybe if I stashed it in Marjory's garage... Awkwardly, I slipped the bike into neutral and tried walking it to the street. I nearly dropped it before I got to the bottom of the drive. With the bum arm, this wasn't happening.

"Fuck it," I muttered, and left it where it was. Angled sideways across the drive, it was even more obvious, and there was nothing I could do about it. Digging my knuckles into the meat of my tingling arm, I continued drunkenly down the lane, finally making it to the Hellcat.

Dropping behind the wheel, I tugged the phone off its charger and called Bobby. His personal line went straight to voicemail. I hung up without leaving a message. This wasn't the kind of thing I wanted in the Cloud, and while I hated putting this through on his work phone, he needed to know what had happened out here—especially if I got myself arrested.

The work phone went to voicemail, as well.

Still ignoring me. Yeah, that was it.

It wasn't because someone had gotten to him already.

Not because he was trapped somewhere.

Or dead.

"Fucking stop," I told myself. My hands were shaking. My head wasn't working right—it felt like it had been shoved through a Vitamix. Belatedly, I stuck the keys in the ignition. Not that I should be driving, but I couldn't stay here.

Hastily, I tapped the number for Remy, switching the device to speaker and balancing it on the dash. He, at least, picked up. The instant he did, a flood of electronica pulsed from the phone, loud enough that I could have been standing right next to him at Club Heaven.

I didn't bother with a greeting.

"There's a problem with a house here at the end of the block," I said. "Basement's a horror show. Human sacrifice, circle, blood. I left bullets everywhere—"

Remy cut in sharply, raising his voice to be heard over the music. "Zaquiel, slow down. It's loud in here." The acoustics shifted as he cupped a hand over the phone. "I can't hear you clearly."

"Shut up," I said. I smacked the steering wheel with the flat of my bad hand. Jagged scissors of nerve pain cut all the way to the bone. "Just listen and shut up."

"Zaquiel, what on earth— "

I took the turn onto Westminster in a squealing arc, practically shouting over his objections. "That fucker killed her, and then he killed her daughter. Strung her up. All for bait." My voice was high and reedy. "Bait for me."

Muttering a comment I didn't catch, Remy traded the thudding bass of Club Heaven's main dance floor for something quieter—probably one of the soundproofed back rooms.

"Where are you?" he demanded.

"Parma," I said, like he should have known that.

"What on earth are you doing in Parma?" In the background, a door opened and closed, briefly filling the quiet with more dance music. A low voice, maybe one of Heaven's no-neck bouncers, asked him something. Remy was on the clock. He covered the mic completely, muffling all but a hint of his terse response. I bashed the steering wheel again in frustration. The car swerved, and I over-corrected, crossing fully into the oncoming lane.

"I went to Marjory's," I snapped. "That bastard killed her. Ripped her fingers off. I..." My air ran out. Sucking a heaving breath, I tried to remember what I'd been saying. At random, I took a turn in the rabbit warren of back streets nestling Marjory's neighborhood. None of the signs looked right.

"Marjory," Remy repeated. "Fuck." The word, from his lips, felt foreign. I had never heard him swear like that before. "Do you mean little Jory—Karl Kazinsky's daughter?"

"Jory?" I echoed. A NO OUTLET sign flashed lazy yellow blinkers. I sped past, barely registering the words. "Karl? Did he write a bunch of love-letters? Guy was kind of kinky."

It was like he didn't hear me. "Explain what's going on, Zaquiel. Start from the top," he demanded. His accent thickened the more annoyed he got—and the more worried. "Who killed Jory? And why?"

"That bastard Zuriel," I said. "He threatened all of them. Every single one."

"You're still breaking up. Did you say Zuriel? Are you absolutely sure? Does he know about Karl's connection to Sal?"

"*Sal?*" I bellowed, completely derailed. "Fuck Sal. When did that Cait Jenner wannabe get tangled up with one of my anchors?" I screeched to a stop as a blinking guardrail blocked my progress. Swinging the Hellcat in a messy U-turn, the wheels spat gravel as I punched the gas. Porch lights flicked on at one of the darkened houses. A silhouette drifted cautiously to the door, and I sped away before I could be spotted.

No one could catch me out here. So many reasons.

"What are you even talking about?" Remy asked.

"He tortured her and killed her because she was my anchor," I said. "If Sal had anything to do with that, anything at all—" Words failed as I choked on rising fury.

"When did you anchor Marjory?" Remy queried.

"When the fuck did you *marry* her?" I shot back. "Does Lil know?"

"That's nothing but paperwork," he responded. "Why would Lil care? The State wouldn't let Jory foster children without a legal husband. That's all she wanted once Samantha died."

"Sammy was a woman?" I asked dumbly.

"Zaquiel, in all seriousness, are you injured?" he persisted. "You really don't sound right."

"Thorns of the king—*Lugallu*," I corrected, but king seemed right, too. The words banged uncertainly around in my brain. A memory—disconnected with the night's events—shivered from scalp to toe. I'd encountered that magic before, or something very like it. The splinter of knowledge was buried so deep, it registered only as unpleasant emotion.

"What?" Remy's voice thundered through the phone.

"Nasty bit of magic." The shivers grew more pronounced. Comprehension remained elusive. "Still can't feel my arm. Not really."

"Zaquiel, listen to me. Is our brother still there?"

"Poofed," I answered. The car swung from lane to lane. Dimly, I realized it was me doing it. "Took Lailah. Tabitha, too." I curled both fists around the wheel, leaving the phone to skitter loose on the dash.

"Lailah? You really are delirious," he muttered. The device started to fall as I took another turn. Traffic lights gleamed up ahead. "Please, just stay put. I'm going to—"

I never got to hear him finish. The light turned red. I tried to brake, but I'd lost track of my speed. Tires screeching, the Hellcat fishtailed through the intersection.

So did a pickup sailing down the cross street.

We both laid on our horns, far too late for anything else. Remy's voice shrilled from the smartphone—all I heard was my name. I swerved hard enough to put the Dodge into a spin. The phone banged against the far window, then clattered beneath the passenger seat. It stopped making noise. Headlights, taillights arced around me in a blur. My seatbelt locked, cutting against my neck as the car banked so sharply, it nearly went up on two wheels. I thought I was going to flip right over. The brakes were useless. My foot was on the floor. A veering Honda, the rusted ass of the pick-up, a utility pole, they all swung by, way too close.

Miraculously, there was no collision.

Tires traded grass for pavement. The Hellcat lurched, then came to a stop, nose pointed into traffic. My head kept spinning for another minute or so. There was a huge neon sign inches from my door.

JESUS SAVES

I cackled madly in its yellow glow.

34

I was still laughing when the driver of the pickup appeared at my passenger side window. I hadn't seen him jog up. He was a big raw-skinned guy in a Steelers jersey. That was funny, too, but for different reasons.

Cupping one hand, he bent and tried to peer through the deeply tinted glass of the Hellcat. With the other, he rapped sharply on the window.

"Hey," he called. "You OK in there?" He seemed rattled, but unhurt. A light scrim of sweat shone greasily on his brow. He rapped again, harder. "Hello?"

I moved and the car lurched forward. With a yelp, he jumped back. Belatedly, I put the thing in park. Gingerly, he approached again, laying a palm against the window. It left a large, sticky print.

From under the seat on that side, my phone started to buzz. My seatbelt was still locked, so I nearly choked myself as I leaned in that direction. I fumbled with the strap and then the closure, finally shrugging free. At least I didn't have to wrestle with an airbag. I spilled across the seat toward his door. Steelers Guy smacked a meaty palm against the frame as I felt around on the floor for the smartphone.

"Come on, man, open up," he said. "I see you in there."

The phone stopped ringing, but then it started right back up. The vibrations rattled against something metal deep under the seat, so the whole thing sounded like a joy buzzer. Still, I couldn't get my hands on it. Only my left hand had any reach, and I could barely feel those fingers. The guy in the Steelers jersey watched my flailing contortions, going from concerned to annoyed the more I ignored him.

"What the hell is your problem?" he demanded. "You nearly killed us both." Angrily, he thumped the Hellcat's roof to get my attention. The whole car jostled. "Are you drunk or something?"

"Go away," I yelled, my voice muffled because I was halfway under the dash.

"I want your insurance information," he said.

"Go away," I repeated. For a minute, I thought had it, but all I gripped was the housing for some of the wires connected with the seat adjuster. With a grimace, I shoved the chunk of plastic back under the seat.

The phone stopped ringing. I waited for it to start up again.

"Open this thing right now, or I'm calling the police." Steelers Guy planted both hands on the doorframe, shaking the Hellcat like he meant to flip it with me inside. I banged the back of my head on the bottom of the dashboard as I jerked up to confront him.

The button to lower the window was right in front of

my nose. I jammed my thumb onto it. Before the tinted glass slid halfway down, Steelers Guy was up in my face and yelling. A long string of spittle bungeed from his lower lip and I slapped it away—we were that close.

"I warned you," I growled. All I saw was red. Then I reached up with my left hand and grabbed him by the throat. My thumb pressed deep against the startled jump of artery. His eyes bulged.

"Whoa. Hey. Shit!" he sputtered.

With casual strength, I pulled him halfway into the car. He had something I needed. I ached for its taste. His gut snagged on the door, legs kicking the side. One arm was trapped at his waist, and with it, he fought to brace himself against the frame. He struggled the other hand up to his neck, prying uselessly at my fingers.

"I got kids, man," he choked.

As his pulse flooded down my arm, I saw them. Two boys and a girl. The boys were goofy meatheads like him, and he loved them, but the girl, Chloe, she was something else. Scary-smart. No idea where she got it. Putting her through college was going to hurt—but it'd be worth every scrounged penny.

Thoughts and memories flashed like dying bulbs in my head, all his. Copper rose at the back of my throat—blood. Like the memories, it wasn't mine. All of it carried healing strength.

His name was Bruce Womack. His friends called him Goose. He'd grown up in Pittsburgh. Still loved all the teams, didn't give a damn what these Brownstown losers said. Someday, when the Nicotine Queen he had to call mother-in-law smoked herself into an early grave, he would finally take his quiet wife and his not-so-quiet boys and that scary-smart daughter whose smile blessed his every morning and return to the city of his birth.

I pulled him closer, drinking the minutia of his life. His one trapped hand thumped rhythmically against the car, slower and slower. In the mirrors of his eyes, I saw my own, a red haze clouding their blue.

No.

This wasn't me. This was the power of the Nephilim icon, reaching from its lonely resting place at the bottom of Lake Erie. I'd killed once under the influence of the Eye. That time, the artifact had saved my life, but I still couldn't justify the cost.

Never again.

With effort, I stopped myself.

"You never saw me," I hissed.

He was weeping. His face went slack. Even that was a power claimed from the Eye—an irresistible command burned directly into his mind.

With a cry of disgust—for myself, not for him—I peeled my hand from his clammy skin and shoved him bodily from the vehicle. He staggered backward, arms windmilling for balance that remained tauntingly out of reach. The imprint of my fingers shone starkly against his weathered skin, the red so deep it looked purple in the sallow light of the church sign.

His legs wouldn't hold him, and he fell with a grunt to the ground. Eyes wide and staring, he lay spread-eagled on the lawn, trembling as if the dry stretch of grass were a snow bank. A dark stain spread at the crotch of his khaki cargo pants and the scent cut sharply through the stink of burned tires still drifting from the road.

Trembling, but for entirely different reasons, I jammed my hand onto the button that sealed the window, then I threw the car into gear and peeled out of there like the Devil from every horror story galloped furiously at my heels.

I'd never met the Devil. Neferkariel was worse.

35

With desperate speed, I drove away from the scene, striving to escape my thoughts. For the first time since fleeing the basement I felt completely lucid—and it hurt. My brain replayed with punishing clarity my attack on an innocent man. The slick pallor of his face. The thudding frenzy of his pulse. The reflected light that spilled from my eyes—not Anakim blue, but crimson.

Halley's "Red Man" had stood at my back, far too close for comfort.

What really stoked my self-loathing was how good it had felt. My head was clear. The ugly burn from the handcuff was mostly healed. I hadn't checked, but I knew the instant I looked in a mirror, all the nicks and scratches from my fight with the cacodaimons would be gone. Even the gash at my neck no longer ached.

There were reasons why the Eye's temptation was hard to resist. But the cost—Bruce had been alive when I'd left him, but I had no idea what kind of lasting damage I had done. Fleeting snippets of his life still floated through my thoughts, crushing with their middle-class sameness. My attack hadn't been focused—the face of his wife, a minor scuffle between twin sons, the bright gifts of his daughter Chloe. How much would the poor guy remember?

Can't go back and fix it.

The thought was empty consolation.

Chased by my guilt—for Bruce Womack, for Tabitha, for Marjory—I picked streets at random, pushing the Hellcat as hard as I dared just to feel the thrum of its power. It didn't help. As soon as I saw signs for the highway, I started across town toward Club Heaven. I needed to talk to Remy before anyone else died because of Zuriel—or me.

Driving almost as fast as my raging thoughts, I crossed from Parma to the Flats in record time. The twin smokestacks of the old Powerhouse jutted darkly against the distant city lights. Rising beyond the industrial fossil, the uplit struts of the Detroit Avenue Bridge glimmered above the curving expanse of the Cuyahoga. The black waters of Cleveland's infamous river trapped a shivering double of the gleaming landmark in their silty depths.

At this hour on a weekend, there was no parking left on any of the narrow streets. I swung around to the main lot. A placard sign declared SPECIAL EVENT RATES, so of course, the cost was doubled. Digging out my wallet, I grabbed a ten and a twenty to pay the bored attendant.

As she slid open the window to her glassed-in booth, the sounds of a captured Pokémon erupted from her phone. Guiltily, she flipped the screen over—as if anybody cared what she did to pass the time all night.

I handed her the money, got a five back as consolation, then pulled forward when the white and orange bar lifted jerkily out of my way. The lot attendant returned eagerly to her game.

The place was packed, and it took several passes up and down the crowded lanes to find a space for the Hellcat. I ended up far from the crimson awning of Club Heaven, wedged between a Caddy and a Tesla.

Before I locked up, I remembered to finally dig my phone out from under the seat. Remy had called half a dozen times. No voicemails, but he'd sent a brief flurry of texts, his typing as precise as his accent.

Are you all right?
Pick up your phone.
Pick up, Zack.
Tell me you're all right.

The last had been sent nearly thirty minutes ago. I raised my thumb, considering a response, but then I stopped. No point. I stood practically at his door.

Arming the alarm, I began the trek across the weather-warped asphalt. The lot was strewn with the detritus of debauched weekends—crushed cigarettes and shattered beer bottles, the dented canister of a whippet, and a pair of women's panties hanging from a fence post like a flag. Whether they flew in triumph or surrender was anybody's guess.

A chest-rumbling throb of dance music spilled from Heaven and into the night, reaching my ears long before I made it to the club's doors. Sure enough, a thick-necked bouncer leaned idly against the bricks, his smart black suit and crisp white shirt making him look like an extra from a Bond flick. I recognized the guy immediately from Sal's usual stable of goons—he'd been in the fight aboard the *Scylla*. I hadn't been near Club Heaven in close to a year, but Captain No-Neck clearly recalled my charming face.

"Westland," he said, no effort to hide his disgust. I wasn't in the mood to be nice, either.

"Ivan," I said. "Or was it Derek." His thick brows beetled with annoyance. "Boris, maybe? All you blood-fed meatshields look alike."

He extended a calloused hand that could have easily palmed my face. "Gimme your ID and shut the hell up."

"I'm the boss's brother. Both of them," I said. "You still need my ID?"

He sneered. "Around here, we follow the law."

I cackled. "Yeah, right." Flipping open my wallet, I played along for the moment, holding the flap with the ID out where he could see it. "That's my face, that's my name. You know I'm older than any of those numbers on that birth date, so stop fucking around and get out of my way."

"Take it out of the plastic," the bouncer instructed. Meanwhile, he waved through a pair of obviously drunk women in clinging black microdresses. They couldn't have been more than twenty.

"You've got to be kidding," I grumbled. I moved to comply, and then just lost it. I didn't have time for his passive-aggressive bullshit, not from a guy my sister held on the same level as a well-trained fighting hound.

Normally, it didn't pay to argue with Sal's security staff. Her bouncers weren't just big, they were also hyped up on Nephilim blood to the point that they barely qualified as mortal. I'd thrown down with a couple of them, and they hit like runaway freight trains.

But after everything else tonight, I didn't fucking care. I got right up in his flat slab of a face.

"You were at the *Scylla*," I said in a hiss. "You know who I am. You know what I can do, and you know what I've survived." He didn't give ground, but his pupils opened wide with a growing flood of adrenaline. Maybe because I'd so recently used the Eye, I could smell the tang of it rising from the blood that jumped at the big artery in his neck. Digging half-moons of hurt into my palms, I clenched my fists and held them rigidly at my sides, fighting to control what I really wanted to do—drain him fucking dry. "I've got business in the club, and I'm going in whether you like it or not. So what you have to ask yourself is how much pain do you want to be in by the end of this conversation?"

Cords straining on his neck, he leaned into my threat, so close, our foreheads nearly touched. I could hear the angry grind of his teeth. His jaw ticked with a barely suppressed impulse to clobber me and then—amazingly—he retreated. Unclipping a walkie at his side, he thumbed the button.

"I got Westland at the front," he barked. "Wave him past the metal detectors once he's inside."

A garbled voice chattered in response.

"Metal detectors?" I inquired. Those were new.

He fixed me with a broiling glare. "Someone shot

the place up about a year ago."

"Wasn't me, and you know it." Striding past him, I stuffed my wallet into my rear pocket and headed beneath the awning. He shouted at my retreating back.

"She's been waiting for you, Westland." From his lips, it was a threat.

I just kept walking. Dealing with Sal was the price of dealing with Remy. But if it led to answers, it would be worth it.

Beyond the double doors, the entrance had been completely remodeled. Gone were the velvet ropes and stained curtains that barely covered the chips in the walls. A daunting chamber of brushed chrome, sweeping columns, black granite, and backlit sections of pebbled glass brimmed wall-to-wall with equally elegant people. Metal rails sunk into the floor corralled their advance toward the blinking monolith of a metal detector—painted with flowing scrollwork so that, somehow, it added to the slick attraction of the room.

Suited security staff, the Nephilim anchors immediately apparent, moved the crowd through the line so no one stood in one place for more than a few seconds. Pocket knives, lighters, chain wallets, and other weapons were located, removed, and politely presented to their owners, all of whom were given the option either to return the items to their cars or to pay an additional fee for a private locker.

Almost everyone paid for the locker. At twenty bucks a pop on top of admission, Sal had a regular racket going.

One of the suited security staff—another beefy lug I recognized from the *Scylla*—waved me over, walkie still gripped in his hand. Skirting the milling crowd, I made my way to his station. The special treatment earned me more than a few dirty looks, especially the way I was dressed. All the coiffed millennials in line sported their club-kid best and, to them, I probably looked two steps from homeless. More self-conscious than I wanted to admit, I put my head down and tried to ignore the prickling heat of their eyes. My beef wasn't with these mortals. To Sal, they were food and cash flow—nothing more.

For Remy it was different, and I was confronted with a poignant reminder of this as I joined No-Neck No. 2 at the front of the line. In a place of honor upon the wall between two strips of lighted glass hung a series of framed photographs. Front and center was a woman whose face I would never forget.

Her name was Alice and she'd worked the door. Anchor or lover to my brother Remy—I'd never thought to ask, although I knew he'd helped arrange her funeral— she'd been one of several casualties in the shooting last year. All were victims of a pair of cacodaimons that had rushed the club while skin-riding the bodies of two murdered cops. The shooters had come for me, but, along the way they'd delighted in ventilating as many people as possible.

The glass on either side of the photos slowly shifted through a soothing spectrum of pastels, a real change from the usual goth palette of Sal's kink bar. Battery-powered votives flickered from little holders in the frames, casting soft illumination across the memorialized faces of guests and staff. I took a few quiet moments to study them each—Alice, the bouncer, one of Sal's human pets, and three other club-kids who I'd only seen in passing at the time.

As the gunfire and adrenaline rekindled in memory, I redoubled all my shields. Sal could build over the bullet holes, she could scrub the blood from the floors, but there was no way to erase the horror of that night. Screams still echoed beneath the pulsing music, at least to my Anakim ears. In the fabric of the Shadowside, the event replayed in an endlessly stuttering loop, layered among the strata of other violent encounters— some supernatural, others tied to mob-hits and similar criminal-world clashes.

Club Heaven was nearly as old as Sal's influence in this town, and within its walls she had played a long and very dangerous game. There were always consequences.

"Come on, get moving," my burly escort said. With the gravel in his voice, he could've moonlighted as a sandblaster. He preceded me into the main room.

The dance floor was a crush of people—unsurprising for this time on a Saturday night. Beautiful men and women ground hip to hip and cheek to cheek alongside other stunning people who seamlessly filled the spaces between the binary. In Sal's club, gender could be as changeable as eyeliner. No one asked and no one cared. They groped and pawed and kissed in the flickering sea of lights and music, drunk on one another's flesh. Those not dancing were packed five deep at the bars.

Overwhelmed by the gyrating mob, I pulled into myself, loathe to touch or be touched—especially with the power of the Nephilim icon still singing in my veins. The bouncer cut a swath straight through the dance floor, giving no shits who he shouldered aside. I wasn't so lucky—the crowd clove together immediately in his wake, and a few of the club's pleasure-seekers sought to grind into me.

I warned them away with a look.

Finally, we reached the far side of the main floor. The observation deck still jutted partway up the back wall. Like the main entrance, it had been remodeled, the industrial steel of its railings replaced with twists of wrought iron and an ornate balustrade that matched the rich wood of the dueling bars. The platform had been expanded to fit a row of little bistro tables, two seats apiece, and these were arranged alongside the railing to facilitate people-watching.

The door leading to the back rooms—the real bread and butter of Club Heaven—remained unchanged. Black and imposing, it was guarded by a burly security staffer who stood so motionless beside the frame, I almost missed her. Chin high, eyes forward, she held her post like a soldier at attention. Her suit jacket hung open to clearly reveal the gun she wore at her side.

No-Neck No. 2 guided me up the stairs to his female counterpart. In flats, she stood easily as tall as me. She wore her dark hair twined tightly in a wealth of skinny braids, all of them gathered into a ponytail that hung heavily past her shoulders.

"Caleb," she said, nodding curtly. Her voice was raised to carry over the pounding of the music. It was deep for a woman and jazz-singer smooth.

"Tanisha, this is Zack Westland," my escort said. He leaned close so she could hear him as he dropped his voice. "Take him back to the sanctuary." Her eyes flicked immediately to the bulge where my second dagger hung awkwardly inside my jacket. I'd never thought to move it, even after I got feeling back in that arm.

"You already frisk this guy?" she asked, incredulous.

"No, they didn't, and I'll save you the trouble," I said. I slipped my hands from my pockets and held my arms out to the sides so she could see everything, if she wanted. "I've got two knives and a gun and no, you can't have them."

The words were hardly out of my mouth before Tanisha surged forward, all flashing eyes and gritted teeth. She went straight for where the blade sagged against my jacket. I brought an arm up to deflect her grasping fingers. In a blur of movement, Caleb stepped between us. Nephilim speed. He shoved Tanisha back a step. A brusque shake of his head warned her against any further outbursts.

"This one's family. He keeps the weapons."

She bristled. "Do they want more trouble?" she snapped. "Because that's how you get trouble, and how people get dead." Her hand lay on her firearm, and never wavered.

"I'm usually the one getting shot at," I said, finally returning my blade to its sheath. "If that happens, you'll be happy I'm armed." She speared me with a look one might reserve for an unstable crate of dynamite masquerading badly as a human.

"Just take him back to the boss," her co-worker advised. The weary note to his voice suggested this wasn't the first time she'd wrangled with him over a point. I wondered how long she would last—and what the fuck she was doing guarding the back rooms.

Not my circus, I reminded myself.

"Fine," she choked. As soon as he had passed me off, No-Neck No. 2—aka Caleb—turned on his heel and started walking away. Tanisha's lips flattened and she glowered at his retreating backside. "Always got me baby-sitting," she grumbled.

"I promise not to explode," I quipped.

She gestured sharply as she got the door. "You walk in front," she instructed. "If you pull a weapon on me, I put you in the hospital. I don't care who you know."

Stuffing my hands back into my pockets, I ambled past her into the familiar black-on-black-on-black vestibule. Leather couches, silver spatter—some things in Heaven hadn't changed. As I stepped across the threshold, a shiver gripped me from top to toe. Even with all my shields held tight, Alice's face flashed before my eyes. This was the very spot where she had died— trying to escape the shooters and get to Remy.

I'd stood beside my brother as he'd cradled her staring corpse.

"What's your problem?" Tanisha demanded. From a pocket inside her suit, she withdrew a keycard. This lounge was little more than an airlock between the public club and Sal's preferred domain. They'd gotten smart and locked it up tight. The last time, there had only been a guard on the door.

He'd died right after Alice.

"Probably better if I don't share," I responded.

With an unhappy grunt, she swiped the keycard and

held the door. "Then how about you move?"

We strode in silence through the maze of back halls, floors, walls, and ceilings all painted black. The only relief was the red on the doors—and there were a lot of them. This portion of Heaven could have passed for a hotel, if not for voyeur-friendly windows and extensive collections of bondage equipment.

She-Hulk didn't bother with small talk, and I wasn't up for it, either. Every step spun me with another sucking wave of déjà vu. Here was where I'd first talked with Remy—really talked, about our different natures and our tangled past. Here was where I'd almost caught the second cacodaimon.

By the time we reached the one door without a number, my palms were slick and I felt ready to jump out of my skin. It wasn't fear, exactly, just a useless wash of adrenaline. Triggers upon triggers lined these otherwise anonymous back hallways and my night had been shit already. My shields took the edge off any psychic impressions, but I had no fix for the storm of sensations roiling inside of my head.

"If you're gearing up to kill my boss, I'll have a bullet through your skull before you can blink," Tanisha promised.

"I'm not." It was barely a breath. I dragged my hands from my pockets and forced myself to keep them open harmlessly at my sides. I didn't turn around to check, but I was pretty sure Tanisha already had her gun out and aimed.

Then the door opened and I stood before Sal for the first time in almost a year.

36

All of my siblings were tall, but Sal was a giantess. Easily six-foot-six in her bare feet, she wore a strappy set of five-inch stilettos, a thong of matching white vinyl—and nothing else. Quickly, I fixed my eyes on her face, the black and red room a dim blur behind her. Six-three myself, I still had to look up. Even ducking, the shoes brought Sal's head to the top of the door.

"Zaquiel," she smiled, and didn't bother hiding her fangs—or anything else. An awkward flush crept over my face. Sal didn't miss it. She only grinned wider. "I'll take it from here, Tan. You're dismissed."

The muzzle of the bouncer's gun brushed the hairs on the back of my neck. "He's still armed, ma'am," Tanisha objected.

Tickled by this, Saliriel laughed expansively. Rich contralto notes echoed up and down the corridor. From my position, I had a great view of her pointy little teeth. It was that or stare straight ahead at the jiggle of far more unnerving attributes.

"If I feared any weapon this one might bring to bear, I wouldn't tolerate his presence in my city," Saliriel said. Languidly, she extended a manicured hand and laid it gently on my shoulder. The gesture appeared almost fond. I fought not to dash it away like a giant, white spider. Sal wouldn't take kindly to the insult, and I had no desire to waste time salving her mood. She was hard enough to deal with as it was, and I wanted to get this done so I could grill Remy. "Step inside, dear brother. It's been far too long," she said. "I'm certain we have much to talk about."

Tanisha didn't easily relent. "I still think I should stay near at hand, ma'am," she insisted.

Holding very still, I fully expected Sal to lunge over me and backhand the new guard for her insubordination. My sister didn't tolerate anyone questioning her whims.

Tanisha, somehow, was different.

"Stand outside the door if you'd like," Saliriel said. She waved one hand with exaggerated dismissal, the other still laying against me. "But once the room is clear, make certain no one else comes in. My discussions with my sibling are private. Understood?"

"Yes, ma'am," Tanisha replied with crisp formality. She had to come from a military background. She had that vibe.

Nodding absently to her underling, Saliriel slipped her hand from my shoulder—but not all at once. It was a protracted gesture, nails gliding audibly along the textured surface of the leather. Despite the jacket, I could distinctly feel the caress and fought hard not to jerk away. Sal maintained a pretense of obliviousness, all the while watching eagerly from the corner of one eye.

Once her hand dropped away, she sighed lightly and glided a few steps away from the door. With the towering figure of my scantily clad sister no longer blocking the entrance, I finally got a good look at the room. The last time I'd been here, the place had been empty, except for two rows of red pillars drawing the eye to an honest-to-whatever-gods-you-worshipped throne.

The throne was still there, perched upon its dais at the far end, with the pillars leading up to it, but the room was far from empty. The roughly fifteen-by-twenty foot space brimmed with people, most of whom I hardly parsed as living things because they held still as statuary. Naked save for strategic bits of chain, rope, velvet, or leather, they posed as ashtrays, tables, chairs, even candelabras, complete with lit tapers blazing from elaborate headgear—and other places.

With one imperious clap, Sal brought the whole room to attention.

"Out! Everyone."

People scurried and the furniture came alive, chairs and stranger arrangements deconstructing as their living components fled. Two among the company collected candles and other decorative objects from the backs, heads, and orifices of their companions, wiping them down and stowing them with rushed efficiency in a chest built into the base of the throne.

Their tableau dismantled, Sal's stable of playthings filed silently to the door. I stepped briskly to one side—the side opposite Sal. Swatting some asses for motivation, Saliriel shooed her pets into the hall. I tried not to stare at the parade of skin, but my brain picked restlessly at the mechanics of living furniture, and how any of them could have possibly enjoyed holding motionless for what might have been hours.

My sister had some weird hobbies.

"Tanisha, be certain that none of them linger," Saliriel instructed. "If any disobey, collect their names and report them to me once I'm finished."

The bouncer's chin dipped in brisk acknowledgement. "Of course, ma'am." If the woman found any of this disconcerting, she did a hell of a job hiding it.

Once the last shivering plaything had scurried out the door, Sal slammed it shut with a bang. Still naked except for those heels and the shiny triangle of panty, she strode close enough to pin me against the wall. We didn't touch, but we didn't have to—I pressed myself against the bricks in squirming reflex.

"It took you long enough," Sal said witheringly. "You, my sibling, are stubborn to the point where I may need to invent a new word."

"Obstinate," I offered glibly. I couldn't help myself. Her eyes glowed with unmasked fury and I refused to flinch. My neck started to kink as I looked up. "Unyielding. Obdurate. Obstreperous—that's always a good one." For months, I'd rehearsed this impending confrontation, but in none of my most bizarre imaginings had it played out with her so disconcertingly naked.

Pink lips curled nastily in response. "How about, 'stupid,'" she said. "Foolhardy." She rolled the syllables decadently upon her tongue, sucking their taste. From her towering advantage, she leaned ever closer and

I resigned myself to the inevitable crush of silicone implants high against my chest—there was only so far I could shrink into the wall. "And, dare I say it," she added, "self-destructive."

If she pressed any closer, I'd be seeking therapy. Before that happened, she whirled abruptly on her heel and strode to the other side of the room. Every toned muscle in the long columns of her legs worked visibly beneath pale and flawless skin. Once at the throne, she draped herself across its ornately carved expanse, legs dangling casually over one of the arms.

"I want to hear it like you mean it, Zaquiel."

"Hear what?" I responded, peeling my back from the bricks and restlessly resettling my wings. The walls of Heaven were more solid than most places, and my not-exactly physical appendages felt slightly crushed. I took a few halting steps toward the dais where she lounged, bristling against this delay.

"Your apology," she prompted.

I almost spit on her. The response was so instinctive, so immediate, I barely managed to hold it back.

"Never," I choked. She regarded me from under a nest of fake lashes. Her eyes were yellow, like a cat's, and they held the same predatory glare—infinitely patient and calculating. Squaring my shoulders, I met her look head-on. "I came to talk to Remy," I said. "Where is he?"

My sister didn't blink, but slowly she shifted her gaze away. With deliberate inattentiveness, she stretched one long leg, minutely regarding the shell-pink polish on her toes.

"Very few are given such an opportunity to redeem

themselves, Zaquiel," she said. "Don't underestimate my anger, should you waste this very gracious gift."

"Oh, get over yourself." It took all I had not to charge to the end of the room and cut the unctuous look from her face. She smiled like she knew it. All of this was a game to her, one I was terrible at playing. She knew that, too. "You want to talk about anger?" I demanded. "Do you have any idea how much that oath of yours has fucked with my life?"

"Zaquiel," she cooed. Idly, she fluffed the tinseled mass of her platinum hair. "It's not as if anyone forced you into it. That oath was your choice."

"You cut a pretty thin line between choice and coercion," I said.

Sal was off the throne in an eyeblink, her demeanor flipping from casual insouciance to acid-spitting rage in less time than it took her to cross the room. Golden fire kindled in her eyes, and she loomed inches from my face, one long finger jabbed painfully into my chest.

"I am not the one who reneged on their word," she hissed. "You promised me the Eye, and you have yet to deliver. We've avoided a confrontation only because I have allowed it." Her voice dropped to a hiss. "No more."

Naked or clothed, Sal was terrifying, especially this fast and this close, yet in the face of all that fury, I surprised myself by holding my ground.

"That thing is at the bottom of Lake Erie," I said. My left hand spasmed as the scar on that palm writhed like a serpent burrowing beneath the skin. Sal's eyes locked on the motion. A chilling smile—nothing like her usual haughty affectation—played at the edges of her lips.

"Is it, now?" she said, holding her face in front of mine, statue-still and creepy as fuck. She didn't breathe. She didn't blink. A chasm of centuries yawned in those pale, yellow eyes and I could practically see the wild ticking of gears in their depths. That feral smile, hungry and inhuman, widened in a flash. All at once, she was moving. She stalked around me in a winding circuit, the click of her heels measuring out their own creeping version of time.

"I can't say what I find more insulting, Zaquiel," she intoned. "That you think I believed you the first time, or that you continue to sell me the same, sorry lie." Like a wolf or a vulture, she continued to circle, the white expanse of her porcelain flesh no longer a distraction. All my focus narrowed to the tension that vibrated down the wiry muscle in her arms, the subtle flick of her gaze as she decided exactly when to pounce.

My own muscles sang with adrenaline, but I held still, waiting to see how this would play out. At last, Saliriel came to a stop in front of me. She didn't pose or get up in my face—not this time. Instead, she held herself loose, as ready as I was for this to erupt into a deadly fight.

"I know you have it." Her voice was a low, inhuman growl, three separate tones at once. "I can smell it on you. I could feel the clinging tendrils of its power the instant you walked into this club."

Mutely, I met her yellow gaze and knew this for a precipice. However I jumped, there was no going back, and the bottom stretched so far out of sight, there was no predicting the fall.

I made my decision.

With fingers that trembled more with shame than with fear, I slowly unclenched my left hand. So there was no mistaking my motion for an attack, I lofted the hand by stages, palm open where Saliriel could see. All the while, the scar ticked and jumped as if it sought to tear from my flesh. A wet heat like blood rushed all down that arm.

"I'm not lying," I said. "But I'm still fucked."

37

"You didn't," she breathed.

"Sorry to say, I did." A little tremor gripped my splayed fingers, but otherwise the lurching of the scar had stopped. I kept the guilty hand raised between us, a rigid gesture of both surrender and salute. Adrenaline drove my heart, its hammer-strokes measuring not fear, but stark relief.

No more hiding anymore, at least not from Saliriel—not on this.

My sister hovered in that gelid pose I'd come to expect from the Nephilim, as if she'd forgotten she had a body. As she digested my revelation, the leaping rush of her thoughts was too great a distraction.

"Do you have any idea what you've done to yourself?" She'd forgotten to breathe, so the words were little more than a hoarse whisper. Shock drained all of her threat. I let my hand drift loosely to my side. Goaded by her failing, I took a deep breath and slowly puffed it out. Then I did it again. I felt steadier for the process.

"I've had a few hints," I admitted. I didn't elaborate. It took real effort to meet her cat-like gaze. "But I didn't come here to bare my soul, Sal. I really need to talk to Remy."

Saliriel also struggled to regain her composure. The ancient mind that peered from beneath her sculpted features already ticked ten scenarios ahead of anyone else.

"Remy's not here." This time, she remembered to breathe. Life returned by stages to her porcelain limbs, and I saw her body as I thought she must—a pretty manikin she happened to ride, useful to a point, but completely disconnected from her true self.

"When did you plan on telling me this?" I demanded. She rolled a naked shoulder, seamlessly resuming her mask.

"Whenever it became convenient, brother mine."

"That's just great," I snarled. "The Eye's old news, Sal. I've got more pressing problems. Things that can't wait—"

"If you think, for an instant, that the Eye is not a pressing concern," Sal hissed, "then you are far more foolish than I have ever assumed, Anakim." With blurring motion, she reached for my arm. I tried to jerk away, half a second too late. Her fingers—cold as iron and stronger by far—dug into the tendons at my wrist. Mercilessly, she bore down on a pressure point until my hand flopped nervelessly open. Unnerving in her focus, she peered at the scar, and all I could think was how much she looked like a hawk about to snap up her prey.

"Why?" she asked. "Why would you even do this to yourself? You've never been one to seek power, Zaquiel, not for ages. Why this? Why now?" As she spoke, she shook me, rattling my arm until my teeth clapped together with transmitted force.

I almost didn't tell her—Sal would certainly use every morsel of information against me, but the secret was out, the big one. No point in clouding the waters with omissions and half-truths.

"Dorimiel stole everything from me with the Eye, Sal," I said. "My life, my memories, every bit of useful knowledge accumulated over millennia of existence." My voice hitched as I staggered in the enormity of the admission. Because of her oath, I'd had no genuine recourse to talk about this to anyone—not my guilt, not my fears, and certainly not my pain. For a moment, I couldn't even go on. My chest tightened as the events on the lake came flooding back—Dorimiel's final attack, Lil's last-minute intervention, my breakneck decision to claim the Eye.

"I could have let that all go, but he'd taken Lailah," I said. "Only Dorimiel knew the passphrase that would release her soul from its prison. I saw no other way to take it from him."

Saliriel shoved me away with a cutting hiss of disgust. Hands fisted in her teased mass of platinum hair, she paced before the dais of her throne, white stilettoes striking the tile in a series of resonate whip-cracks.

"Oh, you stupid, noble, sanctimonious fool," she cried. "Your whole tribe are the blood-drenched, breathing embodiment of that mortal saying about the path to hell."

"Sal," I objected. "He wasn't just dying as I chased him. You saw it. He'd fed on the power of cacodaimons. Their darkness was eating him from the inside out. Any hope to free Lailah and the others was going to sink into the void." It was a sight I couldn't bring myself to describe, all those black and glistening bodies surging from the depths. Dorimiel had called the cacodaimons his new brothers, and the swarm had swallowed him whole.

"What was I supposed to do?" I asked.

"Not. That."

The phone in my pocket buzzed and I jumped as if struck with a cattle prod. One short burst of vibration. Not a call, then, but a text. I remembered Remy's flurry of worried messages, all left unanswered. My hand went to the phone, but I stopped just short of checking it. A sick suspicion—irrational but nagging—clawed from the depths of my brain.

"Where is Remy?" It was a simple enough question, but my voice wavered. My grip tightened on the unchecked phone.

"That again?" Sal demanded.

"Humor me," I said. "I'm stupid, remember?"

"I don't know," she said. "He left."

"When?"

"Zaquiel, I don't monitor his every move."

"Pull the other one," I said. "He's your lackey. You keep track of him. I know you do." In my pocket, the phone buzzed again—a reminder for the text. While Sal dithered around her answer, I slipped the device into my hand. Polite or impolite, I couldn't wait any longer. I had to see.

Remy's name flashed on the screen, but the message was nothing he would write.

ru santa, bro?

My blood ran to ice. Hurriedly tapping my passcode, I stared at the foreign syntax, struggling to decipher its import. Remy's name gleamed atop the text. His number, no doubt. Another message buzzed through even as I studied the first.

cuz u giftwrapped this for me

Dumbly, I fixed on the glowing letters. I couldn't breathe. Sal took my slack expression completely the wrong way.

"You dare insult me with your inattention?" she bellowed. Striding purposefully, she curled her talons to strike the phone from my hand.

Another buzz. Another message. This time, a photo, dim, unfocused. There was so much glistening red, my brain at first refused to parse the face beneath. One sunken eye, azure as the waters of a tropical cove, bulged at the center of the grainy image.

"Fuck," I breathed. "Fuck, fuck, fuck." Faster than Sal could slap for my hand, I shoved the phone in her face.

"What is it now?" she snarled, reeling back from the glowing screen.

"He's got Remy."

The world dropped away.

38

Sal peered minutely at the screen, so close, the blood-drenched image reflected perfectly in the narrowed pupils of her eyes. Spitting like an angry hunting cat, she ripped the phone from my grip, brought it closer, stared some more. She knew as well as I did the startled, inhuman blue of that central feature—probably better.

"Who?" she demanded. "Who dares to threaten what is mine?"

"Zuriel." The Name shivered on the air, cold as his power.

"One of yours," she spat. "Typical."

"Spare me the history lesson," I said. My palms were slick. Restless, I wiped them on my pants legs. "We don't have time for it. This guy's not fucking around."

"Clearly," Sal observed acidly. She looked as if she was going to hurl the slim rectangle of smartphone, but then handed it back with exaggerated care. No further texts came through on the glinting screen—Zuriel had made his point, and thoroughly. I started to type a

MICHELLE BELANGER

response, but what good would it possibly do?

Sal caught the motion and shook her head.

"Don't," she cautioned. Without another word, she turned and strode to an alcove behind her throne. A slim door was set into the wall against one side. She did something to the handle—nothing related to a punchcode or traditional lock—and it swung soundlessly inward. Heels clacking sharply, she disappeared into the shadowed interior. No lights flicked on, but then, Sal didn't really need them.

I didn't even bother to ask what she was doing. Instead, I studied the brutal image on the screen, blowing it up so I could examine every gruesome detail.

Zuriel had been smart. It was a close-up, intentionally angled, just enough for recognition. The bloodied section of Remy's face filled the entire picture so no hints of his surroundings were visible. Without a background, I had no clues on his location. Tilting it this way and that, I tried to glean any useful data from the taunting picture. The lighting suggested another basement, but even that was pure conjecture, based solely on where Zuriel had kept Tabitha.

Killed, I reminded myself. *Where Zuriel had killed Tabitha.* A shiver of guilt swept over me, laced with the bitter bite of sorrow and, with effort, I shoved it away. Guilt was useless, for as much of it as I carried, and the dead I could mourn later—once we'd kept my soft-spoken brother from joining them, piece by piece.

Which raised a very salient question.

"What I want to know," I called to my sister, "is how can Remy look so rough?" Only vague rustlings came forth in answer, followed by the sharp sound of a zipper. She was getting dressed. Finally. "I've shot you guys. Bullets are like bee stings," I continued. "Not even. That's a fuck-ton of blood. He's immortal—next best thing to a vampire. Shouldn't he be healing?"

Sal emerged from the little side room and I almost lost track of my question. From neck to ankle she was clad in heavy, skin-tight leather. The clinging catsuit had a futuristic look, with jointed sections of body armor attached above and beneath her ample chest, down the arms, along the hips. The sectioned armor had a rib-like pattern that made it look like she had killed an Alien queen just to skin her for her chitin. Similar sections of xenomorphic armor ran all down the back of the suit, following both the shape and placement of Saliriel's long spine. I had no idea where the suit hid its zipper—it wasn't visible.

Producing a smooth, black hair tie from who knew where, Saliriel swept her bleached blonde mass into a severe ponytail, completing her transformation into Battle Barbie. The effect was only intensified by a sturdy pair of over-the-knee boots, as armored as the body suit. Like the strappy heels they'd replaced, the boots sported wicked stilettos, steel-bright and gleaming.

"Heels?" I said, momentarily at a loss for anything more coherent. "Don't you have sensible footwear?"

Sal's response was to sweep one leg in a vicious, blurring roundhouse. The heel sliced the air at roughly throat level and could have gone higher with little effort. Air rustled my hair with the nearness of its passage. I barely had time to stumble away before her foot was back on the ground. Her balance never wavered.

"Don't be fooled by the vicissitudes of fashion," she declared. Bending nimbly at the waist, she adjusted a strap at her ankle. "And to answer your previous question, your tribe has hunted mine since the fall of the Great City. What you lack in physical strength, you make up for in magic and cunning." Fluidly, she straightened, striding past me for the door. Aside from the strike of her deadly heels on the tiled floor, her passage was whisperingly silent. Supple and oiled, the leather of her catsuit didn't even creak. "He'll have some item, prepared ahead of time. The zealot Judges always do."

"Shit," I breathed. I knew exactly what she was talking about—I'd worn the damned things myself. As confirmation, I brandished the fading damage at my wrist. "The Thorns of Lugallu."

"What?" At the sound of that name, Sal stopped and rounded on me a foot from the door.

"He had these handcuffs," I said. "Used them on me—called them Thorns of Lugallu."

Thickly, she swallowed. It was rare for Sal's practiced features to betray anything that she didn't want them to, but the momentary slither of fear seemed genuine—and then some. Lips parting, she drew a breath. Resolutely, she composed herself. When she spoke again, her voice was tight and hushed.

"That would do it."

The total absence of canned bravado frightened me. I resisted the urge to check my phone again to study that awful image. Just the taunt and the picture—no demands. No questions. That didn't look good for Remy.

"He can't kill him, can he?" I asked. "Not permanently, I mean."

"Nothing is permanent," she whispered, as if reassuring herself of the fact.

"What aren't you telling me?"

Lightly, she rapped her knuckles against the hard chestguard of protective plates, directly over her heart. "A well-placed strike can discorporate us, if enough power is run through the weapon. I know you've seen this. I've not forgotten how you murdered our sibling Kessiel."

Murder was a funny way of saying "self-defense," but this wasn't the time to quibble. I bit the insides of my lips to keep from saying anything, and let her talk.

"Physical death is unpleasant," she said. "Even though we are immortal, none of us actively seek it. There are costs to our reclaiming. Inconveniences. It takes effort and we can face certain… hurdles."

"Like the handcuffs?"

Her sharp chin dipped once in assent. "If Remy is killed while he's wearing them, they'll interrupt his reclaiming." Grimly, she added, "Depending on how well the bonds are crafted, they may prevent it entirely. That kind of delay is… damaging. He could be lost for centuries."

Mutely, I digested this revelation. I wasn't stupid, though—I knew she was leaving out as much as she revealed. This was Sal, after all.

But something that interfered with the reclaiming— that was no joke.

Each of the tribes had a different way of incarnating. Reclaiming was the Nephilim variation on rebirth. To me, it was the creepiest of all of them. The Voluptuous Ones literally inhabited their blood—vampires of the purest sort—and when they sloughed off their mortal shells, that blood quested forward like a great, crimson parasite. The Nephilim blood-soul would escape to the Shadowside and seek another host—always one of their anchors.

I had no idea if the blood-soul could take over anyone who wasn't an anchor, or what happened to the person rightly born into that anchor's body once the blood-soul came home to roost, and I didn't really want to ask. I'd seen the process play out once with Kessiel, and I still had nightmares about it.

"Why are you telling me all this?" I asked. Nothing was free in her world, especially not information.

"Because tonight, you and I have a common enemy, Zaquiel," she responded. "And, above all else, I want us to win."

39

In the hallway, Tanisha remained stiffly at attention, one arm resting at the small of her back, the other hand lingering on the butt of her pistol. Her head snapped our way the instant Sal hastened through the door.

"Get Caleb on the comms and tell him he's in charge until further notice," Saliriel said crisply. The towering guard—still dwarfed by Saliriel's leather-clad form—didn't even blink. She had the walkie in hand before Sal was completely finished, waiting only to hear if her mistress had any further orders. "After Caleb, call Ava. Have her bring the car around. I want the Denali, not the limo." Again, Tanisha nodded, eyes clear and focused. "Get my weapons and get Javier. You're coming, too. Be prepared for a battle. Remy's been taken."

The first subtle hint of shock touched Tanisha's dark face. Muscles in her throat worked. Beyond that, she stood rock-solid. After the briefest hesitation, she nodded.

"Yes, ma'am."

As the suited guard moved to carry out her orders,

Saliriel motioned impatiently for me to join her in the hall.

"Where are we going, Anakim?" she snapped. "He sent the photo to you. You must have some idea."

"Parma," I said. "It has to be. Remy was on the phone when I crashed—"

"On top of your every other disaster tonight, you've wrecked my beautiful car?" she demanded.

"Are you serious?" I replied. "Forget the fucking Hellcat. It's a thing—irrelevant." With rushed, sweeping steps, Sal began to thread through the maze of back halls. I followed at her heels, for once the one who had to hustle to keep up. Her stride was enormous. "But the last thing Remy heard was a near-collision. We'd been talking about Marjory. When I didn't answer right away, he must have gone to her house, looking for me."

"Off to your rescue again," she growled. "You're going to get him killed, Anakim."

"Not tonight," I vowed.

"You'd better hope not." There was no mistaking her threat.

The crackle of a walkie and Tanisha's marching gait echoed from the corridor behind us. Saliriel paused at an intersection, one black hall leading deeper into the maze of Heaven's back rooms, another angling in the direction of the lounge and dance floor. She canted her head, listening, I realized, to both sides of the walkie conversation. To my ears, Tanisha's ceaseless flow of orders was nothing more than a husky rhythm punctuated by occasional crackles and bouts of silence.

"This way," Sal said after a moment, urging me down the deeper hall. I hesitated, fixed on the door that led to the silver-spattered lounge in the other direction. Sal gave me a hard look, stopping short of grabbing me by the scruff of the neck. I stepped to the far side of the corridor before she could change her mind about it.

"I need to take care of something first." It came out as a half-hearted mutter, reluctance telegraphed through my every word.

"What are you up to, Anakim?" she snapped.

Unhappily, I gestured toward the door. "You've got a club packed with people and energy to spare," I said. "I've got to use that while I can." It hurt to admit, but after Bruce the Goose, I couldn't take any further chances. Not with the hungry curse of the Eye hanging around my neck. I stuffed both fists into my pockets, hoping to hide my left palm before Sal could spot the tic. Her eyes went right to it—I wasn't fooling anyone. After silent consideration, she dipped her head in a subtle, solemn nod. She knew what it had cost me to say even this much.

"Do what you must," she said. "Meet us around front in ten minutes. Be prompt."

Shoulders hunching, I nodded. We both avoided eye contact. Without further comment, Sal hastened down the corridor that wound deeper into her hidden domain. Dressed as she was in her clinging suit of armored leather, she blended seamlessly with the flat black of the ceiling, floor, and walls, until eye-trickingly, she seemed to be a disembodied head bobbing toward the vanishing point.

Lingering at the crossway a moment longer, I struggled with distaste for what I knew I had to do. Month after month, I put off feeding as long as I could—it was the most awkward part of my Anakim nature, a weakness that made me feel like a thief, maybe even a rapist. But Lil had been right. I needed to get my shit together on this. Every tribe had their burden, and all the scruples in the world weren't going to change the fact that my magic required power.

Remy needed me at my best. I couldn't let him down.

I hit the door to the silver-spatter lounge, glad to find it empty. Marshaling my focus, I started peeling away my shields. Layer by painstaking layer, I stripped myself bare, all the while staring at the black leather couch where Remy had taught me how to put the shields up in the first place. My unlikely Nephilim mentor had used the image of a closed fist to help me focus, and now I used that in reverse, pulling both hands from my pockets and uncurling fingers stiff with nerves.

Anxious reluctance spun a knot inside my chest—I didn't like feeling this exposed. The cowl that hid my nature was linked inextricably with my shields. When I dropped the final layer, the cowl went, too. My wings rose reflexively behind me, a wall of living light stretching from one side of the room to the other. On the Shadowside they were a beacon. Without the cowl, anything inhuman could spot me a mile away.

I rushed through the door to the club proper, eager to get this over and be on my way. The first step across the threshold brought me straight through the bitter stain left behind by poor Alice. Her final moments clung like a sticky membrane, and they threatened to drown my thoughts in dizzying waves. Panic, pain, and terror numbed me briefly. Tottering, I made it to the railing and seized the glossy wood as if it were the only thing that could keep me from being swept away.

Below the observation deck stretched the main floor of the club, a writhing mass of bodies molten with glitter and sweat. The music pounded and the lightshow burst in scintillating patterns timed to its driving, electronic pulse. That pulse guided the collective emotions, too—seduction, yearning, passion, naked lust—higher and higher, a heady distillate of mortal pleasure. It surged wildly, as terrifying and awe-inspiring as any tsunami.

Instead of shrinking away from the surging force, for once, I dove in. Emotions closed over me—utterly overwhelming at first. In the rush of sense and feeling, I floundered and nearly lost myself. Drowning felt like this—no up, no down, just whirling disorientation and water all around. I struggled to breathe against the panic. Slowly, distinctions appeared—my thoughts, their thoughts, my feelings, those of the crowd.

This was hardly the first time I'd sipped power from a collection of people, but never in such an intense environment, and never so many mortals at once. With effort, I became cognizant of where I ended and where everyone else began, even as their stolen power coursed through me, rich with all of the different flavors of their minds.

Cresting like a surfer atop a curling wave, I found I could ride it, this wild flood of mortal passion. The surging chaos became harnessed momentum, a great and rolling force that washed over me, through me, and carried me swiftly along. Entranced by the swirling energies that grew increasingly visible the more I drew upon them, I drifted from the observation deck, down the ringing metal stairway, to walk among the crowd.

Bodies pressed around me. I shoved none of them away, but neither did I reciprocate their eager, flirtatious grasping. My focus wasn't flesh. Hands fluttered against the rasp of my cheek, through tousled strands of my hair, and one dancer—male or female, it hardly mattered in this crowd—clung to the sinews of my thigh with enough exuberance that, briefly, their partner followed, murmuring invitations for me to join them.

Breathing deep both their expectation and disappointment, I moved on. My wings spread across the crowd, gossamer beneath the strobes. Rather than over, they passed *through* the swaying, ecstatic bodies, tugging further power from the hidden chambers of their hearts. I dragged that energy into my center, swallowed it down, made it a part of me. Here and there, a head snapped up, eyes fixing vaguely in my direction as some mortal sensed the otherworldly touch. No one seemed to fully understand. Mesmerized by flesh and music, their focus swiftly faded and they melted back into the mass identity of the crowd.

Taut with stolen power, I passed from the dance floor to the still-bustling foyer. Suited guards—two of them clearly Nephilim anchors—warily tracked my progress. Caleb wasn't among them.

As I bee-lined for the exit, the crowd parted before me, and I wondered what the guards saw. To my own perceptions, energy crackled around me in a wild nimbus from top to toe, focused especially around my hands. My cupped palms where I held it felt thick and hot, fingers almost swollen as I soaked in the stolen light. It wasn't an unpleasant sensation, just unaccustomed. There was a sense of saturation and I knew I could only take so much before I had to do something with it.

Blue-white fire kindled behind my eyes as I focused, and a pale haze blossomed across the world. Again I cloaked myself in a cowl, uncertain that the filmy veil could contain so much pulsing light. Then I pulled my wings against my back, and the cascading obfuscation dropped like a soft curtain, muffling me from the world.

Shields next, layers and layers of them. Some to protect, others to distract. I ran my fingers across the thin line of symbols etched into the cuffs of my jacket, along the seam of the zipper, over the tongue of the belt that cinched the creaking leather at my waist. Silently, I renewed the subtle spells—armor that kept things like cacodaimons from piercing my flesh through the coat.

Still, an overflow of energy leapt like lightning in my hands. I touched the pommels of my blades and felt them drink the power, their metal warm and thrumming in their hidden Kydex sheaths.

Finally, I slipped a hand to my inner pocket. All the bouncers tensed, but I only sought the Stylus. I held my other hand loosely open, hoping to telegraph harmless intent. No one opened fire on me—yet. Head down, I kept walking. With one finger pressed against the sigiled case, I fed the intricate weave of magic that hid the ancient artifact. From everywhere and nowhere, the lust and joy of all the dancers continued calling, as if I'd left a piece of myself standing on the main floor of the club.

Ignoring it, I shouldered through the doors to emerge

beneath Heaven's blood-red awning. Power coursed through my finger, refreshing all the magic burned into the little box. As the doors swung shut behind me, the lure of the dance floor faded. Not entirely gone, but dim enough to make it more manageable. Shaking the last dregs of excess energy from my hand, I scattered gleaming droplets like molten sapphires. They cascaded toward the pavement, winking out before making it halfway down. The center of my chest—normally hollow with my persistent state of near-starvation—felt hot, expansive, as if I'd swallowed a star.

It was a wild and giddy sensation. I struggled not to enjoy it.

Around the Denali, every face was fixed on me. Saliriel's eyes reflected not yellow but blue fire, and I knew, in her way, she was seeing everything, no matter how thick my cowl.

"Are you quite finished?" she called with forced nonchalance. She held her mouth tightly and a certain pinched look around her eyes made me think that, for a moment, Saliriel, a Decimus of the Nephilim, was genuinely afraid.

Of me.

The shrinking expression—so foreign on Sal—faded in the blink of an eye, replaced by a haughty mask, as derisive as it was jaded. Her ponytail plumed in the wind, diminishing the effect somewhat.

"Unless you would prefer to delay us further while you pillage more of the power from within my club?" She framed it as a question, the final word hanging upon the air.

"I'm good," I said. My voice hit three notes at once, one of them so deep it registered more as sensation than sound. Swallowing against a rising sense of inhumanity, I curled my fingers around prickling power and stuffed them brusquely into my pockets. Some of the bluish tint to the world faded as I pulled myself together. Nodding toward the SUV, I took a halting step forward. Ava was already in the driver's seat, Tanisha and Javier standing like heavily armed statues on either side of their gigantic mistress.

"Let's go." My voice was my own again. Not that the other wasn't also me.

I just didn't like it much.

40

Sal took shotgun, which surprised no one. She still had to adjust the seat to allow more room for her legs and those wickedly heeled death-boots. This wasn't her regular vehicle—normally she tooled around in the back of a massive limo, when she deigned to leave Heaven at all.

With no desire to sit close to either of the two suited bouncers, I waited for Tanisha and Javier to pile into the back. Javier alone, a flint-eyed, broad fortress of a man with cheeks like pitted granite, took up two peoples' worth of space. Half of that seemed to be the hand-cannon that made all the wrong kinds of angles beneath the lines of his suit. Tanisha let him squeeze himself through the door first, eyes restlessly ticking to me. She looked away just as quickly when she caught me looking back.

"What?" I demanded.

She just shook her head, and angled herself into the far corner of the wide and cushy back seat, leaving a thick, demilitarized zone of space between herself and

Javier. It wasn't easy—on both of them, their shoulders were broad enough to carry a swing bridge. Sitting there next to the massive Latino, Tanisha almost looked like a woman of average size.

I wondered what Sal had been thinking, tapping her for this detail. Tanisha exuded all the cold instincts of professional military, but she didn't parse as an anchor. Since I'd strode from the club, every chance she got she stared at me like my face was turned inside out. I pulled the cowl a little tighter. Maybe it was doing a shittier job than I'd intended.

Tanisha kept staring.

"Fuck it," I muttered and climbed into the middle section, yanking the side door closed behind me.

"Address?" Ava asked. Sal's driver leaned with her fingers poised over a screen built directly into the dash. A brightly colored GPS program awaited her input. I rattled off the street number for Marjory's home, with the warning, "It's a bitch to find."

"I'll find it," Ava assured. She adjusted the brim of her chauffeur's hat, neatly tucking a strand of dark hair behind one ear. Like Tanisha, Ava didn't parse as an anchor—lithe and curvy, she moved like a dancer, when Sal didn't have her in chains. She shouldn't be here, either, I mused. Zuriel would kill anyone he could, in the most excruciating manner that occurred to him.

I buckled in quickly as Ava pulled away from the club, accelerating through the crowded parking lot at a pace that would have impressed even Lil.

Once we were moving, Sal turned around in her seat and held something out. "This is for you." It was a spare magazine for my gun. Baffled, I took it. I didn't even ask how she knew to give me the right caliber. This was Sal, after all. "How many should we expect to fight?" she asked.

"I've only seen Zuriel," I said, "but he's got this charm around his neck. An illusion. I'm pretty sure it's Tuscanetti magic."

Sal gave a derisive sniff. "Those witches sell their magic to the highest bidder." She turned her face to the window, watching the bricks of graffitied buildings streak by as Ava gunned it out of the Flats. "There will be repercussions if I find out which among them is the supplier."

"Veronica," I spat. "I'd bet money on it."

My sister allowed me a sidelong glance. One perfectly plucked brow arched toward her hairline.

"You've crossed swords with Lartha's unwisely ambitious grand-daughter?"

"Great-great-grand-daughter," I corrected.

Sal merely smiled. "Is that what she told you?" Languidly, she returned her gaze to the window, but the chilly detachment was nothing more than an act—I'd seen it before in situations worse than this. Underneath, Sal felt the same driving worry that I did.

"I don't really care what her relation is, so long as she isn't part of this," I said. "Veronica is bad news."

"They all are," Sal agreed. "Now tell me the nature of this Tuscanetti illusion."

"It makes him look like me," I said at length. "But he's just a kid. Sixteen, seventeen tops."

"Anything else?" my sister said. All the others in the car remained stoically silent, save for the crisp, electronic voice of the GPS. Ava took the turn without even tapping the brakes for deceleration, controlling the hurtling Denali on a sharply curving on-ramp with the ease of a stunt driver. The whole vehicle shifted heavily right, Javier's ballast the only thing keeping us from going up on two wheels.

I gripped the seat as the tires squealed.

"He can project the illusion—not just his image, but it also throws his voice." Centripetal force made my own voice strain as I struggled to remain upright—relatively speaking. We merged onto the highway, Ava snaking between a semi and a panel truck in a maneuver I thought impossible for the big SUV. Convulsively, I swallowed.

No one else so much as blinked.

"No clue if there's a limit on its range, but it makes him a bitch to shoot."

"Noted," Saliriel replied.

Smoothly Ava crossed into the fast lane. As she urged the Denali past the ninety mark on the speedometer, a text vibrated on my phone. I twitched, holding my breath as I dug the device from my back pocket. Saliriel caught the motion. Hell, she'd probably heard the buzz even through the muffle of my body.

"Don't respond to that," she snapped. "They escalate once they get a response."

"They escalate if they don't," I replied.

While she didn't concede my point, she broke eye contact. "It pays to draw it out as long as possible," she said to her window.

"He likes it that way," I muttered. Easing a breath between my teeth, I brought up the text, fully expecting another grisly close-up of my captured sibling. But it wasn't from Remy's number. The text was from Father Frank.

> Why is Lil here? She won't go away.

The starkly glowing letters managed to convey his flat annoyance without the benefit of inflection or emojis. Every muscle I hadn't realized was straining abruptly relaxed.

"It's not Zuriel," I assured as I started tapping a response. Saliriel turned in her seat long enough to glower at me while I bent over the screen.

> I asked Lil to watch you both
> You with Halley?

Three dots showed that he was already typing before I hit send. Our responses crossed in the digital ether, overlapping on arrival.

> She's making the family nervous.
> You know how I feel about her.

The padre trusted Lil about as far as he could throw her spectral lioness—which, of course, he couldn't. I was trying to compose something appropriately reassuring and doing a bad job of it when a second message followed on the heels of the first. The smartphone's vibration was a bright burst of sensation in the palm of my hand. It was his answer to my initial text.

Yes. I'm at the Davis house.

Almost as soon as that came through, another rattled the device.

She doesn't need to be here.

Hurriedly, I mashed the delete button until the cursor ate all my painstakingly chosen words, leaving a freshly blank field. Sal was glaring. So was Tanisha. Both their gazes hung on me like weights.

"Domestic troubles?" Saliriel inquired archly.

"Ssh," I hissed. "Let me think." My finger hovered over the tiny on-screen keyboard while the cursor winked tauntingly.

"You better put that thing on silent once we get where we're going," Tanisha warned. "All that buzz-buzz will give your position away in a heartbeat."

"Yeah," I muttered, settling on a foreshortened message. I tapped the words, fixing a couple of ridiculous autocorrects because my spelling went to shit when I rushed on such a tiny surface. Then I hit send.

I'll explain later. Let her do what I asked.
And thank her.

If I knew the padre at all, he was scowling unhappily at his phone, holding the device at arm's length because, even at seventy, he still refused the necessity of reading glasses. But he stopped arguing, as attested by his swift, solitary response, as terse as Father Frank ever got with me.

OK

I was just glad to know they were safe. I tapped a quick thanks, and that was the end of it. Before I put away the phone, I backed out of the series of texts and brought up Remy's bloody photo. That solitary eye, the iris such a startling blue even without all that crimson to frame it... I tried not to think what Zuriel might be motivated to do to those unearthly eyes. As much as I dreaded another text from the sadistic Anakim, I half-hoped he'd send more pictures. I needed more to go on. Aside from heading vaguely toward Marjory's, I had no idea where Zuriel had taken him.

Pressing two fingers against the screen, I spread them in a widening shape to enlarge the photo. Remy's eye dominated the smartphone, a hazy reflection floating in the black of his tightly contracted pupil.

Rafters. Maybe.

Briefly closing my own eyes, I called to mind the blood-drenched cellar where my doppelganger had murdered Tabitha, and then lured me with her cruelly animated corpse. I'd stared long enough at those rafters, trying to yank myself free of that damned metal cuff. The shape and spacing didn't seem to match. Another basement, then—assuming I could trust such a grainy image.

"I know this neighborhood," Sal said suddenly, scattering my internalized images. Blinking, I looked up from the phone. We were already on Westminster, just a turn away from Parmenter.

"Marjory's house is halfway to the second intersection," I offered. "On the left."

The SUV rolled slowly toward the cross street as Ava signaled and turned. Her gaze flicked from the dimmed screen in the dash to the near-total lack of house numbers. Her fingers tightened on the steering wheel—the only sign of her frustration. Guiltily, I felt a brief swell of vindication.

"I bought Karl a house out here when he wanted to start a family," Sal continued. "A solid, working-class neighborhood. Not much seems changed." Her face was turned to the window, but I could see the faint glimmer of her eyes in the glass, yellow as topaz. Brows drawn, she scanned the rows of quiet and nearly identical dwellings.

"Karl Kazinsky?" I prodded. Both the letters and Remy had named him as Marjory's father. Saliriel was habitually tight-lipped about her business contacts. This might be the only time I got her to dish on the subject.

Lightly, my sister nodded, a single dip of her sharp chin. "Karl was one of my accountants," she explained. "If I'm to be honest, he was one of the best, at least since the Porrellos killed Charlie Decker."

Charlie Decker wasn't a name that held any significance to me, but the Porrellos I recognized. A Sicilian family. They and the Lonardo brothers had formed the heart of the Mayfield Road Gang, one of the most influential of local crime families. I didn't harbor any clear memories of Cleveland's infamous *Cosa Nostra*, but Sal's name had come up in connection with them before. In one of its earlier incarnations, Club Heaven had been a speakeasy. It was easy to connect the dots from there.

"You guys hid her. That's why we couldn't find her." Piece after piece clicked together in my head. I felt like an idiot for not consulting Remy sooner, but would he have actually told me anything? Not if Sal had given strict orders for silence. "It's like a Nephilim witness protection program out here."

Sal shifted to face me. Her expression hung somewhere between weary and withering—both emotions fixed firmly on me.

"You jump to such dramatic conclusions," she said, and she sighed. "Karl wasn't any kind of witness, at least not to the kind of thing you're implying. He worked strictly with the numbers."

On Sal's left, Ava squirmed in the driver's seat, one finger stabbing at the GPS screen while she softly muttered profanities. As mine had done, the GPS primly announced our arrival at the house, its marker hovering uselessly in the middle of the street. Again, with that guilty swell of vindication, I tapped Ava's shoulder and pointed.

"The green one," I offered, briefly entertaining the notion that Sal's influence might have buried the location of the little house under lines of hidden code. I dismissed it as improbable. The way Cleveland and its surrounding suburbs had been laid out, it didn't take a conspiracy of immortals to confuse map functions. Ava softly thanked me and banked the wheel toward the drive. Sal was still pontificating.

"Karl had simply gotten tired and wanted to settle," she said. "He was a good worker. He'd earned that chance." Her volume climbed on these last two statements, and I wondered how much of this was for the benefit of the others in the car. "I had Karl set up with a lovely little home, some discreet income, and had Remy make certain no one would bother him. End of story."

"What about his little girl?" I demanded.

"I don't bother myself with trifles, Zaquiel," Saliriel responded. "I put Remy in charge of it and moved on. Once someone leaves my service, there's no reason for me to keep tabs on them."

"Did you have any idea who Marjory is to me?" I demanded hotly.

"Your landlady?" she scoffed, but before I could goad her into an explanation, her hand snaked out and she laid gloved fingers against my lips. I froze at the contact. Knuckles crackled as my hands curled into futile fists. "Enough," she instructed. "Will any of your endless questions lead us closer to Remy?" Pressing even harder against my mouth until I felt the flat outline of individual teeth on the soft side of my lips, she answered her own question. "I think not. Now, get out. Search this house. Do whatever it is you must do to track that rogue Anakim.

"I want him dead within the hour."

Ava and the others poured from the vehicle, the whole Denali rocking as Javier hoisted his vast bulk from the back. Only Sal and I remained in our seats, rigid as statues cobbled from sinew and bone. Her fingers never moved. They were cold, even through the gloves. She was on the verge of saying something else, yellow eyes drilling through layers of my soul. I didn't know what she was searching for, and I didn't want to find out.

With a snarl, I shoved her hand aside.

"Don't touch me," I hissed. "Ever."

Shouldering out from the SUV, I moved around to Marjory's side door. I still had the keys. Motionless, Sal observed from her seat, never taking her eyes from me.

41

Marjory's house felt as empty as I'd left it, except for the faintest hint of Remy's touch upon the handle of the side door. Stilling my thoughts so I could focus all of my senses, I pressed my fingers against the weathered metal and was rewarded with a brief flash of my brother standing almost precisely where I stood. Hair neatly braided, fedora perched upon his head, he wore a light overcoat that snapped against him in the wind. He had keys to the place. As sounds rarely telegraphed through such impressions, imagination supplied their soft jangle as he searched for the proper one.

"He's been here," I said.

"That's useful to know," Saliriel said. She had drifted like a ghost from the passenger side of the SUV and now stood between the vehicle and the house, her pale skin nearly luminescent against the shadows. "But we need his current position to do us any good, Anakim."

"Working on it," I grumbled, striving to dig deeper through the impression, but that was it—one snapshot moment caught faintly on the threshold. Feeling the slump in my shoulders, I withdrew my hand from the door. Tanisha crowded at my elbow.

"We're too exposed out here," she said flatly. "Hurry it up."

I felt a great temptation to shove her away, but she had her holster exposed, hand ready to draw the pistol. Behind her, Javier moved like a mobile slab of mountain, angling himself to bodily shield Sal where she stood. By accident or design, this also shielded my sorry ass, though I was certain that would change the instant anything threatened Saliriel. Javier was literally a walking meat-shield, and while I thought the term derisively, the stony guard approached it as a sacred duty.

Devoid of any expression save a piercing watchfulness, he endlessly scanned our surroundings with bright obsidian-chip eyes. Sal had meant business when she'd picked this goon squad. Even Ava, the driver, was key-up for a firefight, body pressed flat against the Denali and her neat little Beretta aimed toward the sky. Her chauffeur's cap tipped at a rakish angle, allowing one solitary curl to slip out and encircle an ear.

If Zuriel was working alone, we might just steamroll him—but we had to find him first.

Working the key in the lock, I pushed open the door. Before I could step inside, Tanisha shoved to get past me, heaving a snarl of impatience when I didn't immediately surrender my position. She shoved harder, giving me no choice about it. Producing a slim LED flashlight, she crossed her wrists to balance her gun arm so the barrel pointed down the steady beam. Drifting motes of dust turned the light into a solid cylinder of white in the cramped entryway.

Moving in a silent crouch, Tanisha checked the stairs to the basement, tracing a careful circle of light around the hook-and-eye latch that sealed the door. I'd left it like that, and it was good to see it hadn't been disturbed. Making a satisfied grunt that came out as little more than a heavy exhalation through her flared nostrils, the guard pivoted to press her back against the inside wall, crushing the lumpy collection of jackets against their pegs. She aimed gun and light into the kitchen, her dark eyes scouring every cabinet and stick of furniture.

"Clear," she stated.

"I did that the last time I was here," I grumbled.

Her head ticked my way briefly. "That was last time," she said. "Things change, so I do it again."

Reluctantly, I conceded her point, though I still resented the delay. If the time stamp on the first text was anything to go by, Remy had been in Zuriel's clutches for close to an hour. A lot could happen in that span of time. Too much.

Silent as a specter, Tanisha glided up the short span of stairs from the landing to the kitchen, her flashlight cutting through the shadows. I didn't bother pointing out the light switch half-buried under the coats by the door. She obviously didn't need it.

While she explored the physical house, I slid my eyes shut and tried to locate any further impressions left behind by Remiel. Zuriel's weird scrubbing effect made the psychic space feel hollow and cavernous, but I worked it to my benefit, treating it like a clean slate.

Striving for even the faintest glimmer, I unspooled my senses in an ever-expanding net.

Sal became an impatient, crimson flicker looming to my right. Javier, a dull but solid presence that seemed to sink the very ground beside my back. Ava, emotions bright and leaping like a crackling flame. Tanisha, like a serpent gliding smoothly through dark waters, utterly focused on her hunt. One by one, I tasted them—energy, emotion, shape—and, one by one, I shut their presences from my mind.

These loud and keyed-up companions weren't the ones I sought. I wanted Remy who, despite the swirling scarlet of his Nephilim blood-soul, always first presented to me in shades of azure—probably a projection of my own construction, based on the striking color of his eyes. But that bias didn't matter. The language of these perceptions was as psychological as it was psychic, and as long as it got me what I wanted, all of it could be used.

Come on, Remy, where are you?

The icy glimmer of Zuriel's magic spasmed into focus half a second too late. In a brilliant burst, it erupted behind my eyes, tearing a startled yelp from my throat. I clamped my teeth against it. In the same instant, Tanisha loosed a startled hiss. I was already rushing into the kitchen, my hand flicking the light.

"What was that?" Saliriel asked. Wise enough to be cautious, she hung back on the threshold. Javier and Ava went on high alert.

The compact fluorescents of the kitchen stuttered slowly to life. Tanisha stood frozen at the far end, one foot poised on the dull bit of metal flashing where linoleum gave way to the carpet of the living room.

"Don't move," I hissed.

"Do you see me moving?" she replied. She held both gun and flashlight loosely, taking slow and even breaths as if the slightest motion might cause the magic under her to explode. Corded tendons bunched around the jumping artery in her neck.

"Zaquiel, what do you sense?" Saliriel demanded.

"Sssh." Fighting to clear my senses from that initial, searing flash, I approached Tanisha with measured caution. A light scrim of sweat beaded the guard's brow as I studied her. "Where did you step when it happened?"

"Still stepping there," she said tightly. "I'm not dumb. Some triggers get nasty once you take your foot off."

"Fair enough," I responded. Kneeling down, I spread my fingers over the thin strip of metal, sensing but not quite touching the scuffed and pitted surface. A row of sigils flared, arctic-white—Zuriel's work. Not that there was any doubt. My eyes slid shut unbidden to remove the distraction of physical sight, and I tasted the shape and purpose of the spell. Not a ward, exactly. This was something subtle. More complex.

"It won't explode," I assured Tanisha. We were so close, I felt the rush of her relief as my own emotion. Both our hearts resumed a somewhat steadier pace. "But it gave away our position."

"Trip wire," she said. With a grimace she removed her foot, then rolled her neck, looking both chagrined and relieved. "I hate this magic crap."

"Find a different job," I suggested. She only grunted.

Plumbing the lingering energy of the sigils, I satisfied

351

myself that their main burst had been released. The effect was a one-shot, quickly scribed, but still accomplished with finesse. Zuriel was troublingly resourceful. Splaying my fingers, I dared to touch the strip of metal, just to be sure it was inert. No surprises blasted me into my next incarnation.

"It's spent."

"Any other booby traps I should watch out for?" Tanisha asked, beaming her light into the living room shadows. That initial blast still dulled my more distant impressions. All I felt for the moment was our collective knot of anxiousness.

"Not sure," I admitted.

"Check the house and clear it," Sal called from the doorway. "You should have caught that before she tripped it, Anakim."

I bristled at such a direct order. "I'm not one of your goons, Sal."

"You're a dick," Tanisha snapped. "I'm standing right here."

"Nothing personal," I muttered. Wiping the sick feel of Zuriel's magic from my skin, I rose from my crouch on the floor. "He's not going to be here, Sal. You know that."

The decimus buried her worry beneath a chilly hauteur. "If you're so certain about that, do you know where to start looking?"

"Not yet," I admitted.

"Then go." She flicked her hand impatiently. I motioned for Tanisha to precede me.

"I won't miss the next booby-trap," I promised.

"Better not."

We moved forward and, together, we cleared the house, falling quickly into an efficient rhythm. Sal's ebon-skinned shield maiden didn't fuck around. Pausing at every entryway, Tanisha checked for physical threats while I kept all my senses peeled for anything that might escape her mortal eyes. Living room, office, then upstairs to the bedrooms. In every room, we left lights burning behind us. There were no more surprises, but also, no further traces of Remy. Not so much as a flicker.

"I know it was locked, but I'd feel better if we checked out that cellar," Tanisha said.

I grunted unhelpfully, only half listening. All my focus was on the other side. Before we headed back down, I laid my hand against the wall, trying to get a feel for the house as a whole. Tanisha's heat and Sal's expectant impatience knocked against the hollowed-out energy of the place. Ava and Javier, also clustered near the entrance, blended in with Sal.

"This is a waste," I grumbled. "There's another place we've got to check, about a block down the street." No longer trying to muffle my footfalls, I rushed to the bottom of the stairs.

"You planned to mention that *when*?" Tanisha barked after me.

Taking the sharp turn into the hallway, I hustled past the office and into the living room. Two of the three standing lamps burned brightly from their corners. In their yellow light, all the faces turned to corpses on the walls. I rushed toward the kitchen, reluctant to catch sight of that patch of missing carpet where Marjory's body had lain.

I looked anyway. And I froze.

There, smack in the middle of the exposed flooring, lay a coil of gleaming rope, dark and sinuous as a serpent.

Not rope, I thought. It was hair. Remy's hair.

Zuriel had cut away my brother's waist-long braid.

Rationally, I knew it could have been worse—much worse—an ear, a tongue, a hand, even a brilliant, azure eye plucked like an under-ripe fruit from a bloodied socket. Hair was hardly crippling, and yet a sour heat squeezed my throat at the sight of this cruel and petty mutilation.

More disturbing than the hair itself was the issue of its very presence. Tanisha and I had both been through this room. We'd seen the bared patch of floor. The braid hadn't been here—I was certain of it. Which left only the possibility that Zuriel had planted this latest taunt while we searched the rooms upstairs.

It seemed impossible.

Sal stood in the only open doorway. Javier and Ava had watchful eyes upon the street. Even if he'd slunk in through the Shadowside, I had all my psychic senses flung as wide as I could get them. I should have sensed *something.* And yet, here was the braid, mocking proof of our incompetence.

"Fuck me running," I growled.

Sal called from the kitchen, "What have you found?" When I didn't immediately answer, she barked orders like I was one of her foot soldiers, but that only made me clench my teeth in surly defiance. Her mask of arrogant detachment crumbling, she swooped into the living room, blonde ponytail streaming behind her like a tattered standard. She drew up behind me, her towering presence a looming weight against my tucked and hidden wings. As I had, she froze once she saw the plaited insult coiled upon the floor.

"I'm going to kill him," Sal said.

"What's the trouble?" Tanisha asked. The guard had taken the stairs so silently, she seemed to simply appear at the mouth of the back hall. The whites of her eyes sketched bright rings around her irises as she looked expectantly from Sal to me, then finally to what lay upon the floor. Her full lips twitched down. "Is that Mr. Broussard's hair?"

Neither of us answered. The insect buzz of phone broke the thick silence. At the sound, Tanisha's mouth pressed flat with disapproval—despite her request, I'd never bothered to make it completely silent. I'd expected Zuriel to reach out again, had expected some text or blood-drenched photo the instant those alarm sigils had been tripped.

With brittle calm, I reached into my back pocket and plucked out the phone. On the locked screen, the message lingered like a thought-bubble, short and predictably awful.

Wut piece u want next?

Over and over I read those mangled words, my grip tightening until I was in danger of shattering the screen. Sal stood silent behind me, too furious to utter a single sound. As I trembled with impotent rage, I couldn't shake the sense that Zuriel was right there, watching and laughing at us—at me. Some deep, unspoken gnosis clamored that he couldn't resist a spectacle, especially not one of his own design.

I yanked my vision so hard to the other half of reality that black starbursts exploded against my retinas and, for a span of dead seconds, I was completely blind. Blinking until I could see, albeit blearily, I sought any sign of the asshole Anakim—a deepening of shadows in the corner, a blur of pallid wings—but there was nothing. If he was here, he *had* to have come through the Shadowside, had to still be hovering to watch us from that twilit realm. As part of the same tribe, I was connected to that place as much as he was, and still, I could not see him.

"Damn that motherfucker!" I snarled.

As soon as I yelled it, the phone trembled with the palsy of another incoming message.

30 min

I didn't have to ask thirty minutes to what.

42

"We're on a timer now," I yelled, pitching my voice to carry out to Ava and Javier. Tanisha winced at the sudden volume.

"Paint a target on our backs, why don't you?" she snapped. Tension tightened all the planes of her face, broad cheekbones shiny in the living room's brassy light. Behind me, Saliriel said nothing, simply stepping forward to bend toward the desolate coil of shorn hair. The metal of her heels glinted like twin daggers. Her expression was too alien to read.

"He's already seen us," I spat with a vague gesture toward the proof lying right in front of us. While I tapped the timer on my phone to track the deadline, my sister plucked the hair from the floor, twining the black plaits loosely in her long fingers.

The motion was akin to reverence, but my skin crawled weirdly. I knew what it was, knew it had come from Remy, but I had zero desire to touch it. I couldn't explain the feeling. While Sal twisted the hair into a tight, portable knot, I continued peering across to the Shadowside, uselessly seeking signs of Zuriel. Still nothing. I hissed a quiet string of obscenities. "I'm pretty sure he's here right now. I just can't see him."

Sal straightened. One step took her an inch from my chest, towering like the statue of an ancient and very wrathful goddess.

"Seeing such things is your job, Anakim," she snarled. She clenched the knot of hair in one bony hand, and I shied from it for reasons known only to my gag reflex.

"You know how much I've lost," I reminded with quiet heat. "It was one of your tribe that took it from me. I know what's at stake here, and I'm doing the best I can."

Sal drew herself up to her most imposing height—six feet and six inches of pale, leggy vampire, plus lethal heels. She lorded it furiously over me.

"Do better."

I refused to flinch. Words like lava ignited in my throat, the whole, bitter torrent rising to be spat in Saliriel's face. Yet I snapped my jaws shut like a bear trap. Robbed of easy escape, the heat swept down both arms to gather in my fists, where it erupted in a nimbus of crackling energy. I held it there, my potential for violence cupped and ready, telling myself all that anger would soon have focus—but not my sister. No matter how much she baited me, no matter how hard she pushed.

Without a word, I turned my back and started marching for the side door, leaving Sal and all her towering rage for Tanisha to handle. If they followed, that was their choice. I knew where I had to go next.

Javier stood with his back to the door like a one-man blockade, and I crushed the screen door against his shoulders because he wouldn't get out of the way. The man—who hadn't spoken a single word since our departure from Club Heaven—simply looked at me mutely, the obsidian flecks of his eyes tiny in such a great slab of a face.

"Move," I snarled, pushing hard enough to rock him. My voice wasn't human, and I no longer gave a shit.

Javier looked to Ava. The driver nodded very slightly. Her eyes went hooded and a little glassy as she watched me shoulder past, all my power singing around me. A flush crept from the tight collar of her driver's uniform to kiss her cheeks to pink. With all my senses sharp as razors, I couldn't help but taste her arousal. As I swept past her position beside the Denali, it clawed at me, sharp and hungry.

Ava got off on monsters. No wonder she stuck to Sal like glue.

Too angry to feel disturbed or even disgusted, I marched down the darkened street, boots crunching on the husks of dead leaves.

"You coming?" I called over my shoulder.

Ava followed like I'd tugged a leash.

As exposed as we were, nothing jumped us as we made our way. Ava followed a few short steps behind, covering me with her Beretta. The gun sketched a blocky silhouette in her small hands, but she handled it with confident ease. When I glanced back, only her eyes looked a little shocky, darting from house to house and showing too much white. The cloying taste of arousal was still there, and, if anything, it seemed heightened by her fear. I shoved that unwanted awareness from my mind, striding purposefully toward the house where Tabitha—and probably Marjory—had died.

There was no attempt whatsoever at stealth—I just wanted Remy back, and at this point, I was prepared to find a Crossing and fly back and forth across the entire neighborhood until I spotted some sign of the kidnapped Nephilim. Slow and steady was definitely safer, but searching houses top to bottom burned a lot of time.

Anxious, I slipped out my phone to glance at the running countdown.

Twenty-two minutes.

I grimaced, stuffing the phone back into its pocket. No way I should have stood there arguing with Tanisha and Sal. Huge waste of time. Arguing always was.

"Where are we going?" Ava asked breathlessly.

Wordlessly, I pointed to the FOR SALE sign sagging in the unmowed lawn three houses ahead of us. Everything was exactly as I'd left it. Squinting in the crappy lighting that streamed from a distant neighbor's porch, I reassessed that initial impression.

Not *quite* as I'd left it.

My Vulcan lay in a heap across the drive, a few feet from where I'd abandoned it. In a burst, I jogged the short distance to the bike. Ava's footfalls slapped the sidewalk behind me.

A huge scrape cut through the paint on one fender of the Kawasaki, revealing dullness beneath. Another ended in a dent on the gas tank. Trembling around it in the air, I could feel a whisper of violence—not just the obvious evidence scratched into the paint job, but an echo of conflict stamped across the Shadowside.

Steeling myself for a brutal rush of images, I laid all my senses bare and seized the handlebars—

—and my hand was Remy's hand, resting on the grip while the other fluttered near the engine, testing for its heat.

"*Too late. I've gotten here too late.*" Worry verged into fear. Remy had checked Marjory's house because it was the only place he could think of. Tried calling. Tried texts. No answer, again and again. The crash had sounded bad. The silence, worse.

"*And now this. A well-laid trap? But where would Zuriel take him?*"

Remy wished—not for the first time—for skills akin to his brother's. He could sense a few things, but so often felt blind by comparison. How great a gift, to be able to touch a thing and understand what had once transpired. His paltry knack was more a taunt—it showed him just enough to know the world held more. And such a costly effort, but he had to try, needed to see which of his brothers had touched this last, and whether one of them was hurt.

It was like straining to open stitched eyes. But there was something. A lingering spark…

Diving deeper into the vision, I surrendered to Remy's perceptions. My essence on the grips of the motorcycle—

Remiel's version of Anakim sight, translated through Nephilim eyes. Pallid threads of fleeting blue like moonlight on a lake. Gray. Silver. White. A hazy film of aura that shimmered like summer heat. Under all of that, an ancient backbone. Sharp as metal. Clean, with the same glinting bite.

Then something pulled me under, sensation so intense, immediate, I lost myself entirely. No Zack standing beside the scratched-up Kawasaki. Just wave after wave of perception, choking, bitter—

—stabbing, deep into the meat of both shoulders. Swift, so swift, he couldn't react. Daggers—the blades of daggers buried in his flesh. He's driven forward. He faceplants on the bike. The Vulcan topples and he can't get any leverage. His arms refuse to work. There's magic in the weapons—cold and burning all at once. Anakim steel. He knows the taste.

His body strives to fix the damage, but the weapons cauterize even as they cut. Tendons, nerves, and muscles. Down to bitter bone. The agony's enormous and he—

—has the bastard on the ground, but he's got to get the cuffs on quick. They heal fast, the Nephilim, so he'll only get this chance. He got the drop on the bloodsucker, and that's the edge. Stalked him from the house—stroke of luck the fucker tripped the wards. Ruined an hour of work, but what the hell? It's not like they're hard, and look at this.

It's the face, the face in the photo, the one who raised their brother with that dried-up Polish bitch. Just got to get the metal to click—

—shut on his wrists and he screams, not with pain, but with terror. He can't stop it. Can't think past it. Too well, he knows the bite of that magic, had it chew him to pieces as he hung, starving, in chains. And it's happening again, all happening again, no matter that he's better. That, unlike others, he has changed. The effort should count for something. He's loyal. Unfailing. All his debts are—

—payback's a bitch, and this debt's thick as Bibles. It's an eye for an eye and a tooth for a tooth, and this guy's going to suffer because he still can't find Tashiel. And he has to. He *has* to. Maybe when Zaquiel's mentor's hanging in pieces, he'll spill.

Got to know the rules, though. Catch them fast and cut them slow. And he's going to make every slice count for something, just like Tashiel showed him how—

Gasping, I shoved back from the bike, my head spinning with a chaos of conflicting perspectives.

My thoughts.

Remy's.

Zuriel's.

They whirled in a dizzying maelstrom, shifting and so entangled, I could barely separate one from the next.

"Are you all right?"

Ava's question echoed through crashing waves. I concentrated on my breathing. The feel of the concrete driveway under my feet. The sharp half-moons of pain as I drove my nails into my palms. My splintered vision began returning to something like a normal focus—just my thoughts, just my eyes.

"Yeah," I answered. "I'm good."

The breathless rasp sounded anything but. A skeptical Ava hovered near my elbow, caught between grabbing my shoulder to hold me up and stepping back to give me some space. She held the Beretta pointed skyward while she wavered with her empty hand. I didn't like the idea of Sal's pet stunt driver touching me, not even through the jacket, not when I felt like this. Weakly, I waved her away, leaning forward to catch my breath.

"That was weird," I muttered, struggling to unpack the densely layered impressions. Warring snippets of Zuriel and Remy still spun in a confusing miasma around the bike.

Ava watched with wary eyes, lips pursed around a comment. Whatever it was, she never voiced it. A rush of wind stirred the bushes at the nearest corner of the empty house. Incredibly focused, the burst of breeze rattled only the barren branches of what might have been an aging lilac. A tall and sooty shadow appeared, revealing the source of the uncanny wind. The Nephilim could move fast when they wanted. But Sal's fleet passage defied any possibility to track her.

One moment, nothing—and then she was there.

"What have you found, Anakim?" Casting a glance

up and down the street to assure herself of safety, she strolled from her cover with easy grace. Ava stepped back immediately, bowing her head as her mistress approached. She could have said something about what she'd witnessed, but instead she waited for me to speak.

"I have a lead," I answered, "but it's a little confusing."

"Your motorcycle?" Sal sniffed.

"Remy was here," I explained. "He touched it. So did Zuriel. Their impressions are... intertwined. Caught in a moment of struggle. It's hard to get a clear reading."

"More excuses." My sister's eyes caught the faint light of a distant porch lamp, reflecting it back as yellow fire.

"Ma'am?" Tanisha said as she caught up. Her volume strained, she still hadn't quite abandoned a token stealth. She spotted Ava lingering nearby with her Beretta still out and relaxed—but only a touch. "You really shouldn't cluster in the open," she offered.

"Thank you for the suggestion," Sal responded stiffly. She leaned into me. "Dive back into it, Zaquiel. We have no time for squeamish hesitation."

I wanted to punch her—except that she was right. So far this was the biggest breadcrumb the oppressively quiet neighborhood had to offer. If I could manage to navigate the burst of impressions, I could probably get some sense of where Remy had been taken.

"If I pass out, I hope somebody thinks to catch me," I muttered. "Not a big fan of head trauma."

I stretched my fingers to clasp the Vulcan's handlebars. Immediately, the echoes sucked me back in.

43

I drowned in images—a prison. No, *two* prisons, one ancient, one modern, both stinking pits of bleakest desolation. Slouching boys with angry voices. A gleaming dagger. Rusted chains—

—Again. Bound again. He couldn't do it. Too many years spent in that Anakim dungeon, the maddening whispers of promised power clawing in his brain.

An image of the Eye, clear and startling. Not in my palm, but in Remy's. Pale, ferocious, blood dripping from his hands. Clothed in robes, a diadem glinting from his brow. He seemed a different person. I knew him only by the brilliant azure of his gaze.

I shoved impatiently at the fractured memories, striving

to steer the vision toward the events of the last few hours. That was where I'd find my answers. I needed to know where Remy had been taken, not where my brother had been in our long-dead past.

There—a flicker of startled pain and gleeful sadism. In the tangled psychic residue, I caught a replay of the attack on Remy, this time from Zuriel's perspective. So much anger. Jealousy. Betrayal?

And then I lost them. Compressed strata of emotion whirled in an ever-widening gyre. Guilt and trauma bound hunter to victim, both hopelessly entwined around a pivot-point of fear. Remy's fear of imprisonment.

Zuriel's fear of—

—abandoned. He'd been abandoned. It wasn't fair. All the other times, he called and his dad came running. He'd get a lecture, but the charges disappeared. This time, he got told to learn his lesson. So they booked him. Fucking pigs. Stuck him in with twitching junkies and puffed-up hoodrats—all of them his age, but hard. Nasty.

The smell, the feel of people crammed in so tight a space—it made him kind of crazy. Too many voices in his head. That no-lip fuck who just kept staring... He snapped. He smashed that kid to pieces. Made his face a part of the wall. And something happened—a *way* opened up, just as the guards came to beat him.

He learned a lesson, all right. He learned to walk through walls.

* * *

The chaos of densely packed impressions dragged at my own awareness, making it hard to think. I struggled to direct the flow of information, but Zuriel was loud— so loud. The kid had a ton of baggage, and it spilled through everything he'd touched.

More images, punishingly stark. Zuriel murdering his father. He did it as soon as he got out, blind with rage at being left with human trash. He was better than that. *Special.*

He'd used a knife from the kitchen, astounded at how the metal glowed when he gripped it in his hand. Jumped dad in his office. Painted blood across his books. Then the anger left, like turning off a switch. Dizzy and hollow, he ran—left his mother, little brothers, upstairs, all asleep. His head rang with voices, none of them his own. He couldn't touch things. If he did, the world skewed and turned strange. And the gray place—he stayed away from that. It choked him, almost to death.

Tashiel found him, filthy, starving, sleeping in a crumbling mill. The boy believed himself crazy, but Tashiel understood. He handed the boy a better pair of daggers, a set his hands remembered, even if the memories hadn't fully blossomed in his child-brain. Together, they went back and killed the ones he'd left. An old-style baptism, red with his false-family's blood.

Free from mortal obligations, they could be soldiers together once again.

"That fucking bastard!" I snarled. The venom tugged me from the depths. If I'd done something to Tashiel—

killed him or somehow made him disappear, I felt justified in that moment. Tash's idea of mentorship—no wonder Zuriel was a mess. I almost felt sorry for the kid, but he was as much immortal as he was a moody teen. Sympathy couldn't excuse the things he'd done—was still doing. A part of him should have known better. A part of him should have known enough to stop.

Except I knew firsthand the part that was likely to kill with impunity—and without regret. I struggled with it daily.

Shoving away those thoughts, I skimmed the lingering impressions. Sal and the others clustered at my back, distractingly close. They might have been speaking. I didn't hear. All my focus went to blocking them from awareness so I could better read the dirty psychic stain on the bike and pavement.

Finally, I caught the break I needed. The distance helped, and maybe my own anger, so I could parse the lines more clearly between my feelings and those coming from what the struggle had left behind. No further memories whirled to suck me into their vortex, and I saw the faintest trail of Zuriel's bitter, white energy. Pale and fading, it led from the bike to the garage, then further, to the sagging slats of a weathered backyard fence. A smear of what could have been blood—black in this poor lighting—arced across one freshly broken slat.

Beyond the fence stretched another yard and, beyond that, a different street. The properties here were stitched together closely, separated only by a thin line of trees.

How incapacitated was Remy that Zuriel could drag the vampire back to that tree line, ducking with his burden through the gap in the fence? And once he got there, how far could the little bastard get? I could carry Remy without too much effort. Anakim strength wasn't on par with Superman, but it was impressive, nevertheless. Still, the kid was tall, but coltish and lanky. He hadn't finished filling out. Did physics matter? How far could we push past our mortal limitations?

I had no clue.

Suspicion gnawed at me. Bundling Remy into the nearby house would have been easier and made more sense. No trail led that way, no convenient drops of telltale blood, but maybe that was intentional. A gambit to throw me off. The kid was adept at expunging his presence. Except he'd practically gift-wrapped the psychic spillage on the Vulcan. The only thing it needed was a shiny red bow.

Either he'd had too much on his hands with wrangling the vampire, or he'd left the layers of psychic garbage expressly to distract me. I didn't want to set foot in that house where he'd murdered Tabitha—didn't have the stomach to enter that stinking basement again—but I had to know—at least to rule the place out.

"Zaquiel!" Sal snapped. She closed her hand on my shoulder and gave a harsh shake. I smacked her wrist before even thinking about it, whirling to stab a finger into the plates at her chest.

"Don't fucking touch me," I snarled. She didn't even blink when I leaned into her. "I don't want what's in your head inside my head. Not when I'm doing shit like that. You could've messed everything up."

Not remotely chastened, she glowered at me from

the stratosphere. Belatedly, I noticed the cold metal eyes of Ava and Tanisha's pistols, both aimed directly at my head. Javier lingered behind Sal's ferocious women, keeping watch.

"I think he went at least one street over, but we need to check this house first," I said. My voice was tight and I held myself stiffly. "I'm checking my phone now," I added, waiting to dredge it from my pocket. Ava's weapon relaxed, though Tanisha still kept me in her sights. Not sure why she even bothered—at this range, even a crappy shot wasn't going to miss.

The glow of the screen ripped away my night vision and I hissed an unhappy curse. The countdown was still running.

Seventeen minutes.

Time enough to give the place a quick check, then, hopefully, still find Remy before Zuriel decided to shove my brother screaming into his next life.

44

Tanisha insisted on doing the whole sweep-and-clear thing again, creeping with her flashlight through the dark. After the first room, I shouldered her out of my way. We didn't have time for that kind of caution, and I knew where I needed to look.

Only a few hours had passed since I'd been down in that abattoir, but the approach to the basement was rank. The door was closed—I couldn't remember clearly if I'd been the one to shut it on my way out—and when I pulled it open, I gagged on the stink. Tanisha caught up, choking, the whites of her eyes reflecting pale backwash from her LED light.

"That's a body," she said. "Maybe more than one." She took small sips of air, breathing through her mouth.

"No shit," I replied. "Get your light on these stairs."

"You're not my boss, hotshot," she snapped.

"Fuck it," I said. "I got my own." She tensed as I went for my phone. I held the device where she could see it. Letting the countdown run in the background—fourteen minutes—I opened the flashlight app and aimed the beam into the pitchy dark. There was a Crossing down here. I could feel it. That and… something else. Probably residual stuff from the circle. *Maybe.* Beside me, Tanisha twitched as the light caught all the photos messily tacked to the right-hand wall. I'd forgotten them entirely.

"What the hell's all that?"

Grimly, I realized *exactly* what it was. Photos of Tabitha, Marjory… and me as a teenager. The three of us as a group or in pairs. One seemed to be my college graduation photo. There was a picture of Marjory and Remy, smiling together. The last time I'd come down these stairs, I'd been following a trail of blood with only distant candles to light my path. I'd noticed something on the walls, but I hadn't bothered to really look. Now, in the glare of Tanisha's flashlight, there was no missing Zuriel's punishing taunt.

"My brother's sick version of *This is Your Life*," I spat, and I started downward.

"What?" She lingered on the lip of the topmost stair, coughing as the stench rose up.

"Never mind," I called back. "You're probably too young."

"White boy, don't you talk down to me like that," she said. "You don't got that right."

I shook my head, refusing to respond. With determined effort, I shoved the photos from my mind. I could ask Remy about them once we'd saved him from Zuriel.

If we saved him. I counted off another minute before I reached the bottom. *Thirteen.* The beam from my phone's flashlight app found the outermost edge of the jellied blood. The wax from the spent candles spread through the slick pool of black like some kind of creeping fungus, lumpy and pale and wrong.

Tanisha's light bobbed on the wall behind me as she descended the stairs. One step, third from the last, creaked beneath her weight, but otherwise her movements were soundless. I wondered again where she'd worked before signing on with Sal.

Doesn't matter, I reminded myself.

Lifting my own light, I faltered as I finally saw why Zuriel had opted not to bring Remy down to this particular basement.

The place was already full.

"Uh, Tanisha," I said. My voice strained to be quiet, but a part of me was screaming. Quickly, I aimed my light at the floor, hoping I hadn't woken anything up. Backing toward the bottom of the stairs, I forced myself to move slowly. Very slowly. Instinct told me swift motion would be bad. Already on the last step, Tanisha shoved into me—or I stepped back on her. It didn't really matter. We collided.

She cursed and dropped her flashlight. It hit the ground and rolled in a wide and lazy arc, finally coming to rest against a lumpy bit of wax. The thing was durable—nothing shattered and its light never wavered.

The pale beam shone cold against a pair of blood-spattered tennis shoes.

"What the hell is that?" she choked.

I didn't answer immediately, just continued pressing until I drove her against the wall.

"Get back up the stairs," I hissed, hoping the sound

wouldn't carry. We'd already been making too much noise. "*Now.*"

A tremor rocked the nearest sneaker as the foot inside it twitched. Four people of various ages stood together in the dark. The LED's pale upwash painted them in hazy black and white so they seemed like living shadows milling within the circle.

Zuriel had been busy meeting neighbors and making friends—into zombies.

Three men and a woman—none of them Tabitha, I noted with queasy relief—had flickering sigils scored into their chests. Their empty eyes were open, and grisly smiles slashed their throats. Blood drenched each of them, adding considerably to the mess that pooled around their feet. Like silent, lurching hounds, they clustered around the Crossing forged by Tabitha's grueling death.

Guard dogs. I felt sick. *He killed four more people, just to have guard dogs.*

But he couldn't have bound so many people in the time it took me to leave Parma and come back, not while also abducting and restraining Remy. This took planning and preparation. A *lot* of preparation. The oppressive emptiness of Marjory's neighborhood took on ominous significance. Grimly, I wondered how many of its residents he'd murdered in their homes.

As I slowly digested the depth of my brother's sickness, the first figure stumbled forward with ponderous, jerky motions. A middle-aged woman, she was dressed in sweats—the kind that almost certainly said PINK across the butt. She'd probably been out jogging when Zuriel caught her. I could almost hear her screaming from the prison of her flesh. I'd have to help her—help all of them. To consider any other option was beyond cruel. But only later, once Remy was safe.

A second joined the first, his red-billed baseball cap askew on a balding head. Greasy wisps of yellow hair hung like webbing across his face. The LED beam traced his sleepwalk shuffle, and his sagging features became visible in the upwash of my own light.

Tanisha's throat clenched around a scream, reducing the sound to such a high-pitched whistle, I was amazed her vocal chords could sustain it. Rooted in place, she hunched miserably behind me. Whatever she'd signed on for, fighting zombies hadn't been in the job description. Pivoting so I could move around her without exposing my back, I shoved her roughly toward the first step.

"I don't think they can leave the circle," I whispered, "but let's not wait to find out."

Tanisha didn't respond, so I shoved harder. Her whole body twitched. For a minute, I thought she was going to whack me with the butt of her pistol, but then she started moving—slowly at first, then taking the steps three at a time. I was right behind her.

We made it to the top quickly.

From the deep shadows below, the wood of the third step creaked.

"Oh, *hell* no," Tanisha cried, slamming the door. It shut with the thunder of a rifle shot. Slapping wildly at both door and frame, she felt around for any kind of lock mechanism, driving it home with a click.

"Zaquiel?" Saliriel called. She was elsewhere in the

house, but her voice carried, so I couldn't pinpoint her exact location. Maybe the living room. I didn't feel like giving her the guided tour, so I kept my mouth shut. Instead, I hustled for the back door. My mental count had faltered—thanks to zombies. Hoping not to blow my sight too badly, I squinted at the phone.

Ten minutes.

Fuck.

"There's dead in the cellar," I called. "Four, I think. They might be coming up the stairs. Don't care. None of them are Remy. I'm going to the next street over."

Wood splintered loudly. Tanisha yelled and a gun went off. Someone with a surprisingly high and reedy voice—it had to be Javier—shouted in response. I kept running, bursting through the back door, and doubled my speed, pelting across the yard.

Nine minutes.

Through the fence I went. The smear on the wood was definitely blood. In my pocket, the phone buzzed once—a text. I couldn't bring myself to stop and check it. It wouldn't be anything good.

45

The faint trace left by Zuriel picked up on the other side of the fence. Feeling like the psychic equivalent of a bloodhound, I extended my senses in the widest possible net, doing my best to follow where the patchy trail led. I had no doubt it would eventually disappear, but for the moment, it offered at least a hint of direction.

The houses were as eerily silent as on Parmenter, all of them locked up for the night. Here and there, the spectral lights of a television flickered behind thick curtains shut against the late September chill, but otherwise the homes might as well have been abandoned. There were no streetlights to stand as beacons against the dark, although a few of the houses had porch or garden lights that still burned.

Halfway to the first intersection, spattered blood on the pavement told me I was on the right track. Crouching before the irregular pattern, I touched my fingers lightly to the drops. Long dried, though I still felt a hint of Remy's energy, edged with bright notes of panic, fear, and pain.

Senses still wide open, I peered at each of the houses within easy walking distance. Even assuming Remiel didn't struggle, I couldn't imagine his abductor getting far. That meant Zuriel picked a location of opportunity, killing the occupants, or he'd selected a destination ahead of time.

Six minutes.

The dwindling count ran inexorably through the back of my thoughts. As if force could milk their secrets, I pressed my fingers harder against the flaking drops of blood. An irrational urge rose up—to taste the cast-off, press it directly to my tongue and better read the information it contained.

That had to be the Eye talking. Shocked and queasy, I shoved the thought from my head. I would find Remy on my own terms.

All the houses to my right showed signs of occupation, their dreaming inhabitants blissfully oblivious to the troubles of the night. Cars in the driveways. Curtains sighing in the open window of an upstairs room. Faint strains of music, too soft to make anything out. The steady gleam of a porch lamp, surrounded by a frenzy of late season moths.

The other side of the street held more promise. Two of the houses had no visible vehicles and were completely dark. Another had only a watery light trickling from the basement through thick panels of glass. A minivan sat in the middle of that driveway, its nose almost kissing the garage. Decals arced across its back window, starkly white against the darkened expanse. Sighing trees surrendered dead foliage to a sudden gust of wind and something creaked from the center of the yard. I tensed, instantly ready for a fight.

It was nothing but a weathered FOR SALE sign, bent over so far it nearly disappeared in the rustling grass.

Leaving the blood, I bolted across the empty street, a heady rush of adrenaline kicking my heart. Tugging the wilted sign upright, I angled its face toward a weak spill of light. It was the same company as on Parmenter, right down to the dead realtor's face.

This had to be the place.

Five minutes.

46

As I approached the front door, I got my confirmation. Pale sigils flickered in a rough line across the threshold, continuing up either side of the frame. Same story with the front windows. The symbols looked rushed but lethally effective. I recognized a few of the nastier combinations. Zuriel had the place warded to the teeth.

Little shit works fast.

Cautiously, I passed my hand across the door frame—close enough to study the energy of the inscription but not so close to trigger a response. The crackling burn against my fingers told me what I needed to know. I wasn't getting in that way.

Checking the windows, I made my way to the back. Zuriel had tagged everything. The light from the basement shone through narrow strips of glass block, and, while they lacked wards, there was no getting through. Stymied, I threw one leg over the fence that separated the front yard from the back.

From one street over, a swift series of three shots echoed through the night. Nearby, a dog barked wildly in protest. No further sounds followed, but for the first time since separating from the rest of the group, I worried that Sal and her thugs might not be all right.

Four minutes.

As gracefully as possible, I dropped to the grass on the other side, landing solidly on my feet. As soon as I hit, my smartphone vibrated. After those gunshots, I couldn't ignore it. I pressed my thumb on the main button, tapping the passcode, and shielded the glow against my body as the screen came to life.

Two messages. The most recent was from a number not programmed into my contacts. It had arrived after the sounds of gunfire.

Where are you?

One digit off from Remiel's cell, it had to belong to Sal, so at least the decimus was fine. She had my cellphone number, too, though I'd never shared it with her.

Before tapping a response, I checked the other message. Remy's phone. Two words.

Come alone.

The threat was implied, and it was an empty one. Zuriel didn't plan to let him go, even if I made it in time. So it was time to change the game. I pushed the talk-to-text function, whispering quickly into my phone. The message appeared on the screen.

I'm at the house. He says to come alone.
Wards all over first floor. I'm going in from back.

Sal's response buzzed almost immediately thereafter.

You're a fool.

How she typed so quickly with those freakish nails, I
had no clue. Again, I whispered into my phone.

Probably. 103 Whitehaven.

After that text went through, I shut the phone off,
shoving it deep into the inner pocket opposite the SIG
Legion. The hard case of the smartphone jostled for a
moment against the wooden puzzlebox that hid the Stylus,
so I tugged that part of my jacket until the two items settled
into a more comfortable—and silent—arrangement.

Then I ran for a little terrace stretching above a narrow
patio. It wasn't a porch itself, so it didn't have any stairs,
but I thought I could jump high enough to drag myself
over, and there was a window on the second story within
reach of its flat expanse. He couldn't have warded *all* of
the windows—not on the second floor. It was an issue of
economy. He wouldn't have had the time.

Two minutes.

Neither did I—assuming the thirty-minute countdown
meant anything at all. At top speed, I barreled for the
back patio, leaping with all my might at the last possible
second. The jump carried me high—high enough to get
a solid grip on the edge of the overhang, plus enough

momentum to help hoist my weight to the top. It was quick, but it wasn't quiet—the whole structure rattled and creaked in protest underneath my hundred and eighty pounds. I ignored it, hurrying across warped asphalt shingles toward the window.

No wards glimmered around the double-hung frame, and I wondered if that might have been intentional. Ripping quickly through the external screen, I yanked it off and tossed it onto the patio rooftop. The big rectangle of aluminum bounced once, then stilled, making less noise than my boots had.

Digging my fingers into the weathered wood of the bottom sash, I tested to see if I could lift it. There was a simple flip-lock on the inside and while someone had thrown it, they hadn't done a very good job. Only a small corner of the mechanism tucked under the brass lip that held the window closed. Calling energy into both hands, I focused my strength and heaved upward.

The lock surrendered with a tortured-metal screech. From there, the rest was easy. I shoved the bottom portion of the window as high as it would go, clambering awkwardly through the gap. Sheer curtains tangled around me but I just pressed forward, letting my momentum tug them loose. Zuriel had to know I was there, but still I moved as quickly and quietly as my lanky frame would allow. Holding a hand out to help me navigate the darkness, I found a carpeted stairway and followed it down, hoping the access to the basement was close to the bottom.

This fight would end in the cellar. I had no doubt.

Trading the carpet for a tiled hallway, I angled sharply

to the right and checked for a door. It was there—that had to lead to the basement. Pallid light sketched thin lines around its loose-fitting frame. I smelled the blood before I saw it—a smear still tacky on the handle, and a little pool just in front of the door.

I knew from the scent it was Nephilim blood. I could almost *taste* how it was different. With a convulsive swallow, I tried not to ponder *how* I could be so certain, even as the flesh of my left palm began to itch.

Drawing a blade in one hand, I opened the door with the other, getting blood on my fingers and wiping it quickly onto my jeans. The stairs leading down were steep and unusually long, walled all the way to the bottom, so it was impossible to see past the landing. Gray cinder block and puffy pink insulation were the only décor.

Along the descent, rusty smears stood out at shoulder and waist height, dark against generic eggshell white. I went to put my foot on the first step, but caught a glimmer from the corner of my eye. Halting and glancing down, I saw a soft shimmer of magic scribed upon the lip of the step.

I recognized the sigils of an alarm, but there was only one way down, and no way to avoid stepping over Zuriel's little warning system. Any method I might use to pick the spell apart would give off as much energy as the alarm itself.

Not worth it.

Silently, I wished for the convenience of a relic or a Crossing. The Stylus might work as a relic, but to take it from its warded box was to reveal its presence. A dangerous prospect, especially since I was dealing with another Anakim.

I'd shut my phone off, but I knew the countdown app was finished. No more time to dick around. I took a deep breath and planted my steel-toe boot firmly on top of the line of sigils across the step. A pause, then power burst around me like a flash-bang, sending a harsh wind against my clothes and making my ears hum. Otherwise, it was harmless.

Adjusting my grip on the dagger, I loosed a hissing invocation of my Name. At the sound, Zuriel's cackle rose from the depths of the cellar.

"You're thirty seconds late, bro," he called, "but I'll give it to ya."

Ears still ringing, I bullrushed the bottom.

My momentum faltered once I saw what awaited me there.

47

A single light burned in the basement, but I would have preferred the dark. Then I wouldn't have had to see this—my brother's torture.

Remy hung face-forward in an elaborate webwork of rope anchored to a block and tackle high up in the basement's rafters, his shorn hair plastered wetly to his face. There was a cruel art to the bondage, interwoven cords locking every major joint so my brother had no hope of leverage, no matter his vast strength. One thick cord threaded through his mouth like a horse's bit. It yanked his head sharply back, distending his jaw to expose all his teeth. Deceptively delicate, his fangs curled against the wad of damp fiber, partly pinning it in place.

His features were a ghastly mockery of the man I knew, skin stretched so tight across his sunken cheeks, he looked skeletal. His arms winged painfully behind him, elbows lashed together with such severity, the ball joints of his shoulders strained visibly in their sockets. Zuriel had stripped him to the waist, and where it wasn't covered with gore, his skin was white as marble—far too white for anything alive. Vicious cuts covered his chest and limbs, their patterns curving like sadistic arabesques. The edges of the wounds gaped and rippled, the flesh ticking as it strove to knit itself—but there was too much damage, and not enough energy for the task.

The cuffs took care of that.

The Thorns of Lugallu glinted at his wrists, their bitter magic sucking the Nephilim's prodigious power. Not that freedom would have come cheaply, even without the magic writ upon the cuffs. Remy hung in a heavily warded circle, trapping the vampire within as surely as it kept me out.

"What have you done?" I breathed.

Zuriel offered no answer. He just stood beside the captive Nephilim, grinning as if my trussed-up brother were the ultimate big game trophy. His Tuscanetti charm was missing, probably lost in the struggle with Tabitha, so he wore his own creepily youthful face, blue eyes cold and flat and completely absent of anything human. One hand gripped a solitary blade—the same fluted punch-dagger that he'd used in his fight with Marjory's daughter—his pale energy licking brightly along its edges like magnesium flame.

There was so much blood. Remy's body practically wept it, a steady rain of crimson. Dark and pungent, it pooled across the floor, dimpling at the warded edges of the circle, and I strained to imagine how any fleshly being could surrender that much of the substance and still live.

The worst was the stake.

Zuriel had sharpened what might have been an old mop handle, fixing the worn and grainy staff of wood to a stout weight bench positioned in the middle of the floor. Carved all over with gleaming sigils, the wooden shaft had been infused with such deadly power that without a doubt it would drive the Nephilim from his body once it fully pierced his heart.

Remy was partially impaled already, an inch-and-a-half of wood punched through his diaphragm so a slow stream of scarlet trickled down the makeshift pike to add to the spreading mess on the floor. A lead line ran through the block and tackle, connecting all Remy's bonds, and Zuriel gripped it in his other hand. Every time Zuriel moved, Remy shifted downward onto the stake. The wood made obscene squelching noises in the gooey puncture beneath his ribs, and, silently, I screamed for him.

Every instinct clamored for me to rush across the basement and seize my wounded brother, but I knew Zuriel would drop Remy onto that spike the instant I so much as twitched. Even with my speed, I didn't think I could make it past the magic of the circle in time to keep him from being impaled.

Briefly, I considered shooting Zuriel. Without his illusion to wreck my aim, I couldn't miss. Not at this distance. But if he dropped the lead line, that would be the end.

"I was hoping you'd make the deadline, so I wouldn't have to kill him right away," the kid said. Idly, he tugged the thick coil looped around his hand, grinning with hungry fascination at the horror on my face. "Once you know where and how to stick 'em, these guys fade so fast. No fun, really."

With every leashed tremor, Remy's whole body twitched, his face a rictus of anguish. Blood—dark and sluggish—bubbled thickly from the ragged edges of each wound. There wasn't only one puncture, but several clustered together. My breath snagged on a sympathetic ache.

"I'm here," I responded. "Let him go."

The words were a token recitation. I knew that, but I said them anyway. Just standing there felt worse than useless. Vainly, I tried to catch my brother's gaze, to offer some tiny reassurance, but I wasn't even certain he could see me. Remy's eyes rolled to their whites in his head, only a slim crescent of blue visible beneath fluttering lids.

"Is that how you think this works?" Zuriel sneered. "This isn't some kind of hostage exchange, bro. We're way beyond that." With the razor tip of his blade, he opened a fresh line along Remy's bare chest, tracing the soft valley between two prominent ribs. The cut was shallow, mostly for show—Remy barely flinched. "This is pay-per-view. Or maybe, pay-per-*not*-view." Zuriel pressed harder at the edge of the cut, slowly driving his blade deeper. The vampire's skin was already drained so white, it was like watching someone draw blood from a statue. "I ask a question. You answer. I like your answer, I don't cut anything off that's too important. Got it?" As punctuation, he gave the blade a vicious twist. Steel ground against bone and Remy bit down convulsively against the gag.

Numbly, I nodded, because telling him "no" or "stop" was exactly what the little shit wanted. Zuriel craved my pain like a drug, and Remy was his current delivery system. The kid could ask me all the questions he wanted, but none of this was about getting answers. We both knew it. This was torture for the sake of torture.

Flashes of Marjory's brutalized corpse vied with the scene around me, and I strove to think past that horror, to take in the room to its smallest detail, to see some way of getting Remy out in one piece. The lighting was shitty—one brass floor lamp tilting on a dented base, positioned at the farthest corner behind Zuriel. Its tattered shade choked more than it diffused its light, stretching all the shadows weirdly. The basement itself was cavernous, the extra-high ceiling making it feel like some kind of cinder block tomb.

The web around Remy was so elaborate, I wondered how long Zuriel had planned to murder someone in this subterranean space. The weight bench, mop handle, and pulley system might have been happy accidents left behind by the movers, but the extensive coils of rope suggested planning.

So did the circle. Zuriel might not have finished warding the windows on the second floor, but he'd put a shit-ton of energy into that circle. The magic was so tight, it didn't even let Remy's pooling blood escape around its boundaries. I could pick it apart eventually, but it wouldn't be quick.

Remy needed quick. Even without the looming threat of the stake, blood had to be an issue. He'd already lost so much, he looked shriveled.

I can help you.

The words resounded through my thoughts without

warning. Every muscle stiffened. I *knew* that voice. It was the one that had spoken out on the beach, to issue its mysterious warning. Since then, it had been a lingering murmur in the back of my mind, one that had crested close to consciousness once or twice, only I hadn't wanted to acknowledge its presence. Neither clearly male nor female, it felt wholly *other*, patient and alien in ways I could barely comprehend.

I hardly dared to think the Name, but it rose, unbidden.

Neferkariel. The Nephilim primus.

Who else? the voice asked. As if the manic tickling of the scar across my palm wasn't answer enough.

"I owe you a few cuts for ignoring my texts," Zuriel said. He dug his dagger even deeper, then twisted with a flourish. "Rude, bro." Flesh parted and Remy squirmed. The wood of the stake ground against his sternum, and in my mind, that alien presence coiled like a vast boa constrictor, tightening its hold one slithering thought at a time.

This is how it happens, I thought. *This is how I lose everything I am.*

"What do you want to know?" I asked, just to keep the conversation going. If Zuriel noticed I sounded breathless, he didn't care—probably thought my look of naked panic came from what he was doing. I didn't disabuse him of that illusion. Neferkariel's presence pressed harder against the vault of my skull, and my world split-screened between the reality of the blood-soaked cellar and the suddenly crowded realm of my thoughts.

"We'll get to that," Zuriel answered. "But, seriously, bro, can we talk about how you've got a fucking *vampire* for a dad?" He yanked sharply upward, so the spike sucked wetly out of Remy's chest. Then he dropped him just as fast. The stake drove hard into the ragged wound—two, maybe three inches. Not enough to kill, but it was close. "How's that even work?"

"My dad?" I choked.

"Wrong answer!" Zuriel snapped. "Do you think I'm stupid? I saw the photo, you dumbass. That's why I stuck it front and center, so you'd *know* I knew."

Before I could even begin to organize the working parts of a response, words oozed through my thoughts, sucking me away from both Remy and Zuriel. Slow, sweet, suffocating... it felt like I was drowning in honey.

48

I cannot make you do anything you do not wish to do, nor do I have power to stop you from acting against my own wishes, Neferkariel purred. *Were that the case, I never would have allowed the vengeance-drunk Dorimiel to feast on the Unmakers.*

Get out of my head, I demanded. I slammed up every shield, tried every trick I knew as I stood there frozen between the stairs and Zuriel's grisly spectacle. The mental protections helped me focus a little, but nothing made it stop.

It is far too late for that, little Anarch. I could not leave, even if that were my desire.

Every fiber rebelled against those words. I wanted to scream my defiance, to shout that none of it was true. For Remy's sake, I swallowed the anger and the terror and fought to focus on the room.

A bitter taste like ashes rose at the back of my throat, and with weary revelation, I recognized it as defeat. Ever since I'd paid the blood-price to the Nephilim icon, I'd known something like this was likely to occur. Each time I'd tapped that damning power, whether through conscious intention or not, the red monkey on my back had dug his claws a little deeper.

Was it Goose that finally did it? Probably. I'd reached some crucial saturation point and tumbled across my personal Rubicon.

"Time to pay for your mistake," Zuriel sneered. Magnesium fire lasered my attention to his blade. "You know what they say. An eye for an eye and a tooth for a tooth." My stomach clenched. Adjusting his grip on the rope, Zuriel stepped closer to Remy, pressing the burning edge of his dagger along his captive's nearest cheek.

The vampire's flesh sizzled.

Your skepticism is well-deserved, Neferkariel said. *But I can help you stop this so you may focus on the greater threat.*

Greater threat? I wanted to ask, but I couldn't, not in that moment.

All my horror and righteous fury hung upon that gleaming blade. Zuriel angled the tip against Remy's lower lashes, gradually increasing his pressure.

"I think the bloodsucker'll miss his pretty eyes the most, am I right?" The pale skin dimpled, a single drop of crimson weeping around the charged steel.

Remy's breath came in huffing, awful rasps as he tried to strain away. He squeezed his eyes against the weapon. Zuriel only pressed harder.

"No!" I roared. My own dagger blazing, I surged forward, prepared to bull my way through the fucking circle.

I didn't even make it as far as the edge. Zuriel reacted swiftly, whipping his blade away from Remy's cheek. A weeping, blackened slash gaped in its wake. Leveling the weapon in my direction, he bellowed his power.

A bolt of white fire erupted from the tip of the dagger, brilliant and cold as an alien star. The blazing projectile flew straight for my chest, striking harder than any fist. It lifted me, driving me back until my shoulders smacked against the wall at the base of the stairs. Breath rushed out of me in a painful whoosh and all my teeth rattled.

Sliding to the ground like a bug on a windshield, I just crouched there for a moment, aftershocks jolting through my limbs.

"You so much as twitch again, I take them both," Zuriel growled. All the blue of his pale eyes bled to gleaming white. His mortal boy-voice cracked, but two other tones resonated deeply in his chest. The chord they struck was sour.

I give this freely, Neferkariel said. *Listen, and see.*

Before I could resist or even think to object, the clock of the world spun down. Zuriel lofted the dagger, aiming once more for Remiel's poor eye, but he seemed to move in slow motion. Even the flames that licked along the blade rippled with a curious languor, as if they wavered from within a thick fluid, rather than clear air.

My internal perceptions sped in counterpoint—and more than that. Lotus-like, the physical world unfolded, revealing layers of sound and texture I had never imagined, and could not readily name.

The house, above and around us, filled with stealthy sounds. Footfalls. I knew without fully comprehending the faculty, the distinct sound of each person's tread. Tanisha, on the second floor, just beginning to creep from the room with the open window. Ava, on the far side of the house, stopping to bend toward something at the base of the wall. Javier, heavy and plodding, moving into position just out of view of the nearest basement window… and Sal's light step close behind his.

Outside, near Ava's position, there was the soft squeal of rusted metal. A door of some sort, but tiny. A muttered word.

"Ready."

What's the price, you snakey bastard? I demanded, unable to fight the uninvited flood of awareness. *What's the offer I can't refuse?*

I give this freely, Neferkariel repeated.

I still didn't trust it, but that didn't make the perceptions stop. The room around me rippled. Light and shadow shifted, sharpened. Some colors deepened, others faded out.

Odd textural details leapt out from every surface— the steep ridges and valleys in the grain of the rafters, the warp and weft of individual threads in Zuriel's jeans, many of them worn. I could see the fibers there, too, every tiny strip of cotton minutely twisting to make the whole.

Then the circle. To my Anakim eyes, the sigils still glimmered with energy, but I saw *beneath* that, as well— to every stroke and flaw in each individual symbol. Every trace of every physical motion it had taken Zuriel to craft the inscription. The moments where his fingers had shaken, where his pressure had changed, and where the lines skipped uncertainly over cracks in the floor. Most were miniscule, but one or two were large enough to interrupt the crucial flow of energy.

There was a flaw. On the far side, between one and two o'clock in the pattern. It wasn't just a flaw, but an exploit. An irregularity in the cement of the floor, splitting a crucial symbol. Fine threads of Remy's blood trickled through the crack, further separating the lines of energy.

I could get through there.

It would take a few slashes of my blades, but I could do it, and do it quickly. Zuriel would still have some time to react—time enough to drop Remy onto the sharpened spit of wood—so I had to move when my enemy was distracted.

Time resumed its normal pace in limping stages.

The tip of the punch-dagger pressed against the rondure of Remy's closed eye. The Nephilim's skin had bled so pale that the deep blue of his iris sketched a faint shadow against the paper-thin lid. Zuriel leaned close enough to kiss my brother, sick ecstasy twisting his young features. His lips, moist and pink and completely obscene, parted in eager anticipation.

I knew when I had to act. It killed a cringing, human part of me even to consider it, but just looking at Zuriel's euphoric face, there was no better option. His pulse was a war drum. He hungered for the act, utterly seduced by its nauseating cruelty. The moment he did it, all his senses would narrow...

I waited for him to take Remy's eye.

And then I moved to strike.

49

The wet sound was audible, thanks to Neferkariel's gift of heightened senses. I tried not to think about it. If I thought at all, I would stop, and that would defeat the sacrifice. As I blurred across the basement, the power went out. The darkness was immediate and complete.

And yet I could see, not in color, and not in any way I was accustomed to processing sight. Depth, shape, texture, it all spoke an impossible language I nevertheless understood. My Anakim sight remained layered over this, so the glinting lines of the circle sketched an interlocking weave of light against the darkness. Zuriel's dagger shimmered with the same glacial light as his wings.

The Anakim reared back from Remy, startled and infuriated by his sudden inability to see. Like a pale brand sprouting from his knuckles, he lofted his weapon, pouring more energy into its rippling light. I looked away from the dagger, not just to save my night vision, but because I was unwilling to see if any miserable bit of gore were impaled on the tip.

Instead, I focused on his hand with the rope.

Zuriel still clenched the coils that kept Remy from the stake.

Good.

I held power back from my own dagger for as long as I could, tightening my grip while I focused on the patch of the circle where I wanted to be. Thinking of Saliriel's fleet appearance—so fast she might as well have teleported—I pushed harder than ever before to surpass my mortal limits. I sighted the spot like a target, imagining myself already there. Distantly, I knew my legs were moving, but they weren't my focus. There was only the goal.

Pain, bright and brilliant, blossomed immediately under my chest, but I pushed harder. My lungs burned and my eyes couldn't keep up—and then I was there, right where I'd intended. The flaw in the magic hung like a blind spot among the stuttering lines of power, six inches above the floor and no broader than the palm of my hand.

Zuriel hadn't even finished turning his head to react to the wind of my passage. It was as if we moved in separate layers of time. It would cost me—I knew that—and I didn't care. Calling my power with a breathless whisper, I jammed the curved tip of my gleaming blade low into the webwork of energy. First try and I caught the weak point, dead center. In a brilliant blast of blue and white power, I punched right through.

With every ounce of strength I possessed, I ripped upward, gutting the magic as if it were a great beast comprised entirely of lightning. Searing sparks spat wildly around me while jagged bolts snapped across the rippling curtain of force until this whole section exploded inward.

I was through.

Zuriel had barely begun to process what was happening around him. Before he could complete a pivot in my direction, I rushed him, circumventing the laden weight bench in the middle and knocking back his arm with the blade.

With my empty hand, I seized his other arm and its coiled burden of rope, wrenching the cruel leash from his grip. Time began ticking back to its normal progress as we struggled hand-to-hand, but I still caught his every reaction, responding before any blow could connect.

His jacket was warded, like mine, and the leather turned away the first strike of my blade. Rather than waste another, I jammed the butt of my weapon into the taut tendons across the back of his hand. His knuckles spasmed and he almost dropped his dagger. Viciously, I struck the same place a second time, and the weapon clattered noisily to the cement.

Swift as instinct, I kicked it away.

Enraged and clutching a fistful of energy, Zuriel spat the syllables of his Name. Nevertheless, I kept his wrist immobile, and with it the rope. He lashed out, but instead of pulling away, I stepped even closer, turning my head so his strike glanced off my cheekbone. As his knuckles connected, I brought the pommel of my dagger down on his temple like Thor's mighty hammer.

Blood gouted and the ringing crack vibrated all the way up my arm. Zuriel went down and I tore the last few coils from his slackened grip. I kicked him once in the face to make sure he wouldn't wake up any time soon.

Remy was the priority.

As I rushed to grab my wounded brother, one of the basement windows shattered inward, the whole section of glass blocks thudding heavily to the floor. Bits of concrete and cinder block erupted from the hole like shrapnel, pinging walls and floor and hollow ductwork.

Tucked like a diver, Saliriel threaded the impossible narrowness, diving head first and dropping lightly to roll to her feet. Above her, Javier's face and one broad shoulder blocked all starlight, the eye of his gun blacker than any shadow the massive man cast.

I felt the toll for my speed like a furnace in my chest, but I pushed past it, getting my arms under Remy without even stopping to sheathe my blade. Swiftly, I lifted to get him off the deadly pike. He was light, too light, most of his weight spread in the red stain upon the floor, but that was a bitter blessing. His body was knotted like a taut bow in the bonds, making it awkward as hell to hold him.

"Hold on," I breathed. "Please, hold on."

Kicking the weight bench away, I laid Remy gently on the gore-covered floor. The knotted ropes, soaked in drying blood, creaked with every motion. He weakly moved his head, but with a touch, I stilled him. His right eye was a pulpy ruin, and I could see the mess even in this total lack of light. I wished I couldn't. Digging through my pockets, I let my gaze drift elsewhere, but every inch of Remy's flesh was a geography of anguish. The ticks and twitches of his knitting wounds had all but ceased—he was finally fading.

In a rush of wind, Saliriel knelt beside me. With a tenderness I did not expect, she cupped his sunken cheek in one long-fingered hand.

"Oh, my beautiful one," she whispered. "What has he done to you?" With the hand not cradling Remy's cheek, she covered the weeping socket of his damaged eye.

"The cuffs are killing him," I said. "We need to get them off." I began searching through my pockets.

"Does the little beast have keys?" Saliriel demanded. She eyed the still form of Zuriel as if planning his vivisection.

"No, I do." Briefly jangling the sparse ring of keys, I bent to free my brother. Jolts of adrenaline left over from my flurried speed twitched through my fingers. The angle was bad, so I had to yank on Remy's already tightly bound arms to make any kind of headway. A frothing gurgle at the edges of the gag made me keenly aware of his pain. "Would someone cut these fucking ropes already?" I shouted. Then I got the first cuff off.

Still cushioning Remy's battered face with one hand, she clawed at a thick hank of rope. For once, her fierce nails weren't up to the task. "I need a blade," she said curtly.

"Coming," Tanisha answered. The guard's voice was a tight and small thing, as if some of what she'd witnessed had made her shrink upon herself. Even so, she crossed swiftly through the choking dark to offer help. Light sputtered as she reached the edge of the circle. With a startled hiss, she drew back.

I felt around for the lock to the second handcuff. Remy was laying on it. With muttered apologies, I moved him again, still fighting to fit the key. The brow above the mangled socket twitched and, softly, he groaned.

Saliriel traced soothing fingers through his damp, matted hair, refusing to leave his side. "Follow the circle and step around," she called to Tanisha. "There's a way through over here. Follow the sound of my voice and don't press too far forward if you feel static again."

"Yes, ma'am," Tanisha whispered, stepping cautiously in a wide arc.

"How can she see anything?" I hissed.

Sal's response was immediate and pointed. "How can you?"

I turned my face from the question, straining to fit the key through the narrow strip of space between the handcuffs, knots, and Remy's deathly-cold wrists.

"That's what I thought," Sal mused. Pitching her voice to carry, she began calling orders. "Ava, bring the Denali from the other house, and do it swiftly." Wherever Ava was—probably still crouched near the power lines—Sal assumed the driver heard and obeyed. She tipped her face toward the wreckage of the window.

"Javier, I need you down here immediately. You're donating blood."

Without so much as a flicker of a question, the guard rose obediently from his post. Holstering his weapon, he took off at a dead run, moving faster than I would have believed possible for a man of his bulk, even with the benefit of Nephilim blood.

"Use the upstairs window," Sal yelled. "The first-floor wards are still active."

Judging from the sounds, he was already halfway to the patio.

Tanisha made it haltingly through the tear in the circle, dropping next to me in a crouch. She flipped open a wicked tactical blade and wordlessly held it out. Her other hand brushed the shriveled valleys of Remy's ribs. At the chill of his flesh, she jerked away as if burned.

"Jesus," she gasped. "How is he even still alive?"

Neither of us offered an answer. I got the second cuff unlocked, the metal teeth rasping as I pulled it away from Remy's shrunken wrist. Taking care not to jostle the wounded vampire more than necessary, I threaded the cuffs from among the nest of ropes and knots, happy that Zuriel hadn't thought to lash the things into the web of his sadistic cat's cradle. Saliriel looked up sharply as I rose to my feet.

"What are you doing with those?" she snapped.

The lines of sigils glimmered faintly on the metal as I turned toward my wannabe doppelganger. Hungry magic buzzed uncomfortably against my hands, full of devastating potential.

The battered Anakim sprawled motionless where he had dropped, one arm thrown back, the other trapped awkwardly beneath his torso. Blood oozed sluggishly from his temple, mouth, and nose. He wasn't dead—the subtle tick of pulse at his throat confirmed that much— but I didn't expect him to get up and dance a jig any time soon.

"An eye for an eye," I said, ignoring the irony as I moved to bind Zuriel's wrists with the bitter cuffs.

50

Zuriel was waiting. I should have guessed it, should at least have stripped him of the jacket. I knew better than anyone how many handy trinkets that leather could hold. But all my focus had been on Remy—saving him, and then trying to mitigate some measure of my brother's anguish.

Holding the Thorns of Lugallu open like steely jaws, I bent for Zuriel's outstretched arm. Maybe he'd foreseen that, and it was why he'd fallen that way. Maybe it was nothing more than a convenient accident. It didn't matter—as soon as I got close, the little bastard sprang to life, yanking his remaining punch-dagger free from the interior of his jacket.

Two hands, two daggers. That was how it worked for me, and I should have fucking known better with Zuriel.

Hissing his Name like a fatal curse, he drove the bright blade toward my heart. With a cry of my own, I moved in time to block with my forearm, driving the deadly blade away. But he pressed bodily forward, using that startled momentum against me. My stance wasn't stable—I was down in a half-crouch and had been leaning over him just a moment before.

Twisting his whole body, he kicked out my knee. He didn't catch the right part of the joint to break it, but my leg still buckled and, as I caught myself, I skidded on the slick coat of blood.

"Zaquiel!" Sal shouted, but I had neither the breath nor the time to respond. The skid put my back to him, and I fought to blur so I could turn around and meet his blade in time.

I'd spent all my speed to get to Remy and free him.

Agony blossomed deep in my chest, almost dropping me to the floor. Zuriel seized the advantage. Snarling, he launched himself at my midsection, striking fast and low in a series of vicious kidney punches—each tipped with four inches of blazing steel.

It happened so fast.

The warded leather of my jacket turned the first blow, and the second, each failed strike still bludgeoning with staggering force. But there was only so much the magic could do against Anakim steel. Lines of scribed symbols flared along the cuffs and zipper as the power fizzled, then, in a flash, was spent. Zuriel just kept stabbing, shrieking incoherently. Finally, he pierced the armor, the knuckle-blade sinking at an upward angle deep into my flesh. A hot wash of blood flooded down the small of my back, but the rest of me went cold.

I'd seen the length of that punch-dagger, and it felt like he'd sunk it to the hilt.

For a moment, I lost that leg entirely—all feeling

and strength just winked out. Pitching forward, I barely managed to catch myself before I landed on my face. I hadn't even gotten my weapons into play, one fist still clenched around the enchanted handcuffs. As blood pasted my T-shirt to my back and soaked through the waistband of my jeans, I called energy in a breathless rasp, trying to direct some of the power from Club Heaven to staunch the throbbing wound. I had little expectation of success, but I'd healed before with energy stolen with the Eye, so maybe my body would remember how it worked.

Some feeling returned to that leg, and I could move again. That meant it was working—I hoped. I redoubled my focus, trembling through alternate waves of dizzying heat and bitter cold.

While I tried my damnedest not to bleed out, Sal bellowed my Name again. The syllables still rang in the cavernous basement, as a blurring force rocketed past me, buffeting me in its slipstream. Sal, blonde ponytail pluming like some Viking's grisly war trophy, slammed full-force into Zuriel. The other Anakim hit the ground with bone-crunching force. He skidded on his side halfway over the damaged circle, smearing the sigils and further wrecking the sputtering curtain of magic. The whole thing shivered in a cascade of sparks, then collapsed, leaving the basement reeking of ozone over the cloying sweetness of Nephilim blood.

Heavily, I levered myself up on braced palms, striving to breathe through the molten sensation in my back. Slowly, the pain retreated until it was a distant rumble down a long and echoing hall. I couldn't tell if that was the energy working or just shock. Waves of hot and cold continued to shiver through me and I didn't dare reach back to explore the extent of the wound.

Zuriel struggled to crawl further away but mostly ended up squirming uselessly on his belly, elbows and knees smearing weird shapes in the mess upon the floor. Sal was on top of him in an instant, heaving him to his feet by the front of his jacket. With one hand, she continued lifting until his boots dangled half an inch from anything solid. Weakly, he brandished his remaining dagger, the whole blade dark with my gore. Stuttering wisps of energy curled around his fists and glacial light danced faintly on the steel.

Uplit by that pale energy, Saliriel looked like a banshee birthed by the nightmare-forge. Her yellow eyes were incandescent, plump lips skinned back to reveal far too many teeth. Too stupid to know when to quit, Zuriel took a stab at her. With an almost casual motion, her free hand darted forward to intercept the strike. She snapped his blade arm neatly at the wrist.

Bones cracked like branches toppled in a storm. Zuriel howled and his weapon dropped from useless fingers, clattering to the floor. Sal backhanded him to shut him up, and from the crunch, she might have broken his jaw. He spat blood and flecks of teeth. She didn't even flinch. With that chilling smile, she leaned close enough to drag her pointed tongue through the smear of blood at the edge of his mouth.

Zuriel looked ready to puke, but with her other hand on his jacket, he couldn't pull away.

"I shall cut strips of your flesh and feed them to you until you choke upon your own insolence," she promised. "Death with not come swiftly, little Anarch."

Their eyes locked. Zuriel started weeping, cradling the broken arm high against his chest so there was no question Sal could see it. Only I caught the slow, creeping motion of his other hand, fingers straining toward something in his pocket.

All too keenly, I recalled his disappearing act.

"Relic," I hissed.

It was in his hand already, about two inches long, like a foreshortened pen. Without thought or hesitation, I launched myself from where I crouched, scrabbling to tear the item from Zuriel's clenched fingers. Even the echo of pain grew strangely distant. All my attention narrowed to a single focus—the blasted relic. He wasn't going to get away again.

My fingers closed on it, even as Zuriel tapped its power. Smooth and pale and ivory-slick, I recognized it at once as human bone.

Not just any human. It thrummed with a life cut short.

Zuriel had carved this from his father.

51

The world folded as Zuriel and I vied for the relic, competing for control of its stored power. He sought to push through to the Shadowside, and I fought to keep us anchored with the others in the basement.

I was losing. Saliriel wavered in the air between us, fading first to a hazy figure painted in grayscale, then bleeding to a featureless silhouette of scarlet. The rafters and cinder block walls fell away and the shattered remnants of Zuriel's circle grew sharper, taking on substance until the broken filaments of energy glittered like stubs of spun glass sprouting from the floor.

Too much effort, I thought, and with the wound over my kidney, I didn't know what kind of strength I had to waste. So I changed tactics, trying to piggyback on the relic's power.

As it bridged the journey to the Shadowside, punishing images lashed the air around us—Zuriel's attack on his father, the man's torture and eventual murder. Graphic didn't even begin to cover it. I got a ringside seat to the young Anakim's singular capacity for sadism. The relic was drenched in it, sick and bloated, and, as it ripped us both across to the other side of reality, I realized that the miserable death was a fundamental part of its power.

No wonder the thing could carry two of us across, and still not be spent. I could even see how Tabitha had managed to tag along through its wrenching backwash. The relic was strong—obscenely strong.

Human sacrifice had a way of doing that.

The boy hadn't realized it at the time, had no initial understanding of the item's purpose. He'd only felt the knowledge as compulsion, so acute and blinding that he hadn't dared to call it into question.

That is the great tragedy of your tribe. Your knowledge manifests first. The memories of consequence, only later.

Get out of my fucking head. Despite the language, the thought lacked any real force. Everything I had was focused on keeping hold of Zuriel while we made the brain-ripping transition. Stepping to the Shadowside with a relic wasn't a joyride under normal circumstances. Making it a two-for felt like both my brain and stomach were being put through a cosmic centrifuge.

I am waiting, Neferkariel responded.

I didn't dare ask for what, and I couldn't spare him any further thoughts. We were tumbling through the rift and Zuriel came out swinging. Distracted by Neferkariel's yammering, I took a solid blow smack upside the head from one of Zuriel's wings. The force of the strike lit fireworks behind my eyes, nearly knocking me stupid.

As I tried to shake off the damage, the little punk won the tug-of-war with the relic. He managed to stuff it in a pocket, but since Sal had done me the courtesy of breaking his arm, the kid was forced to work one-handed. I still had a good grip on him and there wasn't much he could do about it. Ducking my head against his shoulder to avoid getting clocked with another wing, I drove him forward. As I strained to topple him, pain lanced across the small of my back. Raw and hot, it wasn't as debilitating as before, but it still served as a reminder that things weren't OK.

"Get the fuck off me, bro," Zuriel yelled, flailing.

I didn't waste my breath, just focused on wrestling the kid to the ground. I would have settled for shoving his back against a wall and cuffing him from there, but the walls of the basement—hell, the entire house—were virtually non-existent. About the only solid things on this side of reality were the ward and the wreckage of the circle. Vague shapes like poorly sketched shadows told me where the others stood in the flesh-and-blood world.

Winged, spindly scarlet—that was Sal. Something like a moving block with a head, that had to be Javier hustling down the stairs. Remy was a faint smear on the floor, red like Sal, but dim and spun out, pale streamers of essence sprawled around him like a doll's torn stuffing.

I shivered, realizing we were wrestling inside of all that—the ruin of Remy's blood. For that reason, if no other, I grabbed Zuriel by the throat and shoved hard to push him beyond the circle. The energy glittered like a broken ice castle, all razor-sharp points and brittle edges. They shattered into stardust with a sound like scattered chimes as I smashed my opponent through them. Agony soared hot and swift, but I just kept going.

Maybe the Nephilim Primus kept me up. Maybe it was stubborn desperation.

Spitting insults, curses, and ridiculous jargon, Zuriel got in a few lucky punches, but the way I pressed into him, I kept his leverage to a minimum. With only one good arm, he couldn't effectively pry me off, and I had probably twenty pounds of weight on him—all of it pissed-off, wiry muscle. He tried to brace himself with his wings, but mine were bigger. I countered by bringing them into play, pounding the air to increase our momentum.

He took another futile swing and I scissored his wrist in my elbow, trapping that arm between us. Furiously, he shouted his power, energy spitting from his fingers, but it was a token show, at best. Some of it danced up to snap against my cheek and throat. It stung like a motherfucker, but it was nothing compared to a blade in the back. I twisted to keep his arm locked between us, insulated by the warded leather of both our jackets.

He thrashed and tried worming his fingers inside my coat to dig his nails sharply into my ribs, then quickly withdrew when he got an elbow in the face.

With all my hurt and anger and outrage, I poured on the pain, blue-white fire crackling in a nimbus around the hand that held his throat. Zuriel gave a long, warbling, and very satisfying scream. I wanted right then to slap him in the Thorns of Lugallu, but to grab the cuffs I'd have to release his trapped hand. I didn't think he could do much, not at this point, but—

And what will you do with him then? Neferkariel asked. The words held all the bland detachment of a therapist—or perhaps a scientist, curious but thoroughly uninvested in any particular outcome.

"For fuck's sake, shut up already!" I yelled. The fire around my hand faltered along with my focus. Zuriel choked on the dregs of his scream, then fixed me with the weirdest look. I could almost see a reflection against his pale irises, red as the ominous light of a distant city against a cloudy night's sky.

This one will not stop. You realize that, do you not?

"You mad, bro?" Zuriel whispered. That weird look crawled his features a second time and then, without warning, he vanished from my arms.

52

I thought—reasonably—that he had simply stepped back to the flesh-and-blood world. But, as far as I could measure, we stood in solid bedrock, nowhere near the open vault of the basement. Peering across confirmed this. Behind me, at a distance of about thirty feet, I could just make out the wavering silhouettes of Sal and company. I counted each familiar signature—Sal, Remy, Tanisha, Javier. A fifth had joined them—Ava.

Zuriel was nowhere within sight.

"What the fuck?" Furious, I lashed out at the space he'd so recently occupied, energy still glimmering around my fist.

Blue-white shimmers lingered in the air, outlining... *something*. A slit or seam, suspended amid all the lightless gray of the shadowed limbo. Curious, but with a mounting trepidation, I passed my hand across it a second time. The thing pulsed and trembled at the touch of my energy, like a mouth, pursing to open.

Barely visible, a darker bit of space hovered just beneath the parted surface. A rush of uneasy recognition shivered down to my wingtips and I recalled my conversation with Lailah in Halley's vision of the hidden well. Layers. The Shadowside had layers. I'd been skimming the surface all along. This explained how Zuriel had appeared and disappeared so suddenly.

Are you sure you want to go there? With that wound, your mortal body is dying. Retreat would be safer.

I ignored the annoying voice in my head, determined to wall it from my awareness just like I had the wound he claimed was killing me. It probably was, but that just gave me more incentive to keep pushing. Neferkariel was right on one count. Zuriel wasn't going to stop until he was captured. I was the only one who could go after him.

Drawing on the same capacity that allowed me to step out of the flesh-and-blood world, I took a deep breath, steeled myself, and stepped through the parted curtain toward parts unknown.

A layer of light stripped away—or, perhaps, more appropriately, a layer of dark was added. I wouldn't have thought of the Shadowside as being well-lit. The whole crushing bleakness of that space arose primarily from its lack of illumination and color. Perpetual twilight, starless skies over a world gray as dust—that was the Shadowside as I knew it.

This was darker. The space was a pit around me, and the air weighed heavily upon my wings. The suffocating atmosphere clawed more hungrily, and I knew without having to test it that this layer would eat my strength even faster than the one I'd come to know. Which made me wonder—if Zuriel was losing, why the fuck did he come down here?

Cast-off energy from his wings glistened faintly in the air ahead of me, the only thing of substance that I could see. He'd taken off as soon as he'd crossed over, and there was nowhere to go but up into the desolate excuse for a sky. Twenty, thirty feet above, he arced like a comet, a white tail trailing through the shapeless, choking black.

No telling where he thought he was going. There was nowhere to hide, and I didn't think he could outrun me, regardless of his head start. Even if he escaped to further layers—assuming this descent might be endless—we both had to leave eventually, or face death.

"Not today," I muttered. "Not today." With a running leap, I pounded the air after him, pain a distant clarion ringing against my spine.

Zuriel had dumped a whole lot of energy into his assault on Remy—the ward, the alarm-traps, the near-impassable circle. He'd probably stepped through this nether-space more than once, as well. All of that was costly, and from the way his wings fought to chew the air, he was feeling it.

The broken wrist probably didn't help.

I caught up with him fairly quickly, working even higher so I could drop on him from above. He didn't have his daggers anymore, but I still had mine. If I had to cut the little bastard from the sky, I'd do it. I just hoped it wouldn't come to that. Containing him was more important than killing him.

Dead, he'd just come back.

Still, I'd kill him if he gave me no other option. He sure as hell deserved it.

Below us, the shadow of Parma was nearly featureless. A few roads cut through the unrelieved charcoal of what might have been fields, but most were smudges at best. The rows and rows of identical houses were phantoms, few possessing more substance than smoke. Here and there, the stain of a crossing stood out with the barest hint of color. Red. Always red.

The pigment of anger, of fire, of blood.

Zuriel was pale and sweating when I closed on him, beads forming greasily on his shock-white brow. He'd partly unzipped his jacket, tucking the wounded arm inside the leather like a makeshift sling, but every down stroke jostled it. I could practically hear the shattered ends of bones grinding together—it had to be agonizing.

Drawing my daggers, I tucked and dove, bracing to slam into him from above. He twisted his head around, realized what I intended, and he... rippled. A sucking vacuum shimmered in his wake. He'd gone deeper again.

"Fuck me running," I hissed.

I dove in after him. Another layer, another crushing atmosphere. Shadows congealed as more light stripped away. The half-shadows of houses grew shapeless, as if few things at this level remembered their forms. The air itself swirled thick around us, heavier, a suspension of ink.

I spotted him just ahead. "You can't run forever," I shouted. The dark choked sound and sense alike. The ringing notes fell flat. Zuriel spared me a glinting look. Even his features were pared down to light and shadow, lines and planes.

"Who says I'm running, bro?"

He flickered again.

* * *

Layer and layer, we descended, the pressure grinding with intolerable weight. Each time he crossed deeper, he jumped ahead just enough to force me to rush, so I never fully caught up. That didn't stop me from trying. The wound at my back began to clamor again. Whatever power I'd used to ignore it was flagging.

I tried not to think of the price.

Our flight became more like swimming, then like insects struggling in amber, then beasts drowning in tar. We hung, suspended, our nearly frozen wings the only remaining source of light. That light limned us, traced rough sketches of our bodies, pooled at our hearts. We were reduced to that most basic substance, all else either stripped by the increasing formlessness of the space, or impossible to perceive in the unrelenting void.

"Why?" I gasped, but it was wasted effort. The sound was as flat as if I'd spoken with my face pressed to a wall. Zuriel didn't hear it, or he tuned me out. I was only a few body-lengths away, but moving forward felt like clawing through cold molasses. A breathless effort only gained me an inch.

With his good arm, Zuriel trailed light across shadows, as if he was finger painting on the dark. As I closed on him, a shape took form—the only form visible on this level beyond our thready light of moon and ice.

It was a house, rendered crudely, but recognizable all the same.

Halley's house.

Even as I made the connection, Zuriel blipped from

the darkness and I knew with terrible certainty that he'd reversed his direction, crashing through layers up and up and up. The bastard wasn't running away from anything. He'd been running *toward* her this whole time.

53

"No," I breathed, but words couldn't negate the horror. I had to act—and quickly.

The faint outline of the house beckoned, tugging like an anchor in some direction I could not name. Before I could gather my power to flicker after Zuriel, a terrible, familiar chittering chilled me down to my bones.

Cacodaimon.

My wait is over, Neferkariel announced. *Here is the face of your true enemy, the misbegotten legacy of Dorimiel.*

"What?" I choked.

The sound slithered closer, swift in the darkness and drawn to my light. Two slitted eyes opened in the distance—hardly distant enough. Red as bloody gashes, a membrane flickered and from their depths another color drank the red.

Green. Green as poison, green as sickness, green as a void-touched Nephilim's maddened gaze as he peered down at me and swallowed my memories like candied dates.

"No," I gasped again, even as the very air around me sought to drink my breath. "No, no, no." That chittering cry rose again—high and terrible and almost within reach. Answering ululations resounded from every direction. The darkness filled with eyes.

"Weeee sssseeeee youuuu, Sssskyborrrrrrn," the green-eyed one shrilled. "Weeee wwaaaannt ttooo plaaaaay…"

I gripped my weapons tighter, but against the encroaching dark, their light had grown hopelessly faint. That green-eyed horror—bigger than all the rest—had nearly ended me the other night at the lake. Only its behavior, erratic even for a being of chaos, had kept me from being devoured. And while I still couldn't fathom why the thing had spared me, at least I understood what marked it as so mind-crushingly wrong.

Dorimiel was in there somewhere—or parts of him.

We are not yet prepared for this battle. Run.

I didn't trust the Nephilim primus any more than I could trepan myself, but that was one bit of advice I wouldn't argue. Headlong I fled into the faint sketch of Halley's home, trading darkness for ascending layers of light.

With a knowledge that taunted beyond the periphery of consciousness, I kicked whorls of power behind me and collapsed the open path. The shrilling cries of hungry cacodaimons faded into the black.

54

When I caught up with him, Zuriel stood one layer from crossing into the flesh-and-blood world. Somehow, through that near-endless descent into the crushing void, we'd crossed miles in the mortal world. We were in Little Italy, the echoes of houses clustered among the hills leading up to the towering monuments of Lake View Cemetery.

Cemetery and houses, both crafted with the same dedicated hands, held significant substance in this gray shadow of the world, a welcome contrast to the deep and formless dark I had escaped. Still rattled by my encounter in the depths, I kept an ear out for the cacodaimons' shrill cries. But Zuriel and I were alone in this space.

With one exception.

On the other side of a street that flickered between cobbles and asphalt and bricks, Halley's house stood solid as a fortress with its complex matrix of obfuscations and wards. Lil's lioness lay recumbent on the porch, warily regarding us through one slitted eye. If Zuriel noticed the spirit-guardian, he was too cocky to care.

"You led me right to her," he said. He was missing a front tooth. "And I know what she is. I'm not stupid. Gonna fuck her up good."

"With a broken arm?" I demanded. "No weapons? What, you're going to bleed on her?" Not that I was doing much better.

He patted the front of his jacket, a shit-eating grin on his face. "Your wards can't stop bullets." The lioness took keener interest. "I got your gun, bro, and you didn't even notice."

There was no need to check. Once he'd pointed it out, I couldn't miss the change in the weight of my jacket, the subtle void on that side of my chest.

"You little fuck," I hissed.

"I think I can tag someone before the old priest guns me down." His wings shimmered as he started to step out of the Shadowside.

No.

With a roar of purest fury, I launched myself at his back. Fading dregs of power licked along my blades as I drove them deep into his shoulders—right in the meaty hollow between collarbone and neck. It was a conscious echo of his initial attack on Remiel, and it was wickedly effective.

His wings spasmed and a guttural cry erupted from his throat. Hissing profanities, he jerked and twisted, trying to clap me between the powerful musculature at the joints of his wings, but, with flagging strength,

I crushed myself into the unreachable space along his spine where he couldn't touch me. I knew that weak spot well. I'd had cacodaimons use it on me often enough.

Rage keeping me up, I shoved harder on the daggers, twisting as I felt the metal press through tough layers of muscle to grind on bone. Zuriel bellowed, his voice cracking between registers. The two lower notes that betrayed his inhuman nature echoed dully across the bleak landscape. The lioness twitched an ear, yawning cavernously and hoisting herself to her feet.

She didn't leave the porch, though, positioning her long, tawny body in front of the door. Zuriel tried shifting under me, straining toward the house, but the daggers pinned him in place. This was the end of the line—probably for us both.

Lurching unsteadily, I brought a knee to his kidney, then kicked at the backs of his legs, dragging my weight against his shoulders. Slowly, he sank to the ground, fumbling for where he'd stashed the stolen firearm inside the twin of my jacket. But with my blades sunk through muscle and tendon and nerve, even the unbroken arm wasn't working very well.

He coughed and spat blood—and then he was laughing. Wings sagged, his energy sputtered, blood streamed from the wounds in his back, and he knelt there, laughing.

"What the fuck is so funny?" I yelled, kneeing his kidneys again. My own twinged in sympathy and the world swung.

"I'm just coming back, bro," he said. Blood poured around my daggers. He stopped trying to get the gun and just let his hand drop nervelessly into his lap. He coughed, spat blood, then chuckled, wincing as it shook his pierced shoulders. "You think you're winning or something, but I'll come back." His voice grew weaker with each statement, breath a wheezy rattle. With the angle of my weapons, I'd almost certainly pierced a lung, possibly both of them.

"And I'll find you," he said. "And I'll find *her*. I know what she is now. Took some thinking, but I'm not dumb." He spat again, more froth and blood. I didn't need to press down to keep him on his knees anymore. His strength was flagging—but not his spite. "Anyone you give a rank shit about, I will hunt and cut and kill, over and over again," he swore. I felt its power, as deep as an oath. "Don't you think that's funny? Cause I think it's fucking hilarious."

Disgusted, I yanked both daggers from his flesh. The curved tip of the one on the left snagged a bone, and the splintering grind it made on its way out tore a scream from his throat.

He will not stop, this one.

"Nobody asked you!" I roared. On his knees, Zuriel cackled through phlegmy bubbles streaked with crimson.

"You're not just mad, bro," he muttered. "You're crazy as tits."

But Neferkariel was right. Death would not be the end, not for Zuriel, not for his kind of hatred. I'd known that throughout the entire pursuit. It was why I had chased him, even knowing I probably wasn't making it out myself.

I thought of the handcuffs, still resting in my pocket.

The Thorns of Lugallu—they would have interrupted Remy's reclaiming, delaying it for centuries if he'd died wearing them. Was it the same for one of my tribe? And what would I do once those centuries had passed? Would I even remember in time to save another set of friends and family from Zuriel's blind and fixated wrath?

The kid would just keep coming in one form or another, and Tashiel—wherever he was—would probably join in the fun. So would the rest of my brethren if Zuriel—living or dead—breathed a single word about Halley.

The thought made my marrow run cold. Maybe the Stylus—

With the mental equivalent of clearing his throat, Neferkariel interrupted the thought. As always, his voice was soft and soothing and infinitely reasonable—all the more reason to be suspicious.

Might I point out a more convenient solution?

At my feet, Zuriel was dying in earnest, each breath a sucking labor through the fluids pooling in his lungs. Yet I didn't even need to hear the offer.

"No," I answered flatly.

Would you dismiss an option so swiftly? he persisted. *It does not have to be a bludgeoning weapon. With my help, you can wield it with the finesse of a scalpel.*

The scar on my palm ached down to the tendons, sending little worms of hurt up and down that arm. I dug my nails fiercely into the twitching skin, fervently wishing I had never set eyes on the fucking Icon.

"I'm not Dorimiel," I said. "I would never stoop to that."

Laughter, more sad than bitter, rang within my skull.

435

Once long ago, holding that Icon was the highest honor bestowed upon any member of my tribe, Neferkariel said. *To use it is not to stoop.* Zuriel's head nodded against his chest and his body sagged forward. His wings drooped like ragged curtains around us, trembling beneath their own weight. Soft, almost wistful, the Nephilim continued. *But I will not ask you to trust me, as that would only guarantee the opposite response. You are Anarch, to your very core. You must decide for yourself.*

"Are you finished?"

He elected not to respond. Doggedly, I wiped the mess off my daggers and tucked them both into their sheathes. It took more effort than it should have. My hands were shaking. From Halley's front porch, the lioness peered quizzically, every line of her great, muscled body shimmering with power. Along with Father Frank and me, she and Lil were the only ones standing between Halley and the rest of my bloodthirsty family. The Anakim had hunted children exactly like Halley throughout the Blood Wars.

I hadn't even trusted Remy with knowledge of the girl's existence, and yet here was Zuriel, swearing an oath to make her suffer.

Can you risk that he will deliver? Neferkariel prodded.

"Shut up."

Something went out of me and I dropped to my knees—all the damage, finally catching up as the adrenaline fled. On the side where he'd planted the dagger, the leg of my jeans was soaked to the ankle. I knew what that meant.

A single thread. That is all you must pluck. His knowledge of her existence. I can help you make it disappear.

"No," I croaked. I couldn't catch my breath. "Memory's a web. I know that better than anyone."

"Dafuck you talkin' to, bro?" Zuriel mumbled. Even on his knees, he wavered drunkenly. His skin was the color of ash.

Patient as a predator, Neferkariel circled my failing thoughts.

If you take even that tiny morsel, you will live.

"I don't care about that!" I hissed. It was a lie and he knew it. I was fucking terrified. Not of ending, but of leaving—and failing my friends.

I locked eyes with the lioness and she sneezed philosophically, although whether in commentary on my struggle or the sad state of the two dying men at her feet, I couldn't guess. A spasm wrenched all feeling from my legs, and I clung unsteadily to Zuriel, too stubborn to just curl up and die. What use was immortality if it took me out of the world for decades at a time? If I came back at all, Father Frank would be gone. Halley would be alone. Bobby, Remy, Lailah, Lil—everything I knew, everything I'd worked for would be lost.

"He's a screwed-up, angry kid," I said, bitterly aware that I was rationalizing for my own ears. "Maybe next time, we'll be different."

Zuriel groaned and slumped forward. He tried to laugh again, but instead sprayed blood messily onto the pavement. The red lingered for only a moment as the bricks flickered to stone to dirt to asphalt and back to bricks again. Then the gray drank it up.

You do not believe that.

"No," I sighed. Another spasm wracked me, strangely weaker than the last. "I don't."

Be swift in your decision, Anakim. There is no more time.

My head buzzed with the surging rhythm of my pulse. The thunder of it felt like it should shake the very pillars of the world. With a detached sort of panic, I realized I could no longer see.

"You win," I said. My voice shook.

55

With trembling fingers, I groped for Zuriel's throat. His mind was unwilling—he struggled to the last. He died as Neferkariel helped me pluck the glimmering thread that comprised his knowledge of Halley. As promised, it was targeted and swift.

Power swept through me as my brother expired, the last dregs of his life bolstering my own. My wounds knit so swiftly, the meat and muscle twitched deep beneath my skin. It wasn't a pleasant sensation, but it was nothing compared to the hollow knock of my heart as I drank it down.

Some lines should never be crossed. Still, I crossed them. Immortality wasn't worth a tinker's damn if I couldn't be around to protect my friends.

"Sure. Keep telling yourself that," I muttered and spat copper to the stones. All it took was a touch for me to drain his life. The Eye made feeding too easy. Maybe if I had to close my mouth around his throat, bite through sinew and skin, I'd find it harder to resist.

Maybe.

Once it was over, I gathered Zuriel into my arms and launched myself into the sky. The boy was an awkward weight, all long, dangling limbs, and I strained to remain airborne. Gritting against the effort, I soared to the cemetery, skimming the memory of trees from a countryside long forgotten. Even with the life I'd stolen, the Shadowside gnawed at me, but I refused to leave his miserable corpse anywhere near the Davis house. I wouldn't risk him near Halley, even in spirit.

Deep into the vast acreage of Lake View, I flew with my burden as far as I could safely travel. I alighted in front of the Haserot family memorial. A great bronze angel watched over their graves, so infused with symbolic weight that it broodingly straddled both sides of reality. I dumped Zuriel at the statue's feet, not bothering to be gentle about it. Frisking his corpse, I took back my stolen SIG. I left the hideous relic of his father's fingerbone—couldn't even bear to touch it—and then I gathered his wrists together and bound them with the Thorns of Lugallu.

Maybe it was too late, but maybe it would forestall having to deal with his blind, unreasoning hatred any time soon.

When I stepped back to the skinside, I half-expected the pallid corpse to follow me or, perhaps, fade by stages back into reality like some deceased monster in a horror film. But Zuriel, however monstrous, remained in the Shadowside, stretched before the Haserot angel that wept tears of acid rain.

That wasn't poetry. Weathering had oxidized the

bronze of the life-sized statue to a patina of rich green with accents of purest black. The most remarkable of these markings were tear-like streaks that formed down both cheeks, dripping from the lower lids to the proud line of the statue's jaw. Both the melancholy and the vigilance of the graven figure suited it for watching over this short incarnation of my wayward brother's life.

I thought about saying a prayer, then cackled bitterly at the irony. If I hadn't been damned before, this blatant act of fratricide had surely sealed the deal. Instead, I sought for my phone. Predictably, it was dead, the wards on the case blackened and fried. Not surprising. I'd designed the magical barriers to cushion the technology against a jaunt or two through the Shadowside, not shield it from a descent through the fucking abyss. But I still needed some way to make contact. I had to hear that Remy still lived.

My car was in the lot at Club Heaven—miles away. I didn't have the patience to wait on public transit. Caught in those awkward hours between late night and early morning, few buses would be running, and probably none where I wanted to go. That left one option.

With the copper-salt taste of Zuriel's blood on my tongue, I walked the lonely half-mile to the Davis home on East 124th. I took it slow. Not because I hurt any more. That was the core of my reluctance.

I desperately didn't want Halley to see me after what I had done—especially not if there was any chance she might guess that I'd done it for her.

As I walked, a faint light flirted with the clouds beyond the eastern hill of the cemetery. I put my back to the dawn and followed Lake View's winding paths down to Little Italy. Skirting a pond thick with duckweed, I headed for the blind end of the street next to Halley's. Here and only here, the massive wall that circumscribed the boneyard dwindled to nothing more than a pitted concrete barrier topped with chain link. The whole thing rose no higher than my midsection, and was easily scaled. On the pavement beyond, a profusion of condom wrappers, empty beer bottles, and cigarette butts—mostly the black filters of cloves—bespoke of youthful nights and regular pilgrimages to kiss and revel among the stones.

Once on Halley's street, I couldn't bring myself to approach the house. A light was on in her downstairs bedroom, faint behind thick curtains, and I knew in my gut that the girl was awake and questing for my presence. She had no reason to expect me, but with Halley that didn't matter. Her abilities were unpredictable. Something had given me away.

If the girl was awake, I couldn't go in. The idea of Halley seeing me with blood on my lips was paralyzing. And she would know. In her strange and prescient, impossible way, she would know.

Later. I would have to face that conversation later. I didn't have it in me now. Maybe that was some kind of moral failure, and if so, I didn't know how to fix it. All night, I'd been failing so hard. A part of me was human, crushingly so. There were times when I thought that was the best part of my being—the part that treasured mortal things for their brevity and loved them for their flaws. But my all-too human flaws, right then, felt unlovely—and unlovable.

I hunched in the shadows of dark houses, my fists curled in my pockets because I didn't fully trust the power in my hands. The wind that caught wet tracks upon my cheeks was only half as bitter as the chill that welled within my heart.

"Hey," Lil said, so softly I assumed she was just one more voice clamoring inside my skull. But then she scraped her boot on an uneven bit of sidewalk and I dropped immediately to a fighting stance. I whirled in her direction, hands on the hilts of my daggers, ready to draw.

"Relax," she soothed. Metal glinted in her hand as she tucked a weapon primly in her blazer. It disappeared like a magic trick. Stiletto, by its slender lines. "Lulu said she saw you out here. Thought I'd check."

"Yeah," I responded. Shoving my hands back in my pockets, I angled away from her. She only stepped closer.

"Yeah?" she echoed, rising on her toes. "Is that all I get? You know you owe me big time for this favor. I can't even stand that kid."

"He's dead," I murmured. Wearily, I put my back to her, leaning a leg against a tired fence that protected a king-sized bed worth of yard. "It's over. Halley's safe for the moment. You can leave any time you want."

Lil huffed her annoyance and yanked on my elbow to turn me around. She stopped only when she caught sight of my face. For an instant, she seemed confused, tipping her head up and almost reaching for the moisture on my cheek. Then she stopped herself.

"Zack, are you—?"

She didn't say the word, which was a kindness. Awkwardly, I scrubbed the back of a hand across my eyes. The world smeared. She waited with the same patient intensity of her lioness, full lips pursed around her concern. We stood there, neither quite looking at the other, as the houses woke up around us and the sounds of traffic drifted from the main artery of Mayfield. I didn't talk. She didn't make me. Behind us, over the great hill of the cemetery, the night bled slowly to dawn.

"I need a ride," I said finally. I swallowed the thick taste of salt clutching at my throat. "I have to see Remy. I need to know something good came from this night."

Without so much as a question, Lil led me to her car.

ACKNOWLEDGMENTS

There are always too many people to thank when it comes time to write the acknowledgments. There are all the wonderful and supportive people at the Knight Agency—first and foremost, my tireless book advocate, Lucienne Diver. There's a whole crew at Titan—Miranda Jewess, Becky Peacock, Joanna Harwood, Vivian Cheung, Nick Landau, Laura Price, Paul Gill, Lydia Gittins, Katharine Carroll—with a special shout-out to Julia Lloyd for consistently amazing covers. Steve Saffel, my Dark Editorial Overlord, has helped shape and refine the Shadowside series from the very start—you can blame him for the Icons and all the trouble they've caused poor Zack.

On a more personal note, I would be remiss if I didn't mention all the special people in my life who help keep me sane in between deadlines and book-related stress. From my devoted wife Elyria to the wickedly twisted people in the Shadow Syndicate, my fellow Kheprians, and all my many fans-turned-friends—your humor, timely words of encouragement, and read-aloud sessions help more than you can possibly know. Thank you.

ABOUT THE AUTHOR

Michelle Belanger is most widely recognized for her work on television's *Paranormal State*, where she explored abandoned prisons and haunted houses while blindfolded and in high heels. A leading authority on psychic and supernatural topics, her non-fiction research in books like *The Dictionary of Demons* and *The Psychic Vampire Codex* has been sourced in television shows, university courses, and numerous publications around the world. She has worked as a media liaison for fringe communities, performed with gothic and metal bands, lectured on vampires at colleges across North America, and designed immersive live action RPGs for companies such as Wizards of the Coast. Her research on the Watcher Angels has led to both a Tarot Deck as well as the album, "Blood of Angels." Michelle resides near Cleveland, Ohio in a house with three cats, a few friendly spirits, and a library of over four thousand books. More information can be found at
www.michellebelanger.com

For more fantastic fiction, author events,
competitions, limited editions and more

VISIT OUR WEBSITE
titanbooks.com

LIKE US ON FACEBOOK
facebook.com/titanbooks

FOLLOW US ON TWITTER
@TitanBooks

EMAIL US
readerfeedback@titanemail.com